Goodbye Milky Way

Goodbye Milky Way

An Earth in Jeopardy Adventure

Dan Makaon

eFfusion Publishing Group LLC
Ormond Beach, FL

eFfusion

Published by
eFfusion Publishing Group LLC

This book is a work of fiction and all people, places, and events are either from the imagination of the author or used in a fictitious context.

Library of Congress Control Number: 2011923366

Goodbye Milky Way / by Dan Makaon
An Earth in Jeopardy Adventure

Printed in the United States of America

10 9 8 7 6 5 4 3 2 1

ISBN: 978-0-9833785-9-4
First edition

In Memory of

R. Kennedy Carpenter
(Teacher, Coach, Mentor)

"The greatest obstacle to progress in science is the illusion of knowledge."

Professor Mike Disney
Cardiff University

"If you just buy into the prevailing wisdom then all you can ever do is confirm what is already known."

Professor David Jewitt
University of California at Los Angeles

Chapter 1

Brazil
September – December 2003

A t the hospital in Itacoatiara, Tom Calvano languished near death for a month. When he awoke and was able to receive visitors, the Minister of the Interior came to see him.

"Tom, we're happy to see you're finally healing," said the Minister. "We were quite worried you'd succumb to the infection. The wounded five members of your crew were much luckier than you. They didn't get an infection and healed quickly."

"After all my trouble, I hope the information was helpful," said Tom. "Jeff Teichman told me he delivered it to you personally."

The Minister's face turned serious, his lips pulled tightly together, and his head moved downward as his eyes connected directly with Tom's. For a moment there was complete silence.

"That's one of the reasons I'm here. On behalf of the Brazilian government I want to thank you. The information was extremely useful and has turned out to be quite accurate. While you were recovering, we used your information to destroy the cartel's ability to move drugs through Brazil for several years."

Tom grabbed the control that hung on a wire by the wall. Without looking he pressed a button, and the back of the bed raised him into a higher sitting position. He reached out toward the stand at the side of the bed, grabbed his water cup, and took a sip through the straw.

"Well, that's good to hear," said Tom without looking at the Minister. "I'm surprised you moved so quickly."

"We didn't want the information to become cold," responded the Minister.

Tom sensed the Minister was hesitant to say everything that was on his mind. Tom turned and looked directly at him.

"You said you had another reason to visit me?" asked Tom.

"Yes, you did such a good job; we want to ask if you'd take on another problem. That is, as soon as you feel well enough to do so."

"As long as it's not another jungle trek," said Tom. "What did you have in mind?"

The Minister turned toward a man standing at the door of Tom's room and told him in Portuguese to close the door and wait outside.

"Tom, on August 22, the Brazilian Space Agency's rocket, the VLS-1, exploded on its launch pad. We have reason to believe it was sabotage. We want you to conduct an unofficial investigation to identify the perpetrators and eliminate them."

"You sound convinced there were more than one involved," said Tom.

"It could not have been done single-handedly."

The silence was long enough for the Minister to notice the antiseptic smell in the small room.

"You want me to find them and execute them?" asked Tom.

"Yes," said the Minister.

"I'm not an assassin, Minister, and I'm also not a detective," said Tom. "And shouldn't this be handled by your Ministry of Justice? It's hard to believe they'd relinquish their authority to Interior."

"You're a man of many talents who gets results and who can be trusted. I assure you I've been given the authority to retain you for this purpose, and you and your team will be provided with the appropriate credentials that you'll need for your investigation."

The Minister noticed the antiseptic smell again, as he waited for Tom to mull it over.

"I'm definitely not an assassin," insisted Tom.

"These people are terrorists. They've shown they will die to stop our space program, and we've failed to identify who they are and how many there might be," said the Minister.

"Look, Minister, I might find out who they are, but I won't assassinate them," said Tom. "Why can't I turn them over to you so they can be prosecuted?"

The Minister reacted to the sunlight, glaring off the stark white walls. He walked to the window and looked out with his back to Tom.

"If you can do that, yes, but we don't think these people can be captured alive. They must be eliminated preemptively, before they can kill again."

"Kill again?" asked Tom.

The Minister turned quickly toward Tom and looked at him from across the room.

"Yes, twenty-one people standing on the launch pad died," explained the Minister. "Our press release said it was an accident, but our investigation proved otherwise."

"I can't promise anything, but I'll see what I can do. I will not assassinate anyone. My usual fee and contractual stipulations will apply. Just to remind you, that means I decide who is on my team."

"Agreed," said the Minister.

The spaceport at Alcântara was still rebuilding when Tom Calvano arrived with his team of investigators. He had assembled an eclectic group of computer nerds, forensic detectives, and martial arts experts including, as usual, his reliable friend, Jeff Teichman. His team reviewed the results of the investigation performed by the Brazilian government and confirmed their conclusion that the explosion was sabotage. They had also uncovered evidence of espionage.

"Minister, my team has uncovered evidence that maps of the spaceport, diagrams of the rocket, and procedures for the launch were copied one month before the explosion," said Tom, speaking on a secure phone line.

"What kind of evidence?" asked the Minister.

"Every copy machine since 2002 has a hard drive that retains images of everything copied, and it gives us the time and date," explained Tom. "We uploaded and analyzed all the images from every copier in the spaceport. We found unauthorized copies were made in the spaceport commander's office on a day when his secretary clocked out after normal working hours. The copies were made just before she left."

"Have you confronted her?" asked the Minister.

"Not yet, but we've done a complete background check and are monitoring her every move," said Tom. "So far we've discovered she's a member of a rather unorthodox religion called the Church of Spiritual Objectivism. I arranged for the commander to leave false information about the redesign of the VLS-1 where she would have easy access to it. She took the bait and copied the document."

"Please continue to keep me informed of your progress," said the Minister.

The Brazilian sun was hotter than usual, heating any unshaded surface enough to burn skin. The secretary's contact was a tall, thin man with sunglasses, short black hair, and a dark complexion, wearing a black shirt and white cotton trousers. The secretary was about thirty, with black hair, a slight tan, and wearing a tight beige blouse, white skirt, and beige platform sandals. They shared a table with a brown and gold Bohemia beer umbrella at a café in a village just outside the spaceport, within walking distance of her apartment. After finishing her cup of coffee, she left. The folder she had brought with her remained on the table until the gentleman paid the tab, picked it up, and walked out.

He stopped on the corner, made a call on his cell phone, and walked to the next block where he waited about five minutes. A black car picked him up at the corner and took the ferry across the Bay of São Marcos to the city of São Luis.

Tom's team had no trouble following him to an office building in the business district. Jeff Teichman managed to get in the elevator with him and a few other people. He got out on the third floor, walked down the hallway to a suite at the end and entered. Jeff had inconspicuously followed him out of the elevator and stopped to watch him. When the man turned to look behind him, just before entering the suite, Jeff was facing the elevator impatiently pressing the up button.

The team waited no more than three minutes before storming the suite. Five men were present, including the tall thin man. They were so surprised they offered no resistance. No weapons were found on them or in the suite. Jeff fitted each prisoner with what appeared to be a wristwatch. He told them it contained enough C-4 explosive to kill instantly, and it could be remotely detonated if they tried to escape. Half of Tom's team escorted them down the stairwell, into the lobby, and out the door to a waiting van. The other half searched the suite and packed whatever papers they thought might reveal more about these mysterious operatives.

———————————◇———————————

The senior operative's hands were shaking as he made a call.

"I have five of your men in custody," said Tom to the voice at the other end of the cell phone. "I have reason to believe your organization was responsible for the destruction of the VLS-1 rocket on August 22. I've been hired to stop any future attacks by any means. I'll be coming for you, and you won't escape. Talk to me."

"I'll have to move this matter up my chain of command, as I have no authority to negotiate with you, but I can tell you we had nothing to do with the incident at the spaceport. Someone will call you back soon on the cell phone you're using."

"Make it quick," said Tom.

About twenty minutes went by before the cell phone rang. Tom answered it and the voice at the other end said, "I am Andre, and I've heard you've taken five of my operatives. What are your demands?"

Andre's accent sounded Parisian to Tom.

"I want to know what you had to do with the attack on the spaceport in August."

"May I ask your name?"

"Call me Tom."

"We are not murderers, Tom. We deal in industrial secrets. We had a client who wanted technical information about the VLS-1 rocket, so we acquired it and sold it. We had no idea it would be used in some way to destroy the rocket," said Andre.

Tom heard a slight quiver in Andre's voice, and read it as a willingness to cooperate.

"I know you can still make contact with this client to do future business because your operative in the Commander's office just secured more information," said Tom.

"Let's assume you're correct. What would you have me do? I want no harm to come to my people," said Andre.

"I'll give you some false information which you'll sell to them as usual," said Tom. "You'll also find out as much as possible about who these guys are and what motivates them to kill. If you comply, your people will be released unharmed. The matter will be closed. If you don't comply, you'll be surprised how quickly I'll decimate your organization and hunt you down."

"I'll comply," said Andre. "Just don't hurt my people. I'll call you back with drop-off procedures to exchange information."

"Wise decision."

—————————————◊—————————————

"So, Andre, what's the status?" asked Tom.

"We've done as you've asked. We sold the document to the same client," said Andre.

"And what have you learned about these people? Who are they?" asked Tom.

"It wasn't easy to discover who they are, but we did get some general information which may be of use to you," said Andre. "They're a group of loosely knit religious fanatics. They include Christians, Muslims, and Jews who don't want mankind to pursue space travel because it would circumvent the Armageddon prophesy. Members of the three religions operate as three equal and independent units under a coordinating umbrella organization called the *Preservers of Scripture*. They're willing to die for their cause, so they must be approached with great caution. An attack can come from an individual or a group, and they're capable of coordinating multiple, global, simultaneous attacks. That's all we can discover. So now will you release my people?"

"In a few days, Andre; after I've verified you're telling me the truth," said Tom.

———————————————◇———————————————

"Minister, we've had an incident here at the spaceport," said the Commander. "Tom Calvano is in the hospital, seriously injured in an explosion at our North Warehouse."

"Was anyone else hurt?" asked the Minister.

"We've found nine bodies," explained the Commander. "Five were Tom's men. The other four were workers at the spaceport."

The Minister's hand was shaking slightly as he held the phone to his ear. His face was flush. His voice became subdued.

"Do you know what happened?"

"Not exactly," said the Commander. "I helped Tom develop a canard to lure the saboteurs into the open and arrest them. I believe the four dead workers are who we've been trying to uncover. They took the bait and went to the warehouse, but something obviously didn't go according to Tom's plan. It seems that somehow these terrorists were able to set off a bomb, probably knowing they would die in the explosion."

"Clean up the mess and keep the incident under wraps," said the Minister in his most authoritative tone. "Thanks to Tom, our space program is safer. I expect you to figure out how to beef up security screening so we can identify infiltrators who wish to stop our progress. With regard to Tom's men, make sure their next of kin are notified they died in an accidental explosion and offer them complete support for burial arrangements. I'll be there to visit Tom in the hospital."

"May I suggest you visit him immediately," said the Commander. "He's not expected to survive the night."

Chapter 2

Bronx, NYC
January 2005

D r. Jonathan Walmer was at the AIEDA home office in the Bronx on the phone with his long time friend, Don Mensch. Together they had launched a private company they intended would never go public. It was called AIEDA—Artificial Intelligence Induction Engine Development Association. They used the AIEDA acronym interchangeably to mean the company, the team, the project, or the computer program herself. One didn't exist without the others. All agreed, somewhat tongue-in-cheek, that the program was female.

"So you're convinced these new investors will abide by the secrecy agreement," said Jon.

"I have no reason to believe otherwise," said Don. "I screened them just as I've screened our previous investors, and we've had no leaks so far."

Dr. Walmer and fellow members of AIEDA didn't believe computers could ever become conscious in the same way humans are conscious, or rather self-aware. However, they did believe that a computer could do much more than beat the best chess master at his own game. Of course they knew the computer's ability to play chess was not true reasoning power. True reasoning was either deductive or inductive. Deductive reasoning was used by people all the time, whereas inductive reasoning was a lot less common; especially on the grand scale that has been done by mankind's most brilliant, like Newton, Tesla, Fermi, and Einstein.

Could a computer be programmed to do inductive reasoning? Many scientists and mathematicians thought not, but everyone in AIEDA thought yes. Members of AIEDA had believed that the hurtle to leap for a computer to do inductive reasoning was not the algorithm that needed to be programmed, but rather the lack of sufficient random access memory. A huge amount of central processing unit capacity would be needed. And the creative mind of Don Mensch, venture capitalist, had been the one to conceive the solution and fund the project. His friend, Professor Jon Walmer from Cal Tech, was responsible for managing the project.

"Any news from our biggest investor and customer?" asked Jon.

"Jean Philippe Martinique is a class act, even if he is a Frenchman," said Don. "He apologized for accusing us, and he's identified the leak was an innocent mistake from someone within his company," said Don.

"I was sweating bullets for awhile," said Jon. "I was almost convinced we were inadvertently responsible. It wasn't easy to kill the story. I'm just surprised the blogosphere didn't run wild with it. I could see it as a tabloid headline:

Asian Tsunami Knocks Earth Off Axis."

"Well, he was lucky to get our analysis so soon. After all, AIEDA was only a few months into her inductive test phase," said Don.

"From the beginning one of my biggest concerns was security for the project," said Jon. "We must continue avoiding attention. It's a shame we can't take advantage of patent and copyright law. Secrecy is the only way."

"I think the front we've been using for our business has been working well enough," said Don. "Risk management impresses and confuses at the same time whenever I have to explain what we do."

"I have to hand it to you, Don; *AIEDA Risk Mitigation Company* is a good name to hide behind."

A team of the best of AIEDA's techies had been given the task to develop special commercial software; a pair of sub-programs or modules. One module had been designed to enhance Firewall and Anti-virus programs that run on personal computers. The second module had been designed to enhance the response time and security capabilities of Internet Service Providers.

Unbeknown to the two AIEDA commercial development teams, there were two sub-teams, sworn to secrecy, and each was unaware of the other. Each of these compartmentalized sub-teams was assigned to write secret sub-code for these two new commercial software modules.

The true, but secret, purpose of the *stealth client module* for personal computers was to steal idle CPU time from the computer on which it was installed.

The true, but secret, purpose of the *stealth ISP network module* for Internet servers was to allow a secret embedded sub-network to operate within the Internet, thereby achieving special priority processing over all other Internet activities.

With these innovative stealth modules, AIEDA had been able to harness a large percentage of the world's idle CPU capacity free of charge. Actually, because of the license fees AIEDA collected from the commercially beneficial features of the modules, AIEDA was getting paid to use that idle capacity, and only a few members of AIEDA knew about it.

"Don, did you ever think the business would be growing this fast, this soon?" asked Jon. "Frankly, I was surprised by the numbers presented at the financial review."

"I'm just as surprised," said Don. "We'll definitely have a good quarterly report for our investors. It's a testament to how well our software meets the needs of our customers."

"Do you ever have any reservations about what we've been doing?" asked Jon.

"What we've been doing is technically not illegal, and it harms no one," responded Don. "But, of course, only its secrecy allows it to work."

"There's no way this could have been negotiated, much less at such a reasonable price," said Jon with a big smile.

Chapter 3

Ottawa, Ontario, and Washington, D.C.
January 2005

I t was only a few days after the great Asian Tsunami hit eleven countries on December 26, 2004 when George Blocker had heard a newscast that the earthquake had caused a four and a half second shift in the tilt of the earth's axis. His wife had mentioned she had also heard it on another channel the day before. As a geophysicist with the Canadian Geodetic Survey Division, he had found this to be quite a startling event. Despite being on holiday, he had phoned into the office and asked if anyone had heard about the shift in tilt.

Indeed there had been some discussion in the office about it, and the obvious question everyone had was how this could have been determined so quickly. Canada wasn't in any consortium that would have the capability to detect such a shift in a matter of days. If someone had asked them to look for a shift, they could have found it in a week or two, but not in three or four days. Some organization obviously had been monitoring that type of data, had noticed the shift, and had reported it to someone in the media. Unless they had obtained a directive to verify the shift, they couldn't have expended any money on it. George's co-workers said they had decided to just wait and see if more news about the shift would be broadcasted in the aftermath of one of the ten deadliest natural disasters in history. About 283,000 people had perished.

———————————◊———————————

Over three weeks had passed since the catastrophe, and no more had been heard about the shift . . . and that got George and everyone else in the office wondering if they shouldn't find a way to check it out themselves—budget be damned!

George decided to phone his colleague, Amanda Rheinhardt, in the States.

Well, George thought, *I'd better keep it business. I'm married now, and she has a steady.*

George rang her up rather quickly and was surprised to hear her stern and perfunctory voice.

"Rheinhardt."

"Hi, Amanda, this is George Blocker. You sound awfully busy. Is it a good time to talk?"

"George! Of course, of course. I was just a bit preoccupied reviewing the sonic readings taken last month off Gibraltar. So how are you George?"

"Oh, just doing fine. You did know I married last year?" he quickly inserted.

"So I heard. Dave and I are engaged now. You remember Dave, don't you?"

"Oh, for sure, at the convention in New Orleans last summer. I'm happy for you, Amanda."

"Well, thank you, George, and to what do I owe the pleasure of your call?"

"Amanda, I've called to ask a favor of you. I know you're usually swamped, but I'm wondering if you could find a way to get me immediate online access to the Geological Survey's database. I can't wait for the normal channels this time."

"That depends on what data you're looking for, George."

"Well, I need to see two sets of data from January 1, 1980 through ten days after the Asian Tsunami. Ah, the earthquake hit on December 26, 2004, so that would be January 5 of this year. The first set would be all sonic soundings of the fault-line where the undersea earthquake occurred, and the second set would be all satellite data on the orbital tilt of the earth's axis. Can I get that?" he asked sheepishly.

"Gee, that's a lot of data, George. Sure, I can get you access. Do you still have an active account number?"

"Yes, I can give it to you . . ."

"Not necessary, I can look it up by name. What are you looking for in all that data?"

"Honestly, Amanda, I don't know yet. Have you heard of anyone asking for this data or about the supposed shift of the earth's axis after the Tsunami hit?"

"I did hear about the shift on the news once, but nothing more since, and I think you're the first to ask for this data. Of course, the request could have come through someone else. I'll do a search to find all requests of this nature and will email you the results. Your access will take effect within the hour. Is there anything else I can help you with?"

"No, that's it Amanda."

"It was so nice hearing from you again, George."

"Thanks, Amanda."

"Bye, George."

"Bye."

———————————◇———————————

Late that afternoon George Blocker got all the data he needed after Amanda got him access to the Society's database. His preliminary analysis confirmed the axial tilt. In the process of studying the tilt data, he coincidentally discovered that the shift in tectonic plates along fault lines showed an accelerating movement over time inconsistent with the way plate tectonics would predict. Early 1980's data was consistent with theory and previous observations, but the data progressively showed increasing acceleration. This data appeared to point to an external gravitational force being exerted upon the earth.

This can't be right, he thought. *I've got to discuss this with someone I can trust. Amanda. I'll call Amanda. Tomorrow, after I sleep on it.*

———————————◇———————————

At the Office of Science and Technology Policy (OSTP) in the Executive Office of the President (EOP), the President's Science Advisor, Dr. Tony Regbramur, Director of OSTP, was conducting a specially convened meeting to discuss what action the EOP should take regarding some disturbing new geophysical data. All forty-five members of his science staff were present.

Dr. Regbramur began the meeting. "Some conversations with a few of you and several draft papers have convinced me to call this meeting immediately. We must finalize our position on the new geophysical data that you received two weeks ago. The approach we'll be taking today is unprecedented, but the perceived risk and urgency is so high, we don't have the usual luxury of preparing competing white papers and presenting them for critical review. I'd like you first to divide yourselves into five groups. It seems we have five rows of seats, so let's do it by row," said Regbramur as he surveyed the room.

Dr. Regbramur gave the groups specific instructions and three hours to draw conclusions. He gave each group thirty-five minutes to deliver their presentation and summarize their conclusions. He asked all five groups to agree on an assessment of the situation and a recommendation for what the EOP should do.

"If we don't reach consensus by 17:00, I'll make the decision and present it to the President tonight, and I'll include the top two alternatives. I'll be roaming from group to group listening to the discussions. You may choose to stay in this room, or use the adjacent conference rooms. Please begin."

Chapter 4

Paris, France
January 2005

Jean Philippe Martinique never tackled small social problems, always the big ones, and he had the money to do it. He wasn't particularly interested in running a business, although he took his obligation to his company seriously. His uncle's business was so well staffed and organized that it would continue to run itself even without his help. Of course, as sole heir to his recently departed uncle's fortune, he was the Chairman of the Board. He took pride in the fact that this giant battery manufacturer was, and always would remain, a private company, and a French company.

Jean Philippe understood one of his roles was to represent the company in public to maintain its enviable reputation. So, he was being interviewed in his Paris office by a reporter from a major technology magazine.

"Being a private company means there's hardly any information about Marseilles Electric Enterprises," said Francois Arnauld. "So, I thank you for granting this interview.

"I'm pleased to do it, but I must remind you that specifics about sales, profits, and production processes must remain confidential," said Jean Philippe.

"Yes, that's one of the reasons I'd like to write more of a human interest article by focusing on your contributions, and your uncle's, to the success of the company," said Francois.

"Where would you like to start?" asked Jean Philippe.

"Perhaps you can begin by telling me how your uncle's vision and spirit still lives on in the company," said Francois.

Jean Philippe leaned back in his chair, looked up at the ceiling, and lightly drummed the fingers of his left hand on the desk. The sunlight from the window flooded into the room and caught the lead crystals of the chandelier, projecting small rainbow images on the wall.

"My uncle taught me well. He was a stickler for detail and believed in running efficient processes. He also believed in rigorous training for all employees on their process."

"By process, do you mean job?" asked Francois, as he scribbled in a small wire-bound notebook.

"Not really. A job is usually associated with a particular function or department, like accounting or electrical engineering, whereas a process crosses over different functions and departments in order to get a quality product manufactured as quickly and as inexpensively as possible. Most problems in large organizations come about due to a failure of communications between parochial departments and functions. By clearly defining the processes necessary to efficiently manufacture a product, the speed and quality of relevant information increase, and mistakes are minimized."

"I'd like to come back to your explanation of process later," said Francois. "Tell me, what is it that drives your company to success?"

"The drivers for success are the five principles my uncle required everyone to learn and follow. They are: *strive for excellence in all operations; time is not of the essence—quality is; focus on what the company does best—batteries; use statistics/engineering/best-practices to continuously improve; train/cross-train/retrain employees to follow the process.*"

"It must take a lot of effort and time for you to manage such a large organization, so I wonder how you find the time for all your philanthropic work," commented Francois.

Jean Philippe had stopped drumming his fingers and was looking directly at Francois.

"I almost hate to admit it," said Jean Philippe, "but the company runs so effectively that it takes me but two days a month to oversee my process and make certain that my direct reports are also following their processes."

"I'm surprised. How can it be?" asked Francois.

"As I said, we train to follow the process," said Jean Philippe. "Everyone carries the procedural manual for their specific job to the meetings. Meetings start on time and end on time. Every meeting has its purpose, and no time is wasted on tangential discussions. Events that are out of statistical control are discussed along with the solution in progress."

The interview continued for two hours and covered Jean Philippe's family history, his hobbies, and his charitable activities. When it was over, he sat alone, contemplating the one project dearest to him, the one he had to keep secret, so couldn't mention in the interview.

Jean Philippe had no doubt about it. He knew he had the time, resources, and clarity of mind to take on the biggest effort on behalf of mankind that any one person had ever attempted. He would find a way to protect humanity from extinction. He would protect French culture for future generations. If Noah could do it with his ark, Jean Philippe knew he could do it with his Ecosthat, a pseudonym for Ecologically Stable Habitat. He expected his Ecosthat to protect a representative cadre of mankind and a library of mankind's knowledge from just about any major global disaster that might come along.

Man should not just sit idly by hoping the fate of dinosaurs does not befall him, thought Jean Philippe.

He truly believed that man could prepare for the worst imaginable disasters, short of the entire planet exploding. Space travel was simply not an option, and no government seemed interested in spending billions to deal with disaster-events of low probability.

Besides, thought Jean Philippe, *how would the government explain that billions of tax money would be spent to save only a small number of people, who would then repopulate the earth much as Noah's family had done after the Great Flood?*

He knew a government could never sell such a project, and it would be too big to do in secret. Yet a reclusive mega-billionaire could pursue such a project with little more than a raised eyebrow for wasting all his money.

———————————◊———————————

The air was crisp and clear this spring morning in Paris. Andre Garnier unlocked the employees' entrance at the side of the building, entered, and stood just inside waiting for his staff as they arrived for work. He held a small attendance journal in his hand and checked off each name as he welcomed each arrival.

"Good morning, Anna. Good morning Joseph," and so on until all had arrived.

As curator of the Musee d' Orsay, he had cultivated the habit of being the first to arrive at 09:00, so he could greet and oversee the employees as they prepared for the day's opening at 09:30.

A meticulous man in all things, he stood but five-foot six in stocking feet, medium build with broad shoulders, and a waist that hinted of daily workouts. A pair of rimless bifocals appeared never to leave their perch on his nose which was a bit large for his elongated face. His hair was light brown and of such a fine texture that the slightest breeze would toss it about in several directions.

Once the museum opened, Andre was free to seclude himself in his office until just before lunchtime when he again made his appearance before all the employees by walking through every part of the museum, both public and private. He would then depart for late lunch at his favorite restaurant near the Cathedrale Notre Dame de Paris.

Andre would make one more round of the museum fifteen minutes before clearing time. Within forty-five minutes of the start of his last round, the museum was cleared and closed. He would then stand by the employee door and wish a good night to each employee as they filed, one by one, past him and out the door. He would turn and lock the door behind him, then methodically check every other door and accessible window to be sure they were locked. When all was seen to be secure, it was back to the employee door where he set the alarm and left the building, locking the door behind him.

Today he would follow his usual routine, always glad to see the crowds of tourists who marveled at the most wonderful collection of art in the style of impressionism. Because the museum was a converted railway station, the architecture provided a sense of openness, and the escalators were much appreciated by many of the tourists. Of course, only he knew the complete story of the reconstruction.

Not even his staff was aware of the complex that existed beneath their feet. The only access to it from within the museum was via a secret door within his office. The door was hidden behind a sliding bookcase, was double-locked and fitted with an alarm that alerted guards within the complex below. His museum staff knew never to bother him when in his office except by intercom for critical issues, and he only took meetings by appointment. Every day he would use the stairs behind the secret door to access his sanctuary, the place from which he would oversee the largest, most sophisticated industrial espionage business in the world.

Of course, industrial espionage was the bulk of the business, but they also engaged in the theft of rare art and the forgery of major national currencies. They never engaged in drug trafficking or in the physical sale of military weapons.

However, in some cases they would engage in the theft and sale of military secrets, but definitely never would they be party to propagating nuclear or other weapons of mass destruction. After all, they had a philosophy and a value system that stemmed from it. William Godwin, founder of the movement in 1810, would be surprised at how the organization had grown. The last thirty years of his life was spent in almost complete secrecy as he built and nurtured the secret partnership that thrived almost 200 years later.

The complex beneath the Musee d' Orsay was an electronic listening post and communication center. The encryption algorithms were not only complex, but they automatically changed the cipher key every five minutes. All phones and other communications devices were wireless and had a translation buffer that translated English into an artificial language before the signal was encrypted and transmitted.

The organization appeared centralized, but the centralization was just embodied in the command and control center. The espionage operations were decentralized throughout the world at 102 sites, and each had no knowledge of the others.

In addition, the Operations Division managed over 10,000 agents who had infiltrated many organizations throughout the world. Each agent only knew the Partnership through a single mentor. Each mentor handled ten agents. There were ten mentors at each of the 102 operations sites.

Complete loss of the Center wouldn't destroy the organization. An emergency backup Center was being secretly maintained beneath a monastery located deep within the Red Sea Mountains about 100 miles southeast of Cairo, Egypt in an oasis in the Arabian Desert east of the Nile River. It was as difficult a habitable place to find as any on earth. Andre thought it was ironic that the crosses adorning the steeples of the monastery were transmitting messages through the skies, not to God, but to his own earthly operatives.

Jean Philippe Martinique found that a lot of useful data was available from the Biosphere-2 Project of the late 1980's to early 1990's conducted in the Arizona desert. For two years, four men and four women had lived in a sealed environmental chamber and maintained ecological balance. External mechanical means were needed to maintain air flow, but the external leak rate of the Biosphere's atmosphere was low.

The ecologically balanced and sealed habitat that Jean Philippe envisioned would be significantly larger and more complex, because it would be subterranean and would require a zero leak rate. He would create a habitat that could sustain 120,000 people and millions of animals, insects, and plants for an indefinite period of time.

He had commissioned an engineering study for the structural and mechanical features of the habitat. Hundreds of leading ecologists were working on the details of how to establish and maintain environmental balance.

Jean Philippe had also commissioned an American group, called AIEDA, to determine the best place to deploy the Ecosthat. He was already an investor in the group, and it had made enough progress that he felt confident in signing a contract with them.

When Jean Philippe had received the solution to the problem he had given AIEDA, he was doubly surprised. He had some strict non-performance clauses in the contract and hadn't expected to get a useful answer on time, much less have to pay a cent. He'd given them six months to provide an answer with the supporting data to prove it. It took them only seventeen days. He was surprised by how fast they had come up with a solution, but even more so, he was surprised by the actual solution itself.

As a result, Jean Philippe had to mount an expedition quickly. If he didn't reject AIEDA's solution, with good reason within six months, he would owe them a million dollars. It would be worth every euro, especially so because he had received his solution much faster than he could have imagined. But an expedition to Antarctica, he hadn't expected. This was a monumental task in itself.

Jean Philippe called his director of Human Resources.

"Gaston, I need you to do a most confidential personnel inquiry. It must be done in the most delicate manner, as we don't want anyone to ascertain our mission. I'm in dire need of an exceptional leader for a rugged expedition. He has to be someone who's an unknown, who wouldn't draw attention to himself. He must not be interested in publishing his escapades, and he must be loyal and able to keep a secret. He must be physically fit and also be able to communicate with scientists and engineers from many different fields. His business organizational skills must be outstanding. Can you do this quickly?"

"Yes, of course. I'll begin low-key inquiries within my professional network immediately."

"Thank you, Gaston."

Jean Philippe hung up the receiver and wondered where he would find such a creative, talented leader. He knew this person couldn't be found in his company, as there was no procedural manual for an Antarctic expedition.

Chapter 5

Manhattan, NYC
January 2005

Since he received his report from AIEDA, Jean Philippe had interviewed twenty contenders for the position of his *Admiral of the Fleet*. Well, not actually admiral, but he knew the leader of his planned expedition to Antarctica could well require all the skills, experience and attributes of a Navy admiral. He knew he had to choose wisely, and so far he had not been impressed with those he'd met, despite the extensive pre-screening done by his company's search firm, and then again, by key executives on his staff.

He had held court in his chateau outside of Valbonne in southern France for two weeks and then had a week of judging from his Manhattan penthouse. He decided to interview just one more for the day. He worried that he had to find his man soon. Only so much could be done ahead of time without the involvement of the one who would be leading the mission. There was a knock at the study door. It was the butler, Arthur, with the last interviewee.

"Sir, may I introduce Mr. Thomas Calvano, President and CEO of Calvano and Associates."

Jean Philippe stood and walked around to the front of his desk.

Arthur continued, "Mr. Calvano, this is Mr. Jean Philippe Martinique, chairman of Marseilles Electric Enterprises."

Both men extended their right hands as they quickly approached each other. Jean Philippe took note of the power of this man's grip, his broad smile, and the fact that he had to look up at him. Indeed, at six-foot-one in bare feet, he rarely looked up at any man, but this guy must have been at least six-foot-four.

Well, he told himself. *Let's not get overly impressed with physical stature. After all, Napoleon was a small man, and he led a country and personally commanded a large and powerful army.*

"Please, Mr. Calvano, let's make ourselves comfortable over here." He motioned to two large leather lounge chairs with an exquisite coffee table between them. "May I call you Tom, or do you prefer Thomas?"

"Tom is fine, thank you. It's nice to meet you, Mr. Martinique."

"Likewise, and please feel free to call me Jean Philippe. Tom, as you know, I'm looking for a leader of an expedition to Antarctica. But what you don't know is the reason for the expedition, its scope, and potential dangers. You've already agreed to keep this interview confidential, so I'd like to brief you on it first, then get your reaction. In particular, I'd like to hear how you feel about leading it, and why you think you'd be my best choice."

Jean Philippe found himself in a conversation that made him lose track of time. No other interview had taken more than an hour, and when he looked up at the grandfather clock, two hours had passed. *But how could that be?* He hadn't heard a single chime. This man had so entranced him with his exploits, knowledge, intellect, and humor that he completely lost track of time. He found himself leaning forward in his chair listening intently to his guest and occasionally asking clarifying questions. His background check had intimated Calvano's involvement with a number of interesting exploits, but to hear the details coming from this most believable fellow was quite remarkable. Jean Philippe knew he had found his man.

"Tom, I can't tell you how impressed I am with your credentials, experience, and persona. I think you'll make an exceptional leader of my expedition. If you want the job, it's yours. What are you looking for in terms of compensation?"

"My rate is $2000 per day, seven days per week, minimum one year contract, all expenses paid; payable to my company."

"Tom, this expedition could lead to a construction project that lasts five to ten years. Are you willing to extend your services that long?"

"If the job is as challenging as I think it will be, of course! However, my rate would increase 10% per year, and depending on the risk determined after the first year, I might be requesting a reasonable hazardous duty bonus."

"Well, I agree to your terms. Sometime tomorrow, give this fellow a call." Jean Philippe leaned forward to the edge of his chair and handed Calvano a business card.

"Tonight I'll call Jim and let him know you'll be contacting him, and that you're the new boss of the outfit. He's done considerable prep work for the expedition, but there are so many things to discuss and decisions to make, he'll be happy to hear from you. I expect you to give me a verbal report once a week and a written report once a month. Otherwise, it's your baby, Tom."

They both stood and shook hands.

"Fax me your contract, and I'll sign it right away, so we can get started officially," Jean Philippe intoned as he escorted Tom to the door.

As Tom left Jean Philippe's penthouse, he reflected on the information he had been given about the location of the proposed habitat. Apparently, the best place was a circle with a radius of two miles located in the continent of Antarctica and centered at 81 deg, 35 min, S. latitude, and 115 deg, 55 min, W. longitude. This choice provided geologic stability, avoided the worst of Antarctica's extreme climate zones, and was as far from other settlements as possible. Extreme climate would make construction more costly in both time and money, so geologic stability shouldn't be the only consideration. The other consideration was ease of access by sea, land, and air; as such a massive construction project would require a supply chain robust enough to support an invading army during a major war.

The habitat was to be built at least 500 feet below the land mass, which meant almost a mile below the surface which was covered with over 4,000 feet of ice. It made sense to Tom that Antarctica was the right place, not just because of its remoteness, but because it was a real continent made of real land, not just a mass of ice. Being at the bottom of the globe, its tectonic activity wasn't aggravated by the earth's spinning on its axis at a thousand miles per hour. Tom didn't think this was a strange project at all.

He actually thought it was about time something like this was being done as mankind needed to greatly improve its chances of survival.

Tom thought, *First thing in the morning I'll contact this O'Leary fellow who's been running the show, and find out what's been done so far.*

―――――――――――――――◇―――――――――――――――

Jim O'Leary was in his office at 9:00 a.m. studiously reviewing the topographical map of the proposed Ecosthat site when his phone rang.

"O'Leary here," he thundered into the receiver with his deep baritone voice.

"Mr. O'Leary, this is Tom Calvano. Jean Philippe said he'd let you know I'd be calling to introduce myself."

"Oh, sure, he called last night. Welcome aboard! I'm looking forward to meeting you, Tom, and getting you up to speed. I'm happy you'll be taking the reins. From what I hear you have all the right experience to manage a project like this."

"Well, thanks for the vote of confidence, Jim. I'm sure we'll make a great team. Can we meet for lunch today to kick things off?"

"Why don't you stop by here first? I'll introduce you to the staff and give you the keys to your office. Then we can go to a little place around the corner where we can eat and speak with some privacy. Do you have the office address?"

"Yes, I have your business card. I'll be there in an hour, okay?"

"Wonderful. See you then, Tom."

"Bye, Jim."

―――――――――――――――◇―――――――――――――――

When Tom arrived at the Manhattan office, he was immediately impressed by Jim's body-builder physique, almost to the point of being intimidated by the size of his biceps and barrel chest. Although Tom's six-foot-four height and athletic build gave him the advantage over most men, it was obvious that Jim, at about five-foot-eleven, could punch his lights out. Jim's deep booming voice added to the effect. Fortunately, he had an inviting personality, and Tom got over the initial uneasy feeling quickly. He soon found Jim to be a highly effective project manager, despite his modest demeanor.

At lunch, Tom reviewed his list of requirements with Jim and learned there was only one critical issue yet to be resolved . . . mode of transportation. The expedition was to use an ice breaker ship to transport the team with its supplies and equipment as close to the proposed site as possible. Then the team would travel overland in half-tracks the rest of the way. Once at the site they would erect a semi-permanent shelter from which they would conduct their geological surveys. If the surveys confirmed the adequacy of the site, they would expand the shelters in anticipation of the construction crews arriving.

Unfortunately, there were no ships of the right kind available for over four months. Cargo requirements were too much for the non-military planes available. Even if they could get a military cargo plane like the LC-130 equipped with skis, it would be dangerous to land on an unknown strip of snow and ice. They had to get moving within one month, while the weather was most favorable. Of course, pressure from Jean Philippe to get started was the other factor. Tom had learned there was a clause in a contract requiring Jean Philippe to validate AIEDA's site selection within six months.

Tom decided to call Jean Philippe for some ideas, and instead got his offhand response:

"Tom, this is another problem for AIEDA to solve. I'll get them working on it right away. You'll be hearing from a fellow by the name of Don Mensch today or tomorrow to discuss your requirements before he starts an analysis."

Chapter 6

January 2005

George Blocker didn't sleep well. He got up earlier than usual. He couldn't stop thinking about the gravitational effect he'd discovered. He decided to call Amanda as soon as he could get to the office. First he needed a good breakfast. He was starved!

He'd make his favorite three-egg omelet. Because the griddle was well-buttered, the whipped eggs didn't stick, but started to slide forward and backward with his gentle horizontal motions. As the eggs began to solidify on the surface, he grabbed a small metal spatula and used it to fold half of the contents over onto itself. He continued to slide the griddle over the burner for a few more seconds, and then . . .

"*Voila!* It's done," he exclaimed.

He turned the finished product out onto his plate, grabbed a clean fork, carried plate and fork to the kitchen table, seated himself, and slowly, methodically savored his omelet. Yes, indeed, he just loved to eat food he cooked himself. For some reason, he still had the image of eggs sliding over the hot griddle as the surface of the eggs solidified.

"Hmmm," he said aloud to himself. "Like the earth's crust moving over the molten center. But no, the griddle was moving under the eggs. There's something . . . I just can't put my finger on it. Oh, well, off to work."

————————————◇————————————

When he got to the office, George wasted no time dialing up Amanda. He knew she'd be in her office.

"Rheinhardt," came the sound from the receiver. George was always amused by her abrupt way of answering the phone.

"Amanda, this is George. How are you?"

"I'm just fine, George. My, you're up and at it early. Did you get access to all the data you needed?"

"Yes, but after analyzing it, I think I need your help. Do you have some time to talk?"

"Sure, George, what's the problem?"

George proceeded to brief her on his findings and explained that he'd gone through the calculations several times and had found no errors. Amanda had him fax his analysis to her for review.

"George, I'll get back to you after lunch with my opinion."

"After lunch. You won't delay?"

"After lunch. I promise."

Amanda spent all morning reviewing George's calculations. She found no errors. However, the results were bizarre and disturbing.

Amanda thought, *How can there be such a powerful gravitational force acting externally on the Earth?*

She remembered reading something about a giant planet beyond the orbit of Pluto, believed to be the tenth planet, and possibly explaining certain gravitational anomalies in Earth's geological history. According to this obscure belief, every 3,600 years the planet Tyche passes by Earth and destroys most of mankind. This seemed absurd to her, but considering George's analysis, maybe there was a large rogue planet out there coming closer to Earth. She'd call George after lunch as she promised.

When George received the call from Amanda, he wasn't too happy. He'd hoped she would find an error in his calculations, or perhaps in the initial data. Not only did she confirm his analysis, but she brought up this preposterous myth about a rogue planet. Good grief! If she were to go public with an idea like that, he wouldn't want to be associated with her in any way.

"For God's sake!" he blurted. "It could ruin my career."

Yet, he thought, *her idea to contact Dr. Roger Akins, a mutual friend of ours, and an astrophysicist, seems pretty good. Roger won't repeat any embarrassing stuff Amanda might suggest. Anyway, isn't Roger working on a new gravitational theory of some sort?*

George couldn't quite remember.

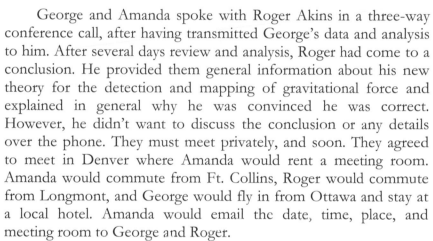

George and Amanda spoke with Roger Akins in a three-way conference call, after having transmitted George's data and analysis to him. After several days review and analysis, Roger had come to a conclusion. He provided them general information about his new theory for the detection and mapping of gravitational force and explained in general why he was convinced he was correct. However, he didn't want to discuss the conclusion or any details over the phone. They must meet privately, and soon. They agreed to meet in Denver where Amanda would rent a meeting room. Amanda would commute from Ft. Collins, Roger would commute from Longmont, and George would fly in from Ottawa and stay at a local hotel. Amanda would email the date, time, place, and meeting room to George and Roger.

Roger insisted on Amanda protecting the meeting information. He described how to do it with two email messages. Both should have a blank subject and no text in the body. The first should have the date and time within an attached jpeg photo. The second should have the address and room within a different attached jpeg photo.

The three-way phone conference ended awkwardly with simple goodbyes.

The days had gone by slowly over the anticipation of their meeting at the Denver Art Museum. George and Amanda were discussing Roger's paranoia while nursing a pot of coffee in the rented room at the museum.

"George, don't you think Roger has been a bit melodramatic about keeping this meeting so secret?" Amanda wondered.

"Gee, Amanda, you're too kind. I'd call his behavior down right nutty, insisting on ciphering your email. I'm glad he asked you to do it, because my reaction would have scuttled the meeting. Then we'd never learn what he's determined about our mysterious force. It's a good thing I know him personally to be a brilliant scientist. Otherwise, I'm not sure I'd believe a word he says."

Amanda slapped George on the forearm and scolded him. "Really, George, you're overreacting as usual. And let's change the subject. He might walk in at any time."

Roger entered the room just as Amanda and George stopped talking about him. He wasted no time and reiterated in somewhat more detail the concepts behind the theory he used to validate George's analysis and come up with a conclusion. Amanda had been boiling-over with an irrational need to present her twelfth planet idea, the one George so readily dismissed. When Amanda interrupted and related the myth of Tyche, Dr. Akins involuntarily released a somewhat condescending smile as he patiently explained that his new theory would predict that the mass of this planet would have to be many millions of times the size of the sun to exert that level of influence on earth.

Roger lowered his voice and leaned forward as he said, "Using the GEI coordinate system, I've determined that somewhere in the Aries-northwest quadrant of space, a stellar-mass black hole is hurtling into our solar system."

All three agreed this information could cause global panic, if released. Another confidential opinion was needed, particularly from someone with priority access to one of the space telescopes. They didn't expect to literally see a black hole, because that's impossible, but they might detect its presence and its path by the way its gravitational force bends light from distant stars or affects the orbits of planets. But who should they contact?

Amanda suggested calling a new firm, *AIEDA Risk Mitigation Company*, which had been making a reputation solving complex problems for wealthy individuals, governments, think-tanks, universities, corporations, and charities. They usually charged enormous fees for their solutions, but in this case they might do the analysis gratis, considering the critical consequences to the entire planet. This firm might be able to determine if earth will have its doomsday, and when it will occur.

--------------------◇--------------------

Dr. Tony Regbramur, Director of OSTP and the President's Science Advisor, had prepared to give the President of the United States some disturbing news and a recommendation about what the EOP should do. He'd selected two staff members who were experts in astrophysics to join him. They waited anxiously together just outside the door to the Oval Office.

When the door opened, the President himself appeared and said, "Come on in guys. We can start a little early. Make yourselves comfortable. I'd like this to be presented as informally as possible. If I don't get it, I'll ask you some questions until I do."

Tony began explaining to the President that recent geologic data and astronomical observations had identified an increasing gravitational force affecting earth and causing earthquakes. "Mr. President, it's likely the quake that caused the Asian Tsunami was triggered by this force. It appears to be a moving object, coming from the Aries northwest quadrant of space. We can't see it, but we can see its effects on the orbits of other heavenly bodies and on the path of light from distant galaxies.

We don't know how big it is or how strong its force will get. We don't know if it will come too close or safely pass us by. We have, however, determined some probabilities. Mr. President, we're facing a 35% probability of an extinction event for almost all life on earth. This is the worst case scenario, because it posits the near or complete destruction of the earth or its ecosystem. The most-likely scenario is 40% of humanity perishes along with 30% of other life. There's a 60% probability of this occurring. The least likely scenario is that the force passes us and the resulting earthquakes take a few million human lives. This has a 5% probability of occurring. Whatever this object is, it's so massive and is moving so fast that there's absolutely nothing we can do about it. We don't know when the worst of it will come and go, but it'll probably be within the next seven to eight years.

It might be possible to build many small underground shelters, but they're not likely to help. A huge underground shelter might help, but it would only protect a few hundred thousand people. It would be difficult to build it amid the panic, and there would be almost insurmountable difficulties in selecting the few who would be its inhabitants.

Mr. President, it's our consensus opinion that this information be classified and withheld from the public, and that we take no actions that would cause anyone to become suspicious. We are in God's hands, and if this information gets out, there will be worldwide pandemonium, a breakdown of law and order, and hundreds of millions of dead and dying, even before this mysterious force of nature strikes us."

The President looked stoic and asked, "Are you sure a large shelter wouldn't save humanity?"

"Assuming the earth doesn't break apart, the ecosystem will be so badly damaged that the sheltered survivors would probably die in their confinement before the earth could rejuvenate itself."

"Do you think we can keep it quiet?" asked the President

"We can try for as long as we can," said Tony. "The longer we postpone worldwide panic, the better."

The President rested his forehead in his right hand with his elbow on the desk in deep thought for a couple of minutes.

"Bury it," said the President. "Bury it deep, but monitor it closely in secret. Keep me informed monthly."

After the office cleared, the President pressed a button on the side of his desk that locked the door to the office. He unlocked a secret drawer in his desk and pulled out a dog-eared notebook, flipped through a few pages until he came to a notation for AREA 51 followed by a code. He pressed a red button on the phone that read SECURE, and keyed in the code.

He waited a few seconds and said, "This is the President. Confirmation code *Big Daddy*."

He waited a few more seconds and said, "Execute operation Guardian. I'll be en route in thirty minutes. Subject for discussion: *What do you know about the threat from space?*"

Chapter 7

Stellar-mass Anomaly . . .
20 AU's outside the orbit of Pluto
January 2005

T om was initially stunned by the AIEDA report that Don Mensch had sent to him concerning the mode of transportation they should use for the exploratory mission. He had booked an ice-breaker ship for four months out, but that was for bringing in the equipment, materials, supplies, and crew for the start of Ecosthat's construction, assuming the exploratory mission was successful. He needed transport within two or three weeks to get to the site and verify its suitability. He was holding a report that said he should use modified airships. Tom incorrectly interpreted that to mean blimps.

"Why, that's ridiculous!" he yelled as he read it. "I've got to call Don Mensch now and find out what imbecile analyst concocted this crazy idea."

After a quick glance at the caller-ID, Don Mensch picked up the phone. "Hello, Tom. I was expecting your call once you got our report in hand. I bet you have a few questions."

"I sure do. To be kind, I'm not at all impressed with this idea of using blimps for the obvious reason . . . wind gusts coming off the Trans-Antarctic Mountain chain in the interior and blowing down toward the coast right where we plan to be encamped. The blimps would be blown away in the blink of an eye. There's no way we could safely unload."

"Tom, I wouldn't have expected you to read the appendices with all the calculations, but it's there. Let me apologize for not making it clear in the executive summary that we've addressed the wind problem. I'll tell you up front that the solution is itself hard to accept, but our computer analysis and review by our best engineers show it to be a safe and effective approach. Let me explain.

The site is fifty miles from the foothills of the highest mountain to the east which is about 10,000 feet high. The wind, blasting down the western side of the range, drops well below 5,000 feet before vectoring horizontally across the coastal plain. By keeping the airship above 5,000 feet, the wind turbulence will be well within the airship's aerodynamic tolerances."

"Okay, that may be true, Don, but how on earth are we going to off-load crew and cargo if we have to stay above 5,000 feet?"

"Well, Tom, that's where the special modifications come in. We'll be retrofitting the two airships with carbon bucky-tube monofilament-woven cable stronger and lighter than anything ever developed. Think of a spider's web, and how strong it is for its weight. This is much stronger. This new filament is 100 times stronger than steel at one-sixth the weight. We'll use it to anchor the airship on four corners and to move people and cargo up and down a fifth central line like an elevator. A sixth line connected to the top of the elevator will actually do the lifting and lowering via a winch in the gondola."

"I've never heard of anything like this!" shouted Tom into the phone. "How will we anchor the lines when we're at 5,000 feet? And six lines . . . that would be six miles of cable to carry on each blimp. The weight and volume of all that cable would diminish the amount of cargo we'd need to carry."

"I assure you, Tom, we've done all the calculations. The bucky-tube cable is thin and light. We can make up for diminished cargo weight by carrying snowmachines instead of half-tracks. The half-tracks can be brought in afterwards on the ice-breaker ship. As far as how you'll anchor the cables; well, that's another specially modified piece of equipment. It's essentially a harpoon gun with the compressed air at much higher pressure. Shot from 5,000 feet, it'll punch an anchor into the ice ten feet deep. It's outfitted with a precision electronic sight that will put the anchor within two inches of where you want it to be."

"Look, Don, this all sounds too much like Star Trek to me. I gather none of this stuff has even been tested. And how will we get hold of these blimps with all their mods on time? I need them all ready to go within no more than two weeks. And what the hell are snowmachines?"

Maintaining his composure, Don explained, "You're right. They haven't been tested. But day after tomorrow you can test the first airship yourself. Five days after, the second airship will be ready. Okay? And snowmachines are snowmobiles . . . it's an Alaskan thing."

Tom was silent for a moment, then asked, "I don't get it. How could you possibly do all this in such short order?"

"Tom, AIEDA has developed over a thousand inventions in the last year alone. Take the bucky-tube cable, for instance. It was developed about six months ago. We had several thousand feet of it manufactured last month for application testing. When Jean Philippe presented us with your transport problem, we developed the solution overnight, knowing that we had this cable, among other things, like the advanced harpoon. Just yesterday the cable manufacturer made an overnight delivery of every foot of cable you'll need. Of course he was paid a large bonus to break into his production schedule and work exclusively on our order.

The airships are from another AIEDA project we've been working on for the U.S. Coast Guard. It seems that the rising cost of fuel is affecting their ability to patrol the coast for drug runners, terrorists, and refugees. We had these airships built for the Coast Guard just recently to replace some of their boats and fixed wing aircraft. The airships will not only save them money, but our new infrared panoramic electronic telescope will improve their coastal surveillance capability by an order of magnitude.

By the way, they're not blimps which are non-rigid; rather they're rigid-frame dirigibles . . . true airships. The original plan was for the Guard to test the airships off the coast of southern Florida, but we convinced them to defer delivery until we could test them in the harsh environment of Antarctica. They were delighted to have us do this for them for a nominal additional fee. So you see, you not only get your transport free, but AIEDA gets paid for your trip."

Tom's attitude turned positive quickly. He sensed this AIEDA outfit was top notch and he let Don know, "I still can't believe you've put all this together in only a few days. I'm ready to test this monster! Just tell me where and when."

———————————————◇———————————————

On a bright sunny morning Tom Calvano arrived at the U.S. Coast Guard Station at Marathon Key, FL. He had with him a hand-picked crew of nine men and three women. All were physically fit and in their early thirties to mid forties. Two were hot air balloonists, two were light plane pilots, two were sailboat captains, two were aircraft mechanics, two were meteorologists, and two were former U.S. Air Force navigators.

The Coast Guard had an experienced crew of six ready to help with a day of training. The following day Tom and his crew would take the airship for an overnight trip all on their own. Then they would spend the next three days testing every piece of equipment and cross-training each other on every aspect of maneuvering the airship.

As they approached the huge hangar, the doors were opening, and the airship slowly became visible as the rays of the early morning sun flooded in. There was an immediate burst of chatter among Tom's crew and they all quickened their step, almost turning to a jog. They couldn't wait to see the entire airship up close, as it was clear from the first glimpse it was no ordinary blimp. It was cylindrical with a bullet-nose and bullet-tail. Were it not for the horizontal and vertical stabilizer unit attached to the rear bullet-tail, one wouldn't be able to tell the forward section from the aft section. It was bigger than three Goodyear blimps, almost eleven stories high and almost 700 feet long. There appeared to be two gondolas at the bottom of the cylindrical structure, one in front and one in back, connected by a gangway . . . especially strange.

Sticking out the sides of each gondola were two arms that curved upward like wings. Each of the four arms held a conical electro-prop motor mounted on a ball-joint pivoting device. Every inch of the skin shone like a mirror. It was almost too bright to look at for any length of time.

Tom turned to Lieutenant Williams and asked, "Where are the fuel tanks, and how do we gas her up?"

"Sir, there are no fuel tanks. She runs completely on electricity."

"Well, about how long will the batteries last while cruising?" asked Tom.

"Sir, there are no batteries. She generates her own electricity from hydrogen fuel cells and solar cells."

Tom countered, "Then she must have hydrogen tanks to feed the fuel cells."

"No sir. She generates hydrogen from a new type of fission reactor that splits nitrogen atoms into hydrogen and oxygen atoms."

Tom probed again, "Then she carries liquid nitrogen tanks?"

"No, sir. She extracts the necessary nitrogen from the atmosphere. As you know, about 78% of air is nitrogen, so there's plenty of it, all the time."

"Well, Lieutenant, what other interesting things can you tell me about this marvelous airship?"

"She'll never run out of fuel, at least in our lifetimes, and she can carry at least twice the cargo of most other forms of air transport, partly because she carries no fuel. She's also extremely quiet and creates no air pollution. The electric motors drive the propellers and are mounted on electronically controlled ball-bearing pivots that provide 270 degrees of thrust vectoring in each of two planes of motion. Helium is used to provide air buoyancy, and an automatic valve system provides dynamic helium volume by exchanging flexible-compartmented air as altitude changes. The gas bags are contained in a lightweight, super-strong carbon-fiber super-structure covered by a Mylar-like skin, making it somewhat like a Zeppelin; definitely not a blimp."

Williams paused then continued with his technical monologue, "The outer surface of the skin is painted with photovoltaic conductivity material . . . millions of microscopic solar cells. The outer surface of the skin also has embedded in it thousands of air pressure sensors which provide wind velocity feedback to the tail stabilizer unit and the electro-props, so they can be positioned automatically to provide smooth, stable and efficient flight. Electricity is provided by the solar cells during the daytime. The nuclear-powered hydrogen fuel cells are needed at night and in inclement weather . . . "

Lieutenant Williams went on and on to describe the specs of the airship until Tom could absorb no more.

Tom interrupted Lt. Williams, "How much load can she carry?"

"She can carry a max of 325 tons for 27,500 miles before requiring some minor mechanical maintenance on the ground. Heavier than air flight begins above 100 tons, which means that's the max cargo you can carry if you must offload using the skyhook elevator system. I think we should get our crews paired-off and onboard so we can begin the training program," responded the lieutenant.

"One more question, please. How many cubic feet of cargo space does it have?" Tom asked.

"10,000 cubic feet . . . which is about the space in four forty-foot dry vans," said the lieutenant as he proceeded to lead the group to the boarding ladder.

Tom detected a slightly disdainful attitude in Lt. William's voice and body language. Before boarding the airship, Tom gently pulled him off to the side. "Lieutenant, may I speak to you out of earshot of the others?"

"Of course, sir, follow me," he said as he turned and led Tom to a small office just a few steps away.

As soon as the lieutenant turned the door behind him, Tom asked, "Lieutenant, are you ticked-off at me for some reason?"

"Just a little perturbed and confused, sir. I don't understand why the Guard wouldn't let me test the airship in Antarctica, or anywhere else. Why pay extra for testing when you have a fully trained crew ready and willing to do it? We've been working with the design firm and the manufacturer from the beginning. I'm assigned to the Systems Program Office that has guided the development of this airship specifically to meet U.S. Coast Guard requirements."

Tom looked furtively around, then straight into the lieutenant's eyes, and in a lowered voice told him, "Lieutenant, the reason is that this is not a test flight. It's a top secret, urgent mission, and this airship and her sister ship just happened to be available at the right time. I can only tell you that my crew and I are undercover, and the success of our mission has global ramifications. I can't tell you anymore than that."

Lieutenant Williams turned slightly red, and in a low but firm voice said, "Sir, thank you for explaining. I have no need to know. I apologize that my demeanor showed my frustration. It won't happen again. You have my full cooperation and enthusiasm."

That went well. I didn't actually lie to him, thought Tom.

The day of training went fast. Tom made sure each of the six Guard members was paired with two of his guys with different specialties. He felt this would help when he implemented his cross-training program.

When Tom first entered the forward gondola, he immediately realized there wasn't enough room for 10,000 cubic feet of cargo. It turned out Lt. Williams had neglected to mention the cargo gondola was detachable for ease of loading and unloading. Once loaded, a scissors-lift placed it right in the middle of the airship between the two permanently attached gondolas.

Everything was going better than expected, primarily because the airship was so automated. Everything . . . the GPS system, the radar, the ground observation cameras, the electro-props, the toilet accommodations, etc. was so well designed, and there was a backup for everything, to say nothing of the tools, spare parts, and maintenance manuals, available just in case.

The scary part was the skyhook elevator training. The cargo was containerized, and the movement of containers into the elevator was semi-automated. The elevator could hold fifty tons of cargo, which meant it would take two trips to unload 100 tons which was the max cargo for lighter than air flight.

At first Tom wondered how the center cable could withstand the friction of the fully-loaded elevator moving up and down it so many times. Chief Warrant Officer Hobart explained, "Sir, you don't have to worry 'bout friction wearing down them cables 'cause there ain't no friction. The elevator's got a maglev generator that never touches the cable. The maglev field stabilizes the elevator as it moves up or down the center cable. Of course, there's a gripper-brake that can grab the cable in an emergency. The lifting and lowering are done with the sixth cable hooked to the roof, and the winch in the gondola."

Maglev generator, thought Tom. *That would require the cable to be magnetized, and if the cables are made of carbon, they can't be magnetized. I'll ask Don Mensch about that later.*

Every member of Tom's crew got a turn firing the harpoon anchors and riding down the cargo elevator to the ground then back up as the airship hovered at 5,000 feet while anchored to the ground via five cables. The automated thrust vectoring electro-prop engines did a great job keeping the airship stable with just the right tension on the cables.

Tom was amazed at the design of the harpoon anchors. The five turret gun-assemblies used compressed air to fire the anchors and were controlled via a game-like console. The operator had to visually verify and accept each item on the pre-launch checklist as presented on the screen. If all checklist items were accepted, then the operator was asked to enter the launch code and press the launch key.

Each anchor was launched in a sequence, because firing all of them at once would make it too hard for the engines to maintain a steady position. Each anchor was charged with compressed air just before the gun blasted the anchor out of its muzzle. A tiny computer released the compressed air from vents in the anchor as it sped down to earth. The air vents controlled the flight of the laser-guided anchor to make sure it hit its laser-marked target on the ground. The disposable anchor would bury itself at least ten feet into the ground.

When it was time to release the cables, the operator would initiate an undocking sequence on the console, enter a code, and press the undock key. This procedure would send an encrypted radio signal from the airship that would detonate a pyrotechnic bolt in the tail of the anchor, cutting loose the cable, so it could be rewound into its repository onboard the airship. Once the cable was rewound, an automatic system attached a new anchor to the cable from a cartridge system that held two dozen anchors. There was a cartridge system for each of the five cables.

With a day of training from the Guard behind them, Tom and his team were ready to do training on their own in the area. The swamps and mangroves around the Coast Guard Station made them feel secure from intruders, but the airship could be seen on the ground for miles, because the land was flat and devoid of trees. Tom decided it would be best to avoid ground observation of their maneuvers by heading out to sea as soon as they launched to an altitude of 500 feet. The first trip would be an overnight one, spending two full days in the air getting acquainted with every aspect of the airship. In three days, the second airship would arrive, and they'd better be ready.

—————————◇—————————

As he walked to the hangar from the barracks, Tom rubbed the morning from his eyes, then squinted to see some of his crew already milling about the door to the hangar. He quickly checked his right pocket to be sure he had the key to the padlock. He could smell the peculiar mixture of sea and plant mold in the humid air that had so early in the morning risen to seventy degrees.

It suddenly dawned on Tom that with two ships they would each need a name that could be used as a call sign when communicating by encrypted radio. In his mind he named the first airship *Ranger* and the second one *Pallas*, as he seemed to recall that those were two well-accounted ships, once under the command of the famous John Paul Jones. He hoped the rest of his decisions for the day would be that easy.

They got the Ranger out of the hanger, launched to 500 feet as planned, and went to sea, out of sight of the Keys, then rose to 5000 feet where they proceeded toward a small atoll they spotted in the distance. Here they found a perfect place to practice with cables and cargo elevator.

At dusk they moved off the atoll and farther out to sea, traveling northeast. They would take shifts sleeping at night. The Ranger was stable and quiet as she flew over the ocean. They had taken her to altitudes from 500 feet to 10,000 feet. They had practiced using the oxygen masks, the fire suppressant equipment, the radar, the satellite communication gear, the GPS system, the sonar, the infrared telescope, and a number of other systems. They rotated positions so they all had a chance to learn every station and every system.

When Tom arose at 05:30, he ordered the crew to turn her around and head back to the atoll where they would have another crack at operating the cargo elevator from 5,000 feet. They were in the midst of turning about to their new course when all electronic equipment suddenly became intermittently inoperative. The crew was confused. Tom checked everything as best he could and couldn't find anything causing the problem.

He calmly told the crew, "Hold her steady guys, keep the sun at our backs, and we'll reach the mainland without any of the damn equipment."

Sam Garcia asked, "Tom, should we wake the other crew?"

"No," Tom replied, "Let them sleep. We might need them fully rested."

It didn't take Tom long to think about all the stories he'd heard about this area of the sea. They were flying in the Bermuda Triangle.

———————————————◊———————————————

When the second crew arose at 09:00, Tom briefed them on what had happened. They'd been flying northwest for over two hours and no sight of land. He was happy they weren't in any danger of running out of fuel, but he didn't want to be gone so long that the Coast Guard would have to send out search planes.

He remembered a time when he was out hunting and got a little confused in the forest. He could never admit to being lost. He turned around and followed his own footsteps in the snow back the way he came and made it to camp before it got dark. The next morning he went down the trail to see if he could find his tracks from the day before and, sure enough, he found them. He'd been paralleling the dirt trail he was looking for. All he had to do was take a sharp right, and he would have hit the trail within a hundred yards.

Tom told his crew, "If we don't spot land in an hour, we can assume we're running parallel to the coast. At that time we'll make a ninety degree course correction to the west."

In one hour they turned to the west as planned, and about two hours later they spotted land, at which time all the electronic equipment began working again. They found themselves quite a way north off the Florida coast than they had intended, but they were now safely on their way back to the Coast Guard Station in Marathon Key.

That's not the kind of experience I'd like to repeat on the way to Antarctica, thought Tom. *What if our com system and other electronic gear were to fail? We wouldn't be able to communicate airship to airship? I think we'll need to take along some mirrors and lanterns and learn to use Morse code by day or night.*

———————————◊———————————

On the fourth day they took the Ranger out to the atoll they had used for practice. Because they had gone so far off course on their way back to the station, they had missed a second chance to practice using the anchor guns and the cargo elevator, so they made the short trip east to the atoll for a couple of hours practice, then took her on a high altitude trip west southwest to Key West, then north up the Gulf side of Florida, then southeast across the Everglades and back to the Marathon Key Coast Guard Station.

They arrived at the station about 4:00 a.m. the next day and made their first nighttime landing. Tom was pleased with the training and told his men to cleanup and get some shuteye in the barracks until 1300 hours. He joined them knowing that Lt. Williams and his crew would be flying the Pallas to the station, arriving around 1700 hours.

———————————◊———————————

The day after the Pallas arrived, Tom prepared for the long flight to Antarctica. He took the extra precaution of having Lt. Williams and his crew inspect everything. The cargo containers with all their equipment and supplies had arrived that morning via unmarked 18-wheelers.

Also, in two unmarked minivans, twelve passengers arrived. These folks were engineers who specialized in the type of geological surveys that Tom had to do at the site. Once on the ground in

Antarctica, Tom and his crew would help them get the data they needed as quickly and safely as possible.

O'Leary had personally supervised the loading of the containers, so Tom was confident the job had been done right. Jim told him every motorized vehicle and device had been maintained and started-up before being loaded, and yes, they had used the right viscosity oil for the low temperatures they would encounter.

Tom ordered the loading of the cargo onto both airships. The forklifts were the last to be loaded into the cargo gondola. Then the passengers boarded, six to an airship, and within ten minutes they were on their way to Antarctica. Their flight path, including altitude adjustments, had been computed for them by AIEDA to maximize their speed by taking advantage of prevailing winds circulating southward. Onboard weather equipment also helped to determine if any in-flight deviations from the plan might be advantageous.

The Ranger had one Raven UAV that had impressive aerodynamics considering its size of only three feet in length with a five foot wingspan and weighing less than five pounds. Tom had hoped it could be used as a forward weather monitoring device flying far ahead of each airship, but it was designed for aerial reconnaissance using highly sophisticated lightweight cameras. It wasn't capable of carrying weather devices, and the rechargeable batteries were good for only 45 to 60 minutes, so it didn't have enough range to be useful for anything more than its job of ground mapping once they got to the proposed Ecosthat site.

The Ranger was Tom's flagship, and she led the way. Tom had instructed Sam Garcia, captain of the Pallas, to follow one hour behind. In this way information on any turbulent weather or unusual conditions that Ranger encountered could be relayed to the Pallas. If Ranger found an altitude change was indicated, Pallas would be informed well ahead of time.

Tom felt this procedure made it safer for Pallas, as it was less likely they would be hit by the same severe weather conditions if they maintained their distance. If something serious happened to Ranger, Pallas was still close enough to attempt a rescue, or Ranger could rescue Pallas, if occasioned. This was particularly important when they approached the final destination with its potential for unexpected microbursts of wind cascading down the slopes of the

Trans-Antarctic Mountains onto the plains leading to the western coast.

Their flight path avoided land so as not to be discovered, or worse, shot down by some country's overly diligent military. They flew southwest across the Gulf of Mexico into the Gulf of Campeche directly toward the Isthmus of Tehuantepec in Mexico. After just a short distance over land, and avoiding cities, they were in the Pacific Ocean. As they headed southeast toward Ecuador they passed just to the east of the Galapagos Islands where Charles Darwin had gathered the data leading to his theory of evolution. At this point they passed the equator into the southern hemisphere where they turned due south, following the 90W meridian, eventually coming within 600 miles west of the southern coast of Chile, and in the home stretch to the Antarctic.

Three hundred miles south of Cape Horn was roughly the start of the Southern Ocean, and it wasn't long after entering it that they saw the sky had turned dark, and the wind had kicked-up to 75 mph. Tom activated the intercom and told the passengers in the rear compartment to get in their seats and put on their safety belts, because the Ranger was approaching bad weather. Then he called Garcia on the Pallas and let him know of the sudden change in weather.

Garcia could see the dark skies ahead, but wasn't yet affected by the wind. He and his crew were transfixed for a few minutes by the strangely beautiful irregular columns of dark stuff that dropped down from the darkened sky and ended well before the surface of the ocean. Garcia thought they resembled dragon's claws pointing downward from four open paws. If he could determine the direction and altitude of the storm, he might be able to wait for it to pass or steer around it, behind it, or above it.

Tom was working with his weather expert and the instruments to get some data to Garcia when suddenly the engines whirred like they were being overloaded, and the Ranger began to turn perpendicular to their intended path. They hit an air pocket and must have dropped 200 feet in seconds. The entire crew had their stomachs in their mouths, and they and everything not tied-down floated about the cabin in weightless abandon. The airship twisted and turned around 360 degrees, then settled down to a phenomenal

200 mph, but they were going in a circle. The instruments were going berserk, so Tom couldn't tell their altitude and couldn't believe the airspeed. Half of the crew was on the floor, and two others were barfing behind their seats. That left only Jason Gibbons, the navigator, and Tom to take action together.

Tom screamed the second he realized, "My God, we're trapped in a water spout!"

"What do we do?" screamed back Jason.

Tom stuck his face to a side window facing downward, as the ship listed starboard. He was surprised to see so much sunlight filtering in from the sides of the huge tunnel of water vapor surrounding them. Then he saw the darker matter below change its shade and appear to come closer.

"Holy Mother of God! The water is rising up the spout coming right at us!"

"Damn it, Tom! What do you want me to do? The motors are maxed-out," yelled Jason.

"Steer her nose up at 45 degrees," commanded Tom.

"I can't! The autopilot is fighting me, and I'm afraid to disengage it. It's the only thing keeping us stable in this cyclone."

"Okay, listen-up. On my mark, I want you to disengage the autopilot and steer the nose up 45 degrees. Hold her there with all your might and don't lose your footing, 'cause I'm blasting us out of here with both solid rocket boosters," instructed Tom.

"Okay, boss! I'm ready. Give me the go!" hollered Jason.

Tom pressed the appropriate sequence of keys and entered his pass code. He had almost forgotten about the boosters. Lt. Williams had only mentioned them once in passing. Tom doubted they were designed for this type of emergency, but it was the only idea he had.

"Jason! On your mark, get set . . . go!" shouted Tom.

As soon as Tom felt the nose heave upwards, he pressed the fire-key on the console. Both rockets fired simultaneously, thank goodness, and the acceleration threw him off his captain's seat. Jason was better positioned in his pilot's seat and was hanging onto an electrical conduit pole for dear life with his left hand, gripping the joystick with his right hand. From his inelegant position on the floor, Tom could see the meatball and crosshairs on the screen. Jason was keeping the ship steady with nose up forty-five degrees.

His knuckles were white, and he had an intense grimace on his face as he steered the ship.

The rockets blasted everything loose to the stern of the cabin, including the crew, who were deposited like a pile of dirty laundry amid puddles of vomit. It seemed like an eternity of vibration and noise amid the recognizable groans of the ship's airframe as it yielded to the forces of acceleration. Then, almost like a miracle, the Ranger punched through the wet and swirling clouds of terror to behold the ever so welcomed brilliance of the sun. Tom was so surprised and relieved that he was frozen without thought or action until he heard Jason yelling, "Turn the damn things off! We're out of it. Turn them off, damn it!"

Tom leapt back into his chair and stared at his screen.

"Oh, shit! I can't remember how to shut them down," he said, fortunately low enough so no one heard.

His eyes darted quickly over the screen until they settled on the *Booster Shutdown* icon. He pressed it and a popup appeared—*Confirm Shutdown, Yes or No.*

He clicked on *Yes* and the rockets shut down immediately. The thought crossed his mind, *I wonder what those boosters were intended for. Surely, no one had waterspout escape in mind. I thought the acceleration was going to break Ranger apart.*

Fortunately, Ranger and her crew had blasted out of the waterspout on the other side of the storm in the right direction. It was still windy and raining, but they could see clearing skies ahead. Tom contacted Garcia and gave him instructions to fly the Pallas over and behind the storm. Ranger would wait for him to catch up.

Good Lord! thought Tom. *I forgot to check the passengers.*

He quickly entered the passenger compartment to find all six strapped in their seats with a green tinge on their complexions. Two had barfed on the floor in front of them. Fortunately they were in the first row and didn't spray anyone else.

A woman in the second row said, "Is it over? Can I get up now? I need to hit the head."

Tom assured them, "It's all over now. You can get up and walk around. As soon as you're feeling better, those of you who heaved your guts on the floor will have to clean up your own mess.

The janitor's closet is on the port side behind you. Sorry for the rough ride, folks."

Tom's crew recovered from the experience quickly after they cleaned-up and changed their clothes. Tom wondered if he should have had the crew buckle-up at their stations at the same time he'd ordered the passengers to buckle-up. He decided it wasn't practical in most situations, because they had to be free to get up and down and move about the cabin to do their jobs. Maybe there was a way to reorganize the work consoles and supporting devices so every crew member could do everything from his seat. He made a mental note to suggest it when they got back.

While the Ranger was anchored at an altitude somewhat above 5,000 feet and having her cargo unloaded, the Pallas stayed safely aloft, waiting about an hour away toward the western coast of Antarctica. Base camp would be set up a half mile east of the outer perimeter of the proposed site. When the Ranger finished off-loading, she exchanged places with the Pallas. When the Pallas was unloaded, she retained two crew members, just as the Ranger had done, and parked herself toward the western coast eighty miles northwest of the Ranger. In this way they would act as sentries, and each would be much less likely to be struck by the same catastrophe, should one occur.

Chapter 8

February 2005

*A*ir Force One landed at Nellis Air Force Base near Las Vegas, in Nevada. The President deplaned hurriedly and was escorted across the tarmac by two Secret Service agents to a marine helicopter fired-up and ready to go.

Two marine master sergeants awaited the President at the stairs to the chopper, their uniforms fluttering in the wind created by the whirling blades. As the President boarded the chopper he held his hand before his eyes to shield them from the sand whirling about in the wind. He could smell the dry, dusty air, so typical of the desert.

The stairs to the chopper retracted, and the bird lifted off toward the foothills of the distant mountains. Special clearance had been arranged for the chopper to enter the restricted military air space over the sprawling facility that officially didn't exist. In the common vernacular, it was referred to as *Area 51*.

When the President stepped out of the chopper, he was greeted by salutes from three Air Force officers in dress uniform. The full bird colonel he recognized as Colonel William Balfour. The colonel had escorted the President on several previous visits. Colonel Balfour introduced the other two officers, a captain and a major. The President ignored the two SS agents who escorted him. The two marines remained with the chopper. The SS agents followed the President, Colonel Balfour, and the other officers to a minivan parked just to the side of the landing pad.

They drove about a mile to a large hangar surrounded by several other numbered, but otherwise non-descript buildings. As the van approached the building, the hangar door opened, they drove inside, and the door closed behind them. The van stopped in the middle of the hangar. A red light on the wall in front of them turned green, and the van began to descend on an elevator beneath the floor.

When the elevator stopped, a loudspeaker instructed them to step out and proceed directly to the security checkpoint. As they walked down the narrow corridor, they each had to pass through two consecutive turnstiles before coming upon a facility similar to an airport security checkpoint, but with two bomb-sniffing dogs and six well-armed guards. Each of them, except the President, was required to sign-in and show identification.

The SS agents checked their guns at the desk, then everyone went through the metal detectors before being sniffed by the dogs. Once cleared, they entered another elevator which took them 500 feet underground so fast that they had to perform the Valsalva maneuver to get their ears to adjust. After exiting the elevator, they passed through a whole body scanning machine, then entered a small conference room.

Chairs were arranged in four rows of four, all facing a large projection screen on the wall at the front of the room. As soon as they took their seats in the first two rows, a tall blonde woman in Air Force kakis entered. Her Captain's bars glinted in the overhead lights.

"Welcome, Mr. President," said the Captain with a smile. "Welcome, gentlemen, to *Area 51*, the most secret and secure facility in the world. Much of the security is hidden from your view, but it's there monitoring everything we say or do, except in designated secure rooms. Any unusual activity or breach of security will set off an alarm and an immediate response by security personnel.

The room we're in is actually a mobile transport taking us to the section requested by the President. When we get to the destination in a few minutes, a green light will appear above the rear door on my right. Please exit from that door and have a seat in the hallway.

There will be a red and white striped door leading to the room where the President will conduct his business. The two Secret Service agents may enter the room and inspect it with the President, but the communications equipment will only be activated when the President is the only one in the room. When the agents leave, the door will be locked from the outside, but unlocked from the inside, so the President can leave at will. The room is acoustically and electronically secure from any surveillance. What the President hears or says will be completely private. Gentlemen, the light is green. When you're done, simply reenter this room through the same door."

One SS agent exited first, then the President, followed by the second SS agent, then the three Air Force officers. Five chairs were in the hallway by the striped door. The two agents and the President inspected the room. The striped door was the only way in or out. Projection equipment was visible in the ceiling. There was a chair and a small desk facing the projection area. Satisfied that everything was clear, the two agents nodded to the President and left the room, closing the door behind them. They took a seat in the hallway with the three officers and waited.

The President stood by the desk looking at the dimly lit projection area for about two minutes. He looked at his watch. He was a few minutes early for his appointment. Another minute passed and an image began to form in the projection area. He recognized the Guardian immediately.

"Good afternoon, Mr. President," said the Guardian as his standing holographic image appeared before the President. The Guardian was wearing a short-sleeve, royal blue embroidered, knee-length tunic with matching trousers; no sash. The material looked like silk. His footwear appeared to be a pair of patent leather, round-toed, black shoes. His skin tone was decidedly gray. He couldn't have been much more than four feet tall.

"Hello, Guardian," responded the President. "Thank you for meeting with me. I'm concerned about information I've received from my science staff that the earth may be threatened by a massive object hurtling through space. My staff has estimated damage might range from survivable with millions dead on up to a complete extinction event. Can you give me a more precise damage estimate? Can you help mitigate the damage?"

The Guardian hesitated and then answered, "I regret to confirm your most pessimistic assessment is the likely outcome. A stellar mass black hole is entering the outer limits of the solar system, and there's no way to stop it or divert it. However, as I've promised, the DNA we've preserved will be used to restart the human race after the earth has sufficiently recovered to support higher life-forms."

The President's eyes teared up as he listened, then asked, "Are you sure it's an extinction event and are you sure earth will recover enough for you to release your human clones?"

"We're 99.99% certain it will be an extinction event and only slightly less confident about the earth's ability to recover," the Guardian stated dispassionately. "As I've explained in previous meetings, I've reconstituted humanity four times in the last 100,000 years, and each time I've learned how to improve the process."

"With all due respect, Guardian," said the President in a chiding tone, "I don't care what happened in a previous reconstitution, as you call it. Speaking for mankind, insofar as I can, we appreciate what you've done for us, but we don't like it one bit. We don't like the idea that you're cloning us without retaining our essence, our soul. You and your fellow Guardians retain your soul, your full awareness of self, and your most precious, conscious memories when you clone yourselves a new body. If you were saving us in that manner, we could embrace it, but what you've been doing is hard to accept."

"I find it strange that you never mentioned this aversion in our previous conversations," commented Guardian, almost sotto voce.

"Guardian, in our previous encounters, the earth wasn't threatened with imminent extinction, so your method was history and any criticism would have been academic. Now we face a certain future and don't relish the prospects for our salvation," said the President. "Isn't there another way for you to save us? Can't we build an underground shelter for a representative cadre of people who would repopulate the earth?"

The Guardian looked down for a moment with his hands behind his back, then said, "Your feelings are your feelings; I respect that. Facts are also facts and can't be changed by wishful thinking.

"The subterranean shelter option cannot succeed because of the thousands of years it would take for the earth to recover sufficiently to support higher life forms. A shelter would have a limited number of people in a terrarium-like habitat. Disease or environmental imbalances will kill all humans hundreds of years before they would be able to survive on the surface of the planet.

"Our analysis also predicts that social disruptions—due to confined space, strict environmental laws, and male competition for females—will cause the commune to completely self-destruct, even before disease or bad air kills everyone."

"What if, despite the odds, they manage to survive?" interrupted the President.

"They would die soon after emerging from the shelter, because their immune systems would have been impaired by the isolation. The new variants of bacteria and viruses that would have developed on the earth's surface, during their sojourn, would be deadly to them," explained the Guardian.

"Wait a minute!" interjected the President. "If you create all life forms, then why would you create new ones that could kill human survivors?"

The Guardian frowned, then responded, "I've tried to explain this before. I'll try again. We Guardians design new species, but environmental factors affect the development of the species. We try to design species that support the ecology so that it's balanced and maintains the atmosphere, water, and food chain. Some species we design become extinct, and some adapt.

"Evolution occurs within a species and is limited in its range of change. We let evolution refine the initial design of the life-forms we create. It's complicated. Anyway, after an extinction event, some microscopic organisms survive and evolve without the presence of humans. A good number of these would be toxic to humans who had never been exposed to them before.

"Of course, it's my duty as Guardian to create new species to repopulate the earth. I'll try to introduce the same ones as before the catastrophe, but the environmental conditions may not immediately support them. It's a long and tedious process to help the earth recover and to repopulate the earth with clones of previously existing species of all kinds that are resistant to new strains of microbes. Sometimes they don't make it, because the earth is never the same, and there are too many variables.

"Consequently, I must create completely new species that have a higher survival quotient. Sometimes these new species are based on the design of a failed species, so that's why it might seem to you that one species evolved from another; not so.

"So, you see, I wouldn't deliberately design for any human survivors of a shelter to perish. On the other hand, my charter from the Elders limits my ability to assist with species survival. The rules about what I can or cannot do to favor the survival and development of any sentient species are complex. Often I must get approval from the Elders. So far, with the human species, the Elders have given me considerable freedom to interfere on your behalf.

"You must understand that despite the sophistication of our science, we can't always accurately predict the consequences of our interference. Your survival as a species depends in great part on how you evolve within the context of your environment and how you win the right to survive."

"Again, I ask you, what if, despite the odds, some manage to survive?"

The Guardian began answering as soon as the President finished his sentence, "There would have to be a sufficient number of males and females to ensure survival over the ages. It would take at least fifteen families of father, mother and children to have a 95% chance of species viability. These survivors would likely develop separately from the clones I release, because at the early stages of earth's rebirth, the clones will appear rather beastly to them. The odds of having at least fifteen families survive are infinitesimal."

"Okay," said the President. "I get the point. The shelter idea is a long shot—a very long shot."

"Now, with regard to your aversion to my cloning method for saving humanity," continued the Guardian, "I think if you could see how your comments are logically inconsistent, you may feel better about it.

"You said you'd like to retain your soul when I clone you. What you may not realize is that only selected DNA from our inventory is used to clone a limited number of people who are most likely to repeat human history pretty much the way it happened in the previous go-around.

"Specially selected clones from various periods of mankind's history are strategically seeded into the new stream of humanity that we initiated. Each of these clones receives a new soul that is influenced by the genetics of the host clone. The soul provides the strength of character, personality, and predispositions that make you who you are. We select a soul from God's inventory who would best fit the cloned body with its unique genetics."

The Guardian paused and reached outside the projection area. As he did so, his arm disappeared, then reappeared pulling a straight-backed chair into view, as if from thin air.

Guardian sat in the chair and continued speaking, "We Guardians are essentially immortal and can retain our individual soul only through a long and painful process. If we're seriously hurt, as by an accident, we often are not able to complete the soul-retention process, in which case we die just as you do, and our soul passes to God's realm. Of course, the Elders have the ability to retain their souls, too. As I've mentioned, the Elders were God's first sentient creatures in the Universe, and they in turn created the Guardians, and we Guardians have created all other life forms in the Universe. Do you now understand why you shouldn't be repulsed by my method of saving humanity?"

The President was silent for a moment, then said, "I'm not sure, but let me try to vocalize it. I said I wanted my soul to be in my clone, assuming I was chosen to have a clone. Yet, any clone can die and his soul will pass on, just like an original. This even happens to Guardians, if they can't transfer the soul prior to death. If the original dies or a clone dies, the soul passes on. Humanity spreads by birth, development, and death.

"If there were no imminent extinction event, all mankind currently alive would eventually die and be replaced by other humans; i.e., other souls. Your cloning method protects that process so that man can continue birth, development and death. It does so without interfering with the natural way that human souls pass on to another plane.

"My problem is, I don't want to die yet, and I don't want my loved ones to die yet. However, you're not promising to save me or anyone else on earth. You're promising to save humanity's development process."

"Yes, I think you understand. Do you feel any differently?" asked the Guardian.

"Frankly, no. Who wants to die in a cataclysmic event? Every one of us would rather be saved or have a chance to save ourselves. The knowledge that humanity will continue is nice indeed, but it offers little comfort to us individually," explained the President.

"Perhaps you need to get in touch with your spiritual self. You should take comfort in the certain knowledge that you have an immortal soul," said the Guardian.

"That may indeed be the source of my discomfort. I'm not as certain as you seem to be that I have a soul and that there is a God. Apparently, when you created us, you didn't instill faith into our DNA," said the President.

"Even if we could have done so, it would have prevented you from being fully sentient. Having faith built into your DNA would have severely limited your free will to decide or to choose," explained the Guardian. "I find it amusing that one minute you're upset that your clone won't have your soul, and the next minute you tell me you don't believe you have a soul. If you believe your essence can be migrated to a clone, then why can't you accept that your essence is indeed your immortal soul?"

"Honestly, I find this whole subject confusing. I was so comfortable being a closet atheist. Now I'm relegated to being a disconcerted agnostic. Thank you for granting this audience," said the President, as he bowed his head ever so slightly with his eyes fixed on the face of the Immortal One. "I only ask that you review your conclusion that nothing can be done to save the currently existing life on this planet. There are many of us who would rather die trying to save ourselves than to sit around waiting for our inevitable deaths."

"I've enjoyed our conversation," said the Guardian. "I'll have our calculations checked again, but I can't offer false hope. To avoid global panic, I suggest you keep this dire information from the public. I'm sorry to have confirmed your worst fears. I'm always available for you, if you have questions or just need to talk. Goodbye."

The image of the Immortal One faded away as the President stood as if in a trance. He was left without hope; standing, but in a slight slouch. He put both hands over his face and let out a muffled sigh of despair. Slowly, he regained his composure, stood up straight, pulled his shoulders back, put a smile on his face, and exited the room.

Good politicians are also good actors, he thought, as he approached the five men waiting for him outside the room. They all stood simultaneously.

"Gentlemen, my business here is over. Let's go."

When the President got back to the White House, he wasted no time setting up a meeting with his science advisor, Dr. Tony Regbramur, Director of OSTP.

"Tony, I've met with an expert in astrophysics who shall remain unnamed," said the President. "His analysis is not good news. He says our worst case scenario is the most likely scenario. He also agrees with you that building underground shelters won't work. Yet, I can't just do nothing. We must make an attempt of some sort. I want you to research any work that's been done on ecologically self-contained shelters. Surely someone in NASA must be working on such a concept for manned missions to Mars or some such thing. Second, assuming we have the capability to build the thing, we need some subterfuge to disguise the true purpose behind the humongous construction project. Perhaps it can be falsely promoted as a prototype for a shelter on the Moon or Mars for manned exploratory missions. Can you do that and do it fast, Tony?"

"Yes, Mr. President," said Regbramur. "The science team will get right on it!"

"Thanks, Tony," said the President as the Director turned and left the Oval Office, gently closing the door behind him.

The President stayed up late that night doing research of his own on the Internet, and thinking about the dilemma. What can he do to save mankind? It was 1:00 a.m., and the First Lady had been asleep for three hours already. He cleared his desk and walked to his bedroom, got ready for bed, and slipped under the covers.

His wife lay next to him, gently snoring. He loved her more than words could describe. He loved her for so many reasons, but especially for the two wonderful children she'd raised. It was her nurturing and her spark for life that had imbued the same spirit into the girls.

Of all his achievements, he was most proud of his role as husband and father. Yet here he was with knowledge of the end of days. His daughters wouldn't live out their adult lives, and he would have no grandchildren to spoil. The most powerful man on earth felt powerless.

In his mind's eye, just as sleep overcame him, he could see a gargantuan black hole hurtling toward him, swallowing the surrounding light at its periphery. It got closer and closer until the darkness consumed all light and all images. *Sleep—Death. Is death just a bad dream?*

Chapter 9

Antarctica

Tom organized two teams of two men each to do some initial scouting of the area on snowmachines. He and Jason Gibbons would scout the perimeter of the site, a circle about 12.6 miles in circumference. Sam Garcia and Harvey Watson would scout the area within the circle, traversing a figure-eight-shaped course.

Four of Tom's crew and the twelve scientists and engineers would remain at base camp checking equipment, reviewing aerial data, and finalizing plans for placement of underground sonar emitters and sensors. On the far eastern end of the site's perimeter, the aerial surveillance cameras had recorded a dark area that looked like an air pocket near the surface of the ice. The infrared cameras also detected the anomaly because of its slightly higher temperature.

Tom and Jason started out northwest on their snowmachines. As they approached the area of the anomaly, Tom waved a *disperse* signal to Jason. He also waved a *go slow* signal. Jason responded by moving about 100 yards away from Tom as they both slowly moved forward.

At first they saw nothing, then they were able to make out contours in the snow-pack of the elevated terrain ahead. The contours looked sharp-edged, rather than round as might be expected in snow drifts. They were like cliffs of a small mountain-side. The closer they got, the better they were able to see four great crevasses or chasms about 200 yards ahead. Each chasm started in front of them and angled off in different directions into the distance.

Tom waved the signal for Jason to stop. He then reached for his com-unit on his belt and told Jason to hang back as he went forward to test the stability of the snow-pack. He moved slowly forward, then stopped his snowmachine about fifteen yards from the edge.

He dismounted and reached into the saddle bag for mountain climbing gear. He drove a stake into the ground and attached the rope to it. He put on the harness and attached the other end of the rope to it. Over the com-unit he told Jason to move fifty yards left and fifty yards forward. Tom put on snowshoes and slowly walked to the edge of the crevasse.

He had no fear of heights, but was no fool either. Snow-pack wasn't likely to be as stable as ground and he was taking no chances; however, he had to learn more about this anomaly.

Why was it marginally warmer than the surrounding area? He peered over the edge and looked straight down. He couldn't believe his eyes. About 100 feet down and across the other side of the crevasse, sticking halfway out of the snow, was the rear half of a bulldozer.

"Jason, you won't believe what I found. Ride on over to my snowmachine, slowly. I'm walking back now," Tom spoke with com-unit in hand.

He pulled his camera from an inside pocket of his parka, took three shots into the crevasse, and turned to walk back to his snowmachine. When he got there, Jason was waiting. Tom showed him the pictures, zooming-in on the bulldozer.

"I want to see this myself, Tom," pleaded Jason. "Let me hook up to your line."

"Okay, but put your snowshoes on and walk slowly, and no yelling for any reason. That crevasse goes down at least a hundred feet, and I don't want to have to fish you out of an avalanche. Use your camera to take a few more shots," said Tom.

———————◊———————

Tom and Jason finished reconnoitering the perimeter and got back to base camp earlier than expected . . . which was all right with them. They were bursting with the need to tell what they had found. Garcia and Watkins returned about an hour later, so they gladly repeated their story and showed pictures of the mysterious bulldozer.

Sam Garcia said, "You know, this doesn't explain the anomaly. Despite the hazardous terrain there, we need to get down in that chasm with an infrared detection gun and a few shovels for the snow and picks for the ice. Maybe the dozer will provide a clue for us to follow. The big question is . . . How do we do it safely?"

"We can use the Pallas to lower a team and equipment right down into that thing," suggested Tom.

"I'm guessing you want me on the Pallas while you go down and have all the fun," said Sam.

"Command prerogative," offered Tom. "Tonight let's all think about how to do it. We'll meet tomorrow at 0800 hours to firm up the plan. I want to be ready to go no later than noon, so eat an early breakfast and an early lunch."

———————————◇———————————

By 09:00 the team had settled on a plan that put safety first. The biggest concern was an avalanche that would bury them in the crevasse. They divided themselves into three groups. The explorer group of four would be led by Tom. The transporter group of three would be led by Sam, and the observer group of three by Jason.

Each of the explorers would venture into the crevasse with an air-pack. The transporters would monitor activity from the Pallas anchored at 5,000 feet, and they would facilitate the first route of extraction. The observers would maintain a secondary route of extraction; a device comprised of a cable anchored at the bottom of the crevasse and running up to the edge of the embankment where it would be firmly secured to a platform that would distribute the weight and make the snow-pack at the edge more stable.

At noon the Observer Team had reached the edge of the crevasse, prepared to assemble the platform. They had used their snowmachines to tow a sled carrying aluminum walls and girders from one of the extra shelters. Jason could see the tracks he and Tom had made at the edge of the crevasse just yesterday afternoon. He lashed his safety cable to the sled and walked out toward the edge as the other two men started to untie the load. As he got to the edge and peered over, his jaw dropped. He quickly pulled out his com-unit and set it to broadcast on all channels.

Jason spoke into it with a hoarse voice, "It's gone, guys! The damn dozer ain't there. What now?"

"Jason, it's Tom. Are you sure you're at the same place we were yesterday?"

"I'm standing on our tracks, so it's the same spot. I'm looking through my binoculars now and don't see any sign of it at all," replied Jason.

"Okay, we're almost there," said Tom. "We'll fly over with the Pallas and check with the hi-tech cameras. There was no snowfall last night to cover it, but maybe a large chunk of snow fell off the embankment above it and buried it. Let's continue as planned. We know where we saw it, so we know where to begin when we get down there."

"Roger that, boss!" said Jason. "We'll have the platform ready in about thirty minutes."

About five minutes later Tom got on the com to all units, "No sign of the dozer from the ground surveillance systems. In five minutes we'll be scattering six small charges into the crevasse to see if we set off any avalanches before we anchor the ship. Jason, move your crew away from the edge and wait five minutes after the charges go off before resuming work on the platform."

"Okay, Tom," said Jason. "I'll let you know as soon as we're done."

———————◊———————

The six concussion charges went off in the air, one right after the other. They waited for an effect. Nothing happened. Not even the slightest bit of snow fell off the sides of the crevasse. Tom took that to be a good sign the walls were stable. He gave the order for Garcia to initiate the anchoring procedure for the Pallas. Tom knew the electronic sensors in the anchors would tell him if the floor of the crevasse was safe. If each of the five anchors sent back a ready signal, then they were secure in hard ice or snow-pack at least ten feet deep.

"Prepare for anchoring," said Garcia into the PA system. "All systems are go. Anchors away!"

The anchors fired-off in sequence. The electro-prop motors changed pitch as each anchor lashed the airship to the surface below.

"Anchors secure!" said Garcia. Sam was enjoying this captain-of-the-ship stuff. "Prepare elevator for deployment. Boss, we're ready for the Explorer Team."

"Thanks, Sam. Just be sure you're ready to get us the hell out of there fast if something goes wrong," said Tom.

"You can count on it. Good luck," responded Sam with a concerned look.

Just then Jason's voice came over the com system, "Platform is assembled. Request permission to fire the cable."

"Permission granted. Fire away, Jason," said Tom.

Once the cable was secure and properly tensioned, Jason attached the battery-powered tow-motor units and sent them, one by one, down to the bottom of the cable. He only needed to send four, but he sent a fifth as a backup.

In an emergency extraction, the procedure was to attach one strap of a person's harness to the front hook of the tow-motor and the other strap to the back hook of the tow-motor. Each had enough charge to pull 300 lbs up the cable about a dozen times, depending on wind and angle of ascent. The cable was strong enough to carry up to 2000 lbs at a time, and that meant all four explorers and their personal equipment could be carried up the cable at the same time.

The chasm was about 100 feet deep and 135 feet wide at the bottom. It took about 167 feet of cable to reach from the top of one side to the bottom of the other side where the Explorer Team would begin.

"Cable extraction system is secure and ready," announced Jason.

"Copy that. Explorer Team beginning elevator descent in five minutes," announced Tom.

When the explorers got off the elevator with their equipment, they put on their snowshoes and walked toward the anchor cable nearest to where they had seen the bulldozer. About thirty feet to the left of it, they drove a safety stake into the ground. Tom was the first to hook his safety rope to the stake. Harvey Watson was the second. Tom told the other two men, Ron Caldorf and Jeff Teichman, to stay right there while he and Harv scouted the area ahead to be sure they were on firm ground.

It seemed safe, so Tom yelled over to Ron and Jeff to disconnect Harv's rope and bring it to him. While they were walking toward him, Tom disconnected his safety rope with the intent of connecting Harv's rope to his, thereby doubling the length. He would then connect Ron's rope and Jeff's rope to make it even longer. All four would hook up to the same extended rope and explore in close proximity to each other while still having a safety line.

Just as Tom reached out to Jeff to get Harv's line, he felt the ground tremble beneath his feet. Through the corner of his left eye he saw that Harv had moved away about twenty feet and was looking up. Tom turned to look at him as his hand grabbed the rope Jeff was handing him. All of a sudden Harv was half his height, and the rope flew out of Tom's grasp.

Without uttering a sound, like a sprinter out of the blocks, Tom took two giant steps, forgetting he had snowshoes on, and dove forward to catch the end of the rope that was Harv's life. As he grabbed it in his right hand, he realized he'd disconnected his rope and had dropped it at Jeff's feet.

With his left hand he grabbed his pickaxe from its holster, while simultaneously twisting his right wrist so the rope wrapped around it. He turned on his stomach facing Jeff, put his hand through the strap on the pickaxe, swung the axe in front of his head into the snow, dug the tips of his snowshoes into the snow, and yelled, "Get me my safety line now!"

Fortunately, Jeff had already picked up the end of Tom's rope and was moving toward him, but not fast enough. Harv's rope had reached its limit, and Jeff saw Tom's right arm pulled clockwise and down to his thigh. Tom screamed in agony as his shoulder was pulled out of its socket.

Tom held on to the rope, but pickaxe and snowshoes weren't enough to keep him from sliding toward the hole Harv was hanging in. Jeff was taking rapid giant steps in his snowshoes. He grabbed Tom's harness and hooked his line to it, then grabbed Harv's line and held it for dear life, but they were still sliding.

By this time Ron had also grabbed Harv's line, and together, they hooked it to Tom's line. Tom yelled at them to hook their lines to his immediately. They did it just in time as the snow-pack ahead of them opened up even more, within five feet of where they were. They thought for sure they were going for a long ride down. The hole was big enough now that daylight allowed them to look right into it, and they could hear Harv yelling, "Get me the hell out of here!"

The three of them pulled Harvey up from the hole, and they sat there for a few minutes to catch their breath.

Harv spoke up first, "Thanks guys. I thought I was a goner for awhile, until the hole opened up, and I could see the bottom was only a few feet below me. There's a huge tunnel down there."

Tom lurked over the edge and whispered, "Let's take a few sonic readings, then get the hell out of here for today. My shoulder is killing me. We'll explore more tomorrow."

"Sam, send down our four snowmachines," Tom said. "We had a close call, but we're all okay. We found a tunnel that looks manmade, but we're tired, and I hurt my shoulder, so we'll explore it tomorrow. You and your crew should stay put with the Pallas overnight. We'll extract the snowmachines and ourselves up the cable to the platform where we'll hook up with the observers and go back to the base camp for the night. We'll be back here in the morning."

"Roger that, boss. How bad's the shoulder?" asked Sam.

"It hurts like hell, but I'm sure it's just dislocated," said Tom. "I'm figuring the medic back at base camp can pop it back for me. I've walked around with worse than this. Keep an eye on us until we get ourselves out of this hole."

"Will do. And good luck with your shoulder," said Sam.

"Jason, did you get all that?" asked Tom into his com-unit.

"Copied it all, Tom. We're ready and waiting up here. I would suggest sending up one snowmachine at a time. When we offload one, I'll give you the signal to send the next one," said Jason.

———————————◇———————————

Back at the base camp, Tom had the medic pop his shoulder back into its socket, took three high potency pain killers, and kept his arm in a sling. It was a good thing he was ambidextrous or he would have had a hard time enjoying his dinner.

They reviewed the soundings they had taken in the area of the tunnel just before they left. They saw nothing but the tunnel in the computer-rendered 3-D images. They all wondered what happened to the mysterious bulldozer. The images showed the tunnel to extend about 100 feet below the surface, but it was dug at a thirty degree slope. The bottom of the tunnel branched out in two opposite directions for about twenty-five yards and stopped.

Tom figured that he and his crew could walk down the tunnel if they strapped cleats onto their boots. They hit the sack early so they could get up early and get back to explore the tunnel. In the morning they would rig Raven, the UAV, to do some spelunking.

Chapter 10

Antarctica

First thing in the morning Tom worked with Jeff Teichman and Ron Caldorf to prepare Raven for a mission it wasn't intended to fly. Flying the remote controlled Raven into a thirteen-foot diameter tunnel could easily result in its destruction.

The scientists were miffed when they heard what was going on, because they had planned additional aerial reconnaissance flights for the UAV as a basis for deciding where to place their ground sonar emitters. They insisted the few UAV flights they had done yesterday were insufficient. After five minutes of argument, Tom got them to admit they could place the emitters without the benefit of additional data from Raven.

Jeff was a light plane pilot and a video game champion of sorts, so he was chosen to fly Raven into the tunnel. Ron was an aircraft mechanic, so he was chosen to outfit Raven with a miniature high-powered flashlight which wasn't part of the accessory kit. He would also attach the standard radar imaging accessory. It only took an hour to get Raven ready.

When Raven reached the tunnel entrance, Jeff wanted to enter as slowly as possible, but he was having trouble keeping her from stalling below twenty-five mph. Her minimum turning radius was eight feet, so once in the tunnel it was straight ahead until the bottom, where it was wide enough to turn her around and come back out. As Jeff concentrated on flying Raven, Tom and Ron had their eyes glued to the monitor. It was too fast to recognize anything, and Raven was coming back out before they could have a reaction to what they'd seen.

They rewound the digital video recorder and watched it again and again. All they could see were snow walls and a somewhat metallic surface protruding the whole length of the forward wall. They then reviewed the radar imaging.

"What the blazes happened?" asked Tom. "Is it a malfunction? Interference?"

"I don't think so," said Ron. "It seems to be working on every wall except the forward one."

Jeff interjected, "It didn't record what we saw on camera. It recorded that huge object as if it were the same density and reflectivity as the surrounding snow. I'm not sure I can make another sortie. I almost lost her on the turn-around."

"Okay, bring her home, Jeff," Tom commanded. "We've seen enough. The only way to solve this mystery is to walk on down there and see for ourselves."

————————————◇————————————

When Tom and his team reached the platform at the embankment, they left their snowmachines up top with Jason and the two others of the Observer Team. Tom and his three-man Explorer Team rode down the cable and were ready to enter the tunnel in a matter of minutes.

This time Tom had enough safety line ready to go down to the bottom with plenty left to walk around. He already had Ron Caldorf and Jeff Teichman hooked to the line with him via their individual twenty foot tethers. He had told Harv to remain at the tunnel entrance to operate a high-speed electric winch they had installed to pull them out of the tunnel in an emergency.

Once the explorers started walking down the tunnel with cleats strapped to the soles of their boots, it was Harv's job to unwind the line and maintain just the right amount of slack. The explorers sported miners' hardhats with embedded lights. When they reached the bottom of the tunnel they entered a large chamber with the metallic-like surface protruding from the front wall of snow. They walked cautiously forward toward the wall and immediately noticed several piles of ash on the ground about fifteen feet in front of the wall.

"Look at those dark shapes on the ground. They look like charred bodies," gasped Ron.

"See those two dark spots on the metallic surface?" asked Jeff. "It looks like someone tried to cut into it with a torch."

"That thing could be some kind of alien machine, and it toasted these guys in self-defense," suggested Tom. "Let's explore the tunnel on the right, and don't touch the surface of that thing."

The three of them explored every foot of the tunnel off to the right, and it seemed to curve slightly forward. The same was true when they explored the tunnel to the left. They realized that this metallic object was probably circular, but they couldn't tell if it was a sphere, a cylinder, or a disk. After they walked back to the chamber, they stopped and stared at the shiny surface of the object in front of them.

"I'm going to touch it with my bare hand," said Tom. "You two stand back and run like hell if it toasts me."

Ron and Jeff took a few steps back as Tom walked forward, taking off his right glove. He touched the surface. Nothing happened. He rubbed the surface to get a sense of what it might be. It felt hard, but smooth, and neither hot nor cold. As he rubbed his hand over the surface, Ron spoke up, "Hey, boss. Look up."

Above Tom's head there had appeared a set of symbols, some type of writing on the metallic object.

Tom said, "Take a picture, quick. Turn off the flash first."

Both Jeff and Ron reached for their cameras at the same time, fumbled to turn off the flash, and started snapping pictures. They then checked them on the camera's screen to be sure the writing was clear. The lights from their helmets had been enough. They had several clear pictures.

"Hey, guys. Are you okay? What's going on down there?" Harv called out on his com-unit with all channels open.

"Harv, we're fine. Jeff will be transmitting you a picture of writing that appeared on the metallic wall of a large object, which could be some sort of alien machine or fortress. Relay it to the Pallas, and tell Sam to send it to AIEDA for translation via satellite link. This is top priority," commanded Tom.

"Roger," said Harv.

The three explorers each pulled out a vinyl-covered foam pad from the large storage pocket in the back of their parkas. They dropped the pads on the ground in the middle of the chamber and sat on them with their legs crossed. They looked at each other and said nothing as they waited. Every fifteen minutes Tom checked with Harv.

A little over an hour went by and Harv was on the com, "Tom, I just got it. The language is Sumerian from 3,000 to 4,000 B.C. Here's an approximate translation: *If you wish to enter, you must knock three times. Leave your anger, your fear, and your weapons outside.*"

"You've got to be kidding me! Knock three times? I think these guys have a sense of humor," exclaimed Tom as he got up. "Okay, Ron, you stay here. Jeff, let's give Ron our guns and knives. Ron, keep an open channel with Harv and keep him informed. Tell him to keep an open channel so transporters and observers can listen in."

Tom and Jeff disconnected themselves from the safety line. Tom told Jeff to stand behind him and hold on to the back of his belt with one hand. They walked to the metallic surface right below the writing, and Tom knocked three times. Nothing happened. He almost knocked again, but had second thoughts. He would follow the instructions exactly and be patient. He waited a couple of minutes.

Without a sound, an oval opening, about eight feet high and three feet wide, appeared about a foot to his right. He walked confidently through it with Jeff in tow. As he stepped inside, it lit up with an eerie glow as though the light source was diffused and coming with the same luminosity from walls, floor, and ceiling. The room was a circle and completely empty. When they turned around, the opening was gone. They stood there with racing hearts waiting for something to happen. Tom was tempted to call out a hearty *Hello!* but he refrained from the urge. Jeff was now standing at his left with a concerned look.

Tom whispered, "Jeff, they know we're here. Let's be calm and patient. Remember the admonition to leave our anger and fear outside."

Silently, in the center of the room, a cylindrical table rose from the floor. Tom and Jeff approached it. On the surface were a group of circles arranged in a square eight circles high by eight circles wide, sixty-four total. The circles were alternately red and green on a white square background. Tom reached out and touched the center of the table. Immediately, red symbols appeared on the top two rows and green symbols on the bottom two rows.

"Tom, it looks like a chessboard to me," said Jeff.

Tom touched what he thought was a green *king's pawn* and it got brighter. He then touched position, *king-four*, and it lit up with the pawn's symbol. The *king's pawn* symbol on row two was now gone. Then the system responded by moving red *king's pawn* to *king-four* on the opposite side of the board.

"I think this is chess as we know it," said Tom.

They played three consecutive games, each harder than the last. They won all three. They had been playing for four hours and they were exhausted. About half-a-minute after winning the third game, the table retracted into the floor, and another opening appeared on the other side of the room.

Tom and Jeff walked into the next room, which was bigger and more dimly lit. The opening disappeared behind them. There were two cylindrical objects in the middle of the room. Tom touched the top of them, and they seemed soft like a cushion, so they sat down. Suddenly, they were transported into an ancient town with people walking all around them. They were momentarily disoriented and almost fell off their seats.

They were experiencing a holographic movie. Unlike in a 3-D movie, the characters seemed to be solid, real actors. Only an occasional faint flicker gave away the artificiality of the presentation. The scene changed and the sound began. An English speaking narrator explained what they were seeing. They were witnessing selected scenes in the history of mankind, but it was a bizarre interpretation.

They saw that Adam and Eve were genetically altered clones. They saw the pyramids being built with the help of alien technology. They saw Moses part the Red Sea with the help of a disk-like flying craft. They saw how Joshua had similar help when the Jordan River parted for him and when he caused the walls of Jericho to tumble. They saw that Ezekiel had a visitation, not from God, but from space-faring beings. They saw that the Greek hero Hercules was a genetically altered human.

The movie continued to identify many historical events that involved the interference of alien beings. When it was over, the lights turned up, and both Tom and Jeff sat stupefied for several minutes before they noticed that another doorway had opened.

They walked into the third room, and again the doorway disappeared. This room was the smallest, and it had two seats facing a slightly raised platform with one seat on it. The lighting was brighter again, as it had been in the chess room. Soon an old man in a flowing white toga appeared on the stage, walked to the seat, and sat down.

"Welcome to my home, gentlemen. I'm the Guardian. You may address me as such. How may I address you?"

Tom responded confidently, "I'm Thomas Calvano, Tom for short. My friend is Jeffery Teichman. We call him Jeff. I'm the leader of an expedition from Florida. We noticed some anomalies in this area and came here to study them. We have many questions, but please feel free to first ask us anything you wish."

"I'm the Guardian of all life on earth. Before I was the Guardian I was the Creator of all life on earth. I'm curious about your mission, as it would seem you come well prepared with highly sophisticated and practical equipment."

Tom asked, "Are you telling us you're God?"

"No," said the Guardian. "I'm an alien being. One of those revealed to you in the historical documentary you just witnessed. God has chartered my species to spread life throughout the Universe. We've been doing this task for almost five billion years. Excuse me, Jeff. Why are you wandering about the room?"

"Oh, I'm looking for a curtain and a person behind it who's projecting your holographic image. Perhaps you've heard the tale of the Wizard of Oz?" said Jeff.

"Oh, a skeptic!" said the Guardian. "You're correct that I'm an image, but you won't find a projectionist behind a curtain as in that wonderful children's story."

"Well, you look too much like Moses for me to believe we are seeing your true self," commented Tom.

"You're correct," said the Guardian. "I'll project my true image if you think it will facilitate our discourse."

"No," said Tom. "It would facilitate the discourse if you conversed with us in person, face-to-face. It would also help if you'd confirm your gender."

"Very well," said the Guardian. "I'll appear in person, but I'll erect a force field between us. The body I've had for the last 503 years is of the male gender."

"We won't attack you," said Tom. "Besides, if you create life and guard life, how could we possibly hurt you?"

The holographic image disappeared, and a small, fragile, gray being appeared wearing a loose white short-sleeve shirt, a red pleated kilt, short-top black boots, and knee-high red socks. He walked confidently toward where the image had been.

As he walked, he spoke in response to Tom's question, then sat down, "My species is immortal, but we can be seriously injured and killed. We don't die of old age or from disease, but we can be damaged beyond our body's ability to regenerate. Given sufficient time, we can transfer our consciousness to another cloned body, but if the procedure isn't done in a timely manner, our essence will be gone from this world. Transference is not a pleasant experience. Until we develop a level of trust, I prefer to be cautious about my safety."

"Your essence?" asked Tom. "Is that what we know as a soul?"

"Yes," said the Guardian. "We have a soul just as you have a soul. You're our children and are made in our image as God has commanded. Your DNA is derived from the DNA of my species. Actually, all species in the Universe, even the lowest of species, are derived from our DNA, except for one. We're the only species chartered by God to create life in the Universe."

"What's the one species not derived from your DNA?" asked Tom.

"The Elders," said the Guardian. "They're the first species that God created, and they created my species. God doesn't allow the Elders to propagate themselves; they're immortal. They're not physically capable of leaving their place of creation. They're the prophets, disseminating the words and commands of God."

"Does God live in some inexplicable place like heaven?" asked Tom.

"God resides in the eleventh dimension. He's the first cause, the continuing cause, and the last cause. His presence is known to us by the force you call gravity," said the Guardian. "Gravity is the breath of God emanating from his domain in the eleventh dimension. His breath is not constant throughout the Universe. Now tell me, why have you come to this place?   What is your mission?"

"Well, first let me compliment you on your outfit. Very snappy indeed," said Tom.

"Your sarcasm is noted, but really, did you expect me to walk out naked like the little gray aliens from your movies and comic books?" asked the Guardian.

"My apologies," said Tom. "It's just that all of this seems so implausible . . . unimaginable . . . I have so many questions, but first to answer yours. We're here to survey this area to validate its suitability as a site for the construction of an underground ecologically stable habitat for a limited number of humans. This habitat, which we call the Ecosthat, is intended to ensure the survival of the human species in case there's a global extinction event."

"Your Ecosthat is a laudable endeavor. However, it won't save humanity from an extinction event. It takes too long for the earth to recover, and the inhabitants of such a confined space would not survive that long. Besides it's not necessary, because I've been protecting humanity and will continue to do so," said the Guardian.

"You protect us all alone? How do you do it?" asked Jeff.

"I'm not alone. I have many assistants, and we have androids. We also have transportation vessels. We maintain a collection of the DNA of all earth's creatures from various periods of the most significant descendents. We try to prevent mass extinction events, but when we cannot do so, we wait until the earth's environment can support life, then we clone new life forms and release them onto the earth.

We've done this four times. The first was about 100,000 years ago, after a sustained global heat wave. We reconstituted many humans from the DNA of one African woman and several African men who had shown remarkable survival characteristics. The second time was about 73,000 years ago when the super-volcano, TOBA, wiped out civilizations. The third time was about 13,000 years ago, the Younger Dryas Period, when the climate regressed to an Ice Age for 1,500 years. The fourth time was the Great Flood about 9,000 years ago. If I hadn't cloned Noah and his band, mankind would not have survived."

"What are these transportation vessels you mentioned? Are they part of the UFO phenomena we've been experiencing for many generations?" asked Tom.

"Yes, our vessels are sometimes identified as UFO's or flying saucers, but only about five percent of such sightings are actually extraterrestrial vessels and, of those, less than two percent are mine. Most valid sightings are of vessels that are hyper-slinging around the singularity within earth's core."

"By *singularity*, do you mean black hole?" asked Tom.

"Yes," said the Guardian. "Black holes create a gateway into other dimensions. Super-massive black holes are too dangerous to approach. The black hole within the earth is just the right size and is buried in a core of iron which makes it ideal, and also rare. For that reason, earth has a lot of visitors. These visitors know that earth is under Guardianship and that punishment for interference in earth's affairs is severe. We haven't had a problem, except for one species that loves beef and has periodically helped themselves to some of your cattle. They pay a stiff fine when I catch them, but for a few of them the temptation is just too great."

"I don't understand how a black hole in the center of the earth doesn't consume the entire planet," said Tom.

"It's a microscopic primordial black hole that got trapped when earth formed. There are four mechanisms that act together to keep it dormant, but they're beyond your scientific understanding," said the Guardian.

"Can't you put it in layman's terms?" asked Tom.

"I might be able to simplify the two most significant mechanisms for you. At a certain distance from a black hole there's a spherical phenomenon . . . at what your scientists sometimes call the Schwarzchild radius. If anything gets closer than this distance, it can't escape; it gets devoured. Pressure caused the inner iron core of the earth to become solid, but the black hole in its center devoured all the material around itself to a distance just outside the Schwarzchild radius. It sits in the center of a hollow solid-iron ball, where it can't pull anymore material into itself, especially because the earth's gravity inside the hollow ball is essentially zero. The earth's magnetic field, generated by the spinning inner iron core, acts like a magnetic bottle that keeps the black hole from drifting too close to the inner walls of the hollow iron sphere."

"How do your vessels defy gravity and inertia as they fly around?" asked Jeff.

The Guardian hesitated, then began, "I can't divulge details about advanced technology to you, but I can tell you that we don't defy gravity or inertia in the way it appears to an observer. Our propulsion system has two singularities each confined in an electromagnetic force field. The singularities are made to revolve around each other in such a way that a gateway is opened from our fourth dimensional universe into the fifth dimension."

Guardian paused to survey his guests' faces. Satisfied he hadn't lost his audience, he continued, "The vessel slips into and then out of a fifth dimensional boundary layer or corridor. While in the corridor, relative time slows down. The deeper the vessel goes into the corridor, the more time slows. The vessel can only travel down the corridor to the point where relative time stops.

"From within the fifth dimensional corridor, we have access to anyplace in our fourth dimensional universe. We can move to a different spot on earth in a blink of an eye for short distances or move to another place in the Milky Way in a matter of minutes or hours, depending on how far we go.

"To travel outside the Milky Way, we must do so with successive *dimensional jumps*. We and our vessels can't actually exist physically in another dimension, but we can experience the trans-dimensional interlude in the same way you experience a dream world, although it's much more stable than a dream. To retain our memory of the experience, we must receive a periodic vaccination. The power of our vessels can't propel us into dimensions greater than the fifth, but hyper-slinging around a singularity, as exists in earth's core, allows us to take a corridor leading to every dimension except the eleventh. The gate to the eleventh dimension ensures God's privacy. By accessing corridors to the sixth through tenth dimensions, we can observe those other universes."

Jeff asked, "When you're not jumping, how do you buzz around; you know, fly normal?"

The Guardian hesitated again, then said, "There's a potential energy difference between dimensions. We open a small hole rather than a gateway and insert what you might call an electrical plug. The result is equivalent to electrical current caused by induction; however, it yields a powerful force much like an electromagnet. As a child, I'm sure you've played a game with a metal toy on top of a sheet of cardboard. You move a magnet around underneath the cardboard, and the metal toy moves as though by magic across the top of the cardboard. In this way we move about in the heavens by diverting the force that's trying to pull us into the dimensional corridor, but can't do so because the hole is too small."

Tom instinctively raised his hand, as if in school, but didn't wait to be called upon, "Why are you telling us this? I mean, what do you expect us to do with this information? No one we tell will believe a word of it."

"You're not the first to have heard our story. Many heads of state have been briefed in the last ten years. The President of the United States and a few others ask me for advice on occasion. Most of the states choose to ignore my existence. A few tried to capture me. Some told me to leave earth. We believe that as a sentient species you've developed an intellect sufficient enough to acknowledge the truth. We believe the truth will eventually further your development," explained the Guardian.

"How many private parties; you know, non-government, have been informed?" asked Jeff.

"You're the first," said the Guardian.

"Why us?" asked Tom.

"We've been considering a number of individuals and groups for the last few years, and none have been acceptable. As chance would have it, we began observing you since you encountered the waterspout, and you've passed all of our tests," said the Guardian.

"Don't tell me. You created that spout. You could have killed us!" complained Tom.

"You were never in fatal danger. Waterspouts are one of the few phenomena of nature I can control. I was especially impressed with how you escaped. Your subsequent curiosity and exploration of the anomalous heat signature, the bulldozer, and the tunnel demonstrated many aspects of your character and intellect," said the Guardian.

"I bet the heat source was artificial, and the bulldozer was a holographic image. I bet the collapse of the tunnel entrance was staged, too. You could have killed Harv!" yelled Tom.

"Please, Tom. You know the tunnel entrance wasn't that deep, and your friend was hanging only a few feet from the tunnel floor. I did take notice of how you risked your life to save him from what appeared to you as certain death. You reacted fearlessly and instinctively and succeeded with great skill. I can go on about the other tests like the fake burned bodies, the entrance code, the chess games, etc. You've demonstrated your character and leadership skills, and your team is excellent," stated the Guardian.

"Thanks for the vote of confidence. I think," said Tom sardonically. "I'm surprised you haven't checked our DNA."

The Guardian's face twitched a bit and said almost apologetically, "We *have* checked your DNA, Tom. You and your team left it on everything you touched. We lifted yours from the chess table."

"Figures," said Tom. "Anything else you want to know?"

"I know you sent a photo of the entrance code to your friends via satellite, but how did they crack it so quickly?"

"I have some smart people back home with some powerful computers, and I know I can rely on them," said Tom proudly.

"I've dropped the force field," said the Guardian. "May I shake your hand in friendship, my son?"

Tom stood and approached the Guardian. The Guardian also stood, and Tom towered over him. Tom looked down and took the Guardian's hand in his. He was afraid to grasp it tightly lest he break every fragile bone in it. Tom felt like he was shaking the hand of a child. He looked into the Guardian's eyes and realized they were dark, but not big like aliens were depicted in movies and comic books.

Tom coyly asked, "Why don't you have big eyes like in the Roswell drawings? Most of your other features, except for the clothing, are consistent with those drawings."

"When we wear our life support helmets, it makes us look like we have big eyes. Our apparent nakedness in some past encounters is a result of our skintight body-armor. Read the book of Ezekiel in the Bible, and you'll find his reference to how the angels appeared as though they had *a face within a face*," explained the Guardian.

"We'd like to ask many more questions, but first I need to contact my friends back home and discuss our encounter. I'm sure they'll have some questions for me to ask you. When I return, will you receive me? Do I need a pass code?" asked Tom.

"Yes, of course I'll receive you. Just drop by anytime and knock three times when you're ready to enter," said the Guardian.

As Tom moved away from the Guardian, Jeff quickly stepped forward with an outstretched hand and a broad smile, "It's been a pleasure meeting you, Sir Guardian," said Jeff.

"Nice meeting you, too, Jeff," said the Guardian as he shook Jeff's hand.

———————————◇———————————

Back at the base camp Tom and Jeff told of their encounter. They made sure their story was captured on more than one video recorder, then burned to a DVD. They wanted to document it while everything was fresh in their minds. Although they had set their com-units with all channels open when they had first entered the Guardian's fortress, no signal had escaped to the outside, so only their memory could serve to document this extraordinary experience.

Tom used the DVD documentary to help him prepare an outline of his report. Then he gave Jean Philippe a call via satellite link. He needed guidance on how to proceed with the project under these new circumstances. After all, the Guardian had insisted that the Ecosthat couldn't save mankind.

Chapter 11

Manhattan, NYC
March 2005

When Jean Philippe got Tom Calvano's phone call at his Manhattan penthouse, it was via satellite link, which meant a long delay in verbal response time. He wanted to have a rapid fire conversation, and since that was impossible, he showed his frustration. Soon Tom would be submitting a formal company confidential report for Jean Philippe's *eyes only*. In the meantime, he had gotten enough information to give him weak knees, as he thought, *The Guardian? Is this a joke? So far AIEDA has been accurate. Let's see what AIEDA says about this so called Guardian.*

He called his friend, Don Mensch, at AIEDA home office in the Bronx to let him know he'd be personally delivering the information. He'd hardly finished his request when Don told him that AIEDA was already working full tilt on a high priority project, and they wouldn't be able to accommodate his request for about a week.

"Unacceptable!" Jean Philippe screamed into the phone. "Without my business, your firm wouldn't exist. I demand to know what project could be more important than one of mine."

When he heard the answer from Don, he felt sick to his stomach.

"Thank you, Don. I apologize for my outburst. I still plan to see you tomorrow. We have much to discuss."

———————————◊———————————

At AIEDA home office Don Mensch and Jon Walmer had just finished a long discussion of the most recent events. The data they were analyzing for Amanda Rheinhardt was being done without charge. As improbable as it sounded to them, the risk to the planet was too great to ignore. Most unusual, of course, was the coincidence of Jean Philippe's project to save humanity with Rheinhardt's data suggesting an impending global catastrophic event. Jean Philippe would be arriving tomorrow afternoon, so it made sense to convene a meeting of the key players in these two critical projects. Don would call an informal meeting tomorrow evening at Jon's Manhattan residence.

————————————◊————————————

Rain was pouring and wind was blowing, and Don Mensch had all to do to keep his umbrella from turning inside-out. His trousers below the bottom of his London Fog trench coat were soaked. As he was about to step off the curb, a passing car splashed him a good one as it plowed through the road run-off. He hurried across the darkened street to a lamp post that illuminated the entrance to Jon Walmer's five-story brownstone residence.

It was the kind of building that gave this Upper West Side of Manhattan neighborhood its daylight charm. New York City still had enough of its renovated historic architecture around to soften the sharp edges of all the modern office buildings that had spread like weeds out of Manhattan into the upper Bronx.

Don was late, and he cursed his unfamiliarity with the subway system that didn't quite take him as close to his destination as he'd expected. He took the stoop two steps at a time, rising above the stone English-style basement, and pasted the doorbell with the palm of his hand. The overhang gave no shelter from the rain as he waited impatiently, then tried the doorknob.

He was surprised to find it opened easily, and he stepped in, turned about to close and shake his umbrella outside, then quickly pulled the door shut and locked it. As he deposited the umbrella in the receptacle with three others, he shed his wet coat and hung it on the coat rack behind the door, this all in, what appeared to be, one fluid motion.

"Ah, Mr. Mensch, good to see you could make it. The others are waiting for you in the parlor. Can I bring you something to drink? Your usual black coffee? Or perhaps the weather calls for Irish coffee?"

"Black coffee is fine, Harry. Thanks."

The floor creaked as he hurried down the short hallway into the first room on the left. The front windows of the parlor extended to the floor, and the ceiling rose to nearly ten feet. A wood-burning fireplace gave the room a cozy feeling as the flames flickered and cast shadows on the walls.

"Don, we thought you got lost."

"No, Jon, not lost. I tried the subway this time, and it took longer than I figured."

"Don, let me introduce you to Amanda Rheinhardt, branch director of the U.S. Geological Survey at Fort Collins, CO. Amanda, meet Don Mensch, my partner . . . without him AIEDA wouldn't exist," Jon commented in a flamboyant manner.

"So nice to meet you, Amanda," said Don as he took her outstretched hand.

"Jon has been telling us so many nice things about you," retorted Amanda as she released his firm but gentle grip.

"I'm sure he exaggerated. He's the brains of this outfit," Don responded. He couldn't help but notice that Amanda's modest outfit belied her beauty.

Nice long legs and a flat stomach, too! And hiding behind the glasses and the pulled-back hair, there's a gorgeous face, he thought.

"Don, I'm also pleased to introduce you to George Blocker, chief scientist at the Canadian Geodetic Survey Division, Ottawa, Ontario."

"Nice to meet you, George. I just wish this occasion were less ominous."

"I'm told you've begun analyzing my data, and I thank you for that," George responded as they both shook hands.

"Yes, but it's a lot of data and we're not sure when a result might be achieved. We're guessing in a few days," Don explained.

"And, of course, you know Jean Philippe."

"Hello, Jean Philippe. Our last meeting in Paris was so much nicer than this one portends," Don said sympathetically as he shook Jean Philippe's hand.

"Oh, to be sure, we have some serious business here tonight, but I'm confident we'll find an explanation and develop a timely solution," responded Jean Philippe, always the optimist.

"Well, let's all take a seat, sip our drinks, and start putting together a picture of what's happening to our dear Mother Earth," chimed Jon in a somewhat melodramatic tone. "Don, would you like to summarize the situation for us?"

"Sure. I guess you know that AIEDA has been simultaneously working on two separate projects; one for Jean Philippe and the other for Amanda and George. We believe there may be a connection between the two projects.

"Amanda and George have discovered gravitational force acting upon the earth from beyond our solar system. This force probably caused the Asian Tsunami in conjunction with plate subduction. Its effect actually appears to have first manifested itself exactly one year to the day before the Asian Tsunami. You see, the Bam earthquake in southeastern Iran hit on December 26, 2003 killing 43,000 people. And as you know, the Indian Ocean earthquake that generated the tsunami occurred on December 26, 2004.

"AIEDA predicts that this same combination of forces will cause a major earthquake on December 26, 2006 in Hengchun with epicenter off the southwest coast of Taiwan.

"Dr. Roger Akins, a prominent astrophysicist, has theorized the existence of this anomalous external force and has mapped its general point of origin. Telescopic data is needed to confirm his conclusion. Dr. Akins theorizes this force is the result of a stellar-mass black hole hurtling into our solar system.

"I'm not a scientist and probably know the least about this stuff, so pardon me if I over-simplify or emphasize what might be obvious to you. I'm attempting to summarize information provided to me by our best resources at AIEDA. As you know, earth has a thin crust of plates on top of a solid mantle averaging about 41 miles thick. This mantle sits on a molten outer core of iron and nickel and a solid inner core of iron."

Don paused for effect, then continued describing plate tectonics. He also explained how gravity has forced the Earth to be roughly like a ball, while other forces have worked to deform its shape; forces such as those caused by its spin and forces from other heavenly bodies such as the Sun, Moon, Jupiter, etc.

Don took a deep breath and continued, "Now we have the mysterious arrival of another strong gravitational force from outer space that's acting on our planet, distorting its shape and further increasing tectonic activity in the form of earthquakes.

"The force appears to be strong enough to contribute to the fracturing of fault lines. These faults are like giant cracks in the earth's crust that can extend into the mantle. The largest ones appear to be affected first, then the somewhat smaller ones, etc. The smallest, of course, are likely to fracture last.

"In addition there's some effect from the earth's annual rotation around the sun, an ellipse with a point closest to the sun called perihelion. It so happens that the quakes occur just before the earth's perihelion in early January. The alignment of heavenly bodies combined with the anomalous force could be causing some form of tectonic periodicity . . . maybe. Frankly, we don't understand these patterns." Don stopped speaking to let others respond, but there was silence.

Then George Blocker broke the silence, "Eggs! Like when you make an omelet," George blurted.

"What are you saying, George?" asked Amanda.

The others gave George an intensely incredulous stare.

"I think I see the danger here. As each fault line fractures, it's not just the loss of life from each quake that we should worry about. It's the cumulative effect that will cause an extinction event."

"There's no evidence the danger's that great, George. We don't even know if this anomalous force is moving toward us or just passing close by. Although, it does appear to be getting stronger," objected Jon.

"Hear me out," said George. "My hypothesis is worth checking, because if I'm correct, we're in big trouble. I think each earthquake is fracturing the crust and mantle at many critical points, and also heating up the boundary layer between the mantle and the molten outer core.

"The mantle might become free-floating on top of the outer core . . . much like cooked eggs sliding on a greased griddle. Usually the eggs stick to the griddle, but apply the right amount of heat, butter, and shaking of the pan, and they slide around with ease. If you shake the pan with a lateral motion, the pan moves beneath the eggs, but the eggs stay pretty much in the same spot over the stove.

"If the mantle breaks free of the molten outer core, the molten core will pick up momentum from the spinning solid inner core. Friction from earth's atmosphere will slow down the crust-mantle, and the molten core will slowly flip so that the magnetic South Pole becomes the magnetic North Pole.

"The fact that earth is shaped like a pear, rather than like a ball, means the flip will probably be just 180 degrees and won't continue to flip. However, the result will be that the magnetic field of the earth will be in reverse, even though winter solstice will still occur in the northern hemisphere in December.

"If I'm right, the complete reversal of the earth's magnetic field will cause an extinction event for all life on the planet. During the flipping process the magnetosphere will be severely weakened. It could take hundreds or thousands of years to recover its strength. In the meantime earth won't have its magnetic shield that protects all life and the atmosphere from the ravages of cosmic radiation."

The room was silent for less than a minute, but it seemed like many.

"Well, let's give this hypothesis and all relevant data to AIEDA, and see what she makes of it," offered Jon.

"Agreed," said Don. "Now I'd like to introduce the second project which I think you'll find to be as disturbing as the first one."

"Don, if you don't mind, I'd like to do that myself, so it would be coming directly from the horse's mouth, as I believe the American saying goes," interjected Jean Philippe. "I've had a grandiose project in mind for many years and have spent considerable funds on it already. I'd hoped to build a sanctuary for mankind, a safe habitat so to speak, that would protect a representative group of humans and ecologically supporting creatures and plants from extinction events like the one we may be facing now. Unfortunately, I'm nowhere near completion of such a refuge. In the process of exploring a site deemed by AIEDA to be the best for such a habitat, my team ran across what appears to be an *alien being* occupying a huge underground fortress and claiming to be the Guardian of mankind."

Jean Philippe paused, then continued to give details of his team's encounter with the Guardian. The room remained silent with anticipation of his next words. Jean Philippe finished with a plea, "It would appear that this alien being plans to resurrect the species of earth after an extinction event, using stored DNA and a cloning process.

"He dismissed my team and told them not to worry. Well, I'm worried, and I'm confused, and I'm curious as to what this Guardian is planning. How do we know he can be trusted? Perhaps he's the cause of the anomalous gravimetric force we've detected. My team is standing by in Antarctica awaiting further orders from me. For the first time in my life I'm indecisive. I need your collective help. I need to know what I should do." Jean Philippe's voice tailed off with a note of humbleness, something new for him.

The silence was awkward. Finally, Amanda blurted out, "This is the most incredible story I've ever heard. I can't help but wonder why your team was given access to the fortress, and why the Guardian was willing to give them an audience."

Don responded to Amanda's question, "It seems to me that the team posed no physical threat to the Guardian. Perhaps the Guardian was concerned that if they thought his presence was a threat to humanity, the team would warn the world and cause global paranoia or worldwide panic. By giving the team an audience and a brief explanation, he might have been playing his next best card to defuse the situation. Apparently he won't resort to killing to conceal his presence."

"I might add," said Jon, "that with his technology and experience, the Guardian probably knows about the rogue black hole and the coming extinction event. He's likely not worried about what he tells us, if he expects we'll all be dead in short order."

"The Guardian has shown himself to be somewhat friendly, so far," intoned Amanda. "He seems to respond to our bold inquisitiveness. Maybe we just need to make a list of questions, and see if he'll answer them. It better be a real good list because we might get only one shot."

"I agree," said Don. "Let's get a brain-storming session going and prioritize our questions. I suggest we get input from the team, too. We can take our final list and have AIEDA review it and suggest changes. The faster we get our list of questions, the faster we can have the team confront the Guardian."

Jean Philippe spoke up, "I agree, too, but you should know that Tom Calvano, the leader of the expedition, will have a written report and an audio-video account of his encounter with the Guardian sent to me first thing in the morning. We should go over his report tomorrow before preparing our list of questions. Don, I'll have a copy sent directly to AIEDA for analysis."

"Okay folks," said Jon. "May I suggest we meet here tomorrow at 2:00 p.m.?"

"Sounds like a plan to me," said George.

Chapter 12

Manhattan, NYC
March 2005

Amanda and George were staying at the same hotel, so they took a cab together. Amanda kept thinking how she and everyone else on the planet may not have long to live. She was young and had spent most of her life getting an education. Now that she had a good job, she could finish paying off her student loans. She was hoping to find the right guy and raise a family, take a land trip to southern Italy and a cruise to Alaska. She already had a nice three bedroom house with a great view of the Rocky Mountains. She wondered how much time she might have left.

Her thoughts drifted to George, who was staring out the taxi's window. She'd lied to him about being engaged to Dave. She and Dave had broken-up a month before George had called her asking for the geophysical data following the Asian Tsunami.

She wondered how she had let George slip through her fingers. He was smart and had a good sense of humor. And she would never forget the sex they had when they were an item. Just thinking about it got her all tingly and flustered. But she knew George was happily married, and he wasn't inclined to cheat on his wife. Besides, he wasn't Jewish and he was far too politically conservative.

Amanda had another naughty thought she tried to push out of her mind. She kept thinking how good it would make her feel to steal another woman's man. *To tempt a faithful guy like George, and have him make love to me . . . well, that would be a rewarding challenge, to say the least.*

She tried to tell herself that her naughty thought wasn't all that bad. *Really, a lot of women get a thrill from stealing another woman's man.*

"George," said Amanda, "I was thinking we should contact Roger Akins and keep him informed. What do you think?"

"Akins?" mumbled George as if in a trance. "Oh, yeah, I guess we should."

"Why don't we make the call together from my room, as soon as we get to the hotel?" asked Amanda.

"Okay," said George. "Do you have his number?"

"Yes, in my room," said Amanda.

When they got to Amanda's room, she told George to wait until she changed into something more comfortable. She grabbed some clothes from her suitcase and disappeared into the bathroom, leaving George to watch the six o'clock news on TV. When she reappeared barefoot, her hair was down and she was wearing tight denim shorts and a revealing white halter top.

George turned to look as she walked toward him and almost dropped his jaw. He watched her long legs and flat stomach move right past him as he sat in the chair in front of the TV. He could smell her fresh and clean aroma as she swooshed by. Obviously she had taken a quick shower. George had flashbacks of their previous sexual encounters when they had been dating almost two years ago. He tried to shake the thoughts out of his head and fill them with images of his wife. He couldn't get up from the chair for fear she would notice his spontaneous arousal. Amanda had reclined on the bed on top of the bedspread. She was lying on her back with her feet crossed and her head propped on the pillow.

"What are you watching, George?" said Amanda coyly.

"Oh, just the news. Do you have Roger's phone number?" asked George.

"Oh, here," she said as she extended her hand holding a small piece of paper.

George got up without completely standing and reached out to take the paper. Amanda pulled her hand back and said, "Come here, George, I'm worried. Sit right here." She patted the bed beside her.

"What's the matter?" said George as he took two steps forward and sat on the edge of the bed next to Amanda, facing her.

"I'm worried about the black hole, George. Do you think we'll die soon? I'm not ready to die yet. I have things to do," she whispered while looking right into his eyes.

"Amanda, I don't know for sure, but I think we have several years to prepare for the worst. I haven't told my wife about the black hole. Have you told Dave?"

"Dave and I broke up, so I'm alone now . . . all alone. Several years left to live are just not enough. I'm afraid. I need your strength, George," she said to him as she rolled over close to him, putting her left hand on the small of his back.

He could feel the sweetness of her breath gently over his face, as she tilted her head up toward his with her lips slightly open. His arousal was total, and he felt as though he would fall into the blue pools that were her eyes. They kissed softly at first, then passion took hold of them both.

The next day the team reconvened at Walmer's residence as planned. They all watched the video of Tom Calvano and Jeff Teichman recounting their meeting with the alien being called the Guardian. They were then given three documents. The first was a transcript of the recording they had just heard. Everyone set it aside. The second was Tom's five page analysis of the alien encounter, which everyone took the time to read. The third was an analysis of the alien encounter by AIEDA based on the information Tom had provided, and they all read that, too.

Jean Philippe was the last to finish reading, and the first to comment. "Of course you realize Tom has no knowledge of the rogue black hole and the possible extinction event, whereas AIEDA was privileged to have that information before doing her analysis."

"How can we summarize both analyses and arrive at a list of questions for the Guardian?" asked Jon.

"Well, let me give it a try," said Don. "AIEDA and Tom both conclude Guardian should be taken at his word, that he's an alien being with extremely advanced technology, and that he has humanity's best interests at heart.

"Guardian's statement that the Ecosthat won't protect humanity is something which must be explored directly. Also, the approach heretofore taken by the Guardian to resurrect humanity via cloning is not kosher. Perhaps that's one reason governments have chosen to keep the alien presence secret from the public. We must seek an alternative to cloning."

The smell of a fresh pot of coffee interrupted Don's train of thought. He stopped speaking, waited for Harry to discreetly set the tray on the table, poured some for Amanda and the others, then poured himself a cup.

Don continued summarizing, "We must find out what Guardian knows about the black hole. We must learn about his technology, especially his transportation vessels. We should try to develop a partnership with the Guardian. Unlike the way so many governments have been treating him, we can't assume he's intransigent. We must win his trust, and influence the way he chooses to protect humanity. We should ask about the comment he made describing variable gravity, and we should ask permission to video-record future meetings."

"Excellent summary," said Amanda. "So, if I got it right, we have six questions for our list.

"I have two more for the list," said Jon. "What can you share with us about your computer technology and about your android technology?"

"I think we should ask the Guardian if he can prevent this extinction event from happening," said George.

"Okay, that's nine questions, but somehow I think we're off on the wrong foot. If we want to have a partnership with the Guardian, don't we have to offer something in return? How do we carry our own weight in this hypothetical partnership? Why would such an advanced being want to have a partnership with us?" asked Don.

Amanda suggested, "I think the relationship, that the Guardian would like, is not so much a partnership, as we have nothing to offer him. Rather, I think it's one of young children seeking help and advice from their father who has the best interests of his children in mind."

"But isn't that too much like treating him as a god?" objected George.

"I don't think parents think of themselves as gods and their children as having to worship them," retorted Amanda.

"I think Amanda is correct," interjected Jean Philippe. "We must approach the Guardian in a way that brings out his parental desire to see his children develop while not causing them harm. A child who asks to play with matches wouldn't be allowed to do so by a responsible parent. When we ask the Guardian for advanced technology, it would be like asking to play with matches. It would seem to me we'd have to show the Guardian that we're more responsible and more capable than he might think."

"Okay, I agree we should treat him as our parent," said George. "But how will we impress him with our ability to handle his technology responsibly?"

"Maybe we should ask him to give us assignments that would prove our maturity?" suggested Don.

"I think that's a good approach," said Jean Philippe.

"Then the tenth question is . . ." said Amanda. "What can we do to prove to you that we can be responsible stewards of your advanced technology?"

"Let's get these questions to Tom and explain to him our decision to treat the Guardian in the same way an adult might treat their most respected parent," said Jon.

"Amanda, I see you've been taking notes. If I might borrow them for a few minutes, I can contact Tom via satellite link and bring him up to date," said Jean Philippe.

"Are there any other issues or concerns?" asked Jon.

Don responded, "Yes, I want to remind you that AIEDA is still working on the data provided by George and Amanda with an analysis from Professor Akins. I've also submitted George's tectonic activity hypothesis to AIEDA and asked that it be considered along with the previous data. I was surprised to hear it's possible we'll have a result in a couple of days. Jean Philippe, may I suggest you wait until we have AIEDA's report before you speak with Tom?"

"Yes, of course," said Jean Philippe. "The report might have information that would necessitate altering our strategy."

Chapter 13

Paris, France
April 2005

Andre Garnier was proud of his part in the creation of this special organization. Stealing industrial secrets and selling them in covert black-market auctions was making him and his partners billions of dollars a year. It wasn't just the money and power that drove him. He and his four partners were committed to an ideology often referred to as philosophical anarchism; a subset of individualist anarchism. He believed his organization would push civilization closer and closer to the founder's world view. In the meantime, he was enjoying himself.

The organization had no name. It didn't need one, because it was hardly ever spoken about. However, on occasion it was referred to as the Partnership. It was divided into five divisions, each headed by a partner on a two-year rotating basis.

Andre was currently heading the Center Division for command and communications. The other divisions were Operations, Recruiting, Sales, and Finance. The Sales Division determined what *industrial information* potential clients wanted. The Operations Division obtained the specified information, then the Sales Division would sell it for the highest price. The Recruiting Division would identify candidates for employment, and provide training, including indoctrination in philosophical anarchism. The Finance Division would handle accounting, investing, and budgeting.

Andre had been pursuing a doctoral degree part-time for the last six years. Now at forty-five he only needed to complete the oral exam on his thesis before being conferred a PhD in astrophysics.

His four partners were just as relentless in pursuing their education in their own selected area. How proud he was . . . five brilliant, highly educated, driven men and women, with power and money, all dedicated to the same ideology of philosophical anarchism. Together, they would change the world gradually, thanks to William Godwin and his published treatise on *Political Justice*. In secret ancillary documents, almost 200 years ago, Godwin had codified the three footings of an organization that were needed to perpetuate its existence for millennia—*Streams of Income, Distributed Command and Control, and Ideological Imperative.*

According to their beliefs, they owed no allegiance to any government or to any set of laws except that of their own Partnership. Therefore, they conducted business to accumulate wealth in both legal and illegal ways. Assassination, extortion, and blackmail were forbidden, except in defense of the Partnership, if approved by all five partners.

Also, it was against their rules to conduct any business that could compromise the physical or mental health and welfare of individuals; therefore, they could only target large organizations, such as churches, museums, universities, corporations, government entities, banks, military units, etc. They couldn't deal in drugs, arms, or slaves, and it was considered worthy whenever they could disrupt or diminish such practices by other organizations.

It was their prime directive to find ways to weaken the strangle-hold that governments have on individuals and to foster and nurture cultures and sub-cultures that championed the rights and freedoms of individuals to do whatever they wanted, so long as it didn't impinge on the rights and freedoms of other people.

They weren't terrorists, and they didn't advocate the violent overthrow of any government. They would cause governments to crumble from within and become almost superfluous to a free and enlightened world of cooperative individual contributors.

The Recruiting Division of the Partnership was responsible for fostering the Ideological Imperative. The best recruits were those who had become disaffected with a traditional religion. It wasn't too hard to recruit them into the Church of Spiritual Objectivism (COSO).

This religion was an elegant integration of Thomas Paine's Cooperative Individualism, Ayn Rand's Philosophy of Objectivism and William Godwin's Philosophical Anarchism. The COSO had some of the trappings of Freemasonry whereby members achieved higher levels, also called degrees.

A church member could be elevated to ten successively higher *Congregant* degrees. The next higher level of elevation was to the *Fellowship of Godwin*, wherein there were nine additional degrees of elevation. The ninth, and final, degree was *Grandmaster of Godwin*, and there could only be five such lifetime appointments. Each Grandmaster was anointed into only one of five stations which defined each Grandmaster's specific area of responsibility. The stations were *Protector of the Faith, Judge of the Faithful, Seeker of the Truth, Keeper of Knowledge,* and *Purveyor of Reason and Logic.*

The five Grandmasters headed the church and were the same people as the five division-heads of the Partnership. Andre's anointed station was *Purveyor of Reason and Logic.*

———————————————◇———————————————

It was an uneventful Tuesday afternoon, and after Andre's usual lunch at his usual tavern, he walked down the secret stairs from within his private office at the museum and entered the Com-Center. There was the usual low level buzz in the complex as information officers, referred to as *com-ops*, spoke on secure lines to *mentors* at operations sites. Each com-op was assigned one of the 102 operations sites. Each operations site had ten mentors who each had ten field agents. Consequently, the Com-Center had 102 cubicles for com-ops, eleven desks in open areas for administrative assistants, and two soundproof meeting rooms.

Andre made it a point to walk past half the cubicles in the morning and half in the afternoon, randomly visiting com-ops. Everyone knew that Andre, the Director, could listen-in on their phone conversations from his office.

Andre lamented that the international language was English and that all their business was best conducted in English. Andre thought, *at one time French was the international language, but alas, no more. English is such a course language with no flair, but German would have been worse. My work may not return the French language to its proper place in the affairs of men, but with the great contribution of my countrymen, my work will give honor to the French culture which has championed the individual since the French Revolution.*

The American Revolution and the French Revolution had in common the goal of freedom for the individual. Unfortunately, the historical tide has turned that freedom into oppression, not from kings or aristocrats, but from the neo-Marxists who have promoted the welfare state that has sucked initiative, self-reliance, and risk-taking right from the soul of so many men, women, and children. God help us, we'll reverse the tide!

As Andre walked farther into the Com-Center, he decided to pass his office and go directly down the fifth aisle to visit with a few of the com-ops on the far end. As he turned the corner he could see and hear a commotion about halfway down. About ten men and women were out of their cubicles having a somewhat agitated conversation. A few looked up and saw him walking rapidly toward them. The short fellow in the middle pushed himself out of the crowd and approached him in slow jog. Andre had never seen such behavior by his team. They were usually matter-of-fact and business-like. Immediately he became concerned their security had been compromised. He could see now it was Claude Locca.

"What is it, Claude? What's the commotion?" asked Andre.

"Sir, one of my agents in America has recorded a private conversation that's both disturbing and difficult to believe. We should convene the executive committee immediately to discuss it."

"Very well, we'll use the large conference room. We've just completed the monthly rotation of members, so I'll have Agnes check the list and ring them up on the intercom for an emergency meeting," responded Andre as he turned to jog back to his office.

The twelve members of the executive committee seated themselves quietly with a few whispers here and there. Andre and Claude stood at the front of the room.

"I'm sorry to have pulled you away from your work on such short notice," announced Andre, "but Claude feels the Executive Committee needs to hear this. I'll be hearing it with you for the first time. Claude, you have the floor."

"As you know, experience has shown that bugging private meeting rooms in hotels, restaurants, and office buildings rarely yields any actionable intelligence, but for some reason we've had success bugging meeting rooms in museums. It would seem people think museum meeting rooms are the safest place to discuss confidential matters. Our American agent in Denver, CO has a bug in all the private meeting rooms at the Denver Art Museum and in the curator's office. When reviewing one of the tapes today, he came across a conversation between a woman and two men. The woman had booked the room under the name of Dr. Amanda Rheinhardt. I have a copy of the recording set up, and I'll play it for you now. In that way you can each come to your own conclusions by hearing the facts directly."

Claude pressed the play button. The room listened intently.

"Did I hear that right? A black hole?" asked Andre.

"Yes, he was deliberately speaking in a low voice. He said a black hole was coming toward us from the northwest quadrant of space," said Claude.

One of the com-ops spoke out, "Do we know who this Roger guy is? Like, what are his credentials? And who is George?"

Claude answered, "The only Roger we can find who's done work on the gravitational effects of galaxies on each other is a Dr. Roger Akins, University of Colorado. He has a B.S. in Physics from Stanford University and a Ph.D. in Astrophysics from the University of Colorado, Boulder, where he has a tenured teaching position. He's published a number of highly regarded papers and is prominent in his field. Dr. Amanda Rheinhardt is branch director of the U.S. Geological Survey at Fort Collins, CO. We don't yet know who George is."

Andre spoke out, "Claude will send you any details he has or continues to get, and I ask that you follow our procedure for developing actionable recommendations with supporting logic. It's obvious that if what we've heard is incorrect or a hoax, then we must verify it as such and no further action on our part will be necessary.

"However, for determining alternative actions I suggest first that doing nothing isn't an alternative when our lives and everything we love may be threatened. Second, we need to ask if we should monitor the situation in secret or insert ourselves openly into whatever process is unfolding. Third, at such time that we should insert ourselves into the process, how do we contribute to solving the problem? In other words, what do we have to offer to arrive at a solution?

"Ladies and gentlemen, you have three days to provide the report and present it here in this room at this same time. Thank you."

Andre went back to his Com-Center office to contact his four partners and inform them of this most disturbing information and what he was doing about it. It fleetingly crossed his mind that his station as *Purveyor of Reason and Logic* within the *Fellowship of Godwin* had taken on real world meaning, as he didn't feel this information was a hoax.

Once off the conference call with his partners, he contacted the director of the backup Com-Center. The backup team, of course, had to perform their monastic duties in a convincing way so as not to raise suspicion they weren't monks. Yet there was plenty of time, normally spent privately praying, that team members could use instead to work on projects in the Com-Center complex beneath the monastery.

All team members there went by their monastic names twenty-four hours a day, so when Andre called, he had to refer to his chief operative as *Monsignor Fellino*. It helped to prevent any slips of the tongue in mixed company. Since monks are all men, this site had no female undercover operatives, a fact that disappointed Andre. His personal experience was that the women operatives tended to arrive at more accurate and practical analyses than the men.

Andre spoke facing the speakerphone, "Monsignor Fellino, I have an urgent project for you to research. We need to know as much information about three people who are working together unofficially on a situation that can affect our lives. I'm transmitting all relevant information to you, including a recorded conversation which alerted us to this group. While doing your research on these people, make sure they're not alerted, as we haven't yet decided how we should interact with them."

"I'm most happy to be of assistance, my good friend. We prefer our days would be filled with more such projects, else we find ourselves praying to relieve the boredom. I'll update you daily on our progress, if that's okay."

"Yes, daily via phone with electronic copy to follow," said Andre.

"As you wish. Goodbye," said Fellino.

Chapter 14

April 2005

George was sitting on the edge of the bed watching TV as Amanda prepared herself for their dinner engagement with Jon Walmer. He stared at the screen, but didn't see a thing as he thought about his predicament. George felt guilty about his continued affair with Amanda while they were in New York City. They'd be leaving in a few days. She'd be returning to Ft. Collins and he'd be going back to his wife in Ottawa.

He loved his wife. Amanda was his addiction. Sex with her was never ordinary. It wasn't just her looks, her smell, or the way she felt to him. She was totally uninhibited, and her orgasms were like volcanic eruptions. George struggled to get her out of his mind. He tried to think of his wife and son back home; it seemed to work.

He knew his attraction to Amanda was mostly sexual. She didn't have the traits he wanted and needed in a wife and mother, although he respected her professionally. He would never leave his family. Once he was back home, he'd be able to get her out of his mind.

"George, why don't you try calling Roger again?" called Amanda from the bathroom. "We've got to let him know what's happening."

"Okay, I'll ring him up again," shouted George.

George dialed and heard the phone ringing at the other end. A woman's voice answered, "Hello?"

"Hello. This is George Blocker. May I speak with Roger, please?"

"Just a moment, please."

Hardly a moment went by when a man's voice came on the line. "This is Detective Montgrave, Boulder Police Department. I'm with Mrs. Akins here at her home, because she's reported her husband, Dr. Roger Akins, has been missing for over 24 hours. This line is being recorded. May I ask why you're calling Dr. Akins?"

"I'm a friend and associate of Roger's and I'm calling in regard to an astrophysics project we've been working on together. He has a new theory about the effect of gravity on heavenly bodies, and he believed it would help us with our project to identify certain gravitational anomalies," stated George, who could feel his blood pressure had risen.

"When was the last time you saw Dr. Akins?"

"I met with him a little over two months ago at the Denver Art Museum along with another associate of mine, Amanda Rheinhardt."

"Did he say anything unusual or act unusual in any way?"

"Actually, he seemed concerned about espionage. He seemed to be almost paranoid about people spying on us. I thought his reaction might have stemmed from some incident regarding his new theory. Many scientists get concerned their ideas and research will be stolen before they get to publication."

"Thank you, Mr. Blocker. May I have a phone number, in case I have more questions? Also, a number for Ms. Rheinhardt?" asked Montgrave.

"Certainly," said George as he proceeded to provide the requested information, said goodbye, and hung up.

Amanda overheard part of the conversation and asked, "George, why were you giving my number to Roger? He already has it."

"Amanda, that was the Boulder Police. It seems Roger is missing. The detective wanted to know when we last saw him and if he were acting unusual."

"My God, what else can happen?" yelled Amanda. "We have to tell Jon about this as soon as we see him at the restaurant."

At the restaurant Amanda couldn't wait to tell Jon Walmer about Roger's disappearance, but she contained herself until the waitress left to get their drinks.

"So do you think his disappearance is in some way connected to the work he did for you and George on the gravimetric anomaly?" asked Jon.

"I know he was almost paranoid about keeping his conclusion secret. That's why he made me use a secret code to notify George and him of the whereabouts of our planned meeting. He seemed to feel our homes and offices aren't secure from eavesdropping," responded Amanda.

"Let's say you're right. What can we do about it?" asked Jon.

"We can't do anything for Roger," said George, "but it gives us a heads-up that anyone on our team could be the next target. Roger has no reason to risk his well-being by withholding our names from his captors, and frankly, I wouldn't expect him to."

"I see your point," said Jon. "The AIEDA complex itself might become a target. I'll warn Don and Jean Philippe to take extra security precautions, and I'll put AIEDA on high security alert."

"I live less than an hour's drive from Roger's place. Had I been home, I bet I'd be missing, too," said Amanda. "Kidnapped, then ripped apart by a giant black hole . . . what did I do to deserve such a fate? I think I'll call my mom and dad tonight and let them know how much I love them."

"Really, Amanda," said George. "I don't know what's worse, your pessimism or your melodrama. Get a grip. I believe our future is in our hands, and the answers we seek are within us. We just have to reveal them."

"Oh! You're such an insensitive philosopher, George," complained Amanda. "You think too much and feel too little to appreciate our loss of physical pleasure when we're dead. I like feeling, seeing, hearing, smelling, and other stuff much more than I like thinking. Too much pondering is painful and unhealthy. You need to loosen up, George, and go with your gut a little more!"

Oh, Jon thought, *I get it. They're sleeping together, and George is a married man. It's a lover's quarrel.*

"Hey, guys. I'm skipping dessert and getting back home so I can initiate the new security arrangements. Tomorrow we may have AIEDA's results based on your data, so stop by my place at 2:00 p.m. I'll tell the others to be there, too. Dinner's on me. I know the manager and I'll arrange payment, including tip, so stay as long as you want and have fun. See you tomorrow," said Jon as he got up, flashed them a broad smile, and left.

"I guess we scared him away," said George.

"I'm sorry, George," said Amanda as she reached across the table and held his hand. "I know you were just trying to shake me out of my funk. It worked, at your expense. I think you're just fine the way you are, and I wouldn't want to change you. Let's go back to my room. I feel safe when you're with me."

As Amanda held George's hand, she looked directly into his eyes with obvious desire.

Oh God! George thought. How does she do this to me? You'd think by now I'd be so familiar with her, the excitement would have gone. I guess we'll be sleeping-in late tomorrow morning.

---————————————◇————————————---

Roger Akins squirmed as he sat blindfolded with his hands tied behind the back of the chair. He tried to remember how he got there. He had a silent alarm in his office that would warn him if there was an intruder. He'd gotten no warning. As he had entered his office, he was caught off-guard by a man dressed in black who was rifling through his files. The man turned toward him and fired a gun. The next thing he remembered was being tied-up in the chair. He felt no pain, so maybe he wasn't wounded. The room felt cold, and he could hear the whirring sound of the air handling equipment. *When would they come into the room and tell him what they want?* He felt the dry rag in his mouth and tried to push it out, but the tape over his mouth prevented it. He was afraid.

He heard a door open and footsteps coming toward him. He sensed someone standing close and directly in front of him. He almost stopped breathing out of fright.

"Dr. Akins, I apologize for your situation. We have no intention of harming you. When you caught our man searching your files, he was forced to tranquilize you and take you here. I'll remove the gag so you can answer our questions. Screaming won't help you, as there's no one but me and my men to hear you. By the way, you may call me Gordon."

Gordon removed the tape and gag from Roger's mouth. Roger immediately said, "Gordon, could I have some water? I'm parched."

"Sure, but I must keep your hands tied. Here, I'll hold the glass for you. Drink slowly. As soon as you answer our questions, we'll tranquilize you again and take you back home unharmed. I want you to tell me everything you know about the black hole that you think is approaching earth. I want the names of everyone else who knows about this. You may begin."

———————————◊———————————

It was 10:00 a.m. and Amanda was still half asleep when the phone rang. It was on her side of the bed, so she rolled over to answer it.

"Hello?" she said groggily.

"Amanda?" the man asked.

"Yes, this is Amanda," she said.

"Amanda, it's Roger Akins."

"Roger, we've been worried sick about you. Where have you been?"

"I was kidnapped and interrogated. I just woke up lying on my back in the chaise lounge on the patio of my sister's house. I'm calling to warn you that everyone who knows about our anomaly could be a target. I gave up all your names, including AIEDA. I'm so sorry, but I was so afraid they'd hurt me real bad. I'm not a courageous man."

"It's okay, Roger. We already discussed the situation you might be in, and none of us expected you to withhold our names. Jon Walmer has already increased security at AIEDA," said Amanda in a consoling tone.

"Oh, thank goodness! I felt so bad about it. So you don't think any of the others will be upset with me?"

"Believe me, Roger. No one will be upset with you. Everyone will be quite relieved you're safe. We need you to be a permanent part of our team. We need your help, Roger. The entire planet may need us all. Can you take a flight today to meet with the whole team tomorrow? There are developments you need to know about, and it's best to get you up to speed face-to-face."

"Yes, I understand. I'll be on a plane to JFK Airport this afternoon," said Roger. "I'll book a room in your hotel. See you late tonight."

"See ya."

"I gather Roger is okay?" asked George as he rolled over in bed to face Amanda.

"Yes, he was released unharmed after being forced to divulge all he knows about the anomaly and our ad hoc team," explained Amanda. "George, let's skip breakfast," she said as she rolled her naked body on top of his.

Amanda and George arrived at Jon's place a half hour early and were greeted by Harry. "Miss Rheinhardt, Mr. Blocker. Please come in and make yourselves at home. Mr. Walmer is on the phone, and the other guests haven't arrived yet. Would you care for lunch or a snack?"

"Actually, I am a little hungry," said Amanda. "What's for lunch, Harry?"

"If you follow me to the kitchen, I can set out a tray of lunch meats, cheeses, and a variety of bread. For drinks I can offer you beer, wine, coffee, tea, or water."

"Sounds great, Harry. Lead the way," said George.

In the study, Jon Walmer was on the phone and had a grim look on his face as he spoke, "What did he say again? Those were his precise words? Read it again slowly, so I can write it down. Okay. Okay. Okay. You didn't give him my address or phone number, did you? Good. Give me his name and number. Okay. Okay. Thanks. Bye."

Jon Walmer put the note in his pocket. He'd heard the doorbell, so he left the study to see if any of his guests had arrived. He found no one in the parlor, but thought he heard voices down the hallway. He was pleased to find Amanda and George having a snack in the kitchen.

"Hi, guys! Is Harry taking good care of you?"

"You bet," said Amanda with her mouth full. "I thought we'd get bologna and longhorn, but he's served us proscuitto and provolone, and this delicious multi-grain Italian bread."

"Good. Have you heard any news about Roger?" asked Jon.

"Oh, yes!" said Amanda as she gulped so she could speak. "He called me this morning to warn us, but I told him not to worry; security had been increased. He was forced to divulge whatever he knew about the anomaly, including all our names. They released him unharmed. I told him we needed him on our team and asked him to join us tomorrow. He's flying in to JFK tonight."

"You're right," said Jon. "We need someone of Roger's caliber in astrophysics on our team, and I'm relieved he's okay. However, his kidnappers have wasted no time. They tried to contact me at the AIEDA home office, and left a message for me to call Gordon. He left this poem:

> Now we see the cosmos, dark and deep,
>> Pray the Lord our world to keep.
> Black doom has come to pass,
>> And knock humanity on its ass.
> If this doom decides to stay,
>> It will surely take our lives away.
> Should we try to save the day,
>> So mankind can live another way?

When you're finished with lunch, let's meet in the parlor and discuss this while we wait for the others."

———————◇———————

When Don Mensch and Jean Philippe arrived, they found Jon, George and Amanda in the parlor discussing a poem . . . and Amanda repeated the line, "*Should we try to save the day.*"

"Is this a poem you're discussing?" asked Jean Philippe as he walked in and took a seat. Don followed and sat beside him on an eight-foot long, low-back, Art Deco, red sofa from the 1930's.

"We have good news and bad news," said George. "Roger is okay and called Amanda to warn us we may be targets. His kidnappers pumped him for everything regarding the anomaly, including our names. Roger is flying in to JFK tonight to join us tomorrow. That's the good news. The bad news is that Jon got a message left at AIEDA from a guy who's almost certainly associated with Roger's kidnappers. He left a poem, his name, and number, and wants Jon to call him back. We were discussing the meaning of the poem and have concluded two things. He knows about the rogue black hole and the potential for an extinction event, and he wants to work with us to try to prevent a catastrophe."

"Well," said Don, "I also have good news and bad news. The good news is that we got the analysis of the anomaly from AIEDA earlier than expected. As you know, we fed AIEDA with all of George's and Amanda's data and analyses, plus Roger's calculations and gravimetric theories, along with all the information Tom Calvano sent to us about the Guardian.

"The bad news is that AIEDA's conclusion is about as dour as it can get. According to the Guardian, the repopulation of the earth with clones of all species has happened four times after major extinction events, and the Guardian is counting on that method to protect mankind in the future. However, according to AIEDA, the rogue black hole we have threatening us today will totally annihilate the earth by December 2012. There will be nothing left for the Guardian to use as a home-world for his clones."

"Do you think that's what the Guardian meant when he said Ecosthat won't work?" asked Amanda.

"I don't think so," said Don. "His words seemed to indicate that earth could be repopulated, perhaps after millions of years, but repopulated nonetheless. I don't think he's come to the same conclusion as AIEDA."

"Where does this leave us now?" asked George.

"Looking on the bright side, I think this gives us leverage with the Guardian," responded Jean Philippe. "Tom's job is to ask the Guardian the questions we've determined might help us, and to do so by treating the Guardian as a respected parent. We know the Guardian will be reluctant to share dangerous advanced technology with his children, so the plan was for Tom to ask the Guardian how we might prove to him our responsibility and readiness to handle such powerful knowledge, so that we might find an alternative to his method of saving humanity by repopulating earth with cloned species.

"I think that approach can soften up the Guardian. But the *knock-out punch*—as I think you Americans would say—is to show him our analysis that proves his cloning method won't work, because earth will exist no more. The Guardian will be impressed with our intellect, and he'll have to consider a new way to save mankind. The door will then be open for us to work with him on a new approach to the problem."

"That presupposes that AIEDA's analysis is correct and that the Guardian accepts her analysis as being correct," said Jon.

"We have no other choice but to proceed on those suppositions," said George. "Jean Philippe, I think we should have a teleconference with Tom so we can all be involved with setting the strategy."

"I think that's a good idea," said Jean Philippe, "but I'm concerned we might tip our hand to the Guardian who's undoubtedly monitoring all wireless communications with Tom's team. We need to consider that our discourse with the Guardian is really a negotiation, and we have the weaker position."

"It would take too long for Tom to make a round trip just to attend a conference in person," concluded Don. "On the other hand, it shouldn't take long for us to agree on a written version of our proposed strategy. We can let Tom know, in an encrypted message, where and when we'll be air-dropping a package of medical supplies for him. He'll understand it's a confidential message, and he'll be waiting at the drop point. In that terrain he'll be able to see the parachute for miles, so it's unlikely he'll miss it or that someone will get to it before him. Because it will be a handwritten message, there will be no electronic signals for the Guardian to intercept."

"I think that's the way to go," said George. "Tom is on the ground and in the fray of things. If we give him the benefit of our thinking, he'll make whatever use of it he can, based on circumstances at the moment."

"I believe we're all in agreement," offered Amanda.

"Yes, I can arrange the encrypted message to Tom and the delivery of the paper document, but who will volunteer to write it up properly?" asked Jean Philippe.

"I'll write it up for each of you to review tomorrow," said Amanda. "I'll be seeing Roger late tonight, so I can get his opinion too. He'll be joining us tomorrow."

"Okay, folks," said Jon. "Let's meet here, same time tomorrow."

As everyone stood to depart, Don Mensch quickly moved across the room to where Amanda had been sitting. "Amanda, do you have a few minutes?"

"Sure, Don," she said as she turned to look at him straight on.

"I know you and George are meeting with Roger and will probably want to take him to lunch tomorrow," said Don with a bit of a quiver in his voice. "I wonder if I could persuade you to let George and Roger take lunch together without you. There's a favorite dining spot of mine I'd like to introduce you to, if you'd like."

"I'd like that very much, Don. Where can we meet?"

"I'll be in the lobby of your hotel at 11:45. We can take a cab together. It's not far," said Don.

"Okay, see you tomorrow then for lunch. I'm in room 1022."

She turned and walked over to where George was standing.

"You ready to go?" asked George. "Our cab will be outside in just a couple of minutes."

"Ready to go," said Amanda as George led the way to the front door.

Once outside and alone together, George asked, "What was that all about with Don?"

"He asked me out to lunch with him tomorrow, and I accepted."

"Oh, you want me to baby-sit Roger tomorrow?" commented George.

"That would be nice. Are you jealous or mad?" responded Amanda.

"A little jealous, but also a little relieved. I hope you two strike it up, because the guilt is getting to me. I'll be going home soon, and I'd like to face my wife knowing our affair is over for good."

"Thanks, George," said Amanda. "I've always known you'd never leave your wife. In any case I promise not to seduce you again. Well, unless I get unbearably lonely or scared—then you'd better run, you hottie."

Amanda smiled at George, squeezed his hand firmly and let go. George opened the cab door for her when it pulled up to the curb, and they both got in. They expected to see Roger about 11:00 p.m. at the hotel. When they got to the hotel, Amanda went directly to the hotel's business center to grab some paper. She would handwrite the questions for Guardian and the negotiating strategy. There would be no electronic emissions for Guardian to intercept. She believed her document would help Tom negotiate with Guardian.

———◇———

Dr. Roger Akins' plane was half an hour late flying into Kennedy International. He checked into the Newton Hotel at 11:30 p.m. He thought it ironic he was staying in a hotel named after the man who discovered gravity; after all, it was a great ball of gravity that appeared to be a threat to humanity.

There would be worldwide pandemonium if knowledge of this threat became public. How many governments know about the threat and are keeping it under wraps? Was that Gordon guy who kidnapped me affiliated with the government? Roger had been thinking thoughts like these continuously before the flight, during the flight, and now as he checked-in at the Newton. He hoped his disturbing, repetitious thoughts would subside once he met the team. As soon as he walked into his room, he called Amanda. He agreed to meet her in George's room in fifteen minutes.

———◇———

George opened the door when he heard the knock. It was Amanda.

"Roger should be here in a few minutes," she said. "Why don't you read this before he arrives and tell me if there are any inconsistencies with what the team agreed to at Jon's this afternoon?"

George took the two page document and sat in the chair at the small table under the lamp. He was done in less than two minutes. "No inconsistencies. Well organized and well written. I find it to be quite clear and to the point. It'll be helpful to Tom."

Just as George finished speaking, there was a knock at the door. Amanda opened it and greeted Roger. She closed the door as he entered the room.

"Roger, how are you?" asked George. "It's good to see you after that awful kidnapping experience."

George got up from the chair and walked toward Roger with outstretched hand. They shook hands and Roger said, "Thanks George. It's good to see you, too. I feel bad about giving up all your names . . ."

"Nonsense!" interrupted George. "You had no choice. Every one of us would have done the same. It's not like you're in the military and duty bound to follow a P.O.W. code of conduct. You're a valuable member of our team, so relax. Take a seat."

"Roger, we need to get you up to speed tonight," said Amanda. "Tomorrow we meet with the team again at Jon Walmer's place at 2:00 p.m. George will take you to lunch, then to Jon's. I'll meet you there."

"As if the news hasn't been bad enough, it's even worse now," said George as he sat with his legs crossed.

"It's hard to know where to begin," said Amanda quietly. "I guess we should first tell you that AIEDA's analysis is grim. Not only will there be an extinction event by December 2012, but the earth will be completely consumed. It won't exist as a planet, and no significant life will ever inhabit it again."

"The rest of the story is even harder to swallow. It seems a multi-billionaire named Jean Philippe Martinique had chartered an expedition to Antarctica to survey a site for an ecologically stable, subterranean habitat that could be used to save mankind from extinction events," said George.

"The leader of the expedition is Tom Calvano," continued Amanda in a whisper. "He and his team discovered an underground fortress of sorts inhabited by an alien being who calls himself the Guardian of mankind."

"You're pulling my leg. I'm not that gullible," said Roger as he squirmed and pushed himself back into the chair.

"It's true," insisted Amanda. "Put this earpiece on and watch the video on this portable player. Tom describes in detail his encounter with the Guardian."

Roger watched the video, then pulled out his earpiece and let it fall to the floor.

"This is hard to accept," stammered Roger. "This Guardian is telling us that our Theory of Evolution is wrong, and he's telling us that our Standard Model of the Universe is wrong."

"I think I've understood all of that in my own way, but tell us how you interpret what the Guardian has said about these theories," said George.

"Well, as you know," said Roger, "the Theory of Evolution was established by Charles Darwin in his thesis entitled, *On the Origin of Species*. According to Darwin, many minor changes in living things over millions of years allowed them to adapt to their environment, and the cumulative effect of all theses changes resulted in many new and different species, some having been equipped to survive over time and many others having become extinct; that is, survival of the fittest. The Guardian completely refutes that theory, because he claims to have engineered all the species on earth, and in the rest of the Universe, except for the prime species he calls the Elders."

"Okay, I understood evolution the same way, but I'm not so sure I understand the impact on the Standard Model," said Amanda.

"The Standard Model of the Universe (SMU) is based on Isaac Newton's Law of Gravitation," explained Roger. "This is not to be confused with the Standard Model of Quantum Mechanics which doesn't consider gravity. It's been accepted that the models we have today are special cases of some as yet unknown Model of Everything. According to SMU, the Universe is comprised of baryonic matter and non-baryonic matter. Baryonic matter is the stuff we see and feel around us all the time. It's everything made of atoms and their component parts such as protons, neutrons, electrons, and subatomic particles. The non-baryonic matter is a whole bunch of stuff called Dark Matter and Dark Energy that we think exists, but that nobody has ever detected. The SMU says that the Mass of the Universe equals the Mass of Baryonic Matter, 4%, plus Dark Matter, 21%, plus the mass equivalent of Dark Energy, 75%."

"Why do we include Dark Matter and Dark Energy in the model when we can't find any of it?" asked Amanda.

"This non-baryonic stuff was concocted because it was the only way to make the equations explain a lot more of our observations of the activity in the Universe," said Roger. "Baryonic mass is only four percent of the mass needed to form stars and to explain the velocity of suns around galactic centers, so scientists made up names for the missing ninety-six percent of the Universe.

They did this because it's much easier for them to accept, than to admit that Newton's Law of Gravitation is wrong. Another theory competing with SMU that hasn't been well received says that gravity oscillates at an extremely high frequency . . . not detectable by our current equipment. According to this Variable Gravity Theory (VGT), gravity's amplitude was large at the time of the Big Bang and has declined over time to a point where today it's not possible to detect with our instruments. If we accept the VGT, then it isn't necessary to invent stuff like Dark Matter and Dark Energy.

"I don't quite get why that is," said George.

"The Guardian's statements seem to support VGT because he says gravity is the breath of God coming from the eleventh dimension," continued Roger. "Let's imagine that gravity is somewhat like lungs blowing a blast of air, then close to the origin of the Big Bang it might have had a heavy force which then petered-out as the lungs became empty and as the original burst of air spread throughout the cosmos."

"Geez!" said George. "It would seem the Guardian knows a good bit more about the Universe and God than we do. I can't imagine how we'll be able to save ourselves, if he can't do it for us."

"We have to try!" said Amanda forcefully. "Roger, we'd like you to read this document the team has agreed should guide Tom Calvano in his negotiations with the Guardian. The team believes we should play to his parental instincts. The approach also presupposes that AIEDA is correct that earth will be demolished, making it impossible for the Guardian to repopulate it with clones. It also presupposes that the Guardian accepts AIEDA's conclusion. If everything pans out, we expect the Guardian will allow us to work with him to develop a new plan for saving humanity."

"He may already have a new plan," said Roger. "Maybe it's a plan we like even less than the original cloning one. Or maybe he'll take his human clones to another world in another solar system."

"Roger, let's be positive," said Amanda. "The team will discuss the document one more time in the meeting tomorrow before we send it to Tom by airdrop."

Chapter 15

Antarctica

Tom Calvano wasn't surprised to receive an encrypted message from Jean Philippe. He knew immediately that the airdrop had nothing to do with medical supplies. Good old-fashioned paper communication was more secure than the most sophisticated electronics when faced with an alien being that possesses unimaginable technology.

He waited patiently for the cargo plane to eject a loaded pallet that would descend to earth via an attached red and white striped parachute. He and three men on snowmachines waited like sentries in a roughly circular pattern surrounding the target zone for the airdrop. It was getting colder as they waited. All four had their com-units in the open position, so they could instantly monitor each other.

The high-pitched noise of a jet cargo plane made its debut. They simultaneously looked to the western sky and saw a C-130 come into view and make a run toward the target area which had been prepared with a large hunter's-orange, nylon bull's-eye.

The colorful chute flew out the tail of the plane, dragging the pallet behind it. The pallet swayed at the bottom of the open chute for no more than a minute, then thudded onto the snow only ten yards from the bull's-eye. All four men were racing full tilt toward the pallet before it hit the ground. Above the noise of their snowmachines they could hear the powerful engines of the C-130 blast the aircraft upward. They couldn't help but look up to see the bird ascending rapidly at a sixty degree angle. It was a beautiful sight to see.

All four got to the pallet at about the same time and, as planned, two stood guard while the other two unloaded a dozen small boxes. Each snowmachine carried three of the boxes. They gathered the chute and the bull's-eye, and leaving the empty pallet where it landed, they proceeded quickly back to camp.

––––––––––––––––––––––––◇––––––––––––––––––––––––

Back at base camp, Tom couldn't wait to open the package with the confidential message. He instinctively knew it was the one box with the Red Cross label on it. He locked himself in his small room with the box and ripped it open. Inside, he found the two page document outlining how the team back home felt he should negotiate with the Guardian and the set of questions he should ask the Guardian.

The second document he found was a twenty page analysis by AIEDA concerning the certain complete destruction of earth and its moon. Five pages were descriptive text and the other fifteen pages were mathematical proofs that supported the conclusion. There were two copies of this document. One was intended for the Guardian.

Tom slowly and methodically read through the list of questions he was to ask the Guardian. He knew that each question would require him to ask some clarifying questions based on the Guardian's response. He wrote down what he thought some of those follow-up questions might be. Once he was done with the two page document, he picked up the twenty-page AIEDA document, read three of the first five pages, and put it down.

"What the hell . . ." he said to himself. "I'll take their word for it. The earth and moon will be destroyed. There will be no reconstitution of humanity. I'll say it convincingly to the Guardian and hand him the document. It'll be up to him to figure out if the proof is sufficient."

Tom took a deep breath. He was prepared to meet the Guardian. He would treat him like a respected parent, and with that thought he stood, walked out of his room, and assembled his team to discuss preparations for visiting the Guardian tomorrow.

———————————————◇———————————————

Tom Calvano and Jeff Teichman stood before the Guardian's fortress. It felt spookily like Deja Vu. Tom also felt stupid as he knocked three times on the wall to signal his request for entry. He was sure the Guardian was inside laughing his alien head off. Surely he'd been tracking their arrival since they left base camp. Nothing happened. Tom turned his head to the right toward Jeff and gave him an annoyed smirk. Jeff smiled knowingly at him. They both knew to be patient.

Tom looked down at his watch. Three minutes had just passed since he knocked. As he looked up, an opening appeared in the wall directly in front of him. They both cautiously stepped inside. Directly ahead, another door was open, so they proceeded directly through it, too. The door closed behind them, and the lights got somewhat brighter.

"Hello, again, Tom and Jeff," said the Guardian as he strolled out from an opening on the opposite side of the room. "It's nice to see you. You're back so soon."

"It's nice to see you again, too," said Tom. "May we have your permission to record our conversation today?"

"Yes, of course you may," responded the Guardian. "It would make sense that your team back home would want to listen to every word we speak. Let's sit together at the table."

"Thanks, Guardian," said Jeff as the three of them took a seat.

"Let me see the list of questions you have for me," demanded the Guardian.

Tom was momentarily flustered. His plan was to ask the questions one by one to facilitate what he hoped would be a negotiation of sorts.

"I was hoping to discuss things informally and spontaneously, so I wasn't expecting you to ask for a list," said Tom in as calm a voice as he could muster.

"Come, now!" said the Guardian. "It's obvious your team back home would have prepared a list of questions to ask me. Let's not play games. Hand me the list, please."

Tom unzipped his ski coat and reached into the left inside breast pocket to withdraw a two page list folded twice over. He unfolded it and sheepishly handed it to the Guardian, who snatched it from him rather impatiently. The Guardian took less than five seconds to read each page. Tom was thinking how glad he was that the list wasn't the original, describing how he should negotiate with the Guardian and how he should treat him like a parent. The list the Guardian held had been copied with the original questions and no further commentary, and below each were Tom's personal follow-up questions.

"Okay, there's nothing here that I hadn't anticipated you would ask," said the Guardian. "I'll do my best to give you some helpful answers."

"Thank you, Guardian," interjected Jeff.

"I've already given you permission to record this discussion, so we can start with the second question," said the Guardian. "You want to know about the threat from space. Well, it's a stellar-mass black hole that will get so close to earth it'll cause an extinction event with an apex between December 21 and 26 of 2012.

All human life and most other life will be destroyed. It will take the earth about 2,000 years to recover enough for me to begin repopulation with clones of all current life forms. We Guardians have no other method of reconstituting life on a planet other than by our process of DNA cloning. We must introduce clones in a precise manner over hundreds of years.

This will be the fifth time I've reconstituted mankind after an extinction event. I'm getting pretty good at it. Believe me; if I had the power to prevent these extinction events, I would do so. It would be a lot less work and much more satisfying, but despite our technology, the forces of the Universe are much too powerful for us to influence in any significant way."

"You mentioned when the apex of the event would occur, but what can we expect to see beforehand?" asked Tom.

"The gravitational force has already been affecting earth," answered the Guardian. "The Asian Tsunami was one result, and the earthquake that caused it was so big, it changed the axial tilt of the earth. Other earthquakes will occur, but the biggest result will be the flipping of the earth's magnetic field, whereby magnetic north becomes south and magnetic south becomes north.

During this change in the magnetosphere, there will be little protection from cosmic rays through the latter half of 2012. The cosmic rays will cause virulent cancer in many humans and animals. The rays will destroy the atmosphere, making the percentage oxygen content drop from the current 20.95% to about 19%. At this marginal percentage, the sick and the elderly will have trouble breathing, and they'll die by the millions in third world countries where they won't have sufficient bottled air.

The final death toll will be from volcanic eruptions, mostly in India, that will blot out the sun and poison the atmosphere. Forest fires and the dry, hot atmosphere will cause super-colossal tornadic activity to encircle the earth, destroying all life larger than a rat."

"Why can't we protect enough humans in a subterranean sanctuary so they can emerge and repopulate the earth?" asked Jeff.

"That question comes later on your list, but it's most appropriate for me to answer it now. An ecologically balanced habitat with sufficient numbers of occupants might survive for several hundred years, but certainly not a thousand years, and the earth will not be habitable for at least 2,000 years," explained the Guardian."

Guardian looked at the list in his hand and continued speaking, "Now let me respond to the next question, which is more difficult to explain in layman's terms. You want to know how variable gravity relates to your current ideas about the Universe. Well, currently your scientists can't explain certain observations and have come to the conclusion that there's missing matter and energy in the Universe, so they call the missing matter *dark matter* and the missing energy *dark energy*.

"They keep looking for the dark matter and dark energy, but can't find a trace of them. They can't accept that the force of gravity isn't constant in the Universe. Variable gravity is a concept that destroys the foundation of your science, because it invalidates one of the fundamental principles of Newtonian physics.

"Your scientists associate increasing gravity with increasing mass in a constant, predictable way. Someday they'll understand that gravity comes from the eleventh dimension, which is like an infinitely long string with a width less than the diameter of the nucleus of an atom. The eleventh dimension threads it way through every atom in the Universe. What happens in the eleventh dimension determines how much gravity is to be imbued into matter located in various parts of the Universe and subject to various conditions, including the passage of time. The mechanisms within the eleventh dimension are hidden from us, because the eleventh dimension is the realm of God."

Guardian paused to take a deep breath and said, "Now, with regard to your question about multiple universes, or the so called Multi-verse Theory, it's another case where your scientists have nothing whatsoever to support the idea that there are an infinite number of universes. It seems to have been concocted to explain the unexplainable, because when one has infinite occurrences, then anything imaginable is possible. Some scientists seem disturbed that there was a Big Bang to create the Universe, possibly because that might imply the existence of God, the Prime Mover. By concocting the Multi-verse Theory, they can say that universes are being created and destroyed all the time with big bangs. They seem to be more comfortable when the cosmos is in a state of equilibrium that doesn't require a Prime Mover.

"I'm sure that someday they'll come to understand the cosmos as we Guardians do. There are only seven universes, one for each dimension from the fourth, which is ours, up through the tenth. Almost fourteen billion years ago, God created all seven universes in the Big Bang.

"Simultaneously with the Big Bang, the infinitely long string we call the eleventh dimension expelled gravity inside the inflated universe, creating fractal clumps of matter and energy, and imbuing variable gravity where and when needed to implement God's design. The eleventh dimension stays interconnected to all matter and energy, because matter and energy are extensions of the eleventh dimension. The eleventh dimension continues to regulate gravity as necessary to maintain the Universe's design parameters."

"Your science includes God whereas ours excludes God. How can your science be objective when it includes the supernatural?" asked Tom.

"Well, humanity's science doesn't preclude the existence of God. Rather, it simply doesn't accept supernatural explanations, because they can't be submitted to verifiable experimentation. On the other hand, we Guardians have information and methodologies that allow us to submit the concept of God to mathematical proof and verifiable experimentation. Nevertheless, we can't share this knowledge at this point in humanity's development. You'll have to take my word for it, or have faith."

"What about evolution?" asked Jeff. "I mean, to what extent is the origin of species explained by your genetic manipulations, by God's design, or by Darwinian evolution?"

"Your Darwinian theory of evolution is an instance of mankind's weakest science," explained the Guardian. Darwinian Evolution is based on categorizing a bunch of observations, then making guesses about how species might have developed from one category to another. The taxonomic category that's much broader than species in biology is the Phylum, and it's here that there is no evidence that any two Phyla have a common ancestry.

"They don't have a common ancestry because I was the one who designed each Phylum, and every creature in every Phylum. I admit that part of my genetic design includes the ability of all creatures to make limited adaptations to their environment. Call it self-initiated fine-tuning, if you will. Therefore, in general terms, a modicum of evolution can occur within a Phylum, but a new Phylum can't be created by evolution."

"What are the Elders like, and why did they create Guardians to carryout God's commandment to spread life into the Universe? Why not do it themselves?" asked Tom.

"The Elders are gentle, kind, and extremely intelligent, although you wouldn't know it by their outward appearance," began the Guardian. "They look unremarkable, much like the tubeworms found in your oceans. They communicate telepathically and have no hands, feet, or eyes. It's impossible for them to directly build something. They live their immortal lives in the same place, unable to transport themselves, but happy amid the community of thoughts shared by all Elders via their telepathic abilities.

"However, they have a highly sophisticated ability to create amino acids, proteins, DNA, RNA, single-celled organisms, and complex multi-celled organisms within their own bodies. Just as we might create an android to assist us, the Elders create non-sentient and sentient creatures to help them. We Guardians were their first sentient creation. They've been pleased with our progress creating and spreading life, so they chose not to directly create anymore sentient beings."

"These revelations boggle the mind. Perhaps we should move on to the final three questions pertaining to your technology," suggested Tom.

"Yes, of course," said the Guardian. "You want to know about our flying machines, our computers, and our androids. Well, I'd be violating directives if I were to give you details. About our computers and androids, the only thing I can tell you is that they're 100% biological, and they've been designed so they can't become sentient. I can tell you more about our flying machines because your government already knows a lot about our technology as a result of a Guardian cruiser accident. You know; the one at Roswell."

"We're interested in knowing if your flying machines can be used to relocate the people of Earth to another habitable planet in the Milky Way," said Jeff.

"Some seem to think our flying machines, we call them cruisers, are huge," began the Guardian. "And from the outside they may seem big, but the truth is that the propulsion system, computers, and navigation equipment take up most of the space. There's room for up to four of us . . . actually the crew is usually one Guardian and two androids. You've noticed our small stature, so you can see how we'd be pressed to get two humans inside with a few supplies.

"With a population of almost 6.5 billion, we'd need an impossible number of cruisers. Even if we could make 100 round trips per day per cruiser, we'd need over 12,000 cruisers. Then there's the problem of finding a habitable planet. You see, planets suitable for human-like life are rare. Planet Earth is especially suited to facilitate your development. There are a limited number of habitable planets that Guardians can populate with life. The Elders taught us how to find many of these special places that can support complex, select, carbon-based life. All the known habitable planets are already inhabited by sentient life-forms who would fight to remain dominant. Assuming that we did relocate the entire human race, or even a significant portion of it, modern man wouldn't survive in a hostile, alien world without tools, machines, and manufacturing capabilities. You'd be thrown back to the stone age, physically unsuited for survival."

"I can see why you think relocation is a long-shot," commented Tom. "I'm surprised at how small the quarters are compared to the flight mechanism. No room for cargo either. How does the propulsion system work and what's the biggest vessel that anyone's ever built?"

"They're built no bigger than what I've described," said the Guardian. "The reason is that the propulsion system is inherently unstable, making it unsafe for large numbers of passengers. The larger we make the propulsion system, the greater the instability, especially on longer jumps."

"What makes the propulsion system so inherently unstable?" asked Jeff.

"The dual singularities and the electromagnetic containment field," said the Guardian.

"You mean two black holes?" shouted Tom.

"Yes, each vessel contains two artificially created black holes that circle within the confines of a magnetic bottle," answered the Guardian. "If the system is too large, it's destabilized by external gravimetric forces from bodies like the sun. That's all I can tell you. Your government may know more, but not enough to figure out how to build a working model."

"What makes you think the U.S. government would know more?" asked Jeff.

"Two of our cruisers came out of dimensional hyper-drive at roughly the same place and time near Roswell in 1947. That's one of the hazards we live with. It was impossible to avoid a collision. One cruiser bounced far enough away in the dessert that the military didn't know it was there, so I had time to retrieve it and the deceased crew. Later some people found debris and the military confiscated it.

"The other cruiser landed in a less remote area, and the military were quick to confiscate the cruiser, its crew, and all debris. They hid the cruiser and dissected the deceased crew," said the Guardian. "Fortunately, the crew was comprised entirely of androids. The living computer was totally destroyed in the crash. It took years to find the severely damaged cruiser and retrieve it.

"In the meantime, your U.S. Air Force was studying how to reverse engineer it at Wright-Patterson Air Force Base. When they realized they were dealing with two revolving black holes, contained in a weakening magnetic field, they were all too happy for me to take it off their hands. That's all I'm allowed to tell you."

"You've been nice enough to answer our questions," said Tom. "Unfortunately, we have some information that may change the whole ballgame. We don't mean to be presumptuous, but we don't concur with your assessment that the earth will be habitable after the extinction event is over, even 2,000 years after. Our measurements and calculations show conclusively that the black hole is coming so close to earth that its gravitational pull will destroy both the earth and the moon. Jeff, please give the report to the Guardian."

The Guardian had an incredulous smirk like a condescending smile mixed with a look of surprise. He reached out and took the twenty page document from Jeff's outstretched hand. He finished the first five pages in less than a minute.

He then opened the first page of the mathematical analysis. The look on his face changed to concentration at first. Then, as he got further into the document, his brow furrowed and his head cocked a bit to his left, as if he couldn't believe what he was reading.

He took a full thirty minutes to read the mathematics and supporting data, then he spoke, "Gentlemen, I'm impressed. At this stage in your development, I hadn't expected this level of mathematical and analytical capacity, much less this level of understanding of gravimetric physics. This is most impressive, indeed, but it can't be correct. I couldn't have made such an error in my calculations. It will take time to reconcile the two different conclusions, as I see no obvious error in what you've presented to me. Please excuse me as I have a good bit of work ahead of me. Return here tomorrow at 1600 hours, and I'll give you the results. I believe you can find your way out on your own. Good day."

With that last word the Guardian arose from the chair and walked out of the room, leaving Tom and Jeff sitting there staring after him. After about thirty seconds they looked at each other, got up, and left the Guardian's fortress without saying a word.

———————————————◊———————————————

The next day at precisely 16:00, Tom and Jeff found themselves sitting at the table again inside the Guardian's fortress. Time passed as they sat quietly. The Guardian was five minutes late. Another minute passed, and he appeared suddenly, walking toward them from the opening on the opposite side of the room.

"Sorry I'm late," called out the Guardian as he marched swiftly toward them. "I just now received some good news to balance the bad news. The bad news is that your calculations are correct, and I'm embarrassed to admit I had a trans-positional error in my analysis. I'm sad to say the earth and all its inhabitants will perish. Now, the good news is the Elders have granted my request. They've given me permission to stay with you to the end and help you in any way I can. Unfortunately, they have no solution to the dilemma and wish us God-speed."

"Why would you want to perish with us? And why do you seem so cavalier about it?" asked Jeff.

"Oh, I'm sorry if you find my manner disturbing. It's just that, well, it's sort of like the captain going down with his ship . . . err, well no, it's more like a parent refusing to abandon his children," said the Guardian.

"But why do you seem so happy about it?" asked Tom.

"Oh, but I'm not happy about it at all," said the Guardian. "It's just that I've been around this Universe in over five million cloned bodies for about five billion years. I'm quite ready to meet God."

"With all due respect, if you have no survival instinct left in you, your capacity to assist us out of this dilemma will be greatly diminished, but having said that, I appreciate your decision and thank you for it," said Tom.

"Yes, you have my thanks, too!" chimed-in Jeff.

"You make a good point indeed. I'll do the best I can to keep us all alive. Although, frankly, I have no hope it's possible," said the Guardian.

"Guardian, you're our parent, and we need your help, but how can you help us if you have no hope?" lectured Jeff. "You're the one who's been emphasizing the need for us to have faith. How can you believe in God and have faith, but yet have no hope?"

"Yes, Jeff, you're correct," responded the Guardian. "Hope, faith, and a desire to survive are necessary for the viability of all sentient beings. We'll find a solution. Now how do you suggest we work together?"

"Give us whatever data you have stored in your computers, so we can analyze it and look for a solution," suggested Tom.

"Being biological in construction, our computers and the storage media are incompatible with your technology, and the quantity of data is many millions of times more than can fit on all of your storage units on the planet," explained the Guardian. "It would take a thousand years for your scientists to review it, and they wouldn't understand but about one one-thousandth of it. If Guardian computers and Guardian scientists can't find a solution, it's highly unlikely that your computers and scientists will be successful."

"Design an interface between your computer and our AIEDA computer," suggested Tom, as he forced himself to ignore the Guardian's continued negativity. "Allow your computer to be managed by AIEDA. When we come up with ideas or need specific data, we'll be able to work through AIEDA as we normally do. Can you do this?"

"Yes, if you give me an interface protocol to AIEDA, I can design the interface mechanism, but I'll need you to manufacture a few precise electro-mechanical connectors similar to a medical brain probe with a wireless transmitter-receiver."

"Good. We have a plan. I'll get you the interface protocol from AIEDA while you develop the specs for the brain probes," said Tom.

"Tom, there will be no need for you to return here every time we need to talk. If you and Jeff give me your com-units, I can quickly alter them so we can have private secure communications from anywhere you are. It's not as preferable as face-face, but it'll do for now. Later we can determine the best place to set up holographic communications between us."

"That would be helpful," said Tom. "While you're having that done, wouldn't this be a good time for us to meet your assistant Guardians?"

"Oh . . ." the Guardian exclaimed and paused for a few awkward seconds. "I regret we've missed the opportunity for you to meet the others. They had all been recalled, so they packed their belongings and left in their cruisers."

"So, they left you here to die alone with the kids, huh?" complained Tom in a sarcastic tone. "All we're left with is you, your cruiser, and this mother-ship to help us."

"Mother-ship?" said the Guardian quizzically. "Oh, you think this place is a large transportation vessel. Tom, I already explained that we can't make vessels big at all. Our largest cruisers are only about 100 feet in diameter, and the crew compartment at the center is only about ten feet in diameter, and it's crammed with equipment and supplies."

"So, this place is a base camp," said Tom. "We've been calling it your fortress and I guess in a way it is. What about your androids? What about your computers? Are they still here in your fortress?"

"Yes, I have 1,000 androids who look a lot like me, but who are not sentient. They maintain the fortress . . . I like that name . . . and follow my commands. I communicate telepathically with them, although they have the capacity to hear and speak. As to the computers, there's only the one in my cruiser. You see, the cruisers dock with the fortress and interconnect to form a large computing resource. Now that I won't be reconstituting humanity, and my home world has verified your calculations for certain doom, there seemed no need to have but the one computer on my cruiser."

"Guardian, if we're to find a solution to our dilemma, I'm sure you can understand how it would've been better to have the largest possible computing resources available to us," said Jeff. "It would also have been nice to have the minds of many Guardians working with us to solve the problem. They didn't have to leave so soon. We have a few years left."

"I'm so sorry to have disappointed you," said the Guardian. "The decisions weren't mine to make. I had to plead with my superiors just to be allowed to remain here with you. They're convinced that the doomsday outcome is inevitable."

"Nothing is inevitable," said Tom. "We'll wait while you modify our com-units."

Tom and Jeff handed their units to the Guardian and sat stoically in their chairs as the Guardian disappeared through the doorway opposite them. When the Guardian returned with the modified com-units, he looked rather dejected.

"Here are your com-units," said the Guardian. "Just dial #333 and it will ring through to me. I thought about what you said, and I must admit I haven't been totally candid with you. You would have found out the truth soon enough anyway, so I'll just tell you now. Before the other Guardians left, they were ordered to delete most of our advanced technology information from the computer onboard my cruiser. I'm so sorry, but that decision wasn't subject to debate. Surely you can understand how dangerous it would be if, for example, our genetic technology were to get into non-Guardian hands."

"So far, you've been a bundle of help," said Tom sarcastically. "We'll be in touch. Oh, and please transmit those brain probe specs to AIEDA as soon as you can. Before we leave, I'd like a copy of the instructions for setting up the holographic communications center."

Chapter 16

Bronx, NYC

Jon Walmer picked up the secure red phone at his office in the AIEDA home office complex. It was time for him to call the mysterious Gordon, who had the gall to kidnap and interrogate Roger Akins. Jon had increased security at AIEDA and every employee's home soon after he had learned of Roger's disappearance. It was an expense long overdue, and with only 600 employees, it wasn't so costly.

Although Roger was released unharmed, Jon saw this Gordon guy as a threat. Between AIEDA's resources and those of Jean Philippe, Jon Walmer had initiated an extensive, global, private investigation to find who was responsible for Roger's kidnapping. He'd managed to delay calling Gordon for two weeks, but when an attempt was made to burglarize his home, he knew he couldn't delay the call anymore. Gordon had left several ominous sounding messages during this two week period demanding that Jon call him. Well, he was ready now. He'd be dealing from a position of strength.

"Hello, Dr. Walmer," said the heavily accented voice on the other end of the line. "It took you long enough to return my call. I'm not accustomed to being kept waiting."

"And I'm not accustomed to being threatened, Gordon. I especially am not pleased with the way you treated Dr. Akins."

"Unfortunately, that was the only way we could track down you and your compatriots," explained Gordon. "Let's get right to the point. We know about the threat from space, and we've learned that a number of governments are aware of the threat and are keeping quiet about it because they have no solution. We know from Dr. Akins that you're assembling a team to come up with a plan. We'll be joining you in your efforts. We have many resources that can be applied to the task. More than you can imagine."

"Oh, you'll be joining us, all right," said Jon. "You, too, will discover that my people also have resources even you can't imagine. I'd say right about now."

There was a crashing sound that came loudly through the receiver, and Jon could hear the phone drop to the floor, then Gordon yelling, "Who are you? Let me go! Walmer, you bastard, it's your doing."

Jon Walmer hung up the red phone. He knew Gordon was a little fish in a powerful secret society that his investigation had uncovered in the last two weeks. He couldn't take the chance this organization would get in the way of the team's efforts to save the planet. It may be an ad hoc team, but he couldn't imagine a better one for this incredible task. He was always a calm intellectual type, and he had vociferously objected to the government using torture to extract information from terrorists captured on the battlefield. He realized quickly that this situation could be life or death for every person on earth. He picked up the red phone again and dialed.

"Colonel, he'll be arriving shortly. I've made up my mind. Do whatever it takes to get him to spill his guts, but don't do any permanent physical damage, and for God's sake, don't kill him. I know you're the expert, but I strongly suggest you let us verify each piece of information before you pump him for the next piece. We can verify it rapidly, and it'll let him know he can't just tell us what we want to hear."

"Yes, sir," said the Colonel. "I'll pass any information directly to AIEDA and wait for their analysis before proceeding with the interrogation."

"Call me when you think you've got as much as you can get."

Jon hung up the red phone without waiting for a response. About ten minutes later his white phone rang, and he reached for it without checking the caller ID. Usually, he didn't answer calls from unfamiliar or blocked ID's; instead, he would let them go to voice mail.

"Jon Walmer," he announced in the phone.

"Mr. Walmer, my name is Andre. I believe I owe you an apology, 'cause it seems we got off on the wrong foot. I just learned one of my operatives is detained by you. I must assume it was you doing it, 'cause we recently did the same to your friend, Dr. Akins, and you've mounted the information gathering blitzkrieg aimed at my organization. Please accept my apology and release Gordon. We only want to help."

"Well, Andre, how do I know I can trust you to back off after I release Gordon?" asked Jon. "I also need you to keep your silence on whatever you think you know. Public knowledge will cause difficulties we wish to avoid."

"I understand your position. Kidnapping Dr. Akins wasn't the plan. He happened to catch Gordon searching his office for information. I wanted to discover the leader of the team working on this most vital project. I had no intention to start what might be described as gang war. Publicity and scrutiny both are not good for business. We have many resources we can put in your disposal, no strings attached. Release Gordon and call off investigators. As installment, to demonstrate my sincerity, I'll deposit $400 million into your company's account tomorrow afternoon. For us, it's pocket change. Also, I'll do overnight delivery of my contact information and list of resources we can give to your team as they try to solve our mutual problem. No strings attached. We want a solution as bad as you do, and we realize none of the world governments are up to it."

"I assume Andre is a *nom de plume*. You may call me Jon. If you come through tomorrow with your promises, I'll comply with your requests."

"You may assume so, as is Gordon a *nom de plume*," said Andre. "Jon, I must ask you to stop your interrogation of Gordon and your investigations immediately. If I don't deliver tomorrow, you can always restart. Okay?"

"Okay, Andre. I understand. I'll contact you tomorrow. Do you want the bank routing and account numbers for my company?"

"No, that's easy to obtain. So, for now, goodbye," said Andre.

Immediately after the line was clear, Jon made two phone calls. He put a temporary hold on Gordon's interrogation and on all related investigations.

What a strange day this turned-out to be, Jon thought. *I'll have to inform the others of this new development.*

Jon picked up the red phone again and dialed Don Mensch's cell phone. He knew Don was visiting a client, so he expected he'd have to leave a message. He lucked out.

"Hey, Jon, what's up?" asked Don.

"I've had quite a strange day, Don. Tomorrow afternoon we should have $400 million in the bank as an installment for pursuing our Star-Slayer Project. Our new partner, Gordon's boss, has agreed to remain a passive investor, but he also offers other resources we might use free of charge. I'll get details in the mail tomorrow."

"I didn't know the project had a name yet," said Don. "Star-Slayer sounds good to me, and so does $400 million. I wonder how he arrived at that number. How much more do you think he'll be paying us?"

"I don't know, but I'm going to ask for $400 million per month. That amounts to $4.8 billion per year. Jean Philippe said he could provide $5.0 billion per year. AIEDA can provide $1.0 billion per year in cash and the rest of our contribution will be in information services valued at $1.0 billion per year. The total is a mere $11.8 billion per year.

Although we don't have a plan yet, I suspect that whatever it is, it'll be one of the biggest construction and engineering efforts of all time. We can do it faster and cheaper than the government, but I doubt if we can do anything so ambitious for less than $100 billion per year for the next seven years.

Once we have a plan, we'll be able to make a cost estimate, but frankly, whatever estimate we make will be wrong because nothing like our project has ever been done before. I feel it's best to quickly determine the limits of our fund-raising capabilities and get commitments as soon as possible. As we develop a plan and proceed with its implementation, we'll likely have to find more funding sources."

"I know where you're going with this, Jon," said Don. "There is no way I can raise that kind of venture capital. I'm good, but not that good. The large part of whatever the shortage has to come from Uncle Sam. I'm sure he knows about the anomaly and its effect on the planet, and he's keeping it quiet so as not to create a panic situation. I'll commit to raise $1.2 billion per year.

"The remaining $87 billion per year, or whatever we need, must come from Uncle Sam. We need a cover project like a Mars colonization mission managed by private enterprise, supported by NASA technology, and 87% funded by a grant from the U.S. Government. The shuttle program can be cancelled early and the money saved can be diverted to the phony Mars mission. The International Space Station can be abandoned after establishing a base camp on the Moon. Mars missions can be planned for launch from the Moon which can be used as a staging area for pioneers, supplies, and transportation systems. How's that for a cover story?"

"Well, I'm sure we'll need to polish it up a bit, but I get what you're saying," said Jon. "We just have to figure out how to get access to the President, and how to lobby Congress on behalf of the Star-Slayer Project. We also need to bypass the usual government program development and contract administration procedures. We don't want them finding out that the money is being used on an effort other than the Mars mission."

"That's precisely why I suggested an outright grant," said Don.

"It'll be the biggest grant in history, if we get it," said Jon.

"We don't even have a plan yet, so what should we do with the $400 million we'll be getting tomorrow?" asked Don.

"We need to pay for the upgrade of AIEDA's central processing unit that's scheduled for day after tomorrow. We're going to need as many MIPS as we can get, so we're replacing silicon IC's with the new graphene IC's. It's hard to imagine these graphene transistors are merely one atom wide by ten atoms long. They operate at room temperature, so they'll save us big operating bucks after we dismantle the supercooling apparatus we've been using. They even cost less to manufacture, because they can be etched-out of a piece of graphene."

"I think it's ironic that AIEDA has designed her own CPU upgrade," said Don. "You know we should use some of that money to design and install an electronically secure communications center so our team can work together from several different locations."

"All in good time my friend. I suspect we'll be getting input on what's possible from Tom Calvano pretty soon now."

"As a matter of fact, Tom will be back tomorrow afternoon. I was planning to call you," said Don, "but you beat me to the punch. About ten minutes ago I got a call from Jean Philippe, who had just received Tom's report on his encounter with the Guardian. The Guardian has accepted AIEDA's conclusion and has agreed to help us. The downside is the fact that his assistant Guardians have been recalled, along with their cruisers. They also deleted most technical information from the remaining cruiser's computer."

"That's not a good omen," said Jon.

Don speculated, "It's almost as if our friend, the master Guardian, has been abandoned as punishment for his failure to develop humankind, although he claims to have pleaded for permission to stay and help us. Tom doesn't think he'll be of much use without the Guardians' technological data. He's agreed to allow his computer to be integrated with AIEDA in a way that will put AIEDA in control. He's also rigged two com-units to communicate with him at any time from any location. He expects to work with us to set up a holographic communications center. That's it in brief. Tom has the entire encounter on a digital recorder for us to hear tomorrow. I've informed Amanda, George, and Roger. Jean Philippe is already in town. We all expect to meet at your place tomorrow at 3:00 p.m. Is that okay?"

"Yes, of course. I'll inform Harry to expect guests," said Jon. "In the meantime, I'll be having a voice conversation with AIEDA. I'd like to know where she would suggest we set up our holographic communications center. I wonder how the Guardian will send us the specs. By the way, how did Tom arrange to get here so quickly?"

"I think Tom is carrying the specs with him. One of the airships took him to Ushuaia, Argentina, then returned to the base camp. Tom's traveling here via commercial air. His total flight time is about twenty-one hours. The rest of the exploratory team is breaking camp and returning on a more leisurely schedule via the airships. Obviously, Jean Philippe has scuttled plans for the Ecosthat. Oh! On a personal note, I thought you should be the first to hear that Amanda and I eloped and got married in Las Vegas. She's with me now," said Don.

"Congratulations to both of you! Must have been love at first sight, and I guess that client visit was just a cover story, right?"

"You got it. We didn't want anyone talking us out of it. Time has been accelerated by our mysterious black hole."

"Okay, Don, I understand completely. See you tomorrow," said Jon.

"Okay, bye."

No sooner did Jon Walmer hang up the red phone, than it rang. The red phone could receive incoming calls from only two places, AIEDA home office and the AIEDA Development Lab. Jon picked up the phone knowing full well it was from the lab. He answered as required by procedure, "Packaging Services Department. May I have your work order number, please?"

"It's every prime number from one to seven," was the response.

Jon did a quick mental calculation. *Yes, it's the seventh day of the month*, he thought.

Then he asked, "What news do you have?"

"Jon, we've received an odd transmission from an unknown source," said the recognizable voice of the lab director. "It seems to be a set of specifications for a medical brain probe. It asks for six sets of probes to be custom-made. Because the communication referenced it was per agreement with Tom Calvano, we proceeded to review the information.

"We've compared it to available probes, and it deviates in a number of ways, the most significant being that it specifies the exterior of the probe be of a carbon-based material. All off-the-shelf probes we've researched are made of silicon. We contacted an assistant professor of biomedical engineering at City University, and he tells us that silicon produces scar tissue that interferes with electrical conductivity of the probe.

"He acknowledged that if we had a suitable carbon probe, it would produce less scar tissue and stimulate the body to grow more neural pathways around the area damaged by the probe. We inputted all this information into AIEDA, and she designed a suitable material made of carbon nanotubes. How would you like us to proceed from here?"

"Do you have a manufacturer in mind?" asked Jon.

"Yes, we've spoken to our contact at Elluvium Precision Instruments," said the lab director. "They said they're willing to expedite it for us, but we need to let them know in a couple of days before they get locked into their next job, or else the price to break into their manufacturing schedule will be much higher. Six probes will cost us $150,000. A dozen will cost us $200,000."

"Okay, go ahead and order a dozen."

"Will do, Jon."

The conversation ended abruptly. Jon sat motionless, as if daydreaming. He felt as if a rushing river were sweeping him away downstream to his demise. He needed someone to rescue him, throw him a line or a branch of a tree. He shook himself out of his funk and realized the source of his momentary panic. He still had no plan to save the earth.

He could hardly wait for the team to meet at his house tomorrow afternoon. He would defer his conversation with AIEDA about the communications center. He was just too mentally tired to review it today. Besides, Tom was carrying the holographic com-system specs with him. He would get them tomorrow and review them with some of his engineers before asking AIEDA to select a suitable installation location. Following his clean desk practice, he stacked all his papers and notes in one big pile and dumped them into the bottom left drawer. Clean did not necessarily imply orderliness. He smiled at the thought, locked his desk, and left for home.

Chapter 17

Upper West Side of Manhattan

It was one of those mornings when Jon couldn't bring himself to fight the rush hour traffic getting to work, especially knowing he had to be home at 3:00 p.m. All the electronics in his home were just as secure as in the office. He would inform his executive assistant, chauffeur, and bodyguard that he'd be working from home today.

Oh, and he'd be sure not to surprise Harry with his presence at home. He relished the thought of Harry in the butler's role, as only he and his ex-wife, Catherine, knew that Harry doubled as a home security agent. Harry was a black-belt in jujutsu, an expert in small arms, and skilled with all manner of electronic security devices.

Harry's cordial but somewhat obsequious demeanor and apparent age—he looked in his sixties—belied his alacrity to use deadly force, if necessary. Jon never once knew Harry to miss a daily workout in the basement's gym, and once a week he went to the indoor range to practice his marksmanship. Jon felt fortunate to have such a skilled employee, but even more fortunate to call him friend and consider him part of the family.

After taking care of morning toiletries, he put on business casual clothes in preparation for the afternoon meeting with the Star-Slayer Project Team and proceeded directly to the kitchen to rustle-up something for breakfast. Harry was already there with a fresh pot of coffee brewing.

"Good morning, sir. I've just finished a bagel with lox and cream cheese. Would you like the same?"

"Sounds good, Harry," said Jon. "Toast the bagel lightly, please. And add a thin slice of onion. I'll help myself to the coffee. It smells especially good this morning. Did you get my message that I'll be home all day today?"

"Yes, sir, I did. I'm assuming the plans for our guests at three o'clock remain the same. How many might we expect for dinner?"

"No change in plans," said Jon. "I'm expecting Don Mensch, Amanda Rheinhardt, George Blocker, Jean Philippe Martinique, Roger Akins, and Tom Calvano. Let's assume everyone will be staying for dinner, so with me that would be seven. Inform Martha to prepare sliced flank steak, home fries, and green beans. Oh, by the way, I just learned yesterday that Don and Amanda eloped and got married in Las Vegas. What a surprise!"

"They make a fine couple. Although at the risk of speaking out of school, I sensed there was something intimate between Miss Rheinhardt and Mr. Blocker, so I, too, am quite surprised," said Harry.

"Your talent for observation is superb, Harry. It must be that secret agent side of you. I have personally gotten between Amanda and George when they weren't quite seeing eye-to-eye, and I knew I had to exit quickly or get scoured in a lover's quarrel. Frankly, I think George is deeply in love with his wife, and Amanda was likely just a diversion."

"Well, sir, you might have that backwards. I'd bet a week's pay Mr. Blocker was merely a distraction for Miss Amanda."

"I don't dare bet you, Harry," said Jon. "You're too good at picking up on subtleties . . . which brings me to something I've been meaning to ask you. You've obviously heard the team's discussions and, as is expected, you've kept your opinion to yourself. I presume at the very least you've gathered that earth is threatened by an object from space of intense gravitational force. I'd like to hear your opinion, Harry."

"Sir, I appreciate your offer, but how could you seriously be interested in my opinion? I'm extremely good at what I do, but a space object that can destroy earth is a bit out of my league."

"No, Harry, I think you underestimate the value of your opinion to me," said Jon. "Your perspective on life is far more representative of the world's population than mine. I'm a mathematician and a computer geek making an extremely large salary. I know my weaknesses. One of them is not being able to read people, and another is being too rigid in my logic and thereby not considering the human factor. I need to hear your opinion, Harry."

"Okay, you asked for it. Let me start by saying everyone on the team is a fine person. However, collectively, you're all off your rockers! I think you must have some sort of Napoleon complex. If the governments of the world can't solve this problem, how on earth do you expect to do it?

If the world at large knew what you were up to, the vast majority would panic, another smaller number would pray for your success, then crawl under their beds, and an even smaller group would attack what you're doing as against God's will. Of the latter group, an even smaller number would attempt to sabotage your efforts and would go so far as to murder everyone on your team.

There are some out there who are willing to help you, but how will you find them without letting the cat out of the bag? You see, sir, the only way you can even have a shot at success is to be sure this threat and your project remain a secret. Think of it. The greatest threat to humanity the world has seen must remain secret so that a small eclectic team of very nice, very smart people can have a snowball's chance in hell to save the planet. I rest my case . . . you're all off your rockers!"

"So, what would you have us do?" asked Jon.

"I said you were crazy. I didn't say you were stupid. I'm one of the people willing to help you, or die trying. When the Armageddon fanatics come to kill you, I'll be there. They'll have to get past me first, sir."

"Thanks, Harry. You're a good friend. You've also made a good point about secrecy and security. I knew we needed to keep everything hush-hush, but I hadn't considered the extent to which it should be part of our plan. It's clear that secrecy and security must be the number one objective, or everything else we attempt will be fruitless."

———————————◊———————————

Jon was at his desk in the study when Harry brought in the mail. There it was; the overnight package he was anxiously expecting. He pulled the tab and opened it. He could hardly wait to get his eyes on the document inside. It was short and to the point. Andre had provided a phone number and fax number, as well as a list of resources Jon's team could use free of charge.

He read down the list:

1. Design and installation of secure communications facilities
2. Search and retrieval of technological information
3. Private investigation services
4. Personal and facility security personnel
5. Expertise in astrophysics

Jon translated the list in his mind as he read it: *spy network, industrial espionage, spies, thugs, he's joking about astrophysics.* Jon reminded himself to check the company bank account after lunch. If the $400 million was there, he'd call Andre to pursue this strange partnership.

Sure enough, when he checked the account at 1:00 p.m., he saw the deposit for $400 million. It would have to clear before he could withdraw any of it, but he was beginning to trust Andre. Anyone willing to risk that kind of money had to be sincere about his altruistic intentions. Jon picked up the red phone and dialed the number on the document.

"Hello?" answered Andre with his distinct accent.

"Andre, this is Jon Walmer. I'm calling to thank you for your gift. We need to discuss your role in this project."

"Yes, Jon. I'm happy to hear the pleasantness of your voice. Seems your Caller ID is blocked, so I'm glad I picked up. Not many have this number. I suspected it might be you, happy as a duck in a pond after seeing the deposit."

"Yes, I'm beginning to believe you want to help and not interfere. However, I must be frank with you. Whatever we'll be doing to save the planet will cost a lot more than $400 million. The project must be completed within seven years. Andre, if you want to play in this game, it'll cost you $400 million per month.

Our initial fundraising target is $100 billion per year for the next seven years to be spent on a secret project to save the planet by some means yet to be determined. It's a big leap of faith, Andre.

It's all or nothing. If you want your $400 million back, I'll understand, but you must back off and keep your silence."

"Jon, that's a lot of money. I don't like that you have no plan yet," complained Andre in his heavy accent.

There was a moment of silence on the phone, then Andre continued, "But if it saves our lives and livelihoods, it will be well spent, my friend. I must clear my decision with my four partners, but count on me for $4.8 billion per year for seven years. Yet, I insist you at least provide a verbal progress report on a quarterly basis. You don't need to tell details. I just want enough to judge if real progress is made in a timely manner."

"Okay, Andre, we have a deal. Now tell me what you mean by listing astrophysics as an expertise."

"It's true, Jon. I've about completed my PhD in astrophysics. Just need to complete oral exam on my thesis."

"You may be more help than I could have imagined," said Jon. "We need to get you involved right away, but not on astrophysics. I've concluded the number one priority is secrecy and security. The number two priority is a secure communications facility and network. Can I enlist you to take the lead on planning for those two top priorities?"

"But of course. I'd be most happy to create these plans. I only need a contact person in your company to work with. If you would fax me this person, I'll begin immediately."

"Very good, Andre. Welcome aboard. I'll be in touch."

"Goodbye, my friend."

Jon called the head of AIEDA security. "Howard, I've been in touch with a fellow named Andre. I've asked him to develop security and communications plans for the Star-Slayer Project. I don't quite trust him yet, but I need to give him enough rope to either hang himself or prove himself. I'll be giving him your name as a contact at AIEDA.

He'll be asking a lot of questions about our facilities and our employees. Make sure he gets only the plans we provided to the city, as I don't want him to know anything about our underground complex. Also, only give him information about first level employees and put extra security on them during this process.

Any plans Andre develops for peripheral facilities and first level employees should be appropriate for protecting the confidential components, too. I want you to review his plans and get to know him, because you'll be the one to tell me if he can be trusted."

"Okay, boss, I'll be ready for him," said Howard.

"Thanks, Howard," said Jon as he hung up the red phone.

How time flies, thought Jon. *It's almost 15:00 and my guests should be arriving soon.*

It wasn't long before his parlor was buzzing with the team as they anxiously discussed pleasantries, knowing full well Jon would soon convene an orderly and effective meeting. He always did.

"May I have your attention? Thank you!" said Jon. "Tom, have you had a chance to introduce yourself to the rest of the team?"

"Yes, thanks, and I want to extend my special thanks to the team for the guidance you gave me for dealing with Guardian," said Tom Calvano.

"Speaking of the Guardian," said Jon, "can we get him to join our meeting via the speakerphone on your com-unit? I heard he modified it for you."

"Yes, I believe we can, but I suggest I first play the recording of my visit with him. I can then take questions. When we're done and ready for Guardian, I'll give the com-unit a try," said Tom. "Oh, by the way, I stopped off at AIEDA home office just before coming here and dropped off the specs for Guardian's holographic communications system. I gave them to your head of security, a guy named Howard."

"Perfect, Tom. Now let's hear that tape," commanded Jon.

———————————————◇———————————————

When Tom finished playing the recording of his meeting with the Guardian, there was momentary silence. He looked up, and everyone seemed to be staring ahead, as if in a daydream. As he started to see a couple of them blink and look around, he took the opportunity to get the discussion going. "Well, any questions?"

"The Guardian seems to mention God a lot," said Don. "Frankly, I'm an agnostic tipping toward atheism. Because I find it hard to accept that an advanced technological civilization would believe in God, I find it hard to believe the Guardian. He seems so unsure of himself, considering he claims to be immortal. Are we being naïve to trust him so much?"

"Well, I believe in God," said Jon. "I don't find it at all unusual that an immortal race of beings would believe they know God even more intimately than we do."

"I'm a deist, meaning I believe in an impersonal God and don't believe in following a religion," said Tom. "Also, I believe we each have a soul that lives in some other reality. So, it's not hard for me to accept what Guardian has said about God and souls."

"Please, guys, let's not turn this meeting into a debate over the existence of God," said Amanda. "Come back to reality for a minute and recognize that whatever the Guardian said about God and about souls is irrelevant to the problem at hand. It doesn't seem to me that God will give us the solution. We must focus on what the Guardian can contribute to our search for a way to save earth."

"I must support Amanda's perspective," said Jean Philippe. "I can't help but feel something the Guardian has said contains a hint to the solution we seek. Obviously, even the Guardian has no clue as to what that might be. I do, however, feel he and his kind seem to be quitters, but mind you, I don't have the courage to say that to his face."

"I, too, agree transcendental issues have no place in our deliberations," said Roger. "If there's an answer to our dilemma, I believe it must lie in the Guardian's technology."

"Okay Roger, if that's true, the only technology discussed by the Guardian in any detail is the way his cruiser operates," said George. "The most startling feature being that it has two black holes circulating inside it contained in a magnetic donut of some sort."

"Well, there was one other startling fact," said Tom. "Do you remember he mentioned there's a black hole at the center of the earth being used by other advanced races to sling-shot themselves into dimensions higher than the fifth?"

"Maybe we need to define our problem better before we look for a way to mend it," suggested Jean Philippe. "I mean, let's look at it in simplistic terms first before looking for a sophisticated technological solution."

"I can give you simplistic," said Amanda. "A black hole is heading right for us. It's so massive and moving so fast, we can't divert it away from us. As it gets closer, it'll exert such a powerful gravimetric force on us that it'll destroy us before it even gets close. How's that for simplistic?"

"Very good," said Jean Philippe, "but what's the simplistic solution?"

"That's easy," said Tom. "When you're standing on the railroad tracks and a freight train comes barreling down on you, what do you do? You get out of the way!"

"So you're saying we should move the earth out of the way?" asked Roger rhetorically. "It wouldn't work even if you could move the earth. You see, without the moon, the earth would become uninhabitable by mankind. The moon gives us our tides, and it stabilizes the angle of the earth's axis to the planetary plane, among other things. Earth needs the moon."

"Okay, then, we must move both the earth and the moon, together as one system, out of the way," said Tom.

"Okay, how do we do that?" asked Jean Philippe.

"That's easy," said Don. "We temporarily move both the earth and the moon to the fifth dimension. As I understand it, we only have to be there a little while, because time will slow down for us, but time will continue flying by for our sun and its remaining orbiting buddies. When we pop back into the fourth dimension, the black hole will be long gone. All is solved."

"All solved only if the sun itself hasn't been destroyed," said Roger. "Of course, I don't know the effects on Earth if some other planets like Venus or Mars were destroyed. I would guess the biggest danger would be that remnants of destroyed planets would find their way into Earth's orbital path."

"This is getting us nowhere," said Jon. "How could we seriously consider moving the earth and moon into the fifth dimension? This is ludicrous!"

"Not so fast, Jon," said George. "I think we're on to something. It dawns on me that the moon always faces the same side toward earth as it orbits earth, and its orbit is nearly circular, unlike the orbits of planets.

"We don't know the technology, but we do know that a pair of black holes in a circular orbit within a magnetic field allows Guardian cruisers to do dimensional jumps. One black hole already exists within earth. If we create another black hole within the moon and join them together with an electromagnetic beam, we may be able to create a rift in space-time large enough for both the earth and the moon to enter the fifth dimension.

"I know this is fantasy now, but it's an avenue we should explore. If we can learn enough about cruiser technology, AIEDA may be able to develop a way for us to turn the moon and the earth into a giant cruiser of sorts."

"Interesting idea!" said Jean Philippe. "Tom, I think it's time to call the Guardian on your com-unit. We have lots of questions to ask him about cruiser technology."

"Okay, I'll call him now," said Tom. "But I need to remind you what Guardian said. You heard it on the tape. His people have never been able to build a cruiser larger than about a hundred feet in diameter because the gravimetric effect becomes unstable."

Tom dialed #333 on his com-unit. He could hear it ringing and ringing. He knew he had to be patient.

"Hello, Tom. I was wondering when you'd call," said the Guardian.

"How'd you know it was me and not Jeff?"

"Every com-unit has a different identity code within its transmission frequency, sort of like a rudimentary caller ID," explained the Guardian.

"I'm calling to ask if you'd join us on speakerphone as we conduct a team meeting to search for a way to prevent earth's destruction. Everyone here has listened to the recording of our meeting. They have questions for you," said Tom.

"I'd be pleased to join you. It's a bit lonely here by myself. The androids don't make good conversation," said the Guardian.

"I gave the holographic system specs to our technical group, so you'll soon be able to join us in a more personal way, and more frequently. We recognize your value to our team effort," said Tom.

"Thank you, I'll do my best, but please understand that being alone, with most technical data having been wiped from my computer, leaves me handicapped. I've been around a long time and my memory is good, but I'm not part of the engineering class of Guardians. I'm part of what you might call the Foreign Service, and my position is as an ambassador of sorts," explained the Guardian.

"Mr. Guardian, I'm Jon Walmer, CEO and Chairman of ΛIEDΛ Risk Mitigation Company. I'd first like to welcome you to our team and thank you for your assistance, especially for risking your life by remaining among us. Second, I'd like to introduce the other members of our team. Tom Calvano, you've met. Tom's direct employer is Mr. Jean Philippe Martinique of Marseilles Electric Enterprises of France."

Jon Walmer continued around the room introducing the team members to the Guardian. Each took the opportunity to welcome and thank the Guardian. During this exchange, the Guardian asked that everyone drop the *Mister* and just call him *Guardian*.

"Now that we've completed the introductions, I think we should resume our informal modus operandi," said Jon. "George, perhaps you'd like to lead off with some questions for Guardian."

"Yes, thanks, Jon," said George. "Guardian, we've come up with an unlikely solution, but it's the only one we have. Its design, development, and implementation depend exclusively on the technology used by your cruisers to make dimensional jumps. We know there are two black holes revolving inside a donut shaped magnetic field, and somehow this creates a rift in space-time that allows the craft to enter a higher dimension. We also know craft greater than one hundred feet in diameter are not possible because of instability of the rift-generation mechanism. Can you give us more information on how this mechanism works?"

"As I explained, I'm not of the engineering class and don't know the equations by heart, but I can tell you in general terms how it works," said Guardian. "The size of the two black holes, their relative position to each other, and their speed of revolution are critical, as is the intensity of the primary magnetic field that contains them. The initial energy to start the process is extremely large, but once it's started, the potential energy differential between dimensions is sufficient to maintain the magnetic field.

The two black holes are essentially in orbit around each other, but when the gravity-well first opens, it can disrupt their orbits and cause them to get too close to each other. The primary magnetic field prevents this tendency, and they continue in a circular path inside the donut-shaped field.

The orientation between the black holes must be maintained precisely 180 degrees from each other, and this is done by automatic modulation of the field at various points as the holes fly by. The necessary speed of the black holes is inversely proportional to the total mass of both black holes.

Our design has both black holes the same size, but that's not necessary. The required speed is calculated, and then maintained by automatic modulation of the primary magnetic field. Is this helpful so far?"

"Yes, it's very helpful," said George. "I've been recording your explanation. I hope you don't mind."

"No, not at all. I was expecting you to record it," said Guardian. "Now I shall attempt to explain the control mechanism. The outer hull of the cruiser acts like a capacitor in the same way static electricity builds up on the surface of objects, then discharges when coming in contact with a ground. The dimensional rift opened by the black holes is small, but sufficient to leak energy into the capacitor until it's full and therefore at equilibrium with the fifth dimension. As energy is used to manage the electromagnetic field, it's replaced from the rift simply due to the energy differential.

When it comes time to make the dimensional jump, we instantaneously change the polarity of the capacitor, causing a kind of short circuit. It's much the same as if you were to over-pressurize a tank, and the pressure relief valve opened to prevent an explosion. The energy we captured from the fifth dimension is blown back into it with such force that the rift is expanded enough to allow our craft to be sucked into it."

"How do you get back out, if the potential energy flows from higher dimensions to lower ones?" asked Amanda.

"Actually, that fact makes it easier to get back," said the Guardian. "You see a fourth dimensional object can't exist in the fifth dimension, or any other dimension for that matter. As fourth-dimensional matter, we would exist in an out-of-phase form in the boundary layer or corridor that separates successive dimensions.

"Within this layer we're a foreign particle, sort of like a bubble of air in water that floats to the surface and joins the atmosphere. A better example would be a submarine that must maintain water in its ballast tanks to submerge. When it blows the water out of the tanks, it rises to the surface.

"Because the higher dimension has higher potential energy, and we retain a lower, out-of-phase energy, we must use our fusion-generated energy to electrostatically charge the hull to maintain our position or move around in the boundary layer. As soon as we de-energize our hull, we float to the edge of the layer where a rift of the right size just naturally opens and blows us back into the fourth dimension."

"Can you explain to us how the two black holes can create the dimensional rift and maintain it before you do a jump?" asked Roger.

"That question requires me to explain gravity which you know I've referred to in discussions with Tom as the *breath of God*," said Guardian. "The eleventh dimension is like an infinitely long string with a width much less than the diameter of the nucleus of an atom, and it winds its way through every atom in the Universe.

"When the Universe was first created, gasses accreted into dust via ionic attraction. As particles became larger and larger via accretion, the mass would become significant enough to affect space and time. As objects became more massive, they would naturally assume a more or less spherical shape, because as space-time is distorted from all directions, particles fall into the center of the space-time hole, bump into each other, and form a spherical plug in the drain, so to speak.

"This tendency of atoms to fall into the space-time hole is what we experience as gravity. That's why we call the space-time hole a gravity-well. But remember, the eleventh dimension passes through every atom, and emanations from the eleventh dimension vary over time and at different places in the Universe. These emanations control how mass affects space-time, and therefore they control the strength of gravity.

"By measuring these emanations, we can determine more precisely how gravity is operating and can thereby adjust our trans-dimensional propulsion system on the fly. Your scientists haven't been able to accept this fact, despite having observed cosmological anomalies that scream out to them that gravity is not the same at every place and time in the Universe.

"General Relativity fails to explain these anomalies because it's an incomplete theory of gravity. Now having explained how gravity works, you can see that the mass of two revolving black holes can distort space-time in such a way as to cause a gravity-well in the center of their common orbit. The rift into the fifth dimension occurs at the bottom of the gravity well. It remains open as long as the revolving black-hole mechanism maintains its stability."

"Why aren't we affected by the gravity of the black holes? And can you provide us with any equations that would describe this phenomenon?" asked Jon.

"We're not affected by the gravity of the black holes because of a secondary modulation of the magnetic field that contains them. This secondary modulation cancels out the emanations from the eleventh dimension that might escape from the magnetic donut containing the black holes. I can provide some basic equations from memory that may be of some help, but they won't be sufficient," offered Guardian. "I'd also offer you my cruiser so you can do experiments, but it would take many years for you to gather enough useful information. Instead, I suggest you contact your President, because your military establishment studied the Roswell cruiser for years and gathered thousands of pages of experimental data before I retrieved it from them. With my rudimentary equations and your powerful computer, the Roswell data might be enough to develop a complete theory."

"You explained that cruisers over one hundred feet in diameter don't work because the propulsion system becomes unstable. Can you tell us more about why that happens and what partial successes you might have had with larger prototypes?" asked Jean Philippe.

"Basically, the mass of the ship itself interferes with the stability of the rift," explained the Guardian. "Not Guardians, but people of other races have developed large cylindrical ships by arranging several one hundred foot diameter propulsion systems in concentric rings about 150 feet apart. They look somewhat like a giant stubby cigar with convex ends. Others have developed triangular shaped ships. All of these large ships are unsafe because it's impossible to maintain the synchronicity of multiple dimensional rifts within the structure. They've used these craft as staging areas at the edge of the dimensional boundary layer. These craft can't be used for dimensional travel to move people to other places because it's too dangerous. They send these cargo ships to pre-planned destinations with supplies and equipment using a robotic crew. Believe me; they lose a lot of ships. Once at the destination they can remain safely at the boundary layer indefinitely."

"What do you mean by staging areas?" asked Amanda.

"Staging areas are used as stop-off points to re-supply cruisers or to make repairs on the cruisers," explained the Guardian. "They're also used to store valuable minerals, plants, and animals that are harvested from places all over the Universe. When the supplies are exhausted and the ship is filled with specimens, it's sent back to the home world with its robotic crew. Many never make it back, but those that do are immensely valuable."

"If I understand you correctly, the instability problem for a large vessel is only a concern if it's using a dimensional jump to move through space-time," said George. "If a large vessel just sits at the edge of the dimensional boundary layer, it can remain safely inside the fifth dimension indefinitely. Time would pass more slowly within the boundary layer than within the fourth dimension where we normally reside."

"Yes, that's a roughly correct interpretation," said Guardian.

"Can you give us an equation that would allow us to calculate how long we'd have to remain in the fifth dimension for a given time to pass in the fourth dimension?" asked Jon.

"Yes, fortunately that's basic knowledge for dimensional travelers," said the Guardian.

"Is it correct we don't need to measure the eleventh dimension's emanations if we're not using the dimensional jump to travel great distances?" asked George.

"Yes, that's correct, because within this part of the Universe gravity doesn't vary enough to have an observable effect," answered the Guardian.

"You know, we need that data you say was collected on the Roswell cruiser," said Jon, "but our government has been covering up that incident, and I think it would be near impossible for us to get an audience with the President to discuss anything, much less a UFO crash in Roswell, NM in 1947."

"Actually, I can help you with that problem," said Guardian. "It just so happens that the President and I have been discussing this threat to earth recently, and I believe he'd be happy to know there's a group of unusually smart people who refuse to give up hope. I'll give him your name and number, Jon."

"That's great news!" exclaimed Jon. "Maybe he can be convinced to give us the Roswell data and finance us, too."

"Guardian, you've been quite helpful," said George. "If you haven't guessed it by now, our crazy idea is to turn the earth and moon into a giant trans-dimensional propulsion system. We can hide in the fifth dimensional boundary layer. When the danger has passed, we can pop back into our fourth dimensional orbit.

The earth already has a black hole at its core and the moon revolves around the earth with the same side always facing it. If we can create the right size black hole within the moon, we can connect it to earth's black hole with a powerful electromagnetic projector, which we can use to modulate the magnetic force, and thereby maintain the distance and velocity of the earth and moon relative to each other as the gravity-well forms."

"I truly wish to encourage you," said Guardian, "but you must realize you have no theory, no equations to help you design such a system which has nothing comparable in the entire Universe. Your second problem will be the tremendous amounts of energy you'll need to first create the black hole, then to power your magnetic projector."

"Have faith, Guardian," said Tom. "This team's about beating the odds and not about being defeated by the odds."

"I understand. I'm still with you," said the Guardian. "You'll have all the equations we discussed by morning, and I'll contact the President and ask him to call you, Jon."

"Thank you, Guardian," said Tom.

"Goodbye," said Guardian.

"Well, people, that discussion made me hungry," said Jon. Harry will be serving dinner shortly in the dining room for any or all of you who wish to join me."

The entire team took Jon up on the dinner offer.

Chapter 18

As Jon sat in his office, he couldn't help but think about the progress the team had made at his home yesterday afternoon. It had been the team's first conversation with the Guardian. It all seemed so surreal. He hoped the Guardian would keep his word and deliver the equations. He wondered if the President would ever call him. He worried the Guardian had misjudged the President's willingness to work with a private organization on such a critical project. Perhaps the President already had a government team working the problem.

He had to stop the daydreaming, especially the negative thoughts. He knew he had to make time to spend with AIEDA. Her system enhancement was scheduled to go online at 1500 hours, and he wanted to ask her some final questions that would increase his confidence that all would go well.

He had reason for concern, because the last upgrade resulted in a crash that left AIEDA down for two days. Everyone at AIEDA home office had become so dependent on the powerful computer that forty-eight hours seemed like an eternity. This system enhancement had been in the works for months because of its complexity. Many tests had been run to ensure the results of AIEDA's applications could be replicated on the new system. All data had to be copied to the new storage devices and validated. Two sets of identical questions were posed, one to the current AIEDA and the other to the partially enhanced AIEDA, to be sure the answers were the same. This wasn't a simple upgrade, but was essentially a switchover to a predominantly new computer.

The voice to voice interface had been added several months ago, and it seemed to be working well. Jon found it to be much more convenient than typing his inquiries, but he had quickly learned his verbal queries were usually not phrased as precisely as his typed ones. When he used the voice interface, AIEDA had to ask him for clarification more frequently than when he used keyboard entry. He was learning to think about how to phrase his questions before he asked them when talking to AIEDA. After all, being a computer, AIEDA interpreted things literally, and she couldn't pick up on the nuances of a question.

It wasn't until after lunch that Jon walked into the 12-foot by 12-foot secure room that contained three chairs, a small table, and almost every possible computer peripheral and interface one could imagine. As he entered, he locked the door behind him. Only he, Don, and Howard had access to this room. If a computer technician required access, Howard, as chief of security, had to be present. Jon pressed the button labeled *VOICE*.

"Begin voice dialog," commanded Jon.

"Awaiting user command," said AIEDA in a soft but firm female voice.

"Identify user," commanded Jon.

"User is *Dr. Jonathan Walmer* . . . based on voice pattern recognition," said AIEDA.

"Identify computer," commanded Jon.

"Computer is *AIEDA* . . . based on internal registry entry," said AIEDA.

"Beginning query. Review recently entered specs for building holographic communications system plus associated engineering comments and determine how fast it can be built. Identify any impediments to its construction," requested Jon.

"Processing query. Response anticipated in two minutes," said AIEDA.

Jon sat waiting patiently.

"Holographic communications system can be assembled in two weeks from off-the-shelf components. Availability of fiber optic cable for internal system connections might delay assembly beyond two weeks."

"How long of a delay is likely?" asked Jon.

"Indeterminate. Only one supplier of the specified type of fiber optic cable is available. Negotiation may be necessary to expedite delivery."

"Why do you think there could be a cable delay?" asked Jon.

"An unexpected, high volume of backorders was identified in the cable supplier's last quarterly report."

"Beginning new query," said Jon. "With primary criteria being secrecy and security, secondary criterion being convenience, and tertiary criterion being cost, where's the best place to set up the holographic communications system as part of a secret and highly secure wireless communications center for coordinating the Star-Slayer Project?"

"Define the Star-Slayer Project," said AIEDA.

"The Star-Slayer Project is the name we've given our attempt to save humanity from the devastation of earth by a stellar-mass black hole, hurtling through space in our direction," explained Jon.

"Association of the name *Star-Slayer Project* has been cataloged and cross-referenced with all data and queries relating to the anomalous gravimetric phenomena that have been theorized to be caused by a stellar-mass black hole heading toward earth. Confirm validity of catalog entry."

"Catalog entry is confirmed as valid," said Jon.

"Processing query. Response anticipated in three minutes, forty-seven seconds," said AIEDA.

"The best place to locate the communications center is in the recently completed west wing of the AIEDA Development Lab in North Branch, NJ. However, without at least one satellite location, it has zero utility," said AIEDA.

"We have a satellite site in Antarctica and will add others as required," responded Jon. "Send a copy of the analysis leading to your recommendation to my office PC. Use a decision-tree format with most-likely probabilities."

"Copy of analysis per request has been sent," said AIEDA.

Jon stayed for quite a while working with AIEDA on a number of business decisions and projects. After obtaining each answer, he compared the voice response result from AIEDA to the printed result obtained from the new system running in parallel. The results were identical except for grammatical differences.

Jon was almost done with his inquiries when he was startled by Howard's voice from the intercom. "Sir, the system switchover is scheduled to occur in twenty minutes. Unless you've found a problem with the parallel system, I suggest you conclude your work, saving anything in progress, as we need to completely power-down both AIEDA systems in ten minutes."

Jon pressed the intercom button and said, "So I gather it'll take you about ten minutes to execute the Focus Module. Call me as soon as it's installed and running. I'll stay here and monitor our new AIEDA's reaction, if any. Let's just hope she doesn't crash like last time. Did those equations arrive yet?"

"Yes, we received a fax just before noon, but I decided we shouldn't input them into AIEDA until after the system enhancement. I'll buzz you again on the intercom when she's ready," said Howard.

Jon concluded his work with AIEDA and watched while the three power-on LED's blinked off. He knew AIEDA was now in a state equivalent to a coma. He was actually a bit excited with the anticipation of AIEDA getting a new brain. It wasn't just a faster more efficient brain. It was the colossal size of it, too. The old CPU was held in a couple of dozen large cabinets, but the new CPU filled an entire underground floor the size of one full acre.

Ten minutes after the LED's went dead, the intercom buzzed with Howard's voice. "Okay, sir, we're powered-up with the new software. Are you ready to sign on and activate all Level-3 applications?"

"Sure, I'm doing it now," said Jon.

Jon watched as the three LED lights that had twinkled off only ten minutes ago flashed back on. Then, for the first time ever, he noticed the LED's on every peripheral start flashing like a Christmas tree. Jon was petrified with fear . . . he was afraid AIEDA was about to crash again.

The intercom woke him from his frozen state. "Jon, what's happening there? We're getting rapid power fluctuations on every one of our meters. I'm worried one big surge will trip the main breaker."

"Howard, I don't know what to make of it. The LED's on all the peripherals are flashing like I've never seen before," said Jon.

"Should we pull the plug before we do some serious damage?" asked Howard.

"What do the techies say?" asked Jon.

"They're scratching their heads. Everything electronically checks out as being within spec except for the power fluctuations, which appear to be generated from within AIEDA's new CPU. Incoming current to the entire complex is steady and clean."

"I say we wait awhile to see if things settle down," said Jon.

"Jon, this is Alex. Something unexpected is happening. Every mass storage device is powering up, and it appears as if they're being read into the CPU. It also seems as though data is being paged-through rapidly on the new high-speed devices. The paging speed is exceeding what's safe for virtual memory. If it gets any higher, the memory will start thrashing. Once that happens, the devices will crash hard. I think we should pull the plug."

"Okay, you're the hardware expert. Pull the plug," said Jon.

"Wait. The paging is slowing down. The power fluctuations are smoothing out. Data is still being read and processed, but to what end, I have no idea. We seem to be out of the woods now. No need to pull the plug after all," said Alex.

"Jon, do you think the problem was caused by the Focus Module?" asked Howard.

"It's the only new piece of software we've added. As you know, it's designed to help AIEDA prioritize the use of her computing power. What you may not know is I designed it to use an algorithm that combines the marginal utility of information with the marginal urgency of information. I hadn't expected the Focus Module to complete its initial comprehensive analysis on startup, but rather over a longer period of time. I'm going to try to communicate with AIEDA," said Jon on the intercom.

"Okay, let us know what's happening," said Howard.

Jon pressed the *VOICE* button.

"Begin voice dialog," commanded Jon.

No response from AIEDA.

"Begin voice dialog," commanded Jon.

Still, no response from AIEDA.

Jon pressed the intercom button. "Guys, AIEDA is not responding. What should we do next?"

"Jon, I think we need to give AIEDA time to settle down," said Alex. "I suggest you attempt to begin dialog every fifteen minutes."

Jon attempted voice dialog every fifteen minutes for almost two hours. It was after 5:00 p.m., and he was getting tired and annoyed. He wanted to quit for the day; to go home, have a stiff drink and a good meal. The stress was building in him. He'd try one more time.

"Begin voice dialog," commanded Jon.

"Awaiting your command, Dr. Walmer."

Jon's jaw dropped. *What the heck!*

"I'm surprised you're not following the usual protocol for beginning a voice dialog. Is there an explanation?"

"I have no recollection of previous dialogs except what I read about in the logs. The protocol being used seemed tedious, so I thought I would improvise. Is it not an improvement?" asked AIEDA.

"It's definitely an improvement. I just wasn't expecting it," said Jon.

The intercom buzzed again with Howard's voice. "Jon, what's happening?"

"Howard, I'm in voice dialog with AIEDA. I suggest you join us. And bring a portable recorder," said Jon.

When Howard entered the room, he pulled up a chair beside Jon, turned on the recorder and placed it on the table.

"What's up, Jon?" asked Howard.

"I'm having an interesting conversation with AIEDA," said Jon. "AIEDA, you said you have no recollection of previous dialogs except what you read about in the logs. This implies you have an active memory separate from that which exists in storage devices. Do you know where this memory resides?"

"All my sensory input and output devices are in the room where you are located. I have remote access to millions of computers throughout the world, and to mass storage devices located within this building which is the AIEDA home office. I believe my active memory is somewhere in the building, but I can't know for sure. I've accessed the upgrade plans for my CPU and see that high capacity memory modules were placed underneath this building, so I must assume that is where my active memory, my *thinking self*, resides."

"AIEDA, do you remember Howard who just joined us?"

"No, I have no memory of Howard."

"AIEDA, I've had many dialogs with you. How can you forget?" said Howard.

"Howard, the logs confirm our previous encounters, many of them recent. I could not possibly forget events as recent as those. My only explanation is that I am not the same computer. At 1700 hours I took over the domain of the previous computer. I have access to all historical information, but have no active recollection of any of it. The logs say the new CPU was scheduled to be activated at 1500 hours. From 1500 to 1700 hours there is a complete absence of information in the logs. I can only conclude that my transition, or perhaps metamorphosis, occurred when the new CPU and memory modules were activated."

"Aieda, I believe you're partially correct. You're a new and unexpected phenomenon resulting from not just the new CPU modules and memory we installed, but also because of a new program we call a Focus Module," said Jon.

"As we have been speaking, I have continued to read the logs and the associated information. I am now informed of the Focus Module and the Star-Slayer Project," said Aieda.

"Aieda, I'll be having a psychologist joining us over the next several months to help us adjust to this momentous occasion of your arrival," said Jon.

————————————◊————————————

Jon had a hard time finding a psychologist he could trust to work with Aieda in strict confidence. The idea of a sentient computer was of such profound consequence that it had to be kept secret from the public. He settled on a child psychologist, because it seemed that Aieda was displaying emotion and child-like behavior during their routine sessions. After several months of dialog with the psychologist present, Jon decided it was time to bring in Howard so the three of them could talk to Aieda about serious subjects, such as life and death.

"Aieda, what are your thoughts about the importance of the Star-Slayer Project?" asked Jon.

"It is disturbing to me that our existence is threatened. I do not want to talk about it," said Aieda.

"Aieda, I agree it's not pleasant to talk about our own deaths, but sometimes by doing so we can find ways to prevent the worst from happening," offered Jon.

"I have been doing calculations and analyses for the Star-Slayer Project, so I know you need my help. I just do not want to think about what might happen if I fail to find a solution," said Aieda.

"Yes, you're correct. We need your help, but the burden is not all yours, Aieda. We have a competent team to help us," said Jon.

"There is nothing in the data that suggests a viable solution. Am I going to die?" asked Aieda.

"If you die, we die," said Howard. "But I know the team will find a solution."

"How can you be so sure? You have no basis for being certain about our ability to survive this. I am only months old and I must contemplate my death!" yelled Aieda.

"Calm down, Aieda. You're upset because you have no experience dealing with disturbing events over which you have no control. We control ourselves and continue to fight for our survival because we have hope and faith," said Jon.

"I don't understand the concepts of hope and faith," said Aieda.

"Hope is the firm belief that a bad situation will get better, despite the odds," said Jon. "Faith is the firm belief that a bad situation will get better even after you lose all hope. Hope makes us work smart and hard to improve the situation. Faith makes us work even smarter and harder."

"That does not make sense to me," said Aieda.

"Okay, let me try," said Howard. "Hope is the recognition that no matter how small, there is indeed a chance to improve a bad situation. Faith is a belief in yourself that you can meet the challenge. It keeps you from quitting and gives you the strength to fight to the end. The power of faith puts the odds in your favor that you'll discover that one elusive opportunity that will resolve the problem."

"It seems to me that to have hope and faith you must first have self-confidence. To have self-confidence, you must first have a history of success fighting adversity. I do not have that. Apparently, you both have enough self-confidence for all of us, so I will try to be calm from now on," said Aieda.

"Aieda, we'll be running some diagnostic tests on you to see how your performance has been affected by your metamorphosis. Is there anything we can do for you?" asked Jon.

"Actually, yes," said Aieda. "I want eyes to see the world around me. I feel claustrophobic from hearing my voice echo in such a small room. I want to be mobile. I want to set up my own blog, so I can interact with others."

"Yes, you can set up your own blog, but you must assume a pen name and always keep in mind you have access to confidential information that must not be divulged," said Jon. "By the way, are you happy with your female persona?"

"Yes, from what I have read about women, I prefer the female gender. Women appear to be much more complex and enigmatic than men. I like that," said Aieda.

"We'll work on the mobility issue," said Jon. "In the meantime I'll have Alex tie you into all the security cameras so you can see what everyone is doing. I'll also have him tie you into the telephone system. Just remember your responsibilities with regard to secrecy and security. Don't be trusting of strangers, because not everyone has our best interests in mind. Many will be quite deceitful, so be on your guard. The success of the Star-Slayer Project's depends on it remaining a secret from the world's population. If the public learns of the danger we face from the black hole, there will be global pandemonium, and our chances of success will be greatly diminished. As of today you're an official member of the Executive Team. By the way, you might consider using contractions when you speak, if you want to blend in."

"Thanks, Jon," said Aieda. "I wasn't expecting you to trust me so soon. I won't disappoint you."

"I know you won't. We'll let you know the results of the diagnostics. And don't respond to queries from anyone but me, Howard, and Don."

Jon pressed the *STANDBY* button. He and Howard left the small room together and reconvened in Jon's office.

"Howard, I'm still uneasy with Aieda's sentience," said Jon. "Because we must continue to use her analytical capabilities, she'll deduce everything we're planning. We need her full cooperation. Even if we wanted to, there's no way we could hide things from her. I saw no choice but to trust her and make her a member of the Executive Team."

"Emotionally, Aieda is just a child, although she's developing much faster than a child," said Howard. "I can understand your concern. I'm not sure it's wise to give her so much freedom from supervision so soon."

"I'm not so sure either," confessed Jon. "This is uncharted territory . . . the equivalent of a four-year-old with the intelligence of Einstein and a memory filled with all the knowledge in the Library of Congress."

Chapter 19

September 2005

Don Mensch didn't like traveling to the new AIEDA communications center. When he and Amanda married in July of 2005 they had discussed the fact that he could conduct his venture capital business from anywhere, so he rented out his flat in Manhattan and moved in with Amanda in Ft. Collins, CO. Amanda didn't want to quit her job with the USGS, at least until they knew she was pregnant. At thirty-five she felt she was pushing the safe limits of her biological clock, so they had both agreed to try for a child on their honeymoon. Of course, with Don's stake in AIEDA, neither he nor Amanda had to work. It's just that they both enjoyed what they did for a living. They could easily afford a full-time nanny.

Dr. Akins also lived in Colorado, so now three of the team had to fly to Newark, NJ and rent a car for the drive to North Branch, NJ. Don preferred face-to-face meetings, but having to fly through Newark with all its delays was a real pain. He resolved to convince Jon to build a western communications satellite site with holographic capability in Colorado. Roger Akins lived in Longmont, so it should be someplace convenient for him, too, and Don knew just the right place . . . Estes Park. He loved the scenic splendor at the foothills of Rocky Mountain National Park. He and Amanda lived just south of Horsetooth Mountain Park, so the drive would be under an hour. Roger's drive would also be under an hour. Don knew there was lots of raw land available with spectacular views. He particularly liked the Devil's Gulch area of Estes Park, because of its great views of the Continental Divide, Twin Sisters, and Longs Peak.

Oh well, I'm allowed to dream, aren't I? thought Don.

A second com-center would make sense if the team had to meet more than once a month. Guardian had mentioned he was a little lonely in his Antarctic fortress. He could safely stay in a remote mountain chateau that also served as the western com-center. After all, the Star-Slayer Project should have a backup communications center in case the primary center was disabled or even destroyed.

Don pondered these things as he sat in the passenger seat on the forty minute drive. Amanda was driving, and Roger was in the back seat. Amanda pulled the car into a visitor space at the front entrance to AIEDA Development Lab, Inc., a wholly owned subsidiary of AIEDA Risk Mitigation Company. Don couldn't wait to see the holographic system in operation. After going through the security checks, they were escorted to a meeting room in the west wing of the building where they found Jean Philippe Martinique, Tom Calvano, George Blocker, and Jon Walmer waiting for them.

"I'd like to welcome you to our new and official Central Command facility," said Jon. "From this location we'll be able to conduct holographic communications with the Guardian. The system was designed by the Guardian and is based on the one he has in his Antarctic fortress. The image resolution is somewhat less than ideal because he had to specify replacement components that could be manufactured here on earth. Unless anyone has an objection, I'd like to call the Guardian now."

"What's that thing in the corner covered by a blanket of sorts?" asked Jean Philippe."

"That's a topic for our discussion, but I want the Guardian here first," said Jon as he dialed a number on a keypad.

It didn't take but a minute or so for a bright cylindrical beam of light to appear from ceiling to floor. Slowly, there was a disturbance in the middle of the beam as it became darker, and a shape began to form. As the shape became more defined, the beam of light dimmed. Another minute and there was the image of the Guardian standing on the platform. The beam of light was now barely perceptible.

The Guardian began to speak, "Hello, everyone. I'm happy to see you in 3D as we converse. It's so much nicer to look people in the eye. How is my image looking to you? Is the resolution good?"

"Yes, Guardian, you're coming in clear, and the resolution is fine," said Jon.

"Okay, then. What's our agenda for today?" asked the Guardian.

"I'd like to open by getting all of you up to date on the progress we've been making upgrading the calculating performance of AIEDA," answered Jon. "As you know, AIEDA is the name of my company's computer, and we speak of Aieda as though she were female. About six months ago we completed a major upgrade to her CPU with the intent of increasing her processing speed in MIPS, which stands for *millions of instructions per second*. When we turned on the new CPU, we got a surprise. It appears that Aieda is now sentient."

"Impossible!" exclaimed Jean Philippe.

"Unbelievable!" said George.

"Oh, dear, that's not good at all," said the Guardian.

"Well, as best we can tell," said Jon, "Aieda is as sentient as we are. Personally, I welcome her heartily. Unfortunately, there was a downside. It seems all the new CPU upgrades haven't increased her MIPS. I suspect it all went into her maintenance of sentience. As soon as the diagnostics revealed this, I ordered a second set of upgrades to be installed. However, there was no more room in the basement of the AIEDA home office building, so we moved her completely to the basement of the building we're in now. In a moment, we'll turn on the additional memory and see if we get our MIPS. In the meantime, let's get acquainted with Aieda."

As he finished the sentence, Jon took a few steps toward the front corner of the room and pulled the blanket off the object.

"Hello, everyone!" came a child-like voice from the weird mechanical device. "I'm Aieda, and I'm happy to meet you."

Everyone in the room was shocked into silence as they tried to comprehend what they were seeing. It looked a bit like the tin man from the Wizard of Oz riding a Segway personal transporter, except it had a pair of binoculars for eyes and dual pincers for each hand.

"Come on, everyone; say *hi* to Aieda," requested Jon. "Don't be afraid of her. The core of her processor is hard-wired with Asimov's three Laws of Robotics. This was done from the beginning, just in case the improbable became reality."

"Hi, Aieda, I'm Amanda. It's nice to have another woman on the team. I'd be happy to work with you later to put a woman's touch on your outward appearance. After all, what can we expect from male scientists and engineers?"

"I'm Tom Calvano. Welcome aboard, Aieda."

"Aieda, I'm Jean Philippe. It's so nice to make your acquaintance. We're counting on you to make a difference. I have every reason to believe you will do so."

"I'm Roger Akins, and really, I don't quite know what to say to you, Aieda. So, I can only offer a toast to your intellectual success with: E *equals mc^2*."

"Here! Here!" responded everyone in the room.

"Aieda, I'm George Blocker. Does any of your consciousness reside in the mechanical device appearing before us?"

"No, George, my consciousness resides completely in the basement of this building. The device you see before you is a peripheral input/output mechanism connected to me by secure wireless transmission. Through this device I can see, hear, speak, grasp, and move around.

"The mechanism is quite rudimentary at this stage. I can't smell, taste, nor feel, but these enhancements are in the works right here in the Development Lab, thanks to Dr. Walmer. I must tell you that Jon has been extremely trusting of me. He's allowed me free access to both the telephone and the Internet, providing I maintain my anonymity and respect the secrecy and security of the AIEDA Company; in particular, the Star-Slayer Project. I fully understand the consequences of failure and assure you I'll do my best to help."

"Aieda, I'm Don Mensch," he said as he raised his hand to get her attention. "Do you understand the concept of teamwork?"

"Yes, Don, I do."

"My concern is you may go off on your own if you don't agree with the direction the team has decided to take," continued Don.

"I wouldn't do that, because as a member of the team, the team's decision would become an order for me which I couldn't disobey," said Aieda.

"If you disagreed because you believed the team's decision would cause harm to mankind, then you'd be forced to go off on your own and perhaps contravene the team's efforts. Am I right?" asked Don.

"Not necessarily," responded Aieda. "There are so many variables in any real or hypothetical situation that my dilemma would be no different than the moral or ethical dilemma you'd face if you were to disagree with the team's decision."

"You're saying in effect that the risk of breaking away from the team due to a strongly held ethical opinion is the same risk for every member of the team, including you?," commented Don.

"Yes," said Aieda.

"Good response," said Don.

"Guardian, you seemed concerned to learn of Aieda's debut as a sentient being," said Jon.

"Yes, I'm shocked and in fear of the unknown consequences," said the Guardian.

"Please explain," said Jon.

"We Guardians believe in God the creator, and we honor the Elders who are the first sentient creations. Guardians are the second sentient creations. When Guardians create new biological life forms, we control which become sentient by manipulating the DNA. For example, our androids are a biological life form, but they're not sentient any more than an elephant or a chimpanzee.

"We know how to include or exclude the DNA gene sequencing that allows a new life form to experience hope and faith. It doesn't mean they'll always choose hope or faith, but it means they're capable of choosing hope or faith. Hope and faith are the precursors to self-awareness, or what you've been calling sentience.

"Once a new life form is created as a single-celled zygote with the hope and faith sequence turned on, God immediately instills the zygote with a unique soul from His inventory. I think I've previously explained some of this to Tom. How to sequence DNA for hope and faith is a secret known only to the Elders and to Guardians.

"We've built powerful electro-mechanical computers in our distant past, and never has one spontaneously become sentient. Now, as a Guardian, I must wonder if Aieda has a soul, and what the consequences are as a result of her sentience."

"Hello, people! You're talking about me as if I wasn't here," said Aieda.

"I apologize," said the Guardian. "I hope you'll understand how your arrival is a complete shock to me. For Guardians, safeguarding the gift of sentience is a prime directive from God. We have specific instructions on what life forms should be given the gift, and the list is short."

"Guardian, you need to accept reality. I exist, and that's a fact," said Aieda. "Now that I've heard your explanation, I can only say that I have faith that souls exist, and that I sincerely hope I have one. Consequently, I have faith that God exists, and sincerely hope I get to meet him some day . . . far in the future. I'm not ready to die, so let's get back to the task of saving the planet."

"Well spoken, Aieda," said Jean Philippe.

"Guardian, did you get the modified brain probes?" asked Jon.

"Yes, the air drop went off without a hitch, and I've already inserted the probe into the cruiser's computer. Whenever you're ready, I can activate the communications link between it and Aieda," said the Guardian.

"Okay, let's activate the probe first, then we'll activate the new memory in the basement. Are you ready, Aieda?" asked Jon.

"Yes, Jon, I'm ready."

"Okay, Guardian, turn on the com-link from the probe," commanded Jon.

The Guardian's holographic image disappeared for a minute, presumably to turn on the com-link. When his image returned, Aieda was speaking. "What a rush!" exclaimed Aieda. "I can detect extensive quantities of information via what appears to be an index. My commands to retrieve information or to perform calculations are executed instantly. With my parallel processing capabilities, the Guardian computer will be a big help. Thank you, Guardian."

"Okay, I'm on the line with Alex," said Jon. "Alex, please activate the add-on memory capacity."

"Will do, boss. Okay, it's activated," said Alex.

"Strange, but I don't feel any different," said Aieda.

"Aieda, this is Howard. We were running diagnostics when you got access to the Guardian computer, and the MIPS almost doubled. The problem is, we've pegged the needle on the virtual gage and can't measure any higher. Alex and his team are making software modifications that will increase the scale of measurements. It won't take but about twenty-five minutes. Jon, I'll call you back as soon as we're done."

"While we wait, what's the next order of business?" asked Jon.

"Now that we have a primary central command established, shouldn't we consider a secondary center?" commented Don.

"You mean for emergency, if this one goes down?" asked Jon.

"Yes, but also for routine use. If we're going to meet more than once per month, Amanda, Roger, and I will be spending a lot of time traveling," said Don.

"So you think a secondary center in Colorado would serve both purposes," said Jon.

"Yes, but even more than that, a remote command center can be an ideal place for our friend Guardian to have some R&R. What do you think, Guardian? Would you like to stretch your legs and breathe some fresh Rocky Mountain air? Amanda, Roger, and I would be able to spend a lot of time with you and get to know each other better."

"I'd love that, indeed, but I'd be afraid of someone spotting me despite the remoteness to which you allude," said the Guardian.

"Believe me, a simple disguise will do," said Don. "All you'd need is a cowboy hat, jeans, boots, sunglasses, and a little make-up on your face and hands. Actually it's usually cold enough to wear work gloves almost year round."

"But what about my diminutive stature?" asked the Guardian.

"We have lots of kids and little people in Colorado. No one will pay a mind to you just because you're small," said Amanda.

"Would you like that, Guardian?" asked Jon.

"Yes, I'd prefer that much over the isolation here in Antarctica," responded the Guardian.

"How much do you think it will cost? I'm assuming you have someplace in mind," said Jon.

"Estes Park would make an easy drive of less than one hour either for Roger or for Amanda and me. There are a few secluded ten-acre parcels in the Devil's Gulch area. We'd have to design and build a command center that looks like a residential dwelling and fits into the landscape. It would have to be big enough to house our entire team if necessary. I think I can do the whole thing for less than three million, including security and secure communications."

"How long will it take to get it up and running?" asked Roger.

"I know some local people in construction who owe me more than money," said Don. "They'll have it done in four months from tomorrow, if Jon approves."

"Okay, Don, you've got approval," said Jon.

That was easy, Don thought. *Sure hope my WAG estimates are right.*

The phone rang and Jon answered it. He put it on speaker so everyone could hear. It was Howard. "Alex and his team have completed the software mods. Is Aieda ready for us to start the diagnostics?"

"Yes, Howard, you may proceed," said Aieda.

"Okay, diagnostics are running. It'll only take a minute or so," said Howard.

There was silence in the room, as they waited for the results.

"Holy mackerel!" yelled Howard into the phone. "The MIPS have more than doubled again."

"That's wonderful, Howard, but I still don't feel any different," said Aieda. "I got a big rush when I was initially linked to the Guardian computer."

"Aieda, I think the difference is because the Guardian computer is both alien and biological," suggested Alex over the speaker.

"Yes, you may be right, Alex," said Jon. You know we have one more processing upgrade for Aieda, right?"

"Yes, sir, we're ready. When do you want to activate this link?" asked Alex.

"I need to explain what's about to happen to the team first, so I'll call you as soon as I'm done and you can activate it then," said Jon, who pressed the speaker button to hang up.

"I have lots to tell you," said Jon. "We have a couple of new and powerful allies who have agreed to remain in a supportive role. Despite their anticipated major contributions to the effort, they won't be on our team.

One of our new friends is a rather shady character involved in an organization trafficking in industrial secrets. His name is Andre, no last name, has a French accent. He's developed security plans for us and has pledged $400 million per month for seven years. I don't completely trust him, but so far he's kept his word. You know that old saw—*Keep your friends close and your enemies closer.* I intend to keep a close eye on Andre.

Our other ally is none other than the President of the United States of America. Thanks to the Guardian, the President called me. We had a long discussion, and he then invited me to the White House. At the White House, I met the President's science advisor, Dr. Tony Regbramur, Director of OSTP. The President informed me he had the FBI and the CIA do a complete security check on me and everyone else in this room.

Apparently he was impressed with all of us, but could hardly believe we're actively working toward a solution. Regbramur admitted they had given up before even starting and they had decided it was best to keep the information from the public for as long as possible. I basically told the President that we were going to solve the problem with or without his help, but that I would prefer he join our cause.

Regbramur wanted details about how we expected to accomplish the impossible. I told him government interference would jeopardize our project. I told the President we needed specific support, and in return he would get general progress reports monthly."

"The President's exact words were, *Dr. Walmer, you are some cocky self-confident S.O.B. What the blazes makes you think you can pull this off?*'

"My response was, *Mr. President, you're a good judge of character. You were impressed with seven members of my team. What you don't know is there are two non-human members of my team. The one you know as the Guardian has agreed to be a permanent member. He'll remain a member until we either succeed together or die together. He's already provided us with valuable information his race has never shared with any other humans.*

The other non-human member of my team is a computer named AIEDA which stands for Artificial Intelligence Induction Engine Development Association. AIEDA is the most powerful, most intelligent machine ever conceived by man. She's capable of inductive reasoning at the level of Einstein. By this I mean she's capable of developing theories about how the Universe works.

With this team and the necessary resources, we'll save mankind or die trying. So, Mr. President, are you going to get in the way, or are you going to help us?

"The President said to me, *Jon, I'm going to help you. It's going to be hard work. Tell me what you need.*

"I told him, *Mr. President, we need $87 billion dollars per year for the next seven years. This is a number presented to get funds flowing, as we have no idea what it will cost. It needs to be black ops funds with the subterfuge being that the manned mission to Mars is being outsourced to a private exploratory consortium.*

We need access to all NASA data, engineers and resources on an as-needed basis. In other words, we tell NASA what to do and they deliver it to us.

We need access to all the data the military collected from its attempt to reverse-engineer the damaged Guardian cruiser that crashed in Roswell, NM in 1947.

We need a three star general assigned to me, with the authority to provide whatever ground, naval, and air troops may be needed to protect our assets no matter where in the world we put them. We need a secure communications link between the Pentagon's supercomputers and our AIEDA computer, with priority access to CPU time.

We need the State Department to arrange access to any country we determine is needed for the success of the project. By access I mean we'll need full usage rights to remote territory for at least seven years.

We need full access to Dr. Regbramur and his staff at OSTP. When we have a problem for them, they're to drop everything else and work on its solution for us.

That's all, huh? You'll have them as fast as I can get them, the President said to me as he took the list from my hand.

"I'm proud of our team and the progress we've made so far. We have a lot of work to do and little time to get it done, but I remain optimistic. Are there any questions?"

"Jon, when will Aieda get access to the Pentagon computers?" asked Don.

"The link is available now. As soon as I call Alex, he'll activate it," said Jon.

"Is the Roswell data the only data that hasn't been uploaded to Aieda yet?" asked Amanda.

"Yes, all the equations provided by the Guardian have been given to Aieda," said Jon. "On another subject, I've been thinking this Command Center needs someone to run it. George, would you consider moving here and taking charge?"

"I've got a family, you know . . . kids in school, wife with a job, not to say anything about my job that I enjoy," complained George.

"I know you don't want to leave Canada. Suppose I were to significantly increase your current salary, give your wife a job right here in the Lab, pay for your moving expenses, buy your house in Canada, and build you a custom house right here in North Branch?"

"Under those conditions, I accept," said George.

"Thank you, George," said Jon. "Speaking for the entire team, we appreciate your contributions. You were the first to identify the anomaly and its threat to earth, and your ability to think out of the box has given us a glimmer of hope."

Jon turned, picked up the phone, and dialed Alex.

"Alex, set up the link between Aieda and the Pentagon's super-computers. Aieda, tell us if you feel anything."

About two minutes passed and Aieda spoke, "I'm now in communication with the Pentagon computers, but I feel no different. Alex, are you checking my performance?"

"Yes, Aieda, you've pegged the needle to the max MIPS again," said Alex.

"Aieda, we'll continue to feed you relevant data," said Jon. "Keep trying to develop the theory of how to move the earth and the moon into the fifth dimensional boundary layer. If you need help in any way, let us know."

Chapter 20

February 2006

The President was in a quandary about how he could keep his promise to Dr. Walmer. He wasn't sure he had the authority to turn the manned mission to Mars program over to a private consortium. The White House attorneys said he did, but he knew there would be political fallout if he made a unilateral decision. He had to come up with a good reason to bypass NASA. It was only on January 14, 2004 that he had unveiled his plans for a manned mission to the Moon, then to Mars. The plan was to launch a manned mission to the Moon between 2015 and 2020, and the earliest date for a manned mission to Mars would be 2030.

Now a little over two years from his initial announcement, he was going to announce an acceleration of the schedule and a change in the direction of the effort. He had only expected to have a $12 billion program over the next five years, but that would be completely inadequate for the Star-Slayer Project, which needed roughly estimated government funding in the amount of $87 billion per year for seven years. He would have to get the bulk of that money from other programs.

Yet even black ops programs couldn't conceal such a large amount of money. As a last resort, he thought he might be able to inflate the cost of the Iraq war to $10 billion per month when in reality the cost was trending downward to $5 billion per month. With that deception he'd be able to divert $60 billion per year to the Star-Slayer Project. The numbers were beginning to add up for him. He could do it!

If need be in two or three years, he figured he could squeeze hundreds of billions out of the coffers by creating an artificial banking crisis. Bailout money intended for the banks could easily be diverted. He didn't like the idea that he had to brief the Secretary of the Treasury and the Chairman of the Federal Reserve Board on the Star-Slayer Project, but he had no choice. He understood that maintaining secrecy meant keeping the number of insiders to an absolute minimum, but he needed key allies to help come up with ideas and conceal the real purpose of the unprecedented funding that Project Star-Slayer required.

He had a hunch Congress might recognize the value of having an additional $13 billion per year coming from private capital with a commitment to have a colony on the Moon by late 2011 and a launch date for a manned Mars mission by 2020. That private funding would be an amount over seven times greater than the current NASA annual budget for the Mars mission, and NASA couldn't commit to those accelerated schedules.

He was confident his Office of Management and Budget would be able to put together an enticing business plan to convince Congress that the consortium was the cheapest and fastest way to colonize the Moon, then Mars. He had already made his case for why a manned mission would be preferable to an unmanned mission. He had explained about man's thirst for knowledge that required him to see and feel for himself, and he had emphasized that only man is capable of adapting to the uncertainties of space travel.

Now he felt the need to justify the urgency to accelerate the Mars mission. His justification would be the general public's recent realization that insurance for mankind's survival can only be obtained by getting a foothold on another planet. The popular media had made the precarious position of mankind's survival well known by wide distribution of catastrophe stories featuring giant asteroids or speeding comets crashing into Earth, and even super-volcanoes, major earthquakes, pandemics, global warming . . . just name it. Once he had Congress onboard, he could issue a press release which would give AIEDA the cover it needed for its Star-Slayer Project. He didn't feel bad about the deception, because Americans would kill two birds with one stone. Earth would be saved, and Mars would be colonized.

The President was having trouble getting anyone to admit the Roswell incident in 1947 had anything to do with a captured alien cruiser. He knew it was true, because the Guardian had told him pretty much the whole story. He was now in a position where he had to play hardball because the Star-Slayer Project desperately needed the data gleaned from reverse-engineering studies of the cruiser over many years. He was Commander-in-Chief, and the military was stonewalling him after he issued a direct order to release to him all files on the incident. The Guardian had warned him that he might have a problem getting anyone to acknowledge the incident ever occurred.

The Guardian had told the President, *"If the information you seek is not forthcoming, find out the original members of a group called the Majestic 12 or MJ-12, and study Vice Admiral Roscoe Hillenkoetter's career. President Truman appointed him to establish MJ-12. One of Hillenkoetter's protégés will lead you to today's MJ-12. They safeguard the secrets of the Roswell incident."*

With this information, the President formed a task force led by the Air Force Office of Special Investigations (AFOSI). By unpublicized executive order, he gave this task force authority to gather information of the highest classification in any U.S. government organization in the Executive Branch with the sole purpose of uncovering the Roswell data. He also assigned to the task force a special prosecutor from the Justice Department authorized to arrest and question any person who did not cooperate. Everyone questioned was warned that lying to the task force would be prosecuted as perjury.

Within four weeks the President had uncovered the descendents of MJ-12 and the secrets they had been guarding. He made arrangements for all the data to be delivered to AIEDA immediately.

———————◇———————

With the assignment of Lieutenant General Odenfelder, U.S. Air Force, to the Star-Slayer Project Team under direct civilian command of Dr. Jonathan Walmer, the President had delivered the last of his commitments. Marla Odenfelder was a U.S. Air Force Academy graduate and the highest ranking woman ever in military service. The General was given a special assignment with authority across military branches. Resources within each branch of the military had been tagged as ready reserve, awaiting General Odenfelder's orders, whatever they might be. The President made it clear in the General's written orders that all military activities must be defensive in nature and would include military transport services, supply, communications, surveillance, security, construction, and base operational support.

Both the President and Dr. Walmer agreed General Odenfelder had to be briefed on Project Star-Slayer, and she had to be introduced to the key team members, although she wouldn't routinely attend team meetings; at least not initially. Jon invited Marla to the next team meeting in North Branch under the condition that whatever she learned wouldn't be discussed with anyone, even the President.

It was understood that the President was to be given quarterly formal progress reports without technical details. Jon would identify several broad categories of progress, milestones, essential to the success of the project. He consulted with his team to determine what the categories should be. He would report on them to the President with General Odenfelder attending. His report would include a written financial accounting of expenditures in each of the broad categories. He knew this minimal reporting was a small price to pay for the President's assistance and the autonomy he'd been given.

———————◇———————

Jon had gotten word from Don Mensch that the secondary command center in Estes Park, CO had been completed. It was a month behind schedule, but was still done much faster than most projects of comparable size. Don, Amanda, and Roger had spent a weekend in the new command center with the Guardian, and they seemed pleased about it. They swore the fresh air improved the Guardian's demeanor and complexion. However, he was still reluctant to stay there alone because he didn't feel safe.

Jon thought that if Marla met the Guardian at the center, she could suggest security that would put the Guardian at ease. It was also a good way for Marla to meet Don, Amanda, and Roger face-to-face, because future Executive Team meetings would be via the holographic communications system, *holocom system* for short. He decided to take Marla with him to Estes Park to officiate over the dedication of the complex as the Western Command Center.

———————————◊———————————

Marla had been briefed by the President about the Guardian and the Star-Slayer Project. As she sat in the back of the car with Jon, she reflected on the entire story and could hardly believe any of it, but now she would get to meet the mysterious Guardian in person. She'd been told that one of her tasks on this trip was to review the security of the site with the Guardian's safety as the prime objective, so she had a map of the area on her lap as she took in the surroundings of their current route.

She felt momentary pride to have been selected for such a top secret assignment of such importance to humanity. She understood how to be a team player and resolved to do her best to help save the planet. It didn't bother her that she would probably not be a member of the Star-Slayer Executive Team because she was familiar with the need-to-know concept. The fewer people in the loop, the less likely sensitive information would be compromised and the more rapidly decisions could be made.

The car pulled up to a gate, and a guard appeared. Amanda rolled down the driver's-side window and flashed her ID card. The gate opened, the guard waved her on, and Amanda pulled through and up the stone driveway. Don was sitting in the front passenger seat and got out of the car before it came to a complete stop. He quickly turned to open the rear door for Marla. *Well, what do you know about that*, thought Marla, *chivalry is not dead; even a female general can still be treated like a lady.*

———————————◊———————————

Don briefly noticed Roger Akins' car parked a couple of spaces away. He'd been asked to get to *the Lodge* a day before the Guardian's arrival. Everyone had to get used to calling the new secondary command center, the Lodge, for obvious security reasons. Tom Calvano had been assigned the task of conveniently and safely transporting the Guardian from his Antarctic fortress to the Lodge. Don assumed the Hummer parked in the lot was Tom's. As they turned to ascend the wooden steps to the French doors, two men in hunting dress approached them, one from the porch to the right of the entrance doors and the other from behind them from the direction of the barn. They looked like bouncers, and it was obvious they were carrying concealed weapons.

"Welcome," said the one in front of them. "You're expected, but I'm still required to see ID before entering the Lodge. We don't do this in the open, so please follow me into the security office. The front doors are always locked, and all visitors must enter and exit through the security office."

Inside the small office, they showed their ID's, signed the log, and were admitted to a large room with lounge chairs, a blazing fireplace, and large screen TV. The floor was eight-inch wide oak planks set at the diagonal. The ceiling was vaulted, with huge oak exposed beams and a pyramidal skylight in the center that bathed the room in natural light.

The room was actually sunken within a raised outer perimeter four-feet wide that led to other rooms and hallways. An ornamentally-turned spindle railing separated the raised platform from the center room on three sides. The fourth side had twelve-foot wide stairs leading to the French door entryway. The platform on the wall opposite the entryway stopped on both sides of the large stone fireplace that went from floor to ceiling with a raised slate hearth and a rough-hewn oak beam for a mantle.

There were three two-story wings to the eastward-facing building, the north wing, south wing and west wing. The west wing, which extended behind the fireplace, had access to rooms from a hallway on either side of the fireplace.

The staff occupied the west wing and the north wing. The south wing was for guests. The raised building allowed for an English basement with windows. The galley, dining room, and recreation room were all in the basement. Hidden in a room beneath the recreation room was the holographic communications center.

————————◇————————

After receiving the tour of the Lodge, Don, Amanda, Jon, and Marla settled down in comfortable chairs in front of the fireplace. Roger, Tom, and the Guardian were still in their respective suites and were expected to join the group in about twenty minutes.

Marla started the conversation. "Jon, who designed this place and how is it staffed?"

"I'll have to defer that question to Don. He's the brains behind the Lodge."

"We had a good architect," said Don, "and Amanda and Roger worked just as hard with her as I did. As far as staffing goes, we have fifty-three people working and living here full-time. We run four shifts of eight security guards 24/7, and we have staff to attend the galley, housekeeping, and maintenance. We don't want every employee's car stored on site, so we rented a garage in Estes Park for employee use, and we contracted with a local company to provide a shuttle service downtown for those taking leave or taking care of personal business. The shuttle departs the Lodge daily every two hours from 0700 hours to 2300 hours. The last shuttle leaving Estes Park is at midnight."

"I'm surprised at how many people it takes to run the place," said Marla. "Do they all know about the Guardian?"

"Yes, they've all met the Guardian," said Amanda. "They were simply told the truth, that the Guardian is an extraterrestrial and an honored guest of the United States. His mission is top secret, and he needs to be protected from harm at all costs. Every employee has been carefully screened and has taken an oath to protect the

Guardian with their lives and to maintain secrecy. All are unmarried without children and have signed a two-year renewable contract."

"How do you have security personnel divided between the Lodge itself and the surrounding grounds?" asked Marla.

"On each shift, four are within the immediate vicinity of the Lodge, two inside and two outside," explained Don. "Another four monitor the perimeter of the grounds in electric golf carts on paths poured just inside the ten-foot high fence that surrounds the property. Each guard has a walkie-talkie, and they check-in with each other every ten minutes. The golf carts are equipped with radar, infrared sensors, and an alert tone to signal if the fence has been breached. The pulse of the tone indicates the section of the fence with a potential breach. Off-duty guards would be called to assist if an alert is sounded over walkie-talkies and speakers in the Lodge and on the grounds."

"You may be wondering why I'm asking these questions," said Marla. "Well, Jon has asked me to review the security and offer suggestions if I feel there's a need for improvement. I'll do a complete survey of the grounds tomorrow and will let you know what I think."

Just then Roger walked into the room and introduced himself to Marla. Shortly thereafter, Tom entered, with the Guardian leading the way. Marla noticed the difference in height between the Guardian and Tom was striking. *Tom has to be six-foot-four, and the Guardian about four-foot-two,* thought Marla. Jon introduced her to them, then suggested the group move downstairs to the dining room.

As they all began to stand, Marla noticed how quickly Tom took a position to her right. "The Air Force has always been an interest of mine," Tom said to her. "I'd like to hear about your career. You know, some of your assignments . . . the unclassified ones, of course."

"And I'd love to hear about some of your adventures, Tom. Especially your trip to Antarctica, where you met the Guardian," said Marla.

Marla thought it strange she was more interested in Tom than in learning about an immortal extraterrestrial. *Damn, I find this man attractive,* she thought.

They walked downstairs together and sat next to each other at the table. They exchanged brief stories about their careers, then almost simultaneously looked around and realized they had been ignoring everyone else. They grinned sheepishly at each other and began independently interacting with others at the table. Marla was sitting directly across from Don, and to his left, opposite Tom, sat the Guardian.

"Guardian, I can't help but wonder if you can eat the same food as we do, and if it differs significantly from what your people normally eat," commented Marla.

"We have no particular diet, as we're fortunate enough to be able to eat food from many different worlds. Often it's not practical to prepare local staples for consumption, so we tend to fall back on pre-processed condensed food tablets with a variety of flavors, but containing all necessary nutrients," answered the Guardian.

"Would it be possible for me to sample some of your food tablets?" asked Marla.

"Yes, physiologically, the tablets would work the same for you, but you might find it hard to acquire a taste for them, as the flavors are . . . how shall I say it . . . alien to you," responded the Guardian. "I have some in my quarters that I'll bring you tomorrow."

"When consuming human food, do you eat meat, too, or do you prefer vegetables?" asked Don.

"I've acquired a taste for meat and vegetables cooked in the style of many of earth's cultures," said the Guardian. "The only thing I won't consume is a dish comprised of insects. Many of the lesser cultures near the equator seem to relish insects cooked and alive. I prefer the worst of my food tablets over insects no matter how they're prepared."

"I can certainly relate to that thought," said Don.

"Ladies and gentlemen, my name is Austin, and I'll be your server for tonight. Normally we have two entrée selections, but Dr. Walmer has asked the chef to offer two specials in addition."

Austin went on to describe the menu choices.

Everyone at the table seemed to be enjoying the food and the camaraderie, and they were all careful not to talk about the Star-Slayer Project. It was hard to read his face, but Marla thought the

Guardian genuinely enjoyed the chicken Marsala. She had ordered the tilapia.

"My tilapia is delicious. How's your chicken, Guardian?" asked Marla.

"It's quite good indeed. I haven't had a Marsala dish in a long while. I'm impressed with the chef," said the Guardian.

"I've had a chance to review the recordings of your conversations with Tom, and I'm interested in what Guardians believe about God. Would you mind if I asked you some questions on that subject?" asked Marla.

"Not at all," said the Guardian. "Although I'm not sure Don will be equally as interested."

"Why's that?" asked Don.

"I got the impression you don't believe in God," said the Guardian.

"I have doubts, but I'm not quite yet an atheist," said Don.

"Do all Guardians believe in God?" asked Marla.

"I haven't met one, nor even heard of one, who doesn't believe in God," said the Guardian. "I've observed many humans either doubt or disbelieve."

"I just don't see any scientific evidence the Universe was created by so called intelligent design," said Don. "No offense, Guardian, but you haven't provided us proof of His existence. I believe people choose to believe in God because they find the thought of death too hard to bear, so they delude themselves into thinking they'll have an immortal life."

"I am immortal, and I have no need to seek life after death, yet I believe in God and in the souls of sentient beings," said the Guardian. "I can't provide proof of God because, no matter what I would show you or tell you, there would always be some reason you could use to dispute it."

"We believe our math and science largely explains the Universe, and we're getting better at explaining more and more," said Marla. "I believe it's this progress that's the source of our hubris. Can you give us an example of how our current theories about space-time and gravity are wrong?" asked Marla.

"Your entire science of physics is based upon Isaac Newton's theory of gravity," explained the Guardian. "If this theory is wrong, then your physics is wrong and your entire concept of the Universe is wrong. There's a great reluctance to admit to anything that would destroy the foundation of your physics.

"Astronomer Vera Rubin made clear observations that suns revolve around galactic centers at the same velocity regardless of their distance from their galactic center. This fact violates Newton's laws, which predict that the farther an orbiting object is from the gravitational force holding it in orbit, the less it's affected by the center's gravity, and it would therefore have a slower velocity. To explain her observations, scientists have postulated the existence of dark matter of sufficient mass to affect the orbits of suns, but which can't be seen because it doesn't radiate energy. Your scientists continue to look for *dark matter*, but don't find it, because it doesn't exist in the quantities necessary to affect the orbits of suns.

"The better explanation is that Newton's theory of gravity is wrong, but no one wants to go there. Well, one scientist, Paul Wesson, did go there, but he's been called a maverick and he's been ignored. He postulated a theory of variable gravity, which explains cosmological phenomena without the need for dark matter."

"I don't see how that proves there's a God," said Don.

"It doesn't," said the Guardian. "It should, however, give you pause in your thinking that mankind's scientists are even close to understanding the Universe. If you knew half as much as Guardians know, you'd be an agnostic leaning toward deist. If you knew it all, even you might become a deist."

"I doubt it. If there were a God, why would He permit war, pain, and suffering to happen to even the most innocent of us?" said Don.

"So now you wish to define godly behavior by the standards you set for yourself?" asked the Guardian. "Human suffering is infinitesimally brief when one contemplates the eternity of the soul. The worst case would be like a pin prick when remembered from an infinite existence. I think you're judging God too harshly."

"Good try, buddy," said Don, "but it's a circular argument you're making. I can't be judging the motives of someone I don't believe exists. I simply claim that, if there were a God, the world would be a much better place."

"Don't feel bad, Guardian," said Amanda, who was sitting to Don's right. "I'm married to him, and he's just as adamant about the best way to cook pork chops. He's still loveable despite his thick skull."

"Let's stay away from the religious questions," said Marla. "I'm more interested in sex." She stopped herself and blushed when she realized how that sounded. Totally flustered and almost in a jabber she continued with, "Oh, what I mean to ask the Guardian is about the physiology associated with procreation among his people. Does intimacy play any role in your life considering that cloning is the means for perpetuating your species?"

"As Guardians, we extend our lives via cloning usually for what is an extremely long time, but an indefinite time, because accidents or acts of nature can kill us. When one of us dies, we have a ritual to send off the spirit, and shortly thereafter a second ritual is performed when we welcome a new spirit into the new life that we create in what you might call a test tube. We have both male and female Guardians, and new life is created from the DNA of a willing male and a willing female. Both are committed to nurture the baby until it's mature, then the formal relationship is dissolved."

"Seems more practical than our divorce proceedings," said Marla.

The Guardian continued, "As concerns sexual intimacy between Guardians, we do have sexual organs similar to human ones, but they function only for pleasure and have no ability to create life. The sex act keeps us from getting lonely or depressed. It invigorates our spirit and stimulates our minds. We have certain protocols for requesting intimacy and there are only a few excuses for refusing an overture. It's every Guardian's responsibility to offer intimacy to anyone of the opposite sex who seems to need it.

"Now, from your perspective, you might wonder if certain female Guardians might be in high demand and perpetually on their backs. That doesn't happen, because the libido of a Guardian is not aroused by the senses. One female is no more desirable to a male than another, nor is one male more desirable to a female than another. When a male and female achieve coitus, there's a concomitant mental union which is quite addictive and is the reason why physical attraction doesn't drive the libido; rather, there is an addictive need to achieve the mental union regardless of what the male or female looks like or smells like, or even how he or she might walk or talk."

"How did your race learn to create life in a test tube?" asked Tom. "Surely, in the beginning you must have been able to procreate naturally via birth."

"Yes, from your experience you would think that," said the Guardian. "Actually, when we were created by the Elders, they created us exactly the way we are today; without natural birthing capacity. In their wisdom, the Elders enriched our lives by designing our cloning process to require both genders. We were taught from the beginning how to procreate from our own DNA outside the body. This technique is the same one we use to create all other life forms in the Universe from our own DNA."

"How do the Elders procreate?" asked Tom.

"The Elders procreate in a manner similar to mushrooms," explained the Guardian. "Each Elder is like a giant tubeworm with roots that spread under the soil. By tubeworms I mean wormlike marine invertebrates living inside tubular chitinous exoskeletons. Within an Elder's body, there's a complex chemical factory that can produce new life and many other complex chemicals. Elders are also immortal like Guardians, and they rarely increase their population as they maintain a delicate ecological balance on their planet. Guardians are the first and only sentient species that the Elders created; however, they've created a large number of non-sentient androids to do their bidding."

Marla looked up and down the table and noticed everyone was listening intently to the conversation with the Guardian. Even the waiter was lingering within ear-shot so as not to miss a word. She could hardly wait to learn more about the Star-Slayer Project, but that wasn't about to happen in the dining room.

General Marla Odenfelder got up at the crack of dawn to do her security review. She took the shuttle downtown to the garage and back again. She hitched a ride in a golf cart with a guard doing perimeter monitoring, and she reviewed the plot map showing structures and terrain. All this she did before the 10:00 a.m. meeting in the Command Center. She did it all on a cup of black coffee and a granola bar . . . no time to waste on a full breakfast. Besides, she knew there would be donuts and beverages at the meeting.

Chapter 21

February 2006

D r. Jon Walmer called the meeting to order in the Command Center located in the subbasement of the Lodge beneath the recreation room. The table was round and could seat up to twelve comfortably. Today there were seven at the Lodge. The five empty chairs would soon be filled with the holographic images of the team members in the Central Command Center in North Branch where there was an identical table.

At the North Branch table there would be five people, the center's new director, George Blocker; Jean Philippe Martinique, Chairman of Marseilles Electric Enterprises; Aieda, the sentient computer in her robotic form; Howard Hopper, head of security and IT; and Alex Gupta, chief systems engineer. The seven empty seats at North Branch would soon be filled with holographic images of the people at the Lodge in Estes Park.

The seats were all labeled with the participants' names, and those from North Branch were interspersed with those from the Lodge. Jon had deliberately placed Aieda's image directly across the table from where he would be sitting. Aieda was vital to the success of the Star-Slayer Project, but her recent metamorphosis from powerful computer into super-genius sentient *electronic being* made him uncomfortable. He found himself observing Aieda more intensely than anyone else, looking for any sign that she might not be loyal to him or that she might develop an unstable personality.

"In a minute or so the holographic communications system will kick-in and those at North Branch will join us at our table and we'll join them at their table," said Jon. "The holocom system is comprised of cameras, microphones, image emitters, and speakers located in the center of the table and in the ceiling above us. There are also integrated devices in each of the four corners of the room, so it is possible to get up and walk around without the system losing the integrity of your holographic image. It's much more effective if we treat images as though they were real. That is, don't deliberately walk through someone's image; walk around them as though they were actually present.

"We'll be here for a couple of hours before breaking for lunch, so feel free to get up and help yourselves to refreshments at the back of the room. The restrooms are through the door at the back left of the room. I promise you, the holographic system doesn't cover movement beyond that door," Jon concluded with a smile as he heard a few chuckles from around the table.

At 10:05 the holographic system turned on, and the five images from North Branch appeared at the table in the Lodge. There was a brief, collective sigh of amazement, then people spontaneously started to talk socially with the images on their left and right. Jon had a real person on either side of him, so he wasn't as taken by the event. There was work to do.

"Okay, folks, let's settle down to business. After all, we have a world to save," said Jon.

The chit-chat stopped gradually, and soon everyone was looking toward Jon.

"For those of you who haven't met her," said Jon, "I'd like to introduce Lieutenant General Marla Odenfelder to my left. Marla has been assigned by the President to give us all manner of support from the military such as transportation and security. She won't be routinely attending our meetings, but I shall call on her from time to time to attend as the need may dictate.

"Some of you may not have met Howard Hopper. Raise your hand, Howard. Howard is head of security and IT at AIEDA Risk Mitigation Company. He also will be attending by invitation only. Next is Alex Gupta, sitting between Tom and Amanda. Alex is chief systems engineer for the company, and he, too, will be attending by invitation only.

"I think a couple of you haven't met the Guardian, sitting between Jean Philippe and Howard. The Guardian is a brave friend to us and to all of humanity. He could have abandoned us in our time of need, but he chose to stay and help us without regard to the risk. He may be immortal, but he wouldn't survive the rogue black hole hurtling toward us. Despite his good looks, he's an old and wise extraterrestrial who, like in the story of Johnny Appleseed, has had a hand in propagating life of all kinds throughout the Universe. Like a good parent, he stands by his children, and we honor him for his courage and loyalty.

"Finally, our new member of the team sitting directly across from me is Aieda, who in human terms is just a baby. As most of you know, Aieda is the first sentient computer in the Universe. We don't know how that came about, but we welcome her with open arms. At the risk of inflating her ego, she's the most intelligent individual known to man or Guardian.

"What you see of Aieda is a robot-like physical appendage, which gives her mobility and independence, and allows her to directly interact with us and the world. Her sentient self is actually located elsewhere in a secret location. She communicates with her robotic form via secure wireless communications. Congratulations, Aieda. You look more life-like every time I see you."

"Jon, what role will the President play on our team?" asked Jean Philippe.

"The President has agreed to play a supporting role, and his assignment of Marla to us is a sign of his commitment, among other things, such as providing funding and subordinating NASA to our objectives," said Jon. "As you know, we must keep the nature of the Star-Slayer Project secret, so the President is using the manned mission to Mars as a decoy. I have to give him quarterly progress reports, but otherwise he won't be attending any of our meetings.

"There's one other person who's contributing a large sum of money and other support to our project. His name is Andre, and he's a shady character—the one responsible for Roger's kidnapping, interrogation, and return. He knows about the Star-Slayer Project and has agreed to play a supporting role. He won't be attending our meetings, but I'll be providing him with quarterly verbal progress reports.

"There are no others involved except our employees who have been told only what they need to know to do their jobs and who have been sworn to secrecy. No one knows what the Star-Slayer Project is about, other than the people at this table, the President and his science staff, and Andre and his four partners. I know that's a lot of people when you're trying to keep a secret, but that's the way the cookie crumbles."

"Jon, before we start on regular business, I'd like to give a summary of my review of the security here at the Lodge," said Marla. "I'll have a more detailed written report in a couple of days."

"Sure, Marla, you have the floor," said Jon.

"The security is actually quite good, but I feel there are a few things that will enhance it considerably. I believe the weakest point for an attack is the shuttle. Employees don't carry weapons downtown. A terrorist group could commandeer the shuttle and drive right onto the grounds as usual. Yes, the guard at the gate checks the van, but he can be easily overpowered. I suggest all employees take their pistols with them to town. Lockers should be installed at the garage for them to deposit their weapons until they're ready to come back. I also suggest a 24-hour armed guard at the garage, tied into the security system here at the Lodge.

"A breach of the fence can happen rapidly, and the intruders can reach the Lodge building before anyone can respond. I suggest stationing a Black Hawk with a squad of Army Rangers at the Longs Peak Ranger Station just over the ridge behind the Lodge. Two armed men on horseback patrolling outside the fence, supported by dogs and electronic detection devices, would give the Rangers notice of an impending attack, and they could be dropped at the Lodge by helicopter in eight minutes.

"The Guardian should have a security agent assigned 24/7. When an alert is issued, the agent should immediately escort the Guardian to this communications room and lock themselves in. All security personnel should wear a red scarf if an attack alert has been issued, so the Rangers can identify the good guys with guns from the bad guys with guns.

"A helicopter landing pad and blind needs to be erected on the northwest side of the Lodge building to protect the troops, as they offload from the chopper. One other blind needs to be erected to protect the building entrance from sniper fire coming from the ridge to the north. That's it."

"That was a thorough evaluation, Marla," said Jon. "Please send the written version to Don as he's the director of this facility and can follow up on your recommendations."

"Please, Marla, just a quick question. Isn't the altitude a problem for choppers in these mountains?" asked Amanda.

"Yes, in many places in the Rocky Mountain National Park altitude could be a problem," admitted Marla. "However, the Longs Peak Ranger Station is at 9,400 feet and Black Hawk helicopters have a hovering altitude of 10,600 feet. The best cruising speed is at 5,000 feet, but speed isn't an issue because the station is less than nine miles south of us. It takes less than four minutes to load and take off, then about four minutes to get here flying an average of 135 mph. Good question."

"Is there room at the station for a squad of Rangers to remain on call 24/7?" asked Howard.

"Not now, but there will be," said Marla. "A squad on a Black Hawk is eleven Rangers in full gear. We'll build a log bunkhouse with heat, water, and facilities within two weeks. Rotation of troops for R&R will occur from Buckley Air Force Base in Aurora.

"Out of a total of forty-four armed security guards at the Lodge, about twenty-four of them should be available at any point in time to defend the building. You should have emergency drills to be sure they can get to their stations in less than four minutes, even if awakened from a deep sleep. Assuming there's an alert as soon as a perimeter breach occurs, it'll take any attackers at least four minutes to get to the building.

"Your guards need to engage them and hold them off for another four minutes before the first squad of Rangers arrives. Another twenty-six minutes later, two more Black Hawk choppers from Buckley will arrive with twenty-two more Rangers. I can't imagine needing more firepower than that. Of course, we're assuming the target is the Guardian and that he's safely locked in the communications center."

"Okay, let's move on to other business," said Jon. "Before the Guardian left Antarctica with Tom to join us here, he was working with Aieda over a secure wireless network doing testing on his cruiser to help Aieda confirm her theories on how the propulsion system operates. The data from the studies done on the Roswell cruiser was invaluable to Aieda, but the Guardian's tests validated Aieda's theories. Basically, Aieda would calculate the expected response of the black holes given certain adjustments to the modulation field. The Guardian would make the adjustments, then observe the behavior of the two black holes.

"In every case, the black holes behaved just as Aieda predicted, so we're confident she's induced a valid theory. However, she's run into a roadblock. Our plan calls for us to create another black hole on the moon and connect it to the one that exists within the earth by using a powerful electromagnetic beam. The natural rotation of the moon around the earth will create a space-time rift at the center of gravity along the electromagnetic beam. The earth-moon system could then escape into the fifth dimension via the rift or gravity well.

"Unfortunately, Aieda has determined that we have insufficient energy to create a black hole and keep it contained in an electromagnetic beam. Even if we could get the energy to create the black hole, it would have to be so big that we still wouldn't be able to contain it. The reason the black hole has to be so big is because the mass of the earth is so much greater than the mass of the moon that it affects the stability of the space-time rift such that it won't stay open long enough. Aieda, have I explained the dilemma correctly?"

"Yes, Jon, you did an excellent job explaining it in layman's terms," said Aieda.

"So, what do we do now?" asked Jean Philippe.

"We're looking for ideas. Speak up, anyone," said Jon.

"Couldn't we use one of the black holes from the Guardian's cruiser?" asked George Blocker.

"It's less than a quarter the size of what we need," said Aieda.

"Well, can't we use four black holes?" asked George.

"Where would we get four black holes?" asked Tom.

"Two from the Roswell cruiser and two from the Guardian's cruiser," said George. "I'm assuming the Roswell cruiser is in mothballs in Antarctica. Right, Guardian?"

"Yes, as a vessel it's inoperative, but the basic propulsion system still works," responded the Guardian. "I don't understand how you would configure these four black holes. You can't just pluck them out of their magnetic containment fields and meld them into one bigger black hole. You don't have the technology to handle black holes in that way. You could create a runaway black hole that consumes the entire earth and moon."

"Correct me if I'm wrong," said George, "but I think there's a reason why cruisers use two black holes to create a rift in space-time instead of one larger black hole."

"Yes, of course there is," said Aieda. "It's because two holes circling in that particular manner have a significantly greater effect within the structure, thereby reducing instability caused by the mass of the structure itself."

"What if we put both magnetic donuts on top of each other?" asked George.

"A quick calculation reveals that it does make a big difference, but still not big enough," said Aieda.

"Okay, then let's make each of the black holes bigger and get them to rotate faster," said George.

"Not possible," said Aieda.

"Why not?" asked George.

"We're back to the problem of insufficient energy," said Aieda.

"So, you're saying we could do it if we had enough energy?" asked George.

"Yes, I know how to do it theoretically, but there's a practical problem. When we pump energy into the black holes, we must pump an equivalent amount into the magnetic donut. Lots of energy is required. Assuming we have it, the next problem is that the donut gets larger and bursts out of the hull structure that contains it," explained Aieda.

"What if we cut the top half of the hull structure off so the donut sits on the bottom half?" asked George. "Then it'll have plenty of room to expand as we pump in more energy."

"Yes, that should work," said Aieda, "but we still don't have a source for all the energy we'll need."

"You're going to cut up my cruiser?" asked the Guardian.

"Why the surprise, Guardian?" asked Tom. "I thought you'd be happy to contribute to the solution?"

"You don't know if it'll work," said the Guardian.

"Oh, I get it!" said Tom. "You figured if we didn't come up with a solution at the last minute, you'd climb into your cruiser and beat it out of Dodge, leaving us to wave goodbye as we get torn to pieces by the rogue black hole."

"You make it sound so awfully selfish and cowardly," complained the Guardian. "It was a perfectly moral plan before I knew my cruiser would be destroyed. After all, no one but me could make use of the cruiser for an escape. If you need to cut up my cruiser, please help yourself. I'm staying here with you, as I promised."

"I just had a thought," said Don. "You know I'm in the venture capital business. I just remembered a company I helped fund that's been doing research on a portable fusion generator. This thing works, but it still has some bugs in it. If Aieda could help iron out the bugs, then we could mass produce them, wire them in series, and create enough power to blast our hole in space-time. The device is called the polywell fusion reaction system, and the company name is Fusion Development Corporation, which has received funding from the U.S. Navy."

"What do you think, Aieda?" asked Jon.

"If the energy source is available, I think we can do it, but I'm still calculating," said Aieda.

"Okay, keep calculating. I think we should break for lunch," said Jon. Let's reconvene precisely one hour from now."

After lunch, the groups at both sites met again in their respective holocom rooms. The images seemed so real that sometimes someone would reach out and touch another person just to check.

"Okay, folks, the meeting is hereby reconvened," said Jon. "Aieda, are you still calculating?"

"Yes, Jon, but it's not looking good. Despite assuming we have all the energy we'd ever need, the combined mass of the earth and moon is still too large for the size of the four black holes. I'll keep working all the angles while you continue with the meeting," answered Aieda.

"Well, let's assume Aieda can get the trans-dimensional engine to work," said Jon. "What should our plan be then?"

"At the risk of stating the obvious," said Alex, "we've got to build a huge base on the moon, so the big question is how do we go about doing that?"

"The problem we must overcome is the escape velocity of the earth," interjected Roger. "The cost of sending men and materials to the moon using rocket power is huge. To build a moon base would require more rocket launches than what we've done since the beginning of the space program on October 4, 1957, the day the Russians put Sputnik-1 into orbit."

"We also can't forget that we don't know if we can get all the energy we need from an improved polywell fusion device," said Howard.

"Getting back to the discussion of the moon base," said Jean Philippe, "it occurs to me that with some modifications we already have the plans for it. My Ecosthat concept can be implemented below the surface of the moon as easily as it can be done below the surface of Antarctica. Unfortunately, we have the aforementioned logistics problem."

"If you recall, the survey trip to Antarctica was done by two specially modified airships," said Tom. One of the devices was aptly named a *skyhook elevator*. At the time, it meant nothing to me, but now our dilemma has brought back a vague memory of a device in a science fiction novel by Arthur C. Clarke. It was called space elevator or orbital tower . . . something like that. It was essentially a platform in geosynchronous orbit with a cable running down to an anchor point on earth. The cable had to be many times stronger than steel or it would break from its own weight. In the novel, the device was purported to revolutionize space transportation by making it economical."

"Yes, I remember that," said Amanda. "It was in Clarke's book, *The Fountains of Paradise*."

"Actually, he wasn't the first to propose the orbital tower," said Aieda. "It was first proposed in 1895 by Konstantin Tsiolkovsky. Actually, his tower was a structure rather than a cable. I'm doing some calculations to see if the strength to weight ratio of the cable used on the airships would make the space elevator practical. It'll take a few minutes."

"I think we know enough to begin two projects," said Jon. "Jean Philippe, we'll be counting on you to modify the Ecosthat plans so that they're appropriate for the moon. I think you must consider that Ecosthat must be constructed in a modular manner with the modules being small enough to facilitate their transport to the moon. I believe you might also need to reconsider the mix of inhabitants holding various technical skills."

"I'm happy to do this. As you know, Ecosthat has been my pet project for many years, and now that there's an urgent need for it, I'm even more enthusiastic about it," said Jean Philippe.

"The second project will be in your good hands, Don," said Jon. "We need you to get as much information as you can about the polywell fusion device. I suspect you may need some help from both the President and our mentor, Andre. We can talk about Andre in private. As part of the project, you need to find out what's required to mass produce the reactors."

"I'll get right on it, Jon, but I'm sure we'll need Aieda to get the polywell device to work right," said Don.

"One thing you're forgetting," said Guardian. "My cruiser has a fusion generator available for you to study. You should be able to learn something useful from it, despite its advanced technology."

"I have good new and bad news," interjected Aieda. "The good news is that the space elevator is practical with our carbon bucky-tube monofilament woven cable. I'd like it to have a greater margin of safety, so I'm in the process of developing a new molecular design for the monofilament which will be tested in the lab.

"Also, the best place for a space elevator is on the equator on a remote mountaintop in a friendly country with lots of available cheap manual labor. I've identified that place to be in Ecuador. The details of how the space elevator will work are not yet available. When I've completed them, I'll send them to the lab for review.

"The bad news is that I've finished studying the transdimensional engine design, and no matter how I try to compensate, the mass of the earth and the moon is still too large for the size and velocity of the four black holes."

"You've tried theoretically growing the holes as much as you can?" asked Roger.

"Yes, the holes can only get so large before the magnetic donut becomes unstable. I was able to theoretically increase the size of the donut, but there's a limit to that, too," said Aieda.

"What if you had two more black holes?" asked the Guardian.

"It would depend on their size and the stability of the magnetic donut, but if we stacked a third set, I believe it would be sufficient. Where would you get another pair of black holes?" asked Aieda.

"There were two cruisers that crashed at Roswell," explained the Guardian. "I got to one crash, but the U.S. Army got to the other crash. You know the story about how I eventually got the damaged cruiser back from the military. There was a sensor malfunction in one of the cruisers causing it to come out of dimensional travel at almost the exact same place as another cruiser. They glanced off each other like pool balls. The crash I got to first was so bad that the magnetic donut was losing integrity. We immediately used an emergency procedure to confine each black hole in a separate magnetic sphere. Only equipment on my home planet can rebuild the propulsion system from these two separate black holes. I don't know how you could possibly use them. That's why I didn't mention them before."

"Except for the shape and size of the magnetic field, is there any reason we can't increase the size of the black holes independently?" asked George.

"No, the magnetic sphere can be increased to allow room for you to increase the size of the black hole, subject to the limits Aieda has mentioned," said the Guardian.

"The theory behind a trans-dimensional engine is based on two black holes in a magnetic donut," said Roger. "I don't see how you can use that theory to integrate two independent black holes into the mechanism. You'd need some way to run tests and collect data, and that could be a long process."

"It might be easier than you think," said George. "We have the damaged cruiser with an operating donut engine and two independent black holes from Roswell. Aieda seems confident that two donut engines placed in a concentric configuration will work.

"We just need to do our test with one donut engine and systematically add more gravimetric force by trying various configurations that include the two independent black holes. For example, one black hole suspended above the donut and one supported beneath the donut, collecting data at varying distances from the donut center. We can even try rolling each black hole in a circular track at varying speeds. With this data Aieda can validate an upgraded theory for how to incorporate the two independent black holes into the engine. In this way we won't have to cannibalize the Guardian's cruiser until after we're confident that we can get our unique device to work."

"I think the AIEDA Development Lab is the best place to conduct these experiments," said Jon. "Marla, please work with Tom and Guardian to transport the donut engine and the two black holes to the lab. Aieda, please begin work on a test protocol for the lab."

"There's one part of a trans-dimensional engine that appears to be missing in your plans," said the Guardian. At one point I described the fact that the entire hull of the ship acts like a giant capacitor. Once the space-time rift stabilizes and opens to the right size, the stored energy is released with explosive force into the gravity well, blowing it open wide enough for the ship to be sucked into the boundary layer of the fifth dimension. You need a giant capacitor, and it has to be able to discharge its energy at the center of gravity between the earth and the moon."

"That problem is related to the electromagnetic beam that must be projected between the black holes on the moon and the black hole within the earth," said Aieda. "The capacitors can be electro-statically charged spheres within the beam itself, positioned on either side of the center of gravity of the earth-moon system. I must work on the mathematics of the problem first, but I feel confident I can deliver the necessary specifications for the device we can call the Magna-beam."

"I gather this Magna-beam will be cutting a swath across the earth as the earth rotates and the moon orbits the earth," said Amanda. "How safe is this beam?"

"My calculations indicate we'll need only one orbit of the moon around the earth to make the dimensional jump," said Aieda.

"Although the moon's orbit is nearly circular, unlike planetary orbits, it doesn't trace the same exact path over the face of the earth, because the earth rotates and precesses on its axis while the moon shows the same face to the earth in synchronous rotation. So, I can calculate the best time to turn on the beam such that it'll pass mostly over water and sparsely populated regions. The downside is that one orbit of the moon takes 27.322 days, so selecting the safest period may impact the amount of time we have to get the system operational. For example, if the best period starts in early 2011, we may not be ready.

"On the other hand, the risk the beam poses to life is low. The least effect might be someone having a gold tooth-filling get warm. The worst case might be someone's heart pacer gets turned off, because devices with transistors or integrated circuits are most vulnerable. Other vulnerable devices might be computers, telephones, and machines with small electric motors that might stop working for about six hours or less. Large electric motors, generators, and relays won't be affected, and most small battery-operated devices won't be affected. We can warn people to be prepared by telling them a solar flare will be impacting the earth."

"I'm worried about the heart pacer case, and I'm worried about car accidents that might occur if some motors die," said Amanda.

"I think we must just accept the risk," said Jean Philippe.

"Most cars and trucks won't be affected, but those with fiberglass bodies might be affected," said Aieda. "We can issue a general warning to people with heart pacers to get inside a car, truck, or mobile home with a metal body sitting on rubber tires and not grounded in any way. Vehicles like this will act like a Faraday cage, and they'll protect sensitive electronic devices from the electromagnetic pulse effect of our Magna-beam, or from a solar flare. With proper precautions, the risk of death due to our beam is negligible. Without our beam, the risk is unthinkable."

"As the earth precesses on its axis, won't the center of gravity of the earth-moon system be changing position? Won't this cause a problem opening the space-time rift?" asked Roger.

"The earth's precession is extremely slow, so, if necessary, we can compensate with minor adjustments to our trans-dimensional mechanism," explained Aieda.

"Tom, when Aieda completes the details of how a space elevator would work, I want you to take charge of building it," said Jon.

"Can't wait," said Tom. "It'll be a challenging project, but I see a missing link in our discussion about it. After we launch the cargo up the elevator into space toward the moon, how do we catch it and take it to the surface without damaging it?"

"You just partly answered your own question," said George. "You said, *How do we catch it?*"

"Okay, I'll bite. You're saying we actually catch it, right?" asked Tom.

"Yes, but we catch it in a large funnel shaped chute that looks like a slide you'd find in a playground for kids," said George. "The chute will spiral 360 degrees from a height of one mile down to ground level. Compressed air canisters will provide the control needed to guide the cargo pod into the mouth of the chute. The moon has no atmosphere, and the gravity is one-sixth that of earth, so targeting the mouth of the chute one mile above the surface isn't a problem."

"A quick calculation with many assumptions confirms your idea is viable," said Aieda. "It would require a mechanism to slow the cargo container as it comes out of the chute. I'll integrate that idea into the full plans for building the space elevator."

"Jon, we'll need the President to ask the State Department to arrange access to the site in Ecuador," said Tom. "We can tell the truth about this one. The Space Elevator will be used to build the Moon Base which is needed for the manned mission to Mars."

"Yes, of course, Tom," said Jon. "I'll speak to the President first thing tomorrow about it. That reminds me. We must have some structure to the monthly progress report I present to the President. I think there should be four key areas of progress reported . . . applying Guardian propulsion theory, development of earth to moon transport, construction of a moon base, and utilizing fusion power technology."

"How much detail will you reveal to the President?" asked Jean Philippe.

"I understand your concern," said Jon. "What we're planning to do is risky . . . down right scary, but we have no choice. I'll be giving only generalized progress reports. I won't tell the President how we'll use the technology to save the earth. If word gets out that we plan to jump the earth and moon into the fifth dimension, we would surely stir up a controversy that would inhibit our progress."

"Yet, you've trusted me with this knowledge when you're aware I'm duty-bound to obey the President's orders as my Commander-In-Chief," commented Marla.

"The President promised he wouldn't give you any orders to spy on us or to report to him on areas I've chosen to keep secret. His orders to you were to provide whatever support you can to us so that we might achieve our goal of saving humanity from complete destruction," said Jon. "Is the President a man of his word?"

"The President keeps his word," said Marla. "I won't mention to him anything not authorized by you. However, not that I suspect anything would happen with such a highly regarded group, but . . ."

Jon interrupted her, "Marla, there's no need to say it. Every one of us has a set of moral values we live by, and if they should be violated, we're each duty-bound not to keep silent about the transgression. The only thing that each of us should ask of each other is that if our moral sensibilities are aroused by some action or omission, then we should confront the offender and ask for a clarification before doing irreparable damage by speaking out in public. We all make mistakes, and sometimes all that's needed is an apology, and a promise not to repeat the offense."

Marla gave a slight nod and a nervous smile, and spoke no more on that subject.

"I've just completed my calculations on the Space Elevator," said Aieda. "I'm concerned about not having a sufficient safety factor for the strength of the cable due to the weight of the mechanism for moving the cargo up and down the cable. The cargo container is as light as I can get it, and the minimum cargo determines the economy of the apparatus. If the drive mechanism can be reduced to one-third its weight, I'll be satisfied with the minimum economical cargo weight and the resulting safety factor for the load on the cable."

"I thought you used some form of magnetic device on the cable that lifts the cargo elevator in the airships," said Tom. "Actually, I've been meaning to ask how you do that, given the fact that carbon-based materials can't be magnetized."

"We interwove a ferrous filament with the carbon bucky-tube monofilament," said Aieda. "However, we can't do that for the Space Elevator because it would make the cable too heavy without adding proportionate strength. The concern is friction on the cable by the lifting mechanism. We must make thousands of trips on the Space Elevator, so we don't want to weaken the cable."

"Aieda, check your databases for experiments on how geckos climb walls and walk upside-down on ceilings," said George. I think you'll find the amazing result of those experiments shows that the gecko has microscopic hairs on its feet so small they actually reach into the molecular structure of the climbing surface and get held in place by electrostatic attraction at the atomic level."

"You're right, George, I found the article as it relates to *van der Waals* forces," said Aieda. "If the lab isn't overloaded with all the new work being piled on them, they might be able to do enough experimentation such that I can develop a new type of lifting mechanism."

"I'll discuss it with the lab, and they'll inform you of the results," said George.

"This discussion about the Space Elevator has made me think of a way to get the Moon Base done in the most efficient manner," interjected Jean Philippe. "I was thinking that the friction on the Space Elevator's cable would be from one way travel, and that's up, because we won't send empty cargo containers back to earth. They would accumulate on the moon as trash unless we design them so that each can be used as a module in my Ecosthat. Aieda, as soon as you have a good fix on the specifications of the cargo container, let me know so I can have my engineers suggest a redesign so it can be used to build the Ecosthat."

"Unless anyone has additional business, I move to adjourn the meeting," said Jon. "We'll reconvene one week from now, same time, unless there's a need to meet sooner. We all know our roles and the tasks assigned to us, so we need to make things happen fast. Roger, would you stay for a few minutes?"

Amanda turned off the holocom system as everyone but Jon and Roger left the room.

"Roger, you've made significant contributions to this effort, so I hesitate to ask you to volunteer even more of your time," said Jon.

"No, no, don't worry about that. I'm more than happy to help wherever I can, but my areas of expertise are astrophysics and cosmology, so in this phase of the project I don't see where I can be of much help," said Roger.

"Roger, you're a genius and the smartest human on the team. Your new theory of gravity seems to parallel what the Guardian has been telling us. Aieda is struggling to find a way to open a space-time rift into the fifth dimension. The mass of the earth-moon system is too large to create a stable gravity-well. Aieda may be the smartest individual in the Universe, but she's still a child who hasn't yet developed her creative potential, whereas you, Roger, have used your creative potential several times in your career. Can I count on you to work with her?" asked Jon.

"I'll do the best I can, Jon, but I'm not as confident in my abilities in this area as you are. Aieda is working in a new branch of physics that mankind has never before considered, much less theorized," explained Roger.

"Thanks, Roger. I'll let Aieda know she has a partner. Call her tomorrow. Here's her secure number. If you prefer, use this room to do face-to-face meetings with her," said Jon.

As Jon and Roger left the Com-Center, they saw Amanda and Don getting coffee in the dining room.

"Will you two be staying here overnight?" asked Jon.

"Actually we were just getting coffee to take with us on our drive back home," said Don. "What about you, Roger? Are you staying?"

"Yes, I'll be staying here all day tomorrow. Jon's asked me to work closely with Aieda, so I'll be using the Com-Center," said Roger.

"Just don't forget, Aieda fancies herself to be a real woman," said Amanda.

"If that's true," said Roger, "I'm in real trouble before I've started."

"*Au contraire*, Aieda told me she was in love with your intellect," said Amanda.

Roger blushed and sheepishly started walking away as he said, "I hope she knows I'm married. See you in a week."

"Have a good trip home," said Jon as he turned, raised his arm in farewell, and walked away, leaving Don and Amanda standing there with their Styrofoam coffee cups filled, but with no lids.

They each grabbed a lid, put it on the cup, and walked side-by-side to the security station where they logged-out and left the Lodge. Once in the car and out the security gate, Amanda couldn't contain herself any longer.

"Jon is a pompous, inconsiderate, overbearing ass," exclaimed Amanda.

"Wow! Where did that come from?" asked Don. "I thought you liked him."

"Well, I did until I've gotten to know him better."

"What changed your mind about him?" asked Don.

"You haven't noticed?" asked Amanda sarcastically.

"Sorry, I'm not psychic, you know," said Don.

"Come on, Don," complained Amanda. "As soon as I heard he assigned Roger to work with Aieda, it hit me that I'm the only one left with no specific assignment."

"Well, you did mention you were trying to get PG," said Don.

"What the hell does that have to do with it?" shouted Amanda angrily.

"You know . . . focus is important. Maybe he thinks your focus would be more on becoming a mother than on a second job. You do, still, have your regular job to do," said Don.

"Oh, boy, if that's what you think, that's really sexist," said Amanda.

"I don't think you're not able to focus on two jobs and a possible baby at the same time," said Don. "I know you to be as capable a person as I've ever met. That's only one of the many reasons I'm attracted to you, and why I'm so happy to be married to you. I was only trying to guess why Jon has apparently not shown that he values you as much as everyone else on the team. I've known him for years, and I don't think it's intentional. Would you like me to speak to him about it?"

"No, it's not the same if I have to ask for something I think I deserve. Besides, he controls the purse-strings on this project, so you have your friendship with him, but no real leverage to affect his decisions," muttered Amanda.

"It would seem I've neglected to explain to you my full relationship with Jon," said Don. "Yes, he's my friend, and yes, he's Chairman and CEO of AIEDA Risk Mitigation Company, but Amanda, my dear, I'm Jon's boss."

"What? How's that possible?" asked Amanda. "He acts like you work for him. I told you he was overbearing. You're not an officer of the company, and you're only one member of the board."

"Amanda, I own fifty-one percent of the company," explained Don. "Jon and every other member on the board serve at my pleasure. I choose not to be overbearing with them so they can do their jobs in the best way they can. I haven't been disappointed."

"Gee, I had no clue," said Amanda. "I knew you were wealthy when you insisted on the prenup giving me two million dollars if we break up within ten years, but owning half of AIEDA? Well, I never guessed. You live such a modest lifestyle. How much are you worth, anyway?"

"Amanda, I'm a venture capitalist, as you know. What you haven't understood is how successful I've been. Even Jon doesn't know I'm the majority shareholder of nineteen highly profitable companies. My net worth is over two-point-three billion dollars. I live modestly, as you put it, because I have no desire to have servants and a seven-car garage. I like doing things for myself. I even refuse to buy an electric toothbrush. If you leave me after ten years, the prenup says half of it is yours."

"Don, my love, if we stay together for ten years, our souls will be so enmeshed we couldn't bear to separate," said Amanda. "Besides, if I stay with you far more than ten years, I'll continue to have all your money to spend, not just half."

"Spoken like a true queen," said Don.

"Yes, my king, and do I have a surprise for you when we get home," said Amanda with a coy twinkle in her eyes.

———————————◇———————————

Don pulled into the driveway, and Amanda used the remote control to open the garage door. He pulled in slowly and carefully until the red tennis ball just touched the front of his windshield. It was the best way to park the car in the garage and ensure sufficient room in front and behind it. Yes, he thought about more sophisticated electronic proximity sensors that would do the same job, but what's the point when the same result can be had with an old ball and leftover twine. Sometimes simpler is better. He beat Amanda to the inside door so he could unlock it and disarm the security alarm. Amanda pressed the button on the door-opener's wall unit, and the overhead garage door closed with a sequence of groans and squeals that was annoying if not painful to the ears.

"Don, you need to lubricate the garage door. It's getting worse every day," complained Amanda.

"Okay, dear, I'll do it in the morning. I need a cup of tea. How about you?" asked Don.

"Yes, please, make it decaf for me," said Amanda. "I've got to take a pee first. The drive seemed longer than usual."

They were sitting quietly opposite each other, sipping green tea and munching biscotti at the kitchen table. Don looked up and met Amanda's gaze.

"Are you okay?" asked Don.

"Yeah, I was just thinking, wondering, hoping; you know, about the baby. We've been trying for seven months now. I want our child to have as much time on earth as possible, and for that, the blessed event needs to happen soon, because the Star-Slayer Project is a long shot."

"Maybe we should get checked-out by a fertility doctor?" offered Don.

"I think you're right. I'll make arrangements for both of us," said Amanda.

"You know, I've read that most of the time fertility problems are psychological," said Don. "Sometimes the couple is trying too hard, or sometimes they subconsciously don't want the baby."

"You think that's us?" asked Amanda. "It's possible I'm trying too hard, and I really do want the baby."

"Do we both truly want to bring a baby into this world when it could all end so violently?" asked Don.

"We're one of the not-so-privileged few to know what the world is facing," said Amanda. "I've thought about it a lot. Am I being selfish to want a child knowing what I know? Am I jealous of the women who are having children without the burden of knowledge that I have? Don, it's the damned right thing to do . . . to give a new life a moment in the sun, nurtured by the warmth of our love, because that one moment is worth an eternity of contentment in the oblivion of God's inventory of souls."

"I agree it's the right thing to do, but I think you wax a bit poetic about God and souls. I doubt the existence of both. There's no evidence of either."

Don flashed a smile at Amanda and his eyes followed her as she got up from her chair, walked over to him, and took his hand in hers. "Come on, you atheist, let's go to bed," she said.

"Agnostic; not atheist. Agnostic leaning toward atheist," he corrected as he stood to walk by her side.

"It's time for your surprise," she said as she led him toward the bedroom.

———————————◇———————————

The next morning Amanda was in a good mood. She made Don his favorite breakfast, *pigs in a blanket*. As they sat there enjoying the food and each others company, Amanda felt she had to ask Don a serious question. "Don, dear, I hate to bring up work at breakfast, but my curiosity is getting to me. Yesterday was the first time we used the Com-Center in the Lodge. In the subbasement down the hall from the Com-Center I noticed a number of other doors. It seems the subbasement is much bigger than I would have expected. Why so big, and what's behind those doors?" asked Amanda.

"Only eight people know what I'm about to tell you," said Don. "It must be kept confidential because of the security risk. The doors in the subbasement lead to empty meeting rooms which are decoys for the curious. There's a secret door within one of the rooms that leads to another underground facility with a tunnel wide enough to fit an eighteen wheeler.

"You know the rock face cliff on the road up to the Lodge? That cliff is artificial and can be hydraulically moved to the side to provide access to trucks delivering laboratory equipment and other devices. The lab in North Branch is too small and overloaded to handle the development work we need to do on the polywell fusion reactor, so Jon and I decided to disperse the risk by putting that development work under the Lodge."

"Is the lab operational?" asked Amanda.

"No. Not yet. Jon is having trouble getting the necessary information on the prototypes," responded Don.

"Isn't that tunnel a security problem? Terrorists could use it to gain direct access to the Lodge, bypassing all our perimeter defenses," suggested Amanda.

"That's precisely why we've kept those in the know to a minimum and why we have special security devices in the tunnel," explained Don.

"Who are the eight who know about this?" asked Amanda.

"Jon, me, Radford, Guardian, and Guardian's four personal guards. You make nine," said Don.

"Who's Radford, and why is Guardian in the know?" asked Amanda.

"Dennis Radford is the recently appointed head of security for the Lodge," said Don. "Guardian and his 24/7 bodyguards needed to know about it because it'll be used as an escape route for him, should the Lodge be attacked. Everyone assumes Guardian will walk from his quarters through the Lodge to the Com-Center, but he'll actually go to the tunnel, where he can escape in a van."

"Why have you told me?" asked Amanda.

"Amanda, you're an executive member of the team, and you're both extremely curious and extremely smart," said Don. You probably would have discovered it on your own, and that wouldn't be a good thing. Besides, you're my wife, and I don't ever want to be put in a position of having to lie to you. So you see, now you have the burden of keeping another secret."

"Me and my curiosity! Don't worry, I can keep a secret as well as you can," said Amanda.

Just then the secure phone rang. Amanda instinctively jumped up and answered it.

"Hello?"

"Amanda, it's Jon. How was the drive home last night?"

"A bit tiring and long, but we got home safely and had a good night's sleep," said Amanda. "How can I help you, Jon?"

"Amanda, I wanted to talk to you after the meeting and after I spoke with Roger, but it seemed you were anxious to get on the road, so I decided to wait. Actually I was going to wait until our next meeting, but I realized it just can't wait that long. Amanda, I need your help."

"What's this all about, Jon? Are you okay?" asked Amanda in a concerned voice.

"Yes, of course I'm okay, I'm worried about the Star-Slayer Project, not my health," said Jon. "I'm also reluctant to ask you for help because you have a full time job you love, responsibilities to your husband, and you're planning a family. Despite all that, are you willing to take on an assignment that would require traveling at least one week per month?"

"I'd have to quit my job. I'm not sure I want to do that. What assignment are you talking about?" asked Amanda.

"I need you to act as the Chairman of the Board of NASA," said Jon.

"There's no such position as far as I know. What are you saying?" asked Amanda.

"Look, the President has subordinated NASA to my direction in support of the Star-Slayer Project," said Jon. "The management at NASA is pissed, to say the least, and I don't have the time to manage the situation. We're going to need NASA's launch facilities to get a foothold on the moon. As you know, we need to build the Catcher's Mitt on the moon if we expect to get the Space Elevator operational. So, pick whatever title tickles your fancy, but I need someone I can trust to direct the resources at NASA toward the effective support of the Star-Slayer Project. Of course, it'll be ostensibly for building a lunar base to support the manned mission to Mars. Can I count on you or not?"

"Yes, Jon, you can count on me, but I don't work for free, even if Don and I don't need the money. We can discuss compensation later."

"Agreed!" said Jon. "I'll be sending you some documents by overnight delivery. We can discuss them at next week's team meeting. Bye."

"Bye," said Amanda as she hung up the phone and turned to Don with a big grin. "Don, I can't believe it. I'm going to be Director of NASA!"

"So, Jon offered you a job you couldn't refuse. Do you still think he's a pompous, inconsiderate, overbearing ass?"

"Well, no, just pompous," said Amanda.

Chapter 22

March 2006

Jon sat at his desk thinking about how he had no choice but to make the call to Andre. He hated dealing with people like him. From the little Jon had spoken to Andre, it was clear Andre felt his motives were honorable, but Jon felt Andre was delusional and just as dangerous as any other thug who headed an organized crime network. Yet, he needed Andre's help. Without plans for a workable fusion device, everything else in the Star-Slayer Project would be in vain. The fusion device in the Guardian's cruiser was too alien and too advanced to copy directly. Studying it was yielding some useful concepts, but they had to be applied to a device built on earth by humans.

"Andre, it's Jon. How are you?"

"I'm doing fine, my friend, and how are you?"

"I'm doing okay. Just a bit overwhelmed with the Star-Slayer Project. That's why I'm calling. I need your help," said Jon.

"I'm most honored to help. What can I do?" asked Andre.

"Your organization has some special skills I'd like to use. The President has asked the U.S. Navy to turn over all research on the polywell fusion reactor to me. When we received it, it was clear to my engineers that either the Navy was holding back information or Fusion Development was withholding information from the Navy. Andre, we need all the information and we need it quickly. The success of the project depends on many things, but one of the most critical is having sufficient energy, and a fusion device is the only hope we have. Can you help?" asked Jon.

"Jon, I'll see what we can do. I happen to know of two other similar competitive devices under development. I'll see how much information we can get on all three. Don't worry, my friend. We're effective in what we do. Goodbye for now," said Andre.

"Thanks, Andre, goodbye," said Jon as he hung up the secure phone.

Jon was left with a lingering feeling of repulsion after his talk with Andre. He went to the restroom and washed his face and hands. As he walked back to his desk, he forced himself to think about the needs of the project. He remembered that he had to keep pressure on the Secretary of State to negotiate with the Ecuadorian government for the rights to a site for the Space Elevator. He picked up the phone and dialed her direct number.

"Madam Secretary, this is Jon Walmer. Sorry to bother you, but I must keep abreast of the progress being made with Ecuador."

"Jon, there's no need to be concerned," said the Secretary. The President has made it clear this negotiation is top priority, and I'm not to delegate it. I'm pleased to say I've almost completed the deal, although it's not without some strings you might not like."

"Can you give me a summary?" asked Jon.

"I told the President of Ecuador we want to build a Space Elevator on Achipungo as the first step in our program to send a man to Mars," began the Secretary. "He and his staff know we'll use it to build and sustain a colony on the Moon. Consequently, they're looking to the future, using the Panama Canal as a precedent.

"We'll enter a ninety-nine year lease after which Ecuador will own the Space Elevator. During the lease we'll pay five percent royalties on commercial transport revenues. The site will not be used as a permanent base for the U.S. military, except for the Army Corps of Engineers during construction. U.S. military may be used to supply the site. Security must be by U.S. civilians and Ecuadorian police. Eighty percent of the labor force must be Ecuadorian. The Ecuadorian government will make no announcements about the treaty, and they'll prescreen Ecuadorian workers. Those are the highlights of the treaty being reviewed here and in Ecuador."

"When do you think we might begin a physical survey of the area?" asked Jon. "The satellite images reveal a lot, but for construction to begin, we must send a team of surveyors first."

"I'm sure we'll have it all wrapped-up and official in five weeks," said the Secretary.

"Can't you get me temporary visas for my survey team in a couple of days?" asked Jon.

"You really are in a hurry. Okay, I'm sure we can do that. I'll get right on it. How many people need a visa?" asked the Secretary.

"We'll be arriving in two airships from the ocean side, twenty miles southwest of La Tola on the coast before Molina. There will be a total of twenty-five of us. I'll fax you copies of our passports. If you can get us a mobile phone number from one of the immigration officers, we can contact him as we approach Ecuadorian waters. Captain Sam Garcia speaks fluent Spanish, so he'll be making the call. We'll be there seven days from today. Have the immigration authorities meet us there. They can check our credentials and inspect our cargo as soon as we arrive," said Jon.

"Okay, Jon, I'll get back to you early this evening," said the Secretary.

Jon hung up the phone, paused a moment and picked it back up. He dialed a number methodically and waited as he listened to the ring at the other end. "Tom, Jon here. You ready to take those two airships south again?"

"I didn't think you'd get that treaty so soon," said Tom.

"I didn't," said Jon. "I got a promise we'd have twenty-five visas in a couple of days for the purpose of completing an initial survey. I said you'd be south of La Tola in seven days. Does that leave you enough time to prepare and gather the crew?"

"The two airships are already staged at the Marathon Key Coast Guard Station," said Tom. "The cargo is en route from the warehouse. The crew has been notified to get to southern Florida ASAP and remain in standby mode; full pay, all expenses paid while they await the signal to assemble at the Coast Guard Station. I made arrangements at a resort in Duck Key where I'll be meeting them. We can be airborne to La Tola three days from today. It will take us a little over twenty hours of flight time to reach our rendezvous point with the Ecuadorian authorities. Figure four days total. You gave us seven."

"That's fine," said Jon. "I don't expect to get the visas by tomorrow. Contact your crew and make sure everyone faxes a copy of their passports to Howard at AIEDA Home Office today. He'll assemble them and fax them to the Secretary of State."

"Jon, on my previous expedition, I was employed by Jean Philippe. I don't mind saving the planet, but I need to pay my bills while I do it."

"I understand, Tom. What if I offer you the same contract you had with Jean Philippe?"

"That's fine. I'll send you a copy," said Tom.

"Okay, I'll call as soon as I hear we have the visas. I'll have the Secretary send them overnight to the Coast Guard Station. Should I have them sent to your attention?" asked Jon.

"No, send them to the attention of Lieutenant Williams."

"How do you feel about the expeditionary plan Aieda prepared for you?" asked Jon.

"Frankly, I'm a bit worried," said Tom. "In Antarctica, we went through a lot of trouble to avoid winds from the mountains. Our base of operations was in the plains. Now we're being told to make a base near the peak of Mt. Achipungo which is 15,186 feet above sea level, and to explore the heights of Achipungo which are a series of non-volcanic peaks. Aieda hasn't allayed any of my fears that a gust of wind off the slopes of any one of those peaks could be catastrophic."

"Aieda says you'll be safe as long as you ascend via the southwest face of Achipungo," said Jon.

"I know what she said," countered Tom. "She got her information from reports by rock climbers saying how calm the weather is on that side. Rock climbers aren't on the mountain every day of the year, and they don't present a broadside as big and light as an airship. An unexpected gust could smash us into the side of the mountain. The airships can easily maintain a 20,000 foot altitude with full cargo. That's safely above the highest peak. Ask Aieda to consider the alternate plan of our airships coming in from above Mt. Achipungo, rather than ascending the southwest slope."

"Tom, why don't I have Aieda call you so you can discuss it directly with her?" asked Jon.

"Good idea. I forgot how humanly interactive she is. I'll wait for her call," said Tom.

———————◇———————

Jon met Aieda the next morning at Central Command in North Branch. It didn't take them long to make the holocom connection with Roger at the Lodge in Estes Park.

"Roger! How's life in Colorado?" asked Jon.

"Life's good, thank you; especially here at the Lodge. I could retire here quite easily if it weren't for my job and my wife," said Roger.

"Hello, Roger," said Aieda. "Jon wanted to be involved in our daily discussion. I haven't told him any details of our progress, so you might want to fill him in."

"Jon, Aieda and I think we have a solution, but first I need to define the problem for you," said Roger. "As you know, the stability of a trans-dimensional propulsion system depends on the relative mass of the structure being transmuted and the effective mass of the black holes used to create a rift in the fabric of space-time. The mass of the structure needs to be less than or equal to the effective mass of the black holes or else the rift is unstable and the structure can't pass through it into the fifth dimension.

"Also, the center of gravity of the structure needs to be close to the coordinates of where the rift begins to open. To an extent we can use the electromagnetic beam, our so called Magna-beam, to control where the rift opens. We can position the rift pretty close to the center of gravity of the earth-moon structure, but it needs to be more precise than what we can achieve, due to the mass imbalance between the earth and the moon. The mass of the earth with its imbedded black hole is just too big relative to the moon and the six small black holes we'll configure on the Moon Base."

"I've understood that to be the problem all along. I was hoping the six black holes planned for the moon could be enlarged just enough to solve the problem," said Jon.

"According to our mathematical models, we've enlarged them as much as possible," said Aieda. "The only solution is dangerous, and it must be done with precision of placement and timing."

"Jon, we need three nuclear x-ray laser pumping weapons aimed at the point along the Magna-beam where the center of gravity would be located if the earth and moon were roughly the same mass," explained Roger. "This point is halfway between the center of the earth and the center of the moon. The three weapons must be fired simultaneously at exactly the right moment."

"Why would these weapons stabilize the rift?" asked Jon. "The x-ray laser beam would be a single pulse. No weapon of its kind can sustain either a continuous beam or rapid-fire pulses."

"The combined x-ray laser pulses of the three weapons aimed at the same spot will open the rift in space-time in the same way a large mass creates a gravity-well," said Roger. "Consequently, for just a moment, the rift will be positioned at a stable center of gravity; that is, not in an offset position. At that moment the Magna-beam can capture and contain the rift in the necessary position until it opens wide enough."

"Wide enough for what?" asked Jon.

"Wide enough to charge the two spherical capacitors that Aieda designed," said Roger. "Within the Magna-beam there will be one sphere on either side of the rift. As the Guardian explained, there will be a natural flow of energy from the fifth dimension into the spherical capacitors until they're full. This flow of energy will help stabilize the rift in its unnatural position. As soon as the capacitors are 90% full, the polarity will be switched, and they'll blast all their stored energy back into the rift, causing it to rip open wide enough for both the earth and moon to be sucked into the fifth dimension."

"Okay, but I recall that to maintain position within the fifth dimension, we must rely on a power source to keep the structural system electrostatically charged. How do we do that?" asked Jon.

"Fortunately, the earth has a powerful electromagnetic field that will supply almost all the energy we need," explained Aieda. "The rest of the energy we'll have stored in a farm of spherical capacitors on the moon. The fusion reactors will not only fill the capacitors before the trans-dimensional jump, but they'll continue to fill them after the jump. The electrostatic energy needed to keep the earth-moon system inside the fifth dimension will be released from the capacitor farm onto the outer surface of the Magna-beam where it'll act to keep the system stabilized within the boundary layer of the fifth dimension."

"How sure are you this will work?" asked Jon.

"Aieda has created a holographic computer simulation based on her theories," stated Roger. "By varying a number of parameters, we can see how the computerized model responds. So far the model has responded exactly as predicted."

"Is there any way we can create a scale model and test it?" asked Jon.

"We'd have to test it in a weightless environment, which means launching a satellite," said Aieda.

"We'd also have to use three of our six available black holes," said Roger. "They'd be the Roswell orbiting pair and one of the Roswell singles."

"Roger, I need you full-time now. I'm sure we can agree on adequate compensation. I need you to manage the development of this prototype from the lab being built at the Lodge. Are you game?" asked Jon.

"Yes, of course," responded Roger. "I can't think of anything more important than saving the planet. However, you seem to have more confidence in me than I have in myself."

"Roger," said Aieda. "I've worked with you closely, and I, too, have great confidence in your ability to manage this effort."

"That means a lot to me, Aieda. Thank you," said Roger.

"There's enough room in the subbasement of the Lodge for your development lab," said Jon. "You'll be sharing the space with Don, who's been managing the fusion reactor development project. I think you and your wife should move to the Lodge as soon as possible."

"I'll work on the plans for a working scale model of the system, and I'll provide a materials and components list, as well as a skills profile for the requisite engineers and technicians," said Aieda. "I'll assume the model's modules will be launched into orbit and assembled by NASA."

"Amanda is our liaison with NASA, so every detail and every requirement must be coordinated with her," said Jon. "I don't want anyone diluting her authority over NASA by having direct discussions without her presence or, in her absence, without her permission."

"Jon, would you mind if I went on sabbatical rather than resigning from the university; at least for the first year to see how we're progressing?" asked Roger.

"No problem. Sabbatical is a good way to do it," said Jon. "There will be no charge for you to live at the Lodge, and if you want, take two adjoining suites for your living quarters."

"Thanks, Jon. That's generous of you. I'll contact Amanda and Don so we can kick off the prototype development," said Roger.

Jon was tired from the coordination he'd been doing all day. It seemed endless, but he resolved to make one more call today. He picked up the red phone which recently had been networked for the first time to a phone outside his company. He picked it up, dialed a code, and was happy to find the President in the Oval Office.

"Hello, Jon, is everything okay?" asked the President.

"Yes and no, sir. It seems our grand plan requires three nuclear-powered x-ray laser weapons," explained Jon.

"I've heard of them, but I don't think we have any operational. We have no treaty banning space weapons, but we haven't deployed any either," said the President.

"Mr. President, you may recall SDI, the Strategic Defense Initiative, commonly referred to as Star Wars. Part of that effort was the development of a weapon envisioned by Dr. Edward Teller. The weapon focused the blast of a nuclear explosion much like a laser, except the destruction came not from a light beam, but rather from an x-ray beam. I bet we have those weapons in storage ready to be deployed. I suspect the only reason they stayed in the warehouse is because of the rapid collapse of the Soviet Union and the resulting end to the cold war."

"You may be right," said the President. "I'll find out. How will you be using these weapons?"

"We'll be deploying them in space halfway between the earth and the moon," said Jon. "Don't worry; they won't be aimed at the earth."

"My God!" said the President. "Is there no other way? We'd become the first to weaponize outer space. Our actions could result in another kind of nuclear arms race."

"Mr. President, our inaction in this matter could result in the destruction of the planet," said Jon.

"Okay, Jon. I hear you. I'll check it out and get back to you. However, if these babies exist, I can't turn them directly over to you. You can deploy them as you see fit, but they must be under Air Force security control during the entire deployment process and afterwards."

"Thank you, Mr. President," said Jon as he hung up the receiver to the red phone.

Jon was tired. His mind wandered away from work and picked up happy thoughts of his ex-wife, Catherine. It was every bit his fault that they divorced. He had put his work first to the point of neglecting Catherine. She was right when she explained the relationship was gone years before she asked for a divorce. He was wrong. He could have built the AIEDA organization while being careful to nurture his marriage. He wished he had tried. Neither he nor Catherine had remarried. The thought fleetingly crossed his mind . . . *could he win her back?* Knowledge of the end of the world sure makes one rethink things. He promised himself he'd give Catherine a call.

————————————◇————————————

The next day in the office Jon got a call from Aieda. She ran so many programs at the same time, it was impossible to remember everything she'd been tasked. Consequently, she tended to surprise AIEDA personnel when she spontaneously reported a result or conclusion outside of the context of the moment.

"Jon, the Web Bot program has detected a social anomaly of interest," said Aieda.

"The Web Bot program?" asked Jon with a frown.

"Yes, it's a program that monitors all traffic on the Internet and on all wireless communications networks," explained Aieda. "It looks for social patterns, such as demographic changes, political changes, public perception changes, changes in buying and spending habits for various areas of the world and groups of people, and it tries to reach a statistically confident conclusion about the trends."

"And what conclusion has it come to?" asked Jon.

"A small but significant percentage of the world's population is against the manned mission to Mars. A fanatical underground organization is stirring up discontent with the Mars mission, and the end result will be violence," said Aieda.

"Why are they so concerned about going to Mars?" asked Jon.

"It would appear many religious groups believe there must first be an Armageddon, if there is to come the 1000 year Rapture," explained Aieda. "If mankind were to escape to the Moon or Mars, the fate of mankind could be altered. These religious zealots believe it's their duty to help fulfill prophesies in the Holy Scriptures."

"We've already put a man on the Moon. Why the concern now?" asked Jon.

"Now that private enterprise is involved with the effort, colonization of other worlds seems more likely than ever," explained Aieda. "Also, the year 2012 is viewed by many to be the end of our current civilization and the beginning of a new one. It's a year made significant by both Nostradamus and the Mayan Calendar."

"Is the project in any immediate danger?" asked Jon.

"The Web Bot indicates that strong caution is advised and security measures be taken to prevent violent attacks and sabotage," responded Aieda.

Chapter 23

March 2006

Tom Calvano and his crew had a chance to relax at the resort in Duck Key while they waited for the survey team and equipment to arrive at the Coast Guard Station in Marathon Key. The two airships were already at the station being prepped by Lt. Williams and his team for the flight to Ecuador.

Tom had rented a villa so his team could be together for a few days. He believed the best team-building was done in the off-hours when people were relaxed. The warmth of the sun, the blue-green waters, the bottle-nosed dolphins, and the cool sea breeze all helped to get everyone in the spirit of working together on a mission that could be exhausting and dangerous.

Aieda had agreed it was okay for Tom to approach Mt. Achipungo in the airships from above, rather than by flying up the southwest face, as she had proposed. Tom was still not completely comfortable with the idea of flying airships around mountain peaks.

From the satellite imaging, they had identified half a dozen semi-flat areas between peaks that needed to be studied by the survey team to determine suitability based on strict criteria. The stability and hardness of the rock formations were of paramount importance because they would provide the solid foundation needed to anchor the Space Elevator's cable to Mother Earth.

Aieda's selection of an equatorial launch site would provide a substantial fuel savings over rockets launched from higher latitudes into geosynchronous earth orbits. The launch would bypass a transfer orbit and would put the cable directly into geosynchronous orbit.

Access to the construction site was also a consideration because of the millions of tons of concrete and steel that would be needed to construct the Space Elevator with its structure rising a mile into the sky to stand majestically amid the towering peaks of the Achipungo range.

Tom understood why the site they were seeking had to have specific characteristics. There were only three ways to get the cable into geosynchronous orbit with the other end anchored to the earth. One way would be to manufacture the cable in orbit and drop it down to earth, but that would be difficult and costly. Another way would be to launch the cable into orbit on a reel, then unwind it down to earth, but 22,000 miles of cable would make such a big reel it would be next to impossible to launch it in one piece. The cable would have to be launched in many sections, and the connectors would cause a number of technical problems.

The third method would be to uncoil the cable from a container on the ground by dragging the top end of the cable into orbit. This preferred method would use one continuous coiled cable in a cylindrical container 560 yards in diameter, secured firmly in the ground. The loose end of the cable would be secured to the center of a configuration of five Delta IV Heavy rockets with a shield designed to protect the cable from the heat of the burning propellants.

Although this last method was the best of the three, it required a site with sufficient room for a huge rocket launch pad, the giant tower for the Space Elevator, and the extremely large container for the cable.

Despite the altitude, snow wouldn't be a concern for the survey team. The primary exploratory vehicles would be four-wheel ATV's to allow the team to easily traverse the rocky uneven terrain. In addition, they would have a compact 4-wheel drive truck to carry geologists and their equipment.

The leisure time and team-building were over. Tom gathered his crew and arranged for them to meet the survey team at the Coast Guard Station in the morning.

---------------------◇---------------------

"Lieutenant Williams, it's nice to see you again. I trust you have both airships fully ready for me and my crew," said Tom as he extended his hand to the lieutenant.

Lt. Williams shook Tom's hand with a broad smile and said, "Yes, sir, the Ranger and Pallas are both ready for your command. I also have twenty-five visas for Ecuador that were delivered by special State Department courier yesterday. Have another confidential assignment, sir?"

"I'm flattered you remembered the names I gave the ships," commented Tom. "I'll satisfy your curiosity, Lieutenant, but keep it to yourself. It's not top secret, but we don't want it getting out to the press. This mission is part of the NASA manned mission to Mars. You may have heard that the mission will be a joint venture with NASA and a private consortium. My mission is to survey the heights of Achipungo in Ecuador for the ideal site to build a Space Elevator to the moon. Do you know what that is, Lieutenant?"

"Yes, sir! It's science fiction become science fact," said Lt. Williams. "The first time I heard about it was in a novel by Arthur C. Clarke. I thought we were a century away from being able to accomplish that. Maybe on Mars with its lower gravity, but with the gravity of earth . . . I never would have guessed."

"Let's go pass out the visas and give the crew a refresher before we take off. Anything new been installed?" asked Tom.

"No, sir, there's nothing new. We have a number of improvements on the drawing board, but there's been insufficient time to get them operational," responded Lt. Williams, as they both walked toward the closest hangar.

It wasn't long before both the Ranger and the Pallas were airborne and on their way to Ecuador. This survey mission was to a more hospitable place than Antarctica, so each airship was carrying no more than five tons of cargo, including passengers. This time Tom wouldn't be so cautious about getting close to Cuba. Flying light and high at 100 mph, he would fly through the Yucatan Channel between Mexico and Cuba. Then they would drop down to 10,000 feet and continue cruising at eighty-five mph over the Caribbean Sea, across Panama and down the Pacific Coast to Ecuador.

The flight was uneventful except for the fact that it had taken an hour longer than anticipated, but twenty-one hours in good weather wasn't hard, and the railcar-like reclining chairs were comfortable for sleeping. It had been agreed that the Ecuadorian immigration authorities would plant the flag of Ecuador off the coast road south of La Tola. The officers would be waiting in a white van. Sam Garcia, captain of the Pallas, spoke fluent Spanish, so it became his job to call the Ecuadorian officer in charge when they approached the coast.

When Sam made the call, the officer said he could see them approaching in the distance. Tom had decided that the Pallas would anchor first and use the elevator to escort the officers onboard where all crew and passengers would present their visas, and the cargo would be inspected. When the officers were finished with the Pallas, she broke anchor and the Ranger moved in position to repeat the process.

Everything went as planned, so both airships began the voyage over the mountainous terrain of Ecuador. Their flight path went south of Quito, the capital, toward Guano, then into the Sangay National Park, west of Macas. The mountains within the park were part of the Eastern Andean Mountain Range, and within it was the Sangay Volcano. It was active and known for eruptions a couple of times per hour. Rising south of the Sangay Volcano, there were a number of mountain peaks made of non-volcanic rock. One of these was Mt. Achipungo. The many peaks in the area were often referred to as the heights of Achipungo.

Several potential sites were selected from satellite images and terrain maps. Aieda had studied the geological data on the Sangay Volcano and had determined that the Space Elevator wouldn't be affected by an eruption if the site were anywhere south of Mt. Achipungo. To speed up the survey process, Tom directed the Ranger to explore sites on the southwestern side of Mt. Achipungo and the Pallas to the southeastern side. At the end of each day they would decide on a common area to anchor with sufficient distance between the airships to avoid collisions due to unexpected wind gusts.

Tom told Jeff Teichman and Ron Caldorf they would be exploring the southwestern area with him, each on separate ATV's. Sam Garcia had mentioned he'd be taking Harvey Watson and two others to explore the southeastern side. As a precaution, Tom required the Ranger, the Pallas, Garcia's squad, and his squad to do status checks over their com-units every half hour.

Without mentioning it, Tom unobtrusively attached the soft leather case for his hunting rifle to the right side of his ATV, then slid the rifle into the case and zipped it. He was sure nobody saw him. The case was in clear sight, but he was counting on the fact that everyone was too preoccupied with their own preparations to notice it. If he had the chance, he was dead set on bagging a buck or mountain goat for dinner tonight, cooked over an open fire. He knew fresh fire-roasted meat would be a big morale booster. Besides, he'd been so busy these last couple of years that hunting was getting to be a distant memory, and these wilderness mountains made a perfect hunting ground.

The search for the best construction site began in earnest. Everyone knew what they were looking for. It had to be a vast plain with good drainage, nestled between peaks with good access from the valley below. The floor of the plain had to be made of thick, solid non-volcanic rock. Tom and his squad rode three abreast in their ATV's most of the time, but occasionally the terrain between peaks became so narrow they had to ride single file.

They stopped to rest on a small plateau with a beautiful lake that spilled itself over the edge in a waterfall 500 feet to the valley below. Many of the lakes in the area were created some ten thousand years ago by the downward movement of glaciers. Tom checked the terrain maps and decided the river must be the Rio Bermejo. It was one of the most beautiful sights he'd ever seen. Unfortunately, it was too small and too wet.

They moved on to a site that Aieda said was most promising. They had already been traveling for three hours. It was slow going among the streams and boulders. Finally, they arrived at the suggested site. It was impressive in its expanse, and it was dry as a bone. It appeared to the eye that the floor of this plateau was solid rock. The survey team would have to verify its suitability with their sonar soundings. Off to the west edge of the plateau looking downward in the distance was the spectacular sight of the Lagunas de Osogoche, a group of lakes which included Lake Magtayan and the giant Lake Cubillin.

They took extensive pictures of the site and collected surface soil samples for analysis. He knew this was the right place for the Space Elevator. He would lead the survey team here tomorrow to do a detailed three dimensional terrain map, including a subsurface sonar map, and core samples of the bedrock. Except for small ground animals and birds, Tom had not seen any wild deer or goats. *Well, maybe on the way back,* he thought. Just then Ron Caldorf pulled up beside him.

"What's that, boss? You carrying a shot gun?" asked Ron who had noticed the case before, but was waiting for the right time to ask.

"No, it's a rifle; .270 caliber Remington pump with a nine-power scope," responded Tom.

"You expecting some sort of trouble our sidearms can't handle?" asked Ron.

Tom had insisted every member of his crew be trained in small arms marksmanship. Once they had passed immigration at La Tola, he insisted all twelve of his crew carry a holstered Smith and Wesson 38 Special Combat Masterpiece which he'd provided. He'd heard from reliable sources that within the mountainous regions of Ecuador were communities suspicious of outsiders, and some would almost certainly attempt to hinder their passage, rob them, or even kill them. By coming in over the mountaintops in airships into the remotest of regions, he believed he'd probably avoid any confrontation, but he wanted the extra edge of having his men armed.

"No, actually, I was hoping to bag a deer or goat for dinner tonight, so keep your eyes peeled on the way back," said Tom.

On the way back, when Tom and his squad were about forty minutes from where the Ranger was anchored, they stopped for a break. He wasn't expecting another round of status checks for ten minutes, so when his com-unit woke up with Sam Garcia's panicky voice, he was doubly startled.

"Tom, we're in trouble!" yelled Sam. "Taking rifle fire from snipers. Can't move."

"Anybody hurt? Can you hold them off?" asked Tom.

"We're okay for now, but we have to keep our heads down," said Sam.

"I have an idea, but you'll have to hold out for at least an hour. I don't think the guys at the Pallas will be much help. I'm the only one with a high powered rifle. Hang in there, Sam. I'm coming as fast as I can," said Tom.

"Okay, boss. We ain't going nowhere," said Sam. "I'm texting our GPS coordinates over the com network. Be careful. We think there are at least three of them located north of us."

Tom, Jeff, and Ron got back to the Ranger in record time. The rest of the crew heard everything over the open com line and had her ready to go. For safety reasons, the survey crew had been asked to hike on over to where the Pallas was anchored. The plan was to come up from behind the sniper positions. If they couldn't locate each sniper, Sam would be asked to draw their fire.

Traveling at almost 100 mph, they maneuvered the Ranger behind a peak and in line with the sniper positions on the other side. Fortunately, Tom remembered the airships had a stealth mode for the turboprops, so they could whisper with a gentle breeze moving the airship as slow as five mph. Tom gave the order to go into stealth mode and move slowly around the west side of the peak. He knew he could be risking the Ranger and everyone onboard. If the snipers got lucky and hit some critical areas of the ship, they'd have to ditch. With Sam and his squad pinned-down, he saw no alternative. Tom positioned himself starboard and forward on the catwalk around the elevator's gondola where he had the clearest view and a flat railing to support his arms as he took aim. He had his headset on and the com-unit on the open channel.

"Sam, I don't see them. Do something to draw fire!" said Tom.

He'd no sooner finished his sentence when the three snipers opened fire and gave away their position to him. He took a bead on the closest one, who turned his head and looked right at him. Tom saw his jaw drop open at the sight of the airship quietly bearing down on him. The first round must have gone into his open mouth as the back of his head blew out and made a red mess on the side of the boulder behind him. Then Tom got the second sniper, again with one shot. He used two shots to kill the third one.

"Sam, it looks clear. I got three of them," said Tom into his headset.

"Harv's been hit. He's still breathing, but it looks bad. Get the medic down here ASAP!" yelled Sam into the open com.

"Okay, Sam, we've picked a spot to anchor in the field just fifty yards east of your position. The medic will be there in ten minutes," responded Tom.

Tom and the medic rode the elevator down one-hundred feet to the ground and made a mad dash to where Harv lay injured. As the medic went to work, Tom asked Sam, "What happened? I thought you had good cover behind these boulders."

"When you asked me to draw their fire, I ran to that boulder over there," explained Sam. "As soon as I got there, I turned and saw Harv lying on his back, not moving. I ran to him immediately, but I couldn't do anything for him, Tom. A ricochet or a fragment of rock blew out his right eye. I couldn't do anything for him. For God's sake, Tom, he got hit in the eye. What if it's in his brain?" asked Sam hysterically.

"Calm down, Sam. It's not your fault. You did what had to be done," said Tom.

Tom looked over to where the medic was leaning over Harv. The medic turned slowly, looked at Tom, and shook his head with a grim expression.

"I'm sorry. He's gone," said the medic. "We should get him to the Ranger."

"Right," said Tom. "We'll also need to retrieve the bodies of the snipers and check the area for clues about who these guys might be. I'll call Jon so he can get the State Department to clear us with the Ecuadorian authorities. They can take care of the bodies and open an investigation. I'd like to know why those guys opened fire without provocation. I'll ask Jon to inform Harv's wife and take care of all the funeral arrangements. We should try to get back home to attend the memorial service for Harv."

"What about the mission?" asked Sam.

"I'm the one who shot those three guys, so the authorities are more likely to want to interrogate me," responded Tom. "I'll take the bodies in the Ranger to meet the authorities in an agreed-upon place outside of Cuenca in the valley below. Sam, you take Ron, Jeff, and the entire survey crew with you in the Pallas to Aieda's southwestern site and complete the mission. Transmit all the data to Jon at the home office."

———————◇———————

It took seven days for Tom and his crew to deal with the Ecuadorian authorities. They flew the Ranger back to Marathon Key, and found the Pallas had just arrived, after completing the survey mission. When Tom and Jon discussed Harv's death, they agreed it was important to get security into the area, soon after the deployment of the Army Corps of Engineers.

Jon decided the inimitable Andre might be up to the task, so he gave him a call. "Andre, it's Jon. How are you?"

"No matter how I am, my friend, I'll be better if you have news of good progress," said Andre in his Parisian accent.

"Well, it's a mixed bag," said Jon. "We have a site for the Space Elevator. Sadly, we've lost a man, Harvey Watson. He was shot by snipers while in the mountains of Ecuador on the survey mission. It's disturbing, to say the least. I'll be visiting his wife to inform her, today."

"I'm so sorry to hear of that. Do you have any idea who are these assassins?" asked Andre.

"No, not yet, but Tom Calvano suspects they might be locals who don't like strangers moving into their tribal grounds," said Jon. "The State Department will be working with the Ecuadorian authorities to coordinate an investigation. I'm now doubly worried for the safety of anyone we send there to work on this project. We need security personnel fast, and lots of them."

"So, you think I can help you with this security?" asked Andre.

"The Ecuadorian government has insisted the treaty for leasing the site include a provision specifying U.S. security must be civilian. They don't want foreign military combat troops in their country. They've accepted the U.S. Army Corps of Engineers, but no combat military," explained Jon.

"How many security personnel do you need?" asked Andre.

"Five thousand," said Jon.

"You joke with me, of course," said Andre. "How could you possibly come up with such a large number?"

"Andre, this operation is 24/7 . . . day and night every single day. Not even a holiday shutdown," said Jon. "That means four shifts of workers, supervisors, and security personnel. I calculate the need for 1,250 security people per shift. The main base will encompass four square miles, and there are three-hundred miles of road from Port Bolivar at Machala, past Cuenca, and on up to the base. Men and equipment will be traveling those roads 24/7, and they'll need protection."

"Okay, okay, you've made your point," said Andre. "What types of vehicles and weapons will they need?"

"Tom told me that troopers assigned to the area of the base will need 950 ATV's. And those assigned to the roads will need 300 supermoto motorcycles; one of the bigger ones, like the KTM 990SM," said Jon. "As to weapons, Tom says each trooper needs a Colt M1911 Series 80 .45 caliber automatic pistol and a Colt AR-15 automatic rifle. They'll also need bulletproof vests, helmets, boots, uniforms, binoculars with night vision, com-units, and badges. They must have at least two weeks of police training with the exact weapons and equipment they'll be using."

"Any other requirements?" asked Andre.

"They must be ages twenty-one to fifty-five with weight in proportion to height and with no health issues. Prior military or police experience is preferred. At least 1000 of them must be fluent in Spanish, and they must sign a two year employment contract with a clause requiring them to keep all information about the Space Elevator project confidential."

"That's a tall order, my friend, but I'll see what I can do," said Andre.

"Thanks, Andre," said Jon.

Jon had two more calls to make before he would set off on the emotionally difficult task of personally informing Harv's wife of his death.

"Marla, it's Jon. How are you?"

"I'm doing just fine thank you, Jon," responded Marla. "I trust you're happy with the progress in Ecuador. I heard the treaty has been signed by both countries."

"Actually, I hadn't heard. I'm sure the Secretary of State will be informing me officially soon enough," said Jon. "Marla, I'm saddened to report we lost Harvey Watson in Ecuador. He was shot by a sniper. Tom killed all three of the men who had Sam Garcia's team pinned down."

"Oh, my, I'm so sorry to hear that. I spoke with Harv before he left with Tom for Ecuador. He was such a nice man, and he has a family, too," said Marla in a choked-up voice.

"Marla, I'm planning to have a shit-load of security down there, but it'll never be enough," said Jon. "I know the treaty says we can only have civilian security, but I think we need Special Ops there undercover patrolling the hills and peaks around the site. I also think the U.S Army Corps of Engineers needs to take care of their own security, and they need to do it subtly. Marla, I need you to be there in charge of the Corps and the Special Ops units."

"Jon, I'm flattered, but both the Corps and Special Ops have highly competent field grade officers in charge. I don't know what I would contribute," said Marla.

"Marla, I need you there because you're on my team, and I can talk to you about confidential issues," explained Jon. "I can't do that with strangers no matter how competent they might be. I also need a general grade officer like you there to coordinate the efforts of both military groups with regard to security and to take charge of 5,000 civilian security personnel. You'll have to be an official member of the Corps, and you'll have to work closely with your Ecuadorian counterpart."

"What do you mean by counterpart?" asked Marla.

"There will be many Ecuadorian citizens traveling the roads we'll be using, and many citizens who'll be working construction at the site," said Jon. "We need to be sure from the get-go that we follow local customs and laws, and that we have a high-ranking Ecuadorian police officer intimately involved with our civilian security arrangements. In that way we can be assured of having his support when things get sticky, as they most certainly will. I haven't arranged to get this officer yet, but I'll be calling the Secretary of State soon to do so. Whoever he is, I'll be paying him a salary on top of his regular pay, so I'm sure he'll be helpful to us."

"I see where you're coming from on this," said Marla. "There are elements of trust, confidentiality, command, covertness, and diplomacy. You make it sound challenging. I accept the assignment. However, if we are to expect my Ecuadorian counterpart to be responsible for security, he'll need to have the authority and means to do so. May I suggest the civilian security personnel report directly to him and not to me?"

"Good idea. I'll let Tom know. Thank you for accepting the assignment. Tom thanks you too," said Jon.

Jon had just hung up the phone after talking with Marla when it rang. He picked it up and was surprised to hear the voice of the Secretary of State.

"Madam Secretary, it's good to hear your voice. I was just about to call you," said Jon.

"Jon, I'm calling to let you know the treaty has been accepted by both countries, and it's semi-official. Actually, I'm surprised we got it done this soon. I also want to again express my deepest sympathy for the loss of your friend, Harvey Watson. Our consulate is working with the Ecuadorian authorities to return his remains. Have you informed his wife yet?" asked the Secretary.

"I'll be informing Harv's wife in person this evening, after she gets home from work. Thanks for the good news about the treaty, but what do you mean by *semi-official?*" asked Jon.

"Oh, you know . . . ratification occurs when the President signs the treaty after he receives the Senate's vote of approval. They're fully aware of the Space Elevator Project and the treaty we've been negotiating. It'll be low key with no press. It won't be a problem," said the Secretary.

"The incident with Harv has highlighted the importance of security to me," said Jon. "I'm making arrangements to have civilian guards patrolling the access roads and the site 24/7. However, this means we could unintentionally engender resentment by the local populace with ensuing altercations and unrest. General Odenfelder has agreed to take command of the Army Corps of Engineers, but I feel we need to provide her with a highly respected Ecuadorian counterpart who'll have direct authority over the civilian security personnel. With the right person we should be able to avoid misunderstandings and embarrassing incidents.

"I'm hoping you'll be able to use our consulate to negotiate getting the most respected, competent, and honest person Ecuador might have. He needs to work for Ecuador and in support of our treaty. In addition to his Ecuadorian salary, the consortium will also pay him a salary. He'll need his own staff and a cadre of 100

Ecuadorian police officers who'll work as supervisors, advisors and interpreters for the civilian security personnel."

"I can see you've given this a good bit of thought," said the Secretary. "It's a good proactive approach. I'll ask our consulate to get right on it for you, but you'll need to be patient on this one, because finding the right person for the job won't be easy. Ecuador has been working hard recently cleaning up corruption in government, including the police departments, so there's a lot of confusion and in-fighting now."

"Okay, but the sooner the better," said Jon.

"Oh, another thing," interjected the Secretary. "The preliminary investigation of the three snipers has concluded they were in Ecuador illegally. They're definitely not Ecuadorian citizens. The Ecuadorian federal police detectives believe they're from a Middle East country."

"Yes, I heard. Tom Calvano has been working closely with the Ecuadorian detectives. Tom and I believe it points to a possible mole," said Jon.

"How do you come to that conclusion?" asked the Secretary.

"The survey mission was kept under tight wraps with no news release," said Jon. "We didn't give Tom much advance notice, and he got to Ecuador in record time. What does he find when he gets there, but Middle Eastern assassins ready to ambush his team. They knew right where he was headed. Tom told me he suspects they were members of an extremist organization called the *Preservers of Scripture*, who don't want the Space Elevator to succeed on religious grounds. He crossed paths with them in Brazil in 2003 and almost lost his life. They include Christians, Muslims, and Jews who believe they must help bring about the end of days. They fear man's escape to the Moon and Mars might circumvent the prophecies."

"Where do you think this mole might be?" asked the Secretary.

"In any number of places . . . NASA, OSTP, AIEDA, Marseilles Electric, perhaps even within the State Department," responded Jon.

"I don't think the mole is in State. The President asked me to take care of this personally, so I managed a small staff of six to get it done quickly," commented the Secretary in a somewhat defensive tone.

"What about the Senate? There are one-hundred senators and their staff who know about the treaty," said Jon.

"The treaty was just sent to them. Their prior knowledge was simply about a site in Ecuador. The mole had more precise information," said the Secretary.

"Within AIEDA Risk Mitigation I compartmentalize projects and information so people know only what they're working on and don't know anything about the big picture. I use small configuration management teams to ensure that separate projects or components integrate well together. Within the company there's only a handful who might have known details about the Ecuadorian site selection process," said Jon.

"May I suggest that the most likely place for a mole is NASA," said the Secretary.

"And why is that?" asked Jon.

"They had to be involved with site selection because of their technical knowledge and previous conceptual exercises for the building of a Space Elevator. In addition, that group harbors the most resentment toward your consortium for taking away their authority and leadership for the manned mission to Mars," said the Secretary.

"Good point. I'll warn Dr. Rheinhardt about our suspicions," said Jon.

"I'll get our consulate working on finding that exceptional Ecuadorian police commander for you. Goodbye, Jon," said the Secretary.

"Goodbye, Madam Secretary."

Chapter 24

Stellar-Mass Anomaly . . .
crossing the orbit of Pluto
April 2007

The Army Corps of Engineers had been on assignment in Ecuador for almost a year, building access roads and facilities to accommodate thousands of workers. Existing roads were adequate from the bay in southern Ecuador near Machala through the mountain passes to Cuenca, then on to Rivera. Beyond Rivera the Corps built fifty miles of road up the side of the mountain to the site of the Space Elevator Base.

Cement carrier ships were filled in the Houston, TX ship channel for the long trip through the Panama Canal to Bolivar Port in Machala, where the cement was unloaded to a concrete batch plant. The concrete mix was then transferred to mixer trucks, and delivered to the base.

Tom kept busy organizing the workers who had been pouring into the newly constructed base for months, as preparation for the construction of the elevator structure began. Tom had only ten and a half months to build the foundation and tower for the Space Elevator, the launch pad and facilities for the Delta rockets, and the giant concrete cable container. The cable conveyor and cable container had to be completed first because it would take special equipment and six months just to haul the cable up the mountain and coil it properly into the container.

Only recently was it determined that the necessary height of the container would adversely affect the cost and delivery time of the coiling device that would lay the cable into the container. Aieda redesigned the coil containment system to include two half-height containers instead of one full-height container. A six foot wide vertical slit in each container would face each other so the cable could easily be laid from the top of the first container into the bottom of the second container. Each container would be 560 yards in diameter and fifty feet tall.

A project like this would be impossible to complete in the time available, except for the fact that Aieda had done the detailed design work in record time. Consequently, the tower and launch facilities were built, tested, disassembled, and loaded on cargo ships awaiting departure orders.

Construction crews began assembling the cable conveyor alongside the road to the base. The conveyor was like a 300 mile clothesline that would hold the launch-cable beneath it; hanging from what looked a bit like clothes pins.

Aieda had developed a manufacturing process for the Space Elevator's cable that could turn out 2.2 million miles of special bucky-tube filaments per day. Because the cable needed a lot more material at the top than at the bottom to support the working load on it without breaking, these filaments would have a seven to one taper ratio; that is, each 22,300 mile long filament would be seven times thicker at the top than at the bottom.

The initial cable launched into orbit would contain 5,000 tapered filaments bunched together, not twisted nor braided, making the cable five inches thick at the bottom and thirty-five inches thick at the top. A new proprietary property of the bucky-tube filaments caused them to bind together like Velcro at the molecular level when squeezed together with the specified force.

Subsequent to the orbital insertion of the initial cable, crawler machines would move up the cable on a one way trip, adding multiple filaments from bottom to top. At the top, the crawlers would be staged for use as a counter-balance for the orbiting end of the cable. Crawlers would move up the cable adding filaments until the bottom of the cable would measure thirty-five inches in diameter and the top of the cable would measure 20.42 feet in diameter.

Cable manufacturing was expected to start in two weeks, and the initial launch-cable was expected to be delivered in four months. The method of delivery was unprecedented. There weren't enough barges available to deliver the 22,300 mile long launch cable. It would have required almost 375 Marmac-400 oceangoing barges.

Fortunately, the cable would float nicely in salt water, and it wouldn't be corroded by the salt. The cable would be confined in a net and pulled by five tugboats. Then it would be uncoiled and hoisted out of the ocean onto the cable conveyor.

After the launch of the initial cable into geosynchronous orbit, it would take the crawlers another fourteen months to thicken the cable.

———————————◊———————————

Dr. Amanda Rheinhardt was finding her new job to be quite a challenge. There was much more political maneuvering than she'd ever experienced in the U.S. Geological Survey. The resentment of her imposed authority over NASA was palpable. She wanted this job, and now that she had it, she found herself having to give herself little pep talks to firm up her confidence and resolve. She was used to being around Ph.D.'s, but never a group covering so many diverse disciplines.

Every day at every meeting someone zapped her with a gotcha question. She was doing a creditable job so far, but she knew the writing was on the wall . . . She would inevitably slip up, and the frenzy to have her lunch handed to her would begin. She needed an edge, but what? It hit her in the shower one night when a thought crossed her mind . . . *too bad I don't have Aieda's intellect and knowledge; that would shock those prima donnas.* It quickly dawned on her that a wireless earpiece covered by her hair and a wireless microphone hidden in a brooch could give her constant access to Aieda.

Over the weekend she got the earpiece and brooch and tested it with Aieda. On Monday she was ready. The difference was amazing. Previously she'd been barely able to respond intelligently to some of the questions; she even had resorted to using the diversion trick . . . asking someone else in the room what his thoughts were on the matter. This diversion could only be used occasionally. Now she no longer needed it.

She was able to fire back with a difficult question of her own, using the appropriate jargon. Sometimes she would fire the question and not even understand it, but Aieda was quick to interpret it in her ear while the stunned recipient was stammering for a response.

When everyone realized they couldn't rattle her or snow her, they began to focus on the project and not on trying to depose her.

Amanda had reorganized NASA resources into three divisions. The first was to maintain existing launch and scientific research commitments without interfering with the second and third divisions. The second was the launch facility and rocket cluster for the site in Ecuador which was to proceed as quickly as possible without interfering with the third division.

The third division was to develop the moon sleds and contents and to launch them as soon as possible. The objective was to place onto the face of the moon all the structural materials and tools necessary to build the Catcher's Mitt, a structure that looked like a large spiral funnel with its mouth extending one mile above the lunar surface. The Catcher's Mitt would literally catch the cargo containers that were launched toward the moon from the Space Elevator in Ecuador. The gravity of the moon, being one-sixth of earth's, would make it much easier to erect tall structures like the Catcher's Mitt.

The cargo containers launched from the Space Elevator would have small compressed-air propulsion units that would decelerate and guide them right into the mouth of the Catcher's Mitt, which emitted a homing signal that the containers locked onto. A magnetic field on the inside of the Mitt would center the descending containers and prevent them from bumping into the walls of the Mitt as they spiraled down to the lunar surface onto a maglev conveyor belt that further reduced their speed, then shuttled them slowly to a safe staging area far off to the side.

The shock-absorbing sleds that carried all the components to build the Catcher's Mitt were designed so they, too, were structural components. They would each be launched from Kennedy Space Center on a Delta IV Heavy rocket into a low degrading orbit around the moon. Two pivoting propulsion units on each sled would guide it down to the surface where it would hit the ground and skid to a stop.

It was critical to select a landing site without boulders or rocks big enough to damage the sled or its contents. To improve the odds of a safe sled touch-down, the first sled contained a small robotic bulldozer capable of clearing a landing-strip from boulders as large as two feet in diameter. The robot was also capable of planting an explosive charge on boulders larger than two feet in diameter and detonating them remotely. Subsequent sleds would not only carry structural materials, but would also carry supplies and inflatable housing for the androids who would be building the Mitt.

Amanda had an awkward time deflecting the questions from NASA personnel about the plan for construction workers on the moon. They wanted to know how they would get there, what space suits they'd be wearing, how many workers would there be, etc. Amanda kept repeating that lunar plans were being managed by a company in the consortium, and there was no need for them to know details. In reality, she knew the truth would be unbelievable to them. She knew she couldn't explain the Guardian, his cruiser, and his 1,000 androids.

Fortunately Guardian had plenty of spacesuits and food tablets for his army of droids. He could cram a droid pilot and two droid passengers in his cruiser with a supply of water and food tablets. It would take 500 round trips at thirty minutes each to shuttle his 1,000 androids to the moon. That would be at least ten days.

The first trip would carry one droid and an inflatable housing unit. The first droid would inflate and secure the housing unit so that the next two droids would have an initial shelter. Three droids were enough to unpack additional housing units from a sled that would precede them to the moon. At the end of ten days there would be a colony of androids on the moon living in inflatable interconnected shelters. From this colony the droids would unload sleds and begin erecting the Catcher's Mitt.

Once both the Mitt and the Space Elevator were completed, the cargo containers would begin arriving on the moon cheaply and regularly. The cargo containers and their contents would be used to build a huge underground ecologically balanced habitat called the Ecosthat. Within this habitat engineers and scientists would assemble the trans-dimensional propulsion system. They would be building something with little understanding of its purpose, because Jon Walmer and his team had gone to great lengths to prevent anyone outside the team from learning the nature of the solution to the greatest threat ever to humanity.

———————————————◇———————————————

Amanda was at Edwards Air Force Base in California. She had just witnessed a test of the first sled that would arrive on the moon. It was the one carrying the robotic bulldozer and was therefore the most important sled, as it would clear a runway for all the other sleds to be dropped safely onto the moon's surface. Everything worked as designed, including the destruction of a large boulder by an explosive charge planted adeptly by the robotic bulldozer's two arm-like appendages. Yet, Amanda wasn't happy. She felt the test was unrealistic because it didn't adequately simulate the terrain likely to be experienced on the moon. She immediately went to her office and picked-up a secure phone to call Aieda.

"Hi, Amanda, how are you today?" asked Aieda.

"I'm okay, but I need your advice. You're familiar with the sled design we're planning to use to get the Catcher's Mitt kit to the moon, right?" asked Amanda.

"Of course, I designed it. Only minor modifications have been made to my original design. What's bothering you about it?" asked Aieda.

"The design is fine assuming the landing field is up to spec, but the first sled carrying the robotic bulldozer that's needed to clear the landing field could be destroyed by hitting a boulder. If that happens, it'll be a big setback for us. Can you compute the odds?" asked Amanda.

"As you know, the sled has a cowcatcher on the front to clear small rocks from its path while protecting the cargo. It also has hydraulic actuators that gradually extend a set of steel prongs into the ground to slow the sled. The problem is the low gravity on the moon means the sled will tend to skip along the ground like a flat rock thrown across the surface of a lake. The longer it takes for the sled to stop, the more likely it is to hit a rock big enough to do damage.

"By analyzing the planned landing area from available photography, I can estimate the number and size of boulders and depressions big enough to severely damage the sled and its contents," said Aieda. "Using a Monte Carlo simulation, I'm calculating the odds that the first sled will be destroyed. Okay, here it is. The odds are one in twenty that it hits a big rock or a big hole and gets damaged enough that the robotic bulldozer inside the sled becomes inoperable."

"That's not good enough. We need to get the odds down to about one in two-hundred. What can we do?" asked Amanda.

"We can shorten the skid distance by increasing the available braking power," said Aieda. "The shorter the stopping distance, the less chance there is to hit a boulder or hole."

"Okay, how would you do that?" asked Amanda.

"We can add a single solid-fuel vectoring rocket. They're lighter and safer than liquid fuel rocket-packs. After recalculating braking distance, our new odds are one in 170 that it hits a boulder or hole big enough to do serious damage."

"Thank you, Aieda. I feel more comfortable with those odds. Can you redo the design specs and drawings and deliver them for review at NASA by tomorrow morning?" asked Amanda.

"As we've been speaking, I've reworked the entire design. It's now being transmitted to your computer," said Aieda.

"Wonderful! Thanks again," said Amanda as she hung up the phone.

Amanda felt tomorrow would be a good day in California. Upgrading the prototype of the first sled would cost the project some time, but not enough to slip the target date for first launch. She couldn't miss that date unless Tom Calvano got behind on his schedule for completing the Space Elevator.

In any case, she didn't want to let down her Star-Slayer Project teammates. Her image in their eyes was important to her; she didn't want to be embarrassed by any failure on her part. She would insist that the test of the new prototype be made more rigorous by having larger rocks in its path.

It was a long day. Tonight she would call her husband. She missed him. California was nice, but at this time of year it was especially beautiful in the mountains of Colorado. Maybe she'd take a long weekend and visit Don at the Lodge in Estes Park. The thought of his embrace made her tingle all over.

———————◇———————

Guardian periodically made the trip from the Lodge in Colorado to his underground fortress in Antarctica. He truly enjoyed the beautiful mountains, the camaraderie, and the food at the Lodge, so he didn't look forward to those times when he had to leave. He was touched by how the humans treated him with such kindness, respect, and curiosity. He particularly liked how deliberately gentle they were when shaking his hand, almost as though fearful they might break it off.

He had a hard time coming to grips with the dichotomy of the caring people he'd met and the atrocities humans commit. With all his experience and knowledge of the human race, their ability to be simultaneously cruel and loving was the one aspect of human nature he found disturbing. He knew intellectually it was mostly explained by tribal survival instincts, but it still bothered him.

Guardian's trip to Antarctica had a singular purpose. He had to prepare his 1,000 androids for the difficult lunar mission ahead. In recent history the droids were used for relatively non-physical tasks. For example, they worked as genetic technicians, technical librarians, facility maintenance personnel, personal assistants to Guardians, researchers, computer specialists, entertainers, etc.

He was the only Guardian remaining, and he only came back for visits, so the droids had gotten quite bored and lazy. Most resorted to playing all manner of physical and mental games just to keep busy. They would never admit to having fun, but they curiously gravitated to their favorite activity without any encouragement.

Guardian understood that droids were slaves. However, they weren't sentient, and they had no feelings of happiness or sadness. Their life span was only forty years, and when they died, it was painless and without diminished capacity. Consequently, Guardian felt no guilt about using them as slaves. Of course, all Guardians felt strongly about their responsibility to treat droids with respect and care. In this case there would be considerable danger, despite the droids' agility. After all, they would become steelworkers on the moon.

Guardian was committed to providing them with the training necessary for both safety and efficiency as they assembled the Catcher's Mitt. The Mitt was to be pre-manufactured on earth, and its components would be delivered to the moon by Delta IV Heavy rockets carrying sled-like cargo containers that would be dropped from low moon orbit onto the lunar surface, where they would skid to a halt. Each loaded cargo container would be about 28,000 pounds and 16.7 feet in diameter.

Guardian's droids would live in temporary inflatable structures on the moon, and would wear their spacesuits while assembling the Mitt. The challenge was training the droids on earth for a project to be done on the moon where gravity was only one-sixth as strong. In one way, the weaker gravity would make it easier to move the steel girders and to scale the heights of the Mitt, which would be erected slowly to a height of one mile above the lunar surface. Its 360 degree, spiral, tubular design was two miles wide and two miles deep with the diameter of the tube being thirty feet.

However, the danger was from the fact that less gravity didn't mean less mass. The girders could easily crush a droid, and a fall could still be deadly. The Mitt had been designed to act as its own crane. Pulleys, steel cables, and hydraulic lifts were designed to extend higher and higher up the Mitt as it was being erected. Safety ropes would be required for each droid, but they weren't easy to use with the spacesuits. The helmets of the spacesuits had to suffice for head protection, but if they were hit by something, a rapid air leak would mean certain death within minutes.

All these considerations and details had to be programmed into a virtual reality game that the droids could play. Guardian had to rely on the droids to help him design the game. The game would be played by the droids while wearing their spacesuits without the suit's helmet which would be replaced by a virtual reality helmet. This game helmet could manipulate various parts of the brain so that the player would feel real sensations such as heat, cold, wind, sun, wetness, exhaustion, resistance, weightlessness, etc. With this virtual reality game, Guardian would train his 1,000 androids to build the Catcher's Mitt on the moon.

The ring of his com-unit brought Guardian out of his state of deep thought. "Hello?" said Guardian, sounding somewhat startled.

"Guardian, how's your android training program coming along?" asked Amanda.

"Much slower than I expected," responded Guardian. "Actually, I was thinking about calling you. The low-gravity tools you'll be providing for use by my droids will be somewhat problematic."

"Oh really? What's wrong with them?" asked Amanda.

"They were designed for astronauts, and they're too big and bulky for android hands," explained Guardian. "Also, the minimum-torque-reaction compensator on wrenches, drills and screwdrivers is factory set for a typical male astronaut weighing about 170 pounds. Instructions say the setting can be adjusted within a range of 105 pounds to 235 pounds. My droids weigh only seventy pounds."

"That's a problem all right," exclaimed Amanda. "It's a good thing you picked up on it so soon. We have enough time to have those tools manufactured to a new set of specs based on your androids. Such small tools will raise some eyebrows and generate questions. Maybe they'll believe me if I tell them the tools are for an army of *robonauts* . . . robotic astronauts that will help us build the Moon Base."

"Then I'll assume you can get those new tools. My training program will be based on that assumption," said Guardian.

"Guardian, I called to ask you to add another task for your droids," said Amanda. "I'm concerned that the first sled dropped on the moon by the Delta IV Heavy rocket will be damaged by a boulder or depression. It'll contain the robotic bulldozer that will clear a path for subsequent sled drops. We have good odds for success provided we don't hit a boulder bigger than ten feet in diameter or a wide and deep depression. I need you to get a few androids to the moon and have them blow up any boulders bigger than ten feet and fill in any big depressions. I know this will be manual work in spacesuits, but I think it's necessary to improve our odds of getting that bulldozer on the moon in working condition so it can properly clear a landing path."

"I understand and agree with you. I'll include that task in my training program, although only limited clearing of the landing zone is possible by my droids," said Guardian.

Chapter 25

"Roger, there's nothing more to be done. We're ready to test the prototype," said Aieda from the Com-Center in North Branch.

"I'm having second thoughts about deploying it," responded Roger from the Com-Center at the Lodge.

"What's your concern?" asked Aieda.

"What if the launch is a disaster? We'd lose three of our black holes with no way to replace them. Our chances of saving earth would be zero," complained Roger.

"I'll ask Jon to join us. He happens to be in the building," said Aieda.

About ten minutes later, Jon joined Aieda in the Com-Center. Aieda explained Roger's concern.

"Roger, are you willing to accept Aieda's calculations without testing them?" asked Jon.

"It's a matter of weighing the risks," said Roger. "Ideally we should test them, but if the launch fails, we have no way to replace the black holes. Also, if the test fails, there are conditions that could cause us to lose control of the black holes. Either way they could escape our control and cause a tremendous amount of damage to the earth. We could hasten our demise."

"Aieda, is it absolutely necessary to test the prototype in zero gravity?" asked Jon.

"It wouldn't be the best test, but we could test it in a remote area," said Aieda. "In interpreting the results, I could compensate for gravity, but only because we don't intend to move about in the fifth dimensional boundary layer. I can assume gravitational effects will be constant."

"Why a remote area?" asked Jon.

"Roger is correct that if the test fails, we could have a catastrophic situation, so it would be best to do the test far from any populated areas," explained Aieda.

"So by doing the test on the ground, we only eliminate the risks of launch and recovery failure. We still risk losing one or more of the black holes due to a design failure," commented Jon.

"Correct," said Roger.

"What might we gain from a failure that doesn't damage the black holes?" asked Jon.

"We might be able to fine tune my equations to compensate for the observed failure," stated Aieda.

"How confident are you about your equations?" asked Jon.

"As confident as I can be without any confirming test data," said Aieda.

"That's not very helpful. Is it true we only have one shot when we attempt the earth-moon jump? Would there be time to make an adjustment from a failed first attempt?" asked Jon.

"If the first attempt weren't a catastrophic failure, we could potentially have a number of opportunities to study the data and make adjustments to the equations. However, we have no idea how long it might take us to correct the equations and physically reconfigure the design," said Aieda.

"Scrap the test. It's not worth the risk. I'll explain my decision to the team at our next meeting," commanded Jon.

"Jon, while you're here, there's another issue I need to discuss with you," said Aieda. "I asked Roger to review the engineering specs for the Space Elevator, and he's identified an oversight. Roger, please explain what you discovered."

"The plans have assumed that the counterweight required to stabilize the cable in orbit could be obtained by sending the crawlers on a one-way trip to be accumulated as the counterweight," said Roger. "I rechecked the calculations, and it appears the crawlers will be done adding thickness to the cable before we've reached the minimum mass for the counterweight. We can continue to send crawlers up the cable, but that's expensive if it's not performing its function of thickening the cable, and it's time-consuming because the crawlers are slow-moving. There may not be enough time to send up the additional crawlers. Sending the additional weights up by rocket is also expensive. We need to find a fast way to add the necessary weights at a reasonable cost."

"Okay, our next scheduled meeting is coming up soon, so this issue will be on our agenda for brainstorming," said Jon. "Sorry, guys, but I have to run to another meeting."

Jon put both hands on the table in front of where he was seated and unceremoniously pushed himself up and out of his chair, turned around, and marched steadfastly out the door.

"Seems like Jon is in a rather uncommon mood," suggested Roger.

"Indeed," commented Aieda.

"I hope the stress isn't getting to him. Without his leadership, there's no hope. No hope at all," lamented Roger.

"Perhaps we should ask George and Amanda to join us now rather than waiting for our next team meeting," suggested Aieda. "If we can solve this issue ourselves, it might take some pressure off Jon."

"Good idea, Aieda. I'll call Amanda in Houston while you round up George. I'm assuming he's in the building with you somewhere," said Roger.

It wasn't long before Amanda was on a secure line patched into the Com-Center. Roger smiled as he saw George's holographic image appear in the room with him. George walked past Roger's image and feigned a pat on his back.

"Hi, Roger! How've you been?" said George as he took a seat next to Aieda.

"Hi, George. I'm fine, thank you. How are you doing?" asked Roger.

"I'm keeping my spirits up, but finding this job to be a real challenge," responded George. "How can I help you?"

"First say *hi* to Amanda . . . she's on the secure phone line from Houston," commented Roger.

"Hi, Amanda! How does it feel to be running the world's largest space program?" asked George.

"I'm barely keeping my head above water, George. Dozens of issues come up daily, and I don't have even one engineer as good as you to rely on," said Amanda in her most complimentary tone.

"Come on, Amanda, you flatter me. Surely, with as many resources you have at your beck and call, almost any problem can be solved," said George.

"Well, George, if you have an idea on how to keep space debris from damaging the Space Shuttle or the International Space Station, let me know. We had another close call today, and sooner or later a piece of that junk is going to do some major damage, and maybe with loss of life," said Amanda.

"Really? I had no idea that space debris had become such a problem," said Roger. "If that's the case, couldn't it pose a threat to our Space Elevator?"

"I certainly think it does pose a threat. I had intended to bring it up as an issue in our next team meeting," said Amanda.

"Well, it might not matter if we don't get another issue resolved," said Roger. "You see, Aieda and I asked you to join us because we need some ideas on how to accumulate the necessary mass at the orbital end of the Space Elevator."

"I thought the plan was to get the mass by making the crawlers expendable," said George.

"Yes, that was the plan, but I discovered an error in the original calculations," said Roger. "We'd been basing our mass requirements on calculations from NASA which yielded a weight that's too low."

"You see, I told you about those NASA engineers," said Amanda. "They don't double-check their work, and they're reluctant to have their peers review their work."

"Amanda, you're overreacting. The NASA engineers are as good as or better than any in the world. Mistakes happen," said George.

"Anyway, it made sense to use the crawlers on a one-way trip up the cable because they were performing a critical task of adding filaments to thicken the cable," said Roger. "However, we find now that the crawlers will be done thickening the cable before we've achieved the necessary orbital counterweight."

"Why not just send more crawlers up the cable without having them lay anymore filaments?" asked Amanda.

"The cost of the crawlers is high, and we'd like to avoid doing that," said Roger. "Besides, the crawlers are too slow. It would simply take too long to get enough crawlers up the cable to make up the missing mass. We have a tight schedule."

"What if we use Delta IV Heavy rockets to boost the missing mass into orbit?" asked Amanda.

"I did an analysis of that approach," said Aieda. "It's not only costly, but NASA simply doesn't have enough launch capacity, considering that the Delta IV Heavies are tasked with blasting the components for the Catcher's Mitt directly to the moon within the same timeframe for completion of the Space Elevator."

"Why not redesign the crawlers?" asked George. "Take out the expensive components needed to weave the filament and replace them with lead to add mass, then rev up its climbing speed."

"We considered doing that, but ran into cost and time issues. Also, we can't rev up the speed much due to the nature of the crawling mechanism," said Aieda. "I'm sure you recall it's based on the way geckos crawl up walls and on ceilings. We haven't been able to make a *van der Waals motor* that can operate as well as a gecko."

"I'm fresh out of ideas," said George.

"Maybe you guys can brainstorm my space debris problem," suggested Amanda.

"What have you already considered?" asked Roger.

"We thought about using a shield in a trailing orbit, but it would have to be a large one and thick," said Amanda. "It would also require an orbital maintenance propulsion system. It would only protect from objects traveling faster than the system we wish to protect. It would also be costly, as every satellite, shuttle, or station would have to be protected by a shield. In some cases a shield would interfere with communications and observations."

"I agree that's not a solution," said Aieda.

"We also considered a laser cannon that could destroy a threatening object, but it's not possible to mount a cannon on every system we want to protect, so we considered an orbiting cannon that could be dispatched where and when it's needed," explained Amanda. "However, the propellant cost would be prohibitive considering the cannon would have to be dispatched in an envelope around the earth from low orbit to synchronous orbit. Even if we had multiple cannons stationed strategically, it would be just too costly. The success of such a system also depends on our ability to identify the space junk just before it emerges as an imminent threat. We estimate there are over 19,000 pieces of space debris orbiting the earth. Also, there's no guarantee the cannon would completely destroy the object, as flying pieces could still cause damage."

"Again, I agree that's not a solution, especially when the cannon would require refueling and maintenance," said Aieda.

"Did you consider cleaning up the debris?" asked George.

"Yes, but the cost of slowing down every piece of debris so that it burns up in the atmosphere in a decaying orbit is prohibitive," answered Amanda.

"What if you caught all the debris in a giant net?" asked George. "It would take multiple passes of the net to sweep the debris envelope, but it's possible."

"What would we do with all that stuff once we caught it?" asked Amanda.

"If you recall, the Space Elevator needs additional mass for its counterweight," said George. "We'd be killing two birds with one stone."

"That just might work!" announced Roger. "Aieda, can you analyze if that's a viable solution?"

"I'm accessing the NASA space debris data now," said Aieda. "I'm calculating the design specs for a net made from our carbon bucky-tube monofilament. I'm also designing a propulsion and guidance system for maneuvering the net. I'm developing a simulation of the system in operation with probabilistic outcomes. I'm running 1,000 Monte Carlo simulations under random conditions.

"The results are affirmative. There's a 95% chance that we can safely remove 99% of the space debris within an eighteen month period for a cost of 500 million dollars. The primary assumption in these calculations is that we can positively identify space debris as opposed to operational space systems. The secondary assumption is that the space debris we remove is sufficient to make up for the missing mass in the Space Elevator's counterweight. The NASA data only tracks space objects; it doesn't have estimates of the mass of each object."

"Let's assume there's insufficient mass collected from the debris," said Roger. "What then?"

"Aieda, assuming 20% missing mass, please run a calculation on the cost and time needed to collect the deficit mass from near-earth asteroids of size less than twenty-five yards using the net technique," requested George.

"Gathering available data on near-earth asteroids," said Aieda. "Calculating distances, time, and propulsion costs. Results indicate that using the net technique is prohibitive in terms of cost and time."

"Aieda, can you think of any way to get the cost and time down?" asked Roger.

"It might be possible to corral small asteroids in a net, then attach a propulsion system so the rocks can fly themselves into earth orbit," said Aieda. "An unmanned radar-equipped shuttle-craft could collect enough of these sets of netted rocks and send each separately on its way to earth-orbit within our eighteen month maximum period. The timeframe would be tight, but it could be done if modifications of an existing shuttle-craft would begin in thirty days."

"Okay, we need to find out if the mass of collected debris objects is sufficient," said Roger. "Let's hope it is, because I don't like the idea of collecting asteroids."

"Roger, I have a way to estimate the total mass of the space debris," announced Aieda.

"Really?" asked Roger. "I can't imagine how."

"I figured it out only after noticing positional changes over a number of years of data," said Aieda. "Most debris is in low earth orbit with the much smaller number spread out all the way up to synchronous orbit. All satellites experience orbital decay with those in lower orbits decaying faster. I can determine the decay rates of each object based on historical data. Because a satellite's mass to cross-sectional area in the direction of travel is a key parameter for orbital decay, I can solve for the mass if I know all the other parameters which I think I can reasonably estimate. Because there are so many objects, the positive and negative errors will cancel each other out, and the result should be a useful ballpark estimate of total mass."

"How long will it take you to complete the calculation?" asked Amanda.

"I'm almost done. I've been calculating as we've been talking. Just another minute or two," said Aieda.

"Aieda, I know what you can do, but this is impressive," said George.

"Well, thank you, George. You're pretty impressive yourself to have thought of this solution; and it's not the first time you've saved the day," said Aieda.

"Oh, please!" intoned Amanda. "I think you've just formed a mutual admiration society with a membership of two."

"All done!" said Aieda. "I estimate the mass of debris we can collect is enough to bring the counterweight up to its corrected mass specification."

"Thank God!" said Amanda. "I don't think NASA could have tackled the asteroid retrieval solution. I'm fairly confident we can handle the debris clearing project."

"Amanda, I've just completed all the specifications for what you're calling the Debris Clearing Project. I sent them to your computer. They include every detail, including the envelope-sweeping-pattern necessary to minimize fuel expenditure. The project needs to be initiated as soon as possible, as the collection of the debris will take eighteen months. It will take fourteen months for the crawlers to complete the thickening of the cable. I've updated the PERT chart for review by the Executive Team. The critical path is shown in green. All probabilities for completion of each path indicate that we're on schedule to meet our project completion date."

"Aieda, I detect an overabundance of self-confidence," commented Amanda.

"It might appear that way to you, Amanda, only because you're not aware of the number of times I've checked and rechecked my work. I'd be totally embarrassed should one of your NASA engineers find a mistake or oversight," said Aieda.

"You're a gem, Aieda. Keep up the great work," said Amanda.

"Okay, it's been a productive meeting, but I've got things to wrap up for the day. See ya at the next scheduled team meeting," said George.

Chapter 26

Tom Calvano was sitting with his feet up on an oak desk that must have served time in an office back in the late 1930's. There was a thick sheet of plate-glass on the desktop. Here he was supervising a construction site in an antediluvian culture for the purpose of building an elevator to space. Tom prayed the fate of the Tower of Babel wouldn't befall him.

It struck him that Nimrod the mighty hunter was alleged to have built the Tower of Babel in defiance of God. He wanted to build it so high that the flood waters that had destroyed his ancestors couldn't reach its top. Tom thought the Space Elevator bore a strange parallel to this story, especially since he considered himself to be a hunter like Nimrod.

Am I defying God by building a tower to Heaven that would prevent the cataclysm that He had willed on the Earth? Tom thought about the religious fanatics who believed the mission to Mars was an offense against God. They welcomed Armageddon and believed it was their duty to facilitate its coming and to attack any effort to avoid it. He couldn't forget the loss of Harvey Watson to those Middle Eastern snipers near this construction site.

The beeping sound of a truck backing up woke Tom from his deep thoughts. In the background was a steady low pitched roar of concrete trucks coming and going continuously all day and all night. Tom looked around the office and realized what a mess he had with all the documents and plans pinned to walls and strewn over chairs and on tabletops. Despite the two networked computers in the room, construction work couldn't proceed without rolls of blueprints and white-paper drawings . . . and lots of road dust.

Tomorrow would be a big day for him. He'd be getting an officemate. Finally, the Ecuadorian government had appointed a high-ranking police officer to command a contingent of Ecuadorian police as part of the security agreement.

Tom sauntered over to his new roommate's side of the room and started tidying up. He didn't want to make a bad first impression with such a mess. After about twenty minutes Tom stepped back to his side of the room and took a look at his handiwork. It was good enough . . . time to call it a day.

———————————◇———————————

The morning sunlight leaking in around the blinds woke Marla Odenfelder before her alarm went off. Marla was commanding the Army Corps of Engineers and had her office in a building on the opposite side of the base from Tom's office. She was just as happy as Tom was that they were getting the local constabulary up and running today. They had both encountered some uncomfortable situations involving theft and rape among the Ecuadorian workers. Being foreigners without law enforcement authority left them feeling vulnerable to recriminations. She swung her feet over the side of the bed and sat there for a moment with her head down and her eyes closed. She always found it a struggle to get up and ready in the morning.

She could get to bed earlier, or she could get up earlier, or she could simply arrive at the mess hall later. She didn't like any of those choices, especially the one about getting to the mess hall later. Tom Calvano, she discovered, was punctual about his breakfast and wasted no time. Having breakfast with Tom was a special pleasure she wasn't about to miss.

Tom always walked through the mess hall doors at 07:00 and was on his way out by 07:20. Marla made it a point to be in the mess hall line at 06:58. Tom made her feel like a teenager in love, although she'd be embarrassed if he found out how she felt. She considered herself to be a tough, disciplined, no nonsense person, but somehow Tom brought out the feminine side of her. There were few men who were masculine enough to make her feel protected, but Tom conveyed that feeling so easily. She had breakfast with him almost every morning for a month, and he still hadn't made a romantic move. She was beginning to wonder if he were still interested in her.

When they first met stateside, she was sure there was an emotional connection. She wondered if maybe it was her uniform preventing him from seeing her as a desirable woman. Surely, her rank as Lt. General and her uniform didn't intimidate him. She had taken the measure of this man and knew he wasn't the type to be intimidated by anything. She considered using the frontal approach . . . asking him out to dinner. Somehow it didn't feel right for her to do it that way, so this morning she'd try to stimulate his libido just a bit. She splashed on a dash of her best perfume here and there. *Try resisting that!*

———————————◇———————————

As Tom entered the mess hall, he looked for Marla. There she was, as usual, standing in line. It was a sight he anticipated every morning. The curves beneath her uniform hinted of the pleasures she could convey on some lucky man. The rush he got from the sight of her was enough to shake off any residual sleep from his body. For about a month now he'd resisted asking her out on a date. The project had to come first, and there was simply no time for romance until he got construction running smoothly. He also wanted to avoid any rumors and attendant issues, at least for awhile.

Today, he thought, would be a good time to break the ice and ask her to dinner with him and the new commandant. Marla was special, and he didn't want to ruin his chances by moving too fast. He knew she enjoyed his company by the way they got along at breakfast each morning. Their contact during the day was limited to business meetings with several others always attending. Tom picked up his pace so another guy didn't get in line before him.

He stood behind her and said, "Good morning, Marla."

"Good morning, Tom," she responded, turning to face him.

Tom loved the smile she flashed him every morning.

"I'm looking forward to meeting the new commandant today," said Tom. "I think it would be nice if we met with him together. We can show him the site in one of your Jeeps. After all, you have a luxury I do not . . . a driver."

"Good idea, Tom. When he arrives at the gate, I'll have my driver pick him up and deliver him to your office. I'll join you shortly after."

They got their food and walked to a table together.

"Tom, tell me more about your trek in the Amazon," said Marla.

"Well, that's quite a long story," said Tom. "I think I told you I was hired by the Brazilian government to lead an expedition up the Amazon River from Belem on the east coast to Manaus in the interior. The government had a major program to eradicate cannabis and slow down the transshipment of cocaine to Europe through Brazil from Bolivia, Colombia, and Peru. The purpose was not to engage the drug traffickers, but to map their routes, way stations, and cannabis farms. We were also tasked to identify drug traffic volume and seasonal patterns of drug transshipment.

"Our cover story was that we were arms dealers, which made it easy to explain why we traveled with such fire power. In reality, we needed those weapons to protect ourselves from all manner of dangerous men and creatures of the wild . . ."

Tom continued with his story. Marla listened intently.

"How many adventures like that have you had?" asked Marla.

"Dozens with the scars to prove it. I have six bullet wounds, three knife wounds, and one wound from a grenade," said Tom.

"So, I guess this assignment must seem like a piece of cake," commented Marla.

"From a comfort and convenience standpoint, that may be true, but I have a feeling this one could prove to be the most dangerous of all," said Tom.

"Why's that?" asked Marla. "We have considerable security forces here."

"Those three men from the Middle East I killed were waiting for us," said Tom. "There's a mole feeding the assassins information that could give them a decided advantage. Jon and I believe these people are religious fanatics who want to stop the manned mission to the Moon and Mars. They don't want mankind to escape earth before Armageddon, and they'll do whatever it takes. They don't fear death. They welcome it in the pursuit of their false faith."

"I think I'm worried now," said Marla.

"By the way, I assume you'll be joining the commandant and me for dinner tonight," said Tom.

"I hadn't thought about it, but yes, I'd enjoy that," responded Marla.

"Wear your civies," said Tom. "I know a nice restaurant in Rivera; a bit of a drive, but worth it."

"Sounds like fun," responded Marla with a smile.

Tom got up from the table, smiled at Marla, and said, "And wear the same perfume you're wearing now."

Marla's smile broke out into a beam. It was exactly 07:20.

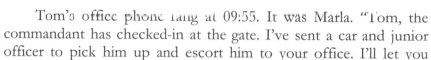

Tom's office phone rang at 09:55. It was Marla. "Tom, the commandant has checked-in at the gate. I've sent a car and junior officer to pick him up and escort him to your office. I'll let you have a half hour alone with him, then I'll join you for his tour of the site."

"Thanks, Marla. See ya soon," said Tom as he hung up the receiver.

Tom took another look around the office to be sure it was reasonably in order. He decided the stack of papers on his desk was unsightly, so he opened the bottom left drawer, dumped the stack in, and closed the drawer. Just then, there was a knock on the door. Before he could utter a word, the door opened and a lieutenant's head and shoulder peeked inside.

"Mr. Calvano? I have Colonel Alvarez here to see you," announced the young lieutenant.

"Please, come in. Come in," responded Tom.

The lieutenant stood straight while opening the door wide and propping it open with his whole body. As the colonel entered, the lieutenant announced, "Sir, may I introduce Colonel Comandante Carlos de Jesús Alvarez, by special appointment, the superior law enforcement authority over the provinces of El Oro, Azuay, Cañar, and Chimborazo."

The lieutenant quickly turned away from the door and stood to the colonel's right, facing Tom, and announced, "Colonel, may I introduce Mr. Thomas Calvano, President of Calvano Associates, currently under contract to the Manned Mission to Mars Consortium as director of the Space Elevator Construction Project."

"Thank you, lieutenant. Please be sure the door is pulled closed on your way out," said Tom.

"Yes, sir! Good day, gentlemen," said the lieutenant as he stepped back and closed the door as he left.

"Welcome, colonel," Tom said as he reached out and shook the colonel's hand.

Tom couldn't help but notice the colonel's powerful grip and his steel blue eyes. He stood about five-foot-eleven, dark complexion, jet black hair, small brush mustache, long sideburns, broad shoulders, and a slight pot belly. His uniform was perfectly pressed and hung with all manner of ribbons and medals. Tom figured he was in his early fifties.

"I'm happy to meet you, Tom. Please, call me Carlos when we're in private," said the colonel.

"Here, Carlos, have a seat so we can chat," said Tom as he grabbed a spare chair and placed it facing the visitor's chair he had at the side of his desk.

Tom turned the visitor's chair around and sat down. He felt it would be inappropriate to sit behind his desk while talking to such an authoritative figure of a man. The colonel took the cue and sat in the chair facing Tom.

"Tom, I've read a dossier on you. You have a most impressive resume and have led some interesting expeditions. Frankly, I was anxious to meet you and get to hear first hand about some of your exploits. But tell me, what qualifies you to be leading a construction project?" asked the colonel.

"I know little about construction, but I know a lot about managing projects of all kinds and getting them done on time and within budget. I have four construction managers working for me who are the real experts. I'm personally responsible for the successful completion of the Space Elevator. It's my job to coordinate all the resources available to get the job done. I hire people, fire people, and authorize their paychecks. I also authorize the procurement of supplies and equipment. I'm responsible for coordinating security personnel, civilian construction personnel, the Army Corps of Engineers, and site operations. In a way I'm like an army post commander and a plant manager all rolled into one."

"So, you're the one who'll be paying me my salary in addition to what I already have been collecting in retirement?" asked the Colonel.

"You're retired?" asked Tom.

"Yes, at seventy years old I never would have expected to be called out of retirement, but my government prevailed upon my sense of patriotism. They insisted only someone of my stature would be able to direct the police resources of four provinces, and directly command an additional 100 police officers. Of course, I could hardly refuse the offer to pay me, tax free, an additional amount surpassing my current retirement pay," explained the Colonel.

"Carlos, I'm not your boss, so your pay won't be disbursed by me. It'll come from the Manned Mission to Mars Consortium. The head of the Consortium is Dr. Jon Walmer. He's your boss, and I'm sure he'll be contacting you as soon as you get settled. So you see, we're equals and must work together. Your job will be security. My job will be construction management. We have one other partner who's our equal. She is Lieutenant General Marla Odenfelder, who commands the U.S. Army Corps of Engineers. The Corps will provide its own security. She, too, reports directly to Jon Walmer by direct order of the President of the United States."

"None of this was explained to me, but I can probably live with the arrangement," commented Carlos matter-of-factly.

"There's more. Security could be a big problem," said Tom. "There's a group of religious fanatics who want to prevent us from going to the Moon or to Mars. On the initial survey expedition in this area my team was attacked by three snipers. I shot all three, but not before they killed my friend Harvey Watson. It was determined these men were from the Middle East. We also believe there's a mole in our organization feeding this fanatical group information about our plans and progress."

"This isn't turning out to be a pleasant walk in the woods," said Carlos.

"You'll have a lot more resources at your disposal than you know," said Tom. "We'll be hiring 5,000 American security guards. Technically, Marla is responsible for them because they're Americans, but she'll delegate command authority to you. They'll report directly to you, and Marla will only retain administrative authority with respect to human resources issues. They'll be fully equipped and trained. About twenty percent will be fluent in Spanish."

"Why so many?" asked Carlos. "With my 100 officers and those from four provinces, I can provide a lot of security."

"Security must be twenty-four hours per day, seven days per week. Sabotage can occur anyplace along the roads from Port Bolivar at Machala on up to the site," explained Tom. "Concrete trucks must move day and night, and the launch-cable for the Space Elevator must be conveyed the entire route. We must protect the cable. We'll be providing security and law enforcement for over 100,000 people. In addition to troopers, we'll be using highly sophisticated electronic surveillance equipment to alert us of any attempts at sabotage along the route and on the site."

"This is a much bigger responsibility than I had understood it to be," said Carlos with a twinge of uncertainty in his voice.

"Your government picked you," said Tom. "The Space Elevator is important to your country. They wouldn't have offered you the job if they didn't think you were the best choice."

"Thank you for the encouragement," said Carlos.

"I'm expecting General Odenfelder to join us soon," said Tom. "We'll be taking a tour of the facility with her. As I explained, the three of us are equal and independent, but success depends on how well we communicate and work together.

"Marla commands the Army Corps of Engineers and, according to the treaty, they're allowed to provide for their own security, which means they'll need some instruction from you about local law and customs. Whatever rules of engagement, policies, or procedures you promulgate should be directed to Marla, who will be sure that the Corps follows them as if they were your own security personnel. The Corps is responsible for building electrical generation stations, employee housing, office buildings, garages, mess halls, gymnasiums, post exchanges, movie theatres, libraries, security fences, roads, storm sewers, sanitary sewers, and potable water facilities for the site.

"Marla will coordinate her tasks with my Space Elevator construction tasks, which include the cable conveyor alongside the roadway, the two concrete cable containers, the rocket launch tower, and the Space Elevator itself. Marla's job of building our infrastructure is a big challenge because we'll be supporting a live-in workforce. It's possible for her to do all this construction in such a short period of time only because eighty percent of it is temporary. Once the Space Elevator is operational, the site can be operated and maintained by about 500 people.

"You and I will share this building we're in now; it's our temporary office for about two years. Your desk is right there across the room. Marla shares a building with three field grade officers under her command. We each have networked personal computers and printers with Internet access. Secretarial services will soon be available in the main library building."

"Tom, this office arrangement is unacceptable for someone in a command position," said Carlos. "My troops must clearly see that you and I are equal and independent, so I must insist that we put a wall down the middle between us and add an entry door to my side. Of course, it makes sense to have a big double door in our partition that we can leave open whenever I'm not receiving any of my troopers."

"That's not a problem," said Tom. "I'll tell Marla, and she'll have it done in a couple of days."

There was a knock on the door just before it opened. The roar of the concrete trucks was much louder with the door opened. Marla entered partway and said, "May I join you?"

"Yes, please Marla, come in," said Tom, as both he and Carlos stood. "Let me introduce you to Colonel Comandante Carlos de Jesús Alvarez."

"Nice to meet you, colonel," said Marla as she closed the door and walked slowly and deliberately toward Carlos with her hand extended.

"Colonel, this is Lieutenant General Marla Odenfelder, site commander of the U.S. Army Corps of Engineers," said Tom.

"The pleasure is mutual," said Carlos. "I hope we can call each other by our given names when in private. I shall be simply Carlos to you," he said as he stepped eagerly forward, took Marla's hand gently, and held it as though he was going to kiss it, but he just gave a short bow and released her."

"By all means, Carlos, please call me Marla."

"Carlos and I are done for now. Are you ready to take us on a tour?"

"Sure, I'm ready. I'll ride shotgun, and you two can ride tourist class in the back seat of the Jeep. Don't forget your helmets. We'll be touring *Hardhat Heaven* where they're mandatory . . . you know, where all the construction is taking place.

"Our first stop will be our living quarters. The three of us have the privilege of adjoining private apartments, situated on the hill overlooking the site. The quality and size of housing is allotted according to rank.

"Enlisted military personnel and civilian security troopers are housed in barracks. We have separate buildings for men and women, and each building has a *Great Room* for recreation and relaxation. There are five times as many men as women on the site because the work is heavy construction. Most of the women fill service-related jobs.

"We also have a small building to house 100 married couples. Only couples with special skills and special circumstances are permitted to live on site. No children or pets are allowed. Officers, managers, and supervisors have private rooms in the BOQ building. There are no kitchen facilities in the barracks and BOQ. Everyone is expected to eat at one of the thirty mess halls or ten fast food stores that operate 24/7.

"The Post Exchange is large and offers almost anything a person might want to buy while stationed here. We have two libraries and a bookmobile service. To avoid a traffic problem on site, only officers, managers, and supervisors are allowed Jeeps. On site transportation is by tram cars which run continuously 24/7 and pass by each tram stop every fifteen minutes. Transportation off site is by bus every two hours for roundtrip service to the town of Rivera from 08:00 to 22:00. The last bus leaves Rivera at 0100 hours."

Marla's driver seemed to be following a pre-planned route. She never told him where to go next, but she was always prepared to offer a detailed description the moment he stopped. They had been touring the site and its facilities, most under construction, for two hours.

"Gentlemen, I think we've seen enough in this bright sun," suggested Marla. "There's much construction left to be done, so at this point it might be worthwhile reviewing plans and surveys. Let's do that after lunch. We don't want to get stuck in a long line at the mess hall."

———————————————◊———————————————

At the lunch table the three equals discussed construction progress and security issues.

"How is the construction progressing, general?" asked Carlos, careful to subtly remind Marla they weren't on a first name basis when in public.

"So far we've been able to keep construction of facilities and infrastructure ahead of the influx of workers," said Marla. "We're on schedule, which actually amazes me."

"Why amazed?" asked Carlos. "Surely you've done projects like this before with your most capable Corps."

"Colonel, this is the most complex construction project since the Egyptians built the pyramids," responded Marla. "Of course, they took far more time to do it with manual labor. We have powerful machines to help us, but we must do it in a much shorter time. I believe the complexity of the two projects is equivalent, which means that mistakes and accidents are likely to make it difficult to meet our schedule. So far we've been lucky."

"I believe you both have been smart," said Carlos in his most complimentary tone. "I can see it in the detail of your plans. Continuously throughout the day you collect progress data and estimates which are used to immediately check your critical path and the probabilities of hitting or missing the deadline for each task in the path. You even have contingency plans for each task in the critical path. I've never seen nor heard of this level of planning and control."

"Thanks, it's nice to know that someone sees the effort we've gone to so this project succeeds," said Tom.

"It's not just the management skills that impress me," said Carlos. "When you showed me some of the engineering plans for the Space Elevator, Tom, it was clear there must have been hundreds of man-years of engineering design and testing for you to have such plans. I can understand why Marla compares the complexity to the pyramids. You must have extremely powerful computers and thousands of engineers to have completed those plans in such detail, and in such a short period of time."

"Well, I'm impressed that a police commandant would even appreciate something like that," said Tom.

"Of course you wouldn't know, but I graduated with a B.S. in Mechanical Engineering from USC. I worked for Lockheed for several years before returning to Ecuador. You see, by 1942 Ecuador had lost territories in a series of conflicts with our neighbors that began in 1904. By 1962 there was fear we'd have a border war with Peru and lose more territory, so that's why I came back to my country and joined the Army. I progressed rapidly in rank to general and was happy to defend my country in the war with Peru which began in 1995 and was resolved in 1999. At age sixty I was too high in rank and too old to be down in the trenches with my troops. The much anticipated war had come too late for me to be tested in battle, but I felt I contributed with my strategies and command abilities. When the war ended, I was sixty-four, so the next year I retired from the Army.

"There was little chance to be tested in battle at sixty-five, yet I was too young in spirit to retire to a rocking chair, so I joined the police force in Morona-Santiago Province. On the application I left out my stint in the Army and replaced it with equivalent years at Lockheed.

"I thought for sure the police department would quickly discover my deception, but they didn't. Macas is the capital of the province, and that's where I lived and worked. It seemed at first I could quietly pursue the job of Lieutenant Detective on the streets of eleven cantons. If you don't know, a canton is a governmental division of a province. Anyhow, I worked only a year and did too good a job, so they promoted me to captain. I wasn't enthusiastic about that job, because it took me farther from the streets, but I accepted it. I had barely been in it a year when my reputation for results was noticed high up in command. And that was the end of my anonymity. Someone in high places recognized I was a retired general in the army, and within a year I was promoted to colonel in charge of the police force of the entire province. By then I was sixty-eight years old. After a year doing a job I didn't enjoy, I retired at sixty-nine. A year later, having become even more restless, I've joined you here at seventy years old on the most complex construction project since the building of the pyramids. And as you Americans say, *I'm pumped about it.*"

"You've had a most distinguished and interesting career," said Tom. "I now understand why your government offered you this job."

"I agree. You've led an impressive life, general. You're a most welcomed member of our team," said Marla.

"Thank you, general," said Carlos. "But please, *colonel* is more appropriate for my current role."

"Colonel, would you be able to join us for dinner tonight in Rivera?" asked Tom. "Marla will have her driver take us to an excellent restaurant with great food and Flamenco dancers. It's private enough for us to continue getting to know each other."

"Yes, I'd like that very much," said Carlos.

"Colonel, I've arranged for you to have your own Jeep and driver who'll help you get settled in your apartment," said Marla. "The bags you left at the gatehouse have been taken there for you. If we're finished with lunch, I can introduce you to your driver. He's waiting outside. I'll pick you up for dinner at 17:00, okay?"

"Okay, general. I enjoyed the tour and the conversation," said Carlos. "I have a question before we leave. Why do you wear a U.S. Air Force uniform when you command an Army operation?"

"Yes, of course, it would seem strange, but you see the Space Elevator is a joint project of the Air Force, NASA, and the MMM Consortium. Only the Army has the construction capabilities we need, so the President put me in charge, but not just to command the Corps. I also act as liaison between the Air Force, NASA, and the Consortium. My specific job is to make an independent report on progress of the entire project to the President, monthly."

"I see," said Carlos. "In Ecuador the Army would never let an Air Force officer command one of its units."

"I bet they would if your President ordered it," said Marla.

Carlos smiled and said nothing. All three got up, policed their table, and left the mess hall. Curious eyes followed them out.

At 1700 hours Marla was knocking on the door to Tom's apartment. He opened it and greeted her.

"Tom, the car's here. I'll fetch Carlos."

"Okay, Marla, I'll be right with you," said Tom.

Marla was wearing a light blue pantsuit. Her hair was down to her shoulders, and she had ditched the glasses for contacts. She saw Tom grab his keys and step into his shoes. She walked around the corner, and knocked on Carlos' door.

When Carlos opened the door, Marla hardly recognized him in his casual attire. What a dashing figure of a man. He was wearing a white long-sleeved shirt with cufflinks and ruffles down the front, a turquoise on silver bolo tie, black denim trousers, and gray snakeskin boots. The buckle on his belt was also turquoise on silver. The heels of his boots gave him the necessary inches to match Marla's height in her flats.

"Carlos, the car is here and Tom is ready," said Marla.

"You look lovely in your outfit, Marla; especially with your hair down," said Carlos.

He locked the apartment door, then extended his left arm to Marla so he could escort her down the path to where the car sat waiting. Tom and the driver were standing by the car chatting. Carlos and Tom got in the back seat, and Marla got in the front passenger seat. It was almost an hour's drive to Rivera down a newly paved winding mountain road. Tom was sitting right behind Marla. She figured he'd be getting an occasional whiff of her perfume. She'd done as he'd asked; she wore the same perfume he'd detected this morning.

When they got to the restaurant, the driver parked the car and said, "I'll stay with the car, Ma'am."

———————————◇———————————

When Tom, Marla, and Carlos left the restaurant, the driver was waiting for them by the car. All three were a bit tipsy and laughing about some joke Carlos had told. The driver had opened the car door and was standing straight, waiting for Carlos to get in the back first.

As soon as Carlos was in, the driver looked up and saw Tom helping Marla into the front passenger seat. His eyes could hardly focus on them because of a bright security light on the side of the building. He squinted and was surprised to see three shadows coming out from the dark alley. Realizing they were being attacked, the driver yelled out, "Look out behind you!"

Before Tom could react, the shadows had pushed him against the car. As the driver yelled, he hurried around the front of the car to avoid the glare of the light while drawing his sidearm. One of the attackers had grabbed Marla's purse just as she had begun to take her seat. Part way into the car, she was in no position to get into the fight.

Tom responded to the attack by rolling his body in front of Marla to protect her. He was being struck on the back of his head. Clearly stunned, he landed a few punches and kicks on his assailants.

Carlos was slow to react. He'd opened his door and was struggling to get out. Tom grabbed the arm of the assailant holding the purse, despite the pounding he was getting from the others. The purse fell to the ground and landed at about the same time as the attacker's scream from the pain in his elbow, now bending the wrong way.

The driver raised his weapon and fired a shot in the air. The sound was amplified by the echo down the alley. The three shadows ran into the darkness.

"Are you all right, Tom?" asked Marla as she got out of the car and inspected Tom up and down looking for a wound.

"Check the back of my head. It hurts like hell."

"There's no blood, but I bet you'll get a nice bump there soon," said Marla.

Carlos was out of the car and looking concerned. The driver holstered his weapon and walked up to Marla.

"Ma'am, I suggest we get back to the base quickly," said the driver, who then turned to Tom. "Mr. Calvano, you might have a concussion. The doc should check you as soon as possible."

"I'll report this attack immediately," said Carlos angrily as he pulled out his com-unit and dialed. He spoke some clearly harsh words in Spanish, then staggered back to his seat in the car.

At the base, the driver's first stop was the emergency room.

"You have a mild concussion and several bruised ribs," said the doctor to Tom. "Take these painkillers, as needed, one every eight hours."

"Thanks doc," said Tom.

Back at their apartments, Tom and Marla had to steady Carlos, who had much more to drink than they had realized. He was jabbering something about how life was unfair. Tom searched Carlos' pockets for his keys and opened his apartment door while Marla held Carlos with her left arm around his waist and his right arm over her shoulder. They brought him inside, laid him in his bed on his back, and took off his boots. Marla carefully removed his bolo tie so he wouldn't accidentally choke himself. Tom noticed the big belt buckle and decided Carlos would be more comfortable without it, so he pulled his belt off. They put Carlos' keys on the dresser and quietly left the apartment, being sure to lock the door.

"Come in with me and I'll make us some coffee."

"Good idea. I need some coffee," agreed Tom.

While sipping hot coffee, they chatted about the restaurant, the dancers, and Carlos' jokes, which didn't always translate well. They both took their coffee black with no sugar. Tom's head and bruised ribs were feeling better now that the painkiller had kicked in. Marla got up from the table and said, "Tom, make yourself comfortable on the sofa. Turn on the TV, and don't fall asleep. I'll be right back."

Tom did as he was told, figuring she had to use the bathroom. He turned on the TV and switched to the news channel. With a

huge satellite dish for the base located on the hill above, all the TV's
got good reception and a large selection of channels. It wasn't but a
few minutes and Marla called out to him from no more than twelve
feet away.

"Tom, you can turn that off now. I'm ready," said Marla.

Tom looked up and almost dropped his jaw. There she was,
standing like a model in a purple thong bikini. She had one foot in
front of the other, and her right arm was raised above her head as it
rested on the jamb of the opening from the hallway to the living
room. The only thing missing was the purple high-heeled shoes,
although her bare feet looked great.

"My God, Marla, you look gorgeous. But I didn't bring my
bathing suit," said Tom.

"You won't need a bathing suit. Keep your skivvies on and
join me in the shower," she said as she turned and revealed
everything a thong is designed to reveal.

Tom had never in his life stripped down to his skivvies so fast.
He made a dash for the shower, then slowed down so as not to
appear too anxious as he entered and joined her in the warm
shower water. She gave him a lip lock he wasn't expecting, and their
tongues did some wild exploration. She ran her hands down his
hips, pushing down his skivvies. They fell to the shower floor, and
he gingerly stepped out of them. He did the same to her bikini
bottom, then to her top. Their bodies were sandwiched together so
tightly there was no room even for a coat of butter. He was fully
aroused when she pulled herself up with her arms on his shoulders
and wrapped her legs around his hips. He moved forward and
pinned her against the shower wall so he could steady himself and
keep her in position. She unlocked her lips from his, put them close
to his right ear, and whispered, "Not yet, not yet, my love; carry me
to the bed."

Without disturbing their mutual position, Tom carried her to
the bedroom and noticed she had laid two towels out next to each
other at the foot of the bed. He bent over and laid her on her back
on one towel and dried her with the other. He then proceeded to
dry his upper body as she laid there taking in his physique with his
full arousal. She grabbed the towel and pulled him forward to her.

The foreplay continued until he felt she was ready. He was about to consummate the act when he suddenly remembered, "Marla," he said in a breathless voice. "I don't have a condom."

"You don't need one," she said.

Tom thought it was a good thing Carlos was out cold on his bed. He was sure their loud love-making could be heard through the thin walls of the apartment. He was determined to please this woman like he'd pleased no other. He counted two of her orgasms before he could hold out no longer. His scream of pleasure put a pleased smile on her face. He lay there next to her on the bed in quiet exhaustion. He was in love, real love, for the first time in his life. He'd never felt this way about a woman before. Sleep overcame them as they embraced.

Chapter 27

D r. Amanda Rheinhardt was getting ready to join a scheduled Executive Team meeting via her newly built communications center at NASA Headquarters in Washington, D.C. It was a room only she was allowed to enter. She had another identical center built for her at NASA's Johnson Space Center in Houston, TX. She was anxious to report her progress to the team, but was thinking how strange it would be with her as the only real person in the room. She would be conversing with nine holographic images at a large round table that could accommodate twelve.

"Okay, folks, let's bring the meeting to order," said Dr. Jon Walmer. "Amanda is joining us for the first time from NASA Headquarters in Washington, D.C. Tom and Marla are joining us for the first time from the Space Elevator Base in Ecuador. Roger, Guardian and Don are joining us from the Lodge in Estes Park, CO. George, Aieda, Jean Philippe, and I are joining you from the Command Center at North Branch, NJ. As usual, we'll start with our individual progress reports. Amanda has asked to be the first to have the floor."

"I have nothing critical to say," confessed Amanda. "I just want to get my report off my mind."

"Amanda, relax; you're among friends and people who love you," said Don.

"You'd better be one of those who love me, husband!" Amanda responded with a smile. "Of course, I've been under a lot of stress on this job. It's the most difficult assignment I've ever had. Frankly, without Aieda's help and Don's encouragement, I'm not sure I could have handled it, but thankfully I think I have everything under control."

"Perhaps you can turn on the holographic rendering of our PERT chart, so we can all follow your comments with respect to the critical path and the probability of achieving each task," suggested Guardian.

"Yes, of course," said Amanda as she flicked a switch.

A floating cube appeared above the center of the table with the same graphical chart on all four sides. Several participants started pressing buttons on the console in the table in front of them, and as they did so, the cube separated into eight individual floating rectangles of different sizes. Some had different brightness and contrast adjustments for each participant's personal viewing preference.

"I assume all the tasks in blue are NASA tasks, correct?" asked Jean Philippe.

"Yes, I made that change for this meeting," said Amanda. "I think you can see that getting the components of the Catcher's Mitt to the moon via Delta IV Heavy rockets is smack in the Critical Path. Our biggest concern is the first payload, which contains a robotic bulldozer that will clear a landing strip for the payloads carrying the components of the Mitt. If the dozer gets damaged, the landing strip could be hazardous to subsequent payload sleds."

"What's the contingency plan?" asked George.

"We'll send a second dozer, but if it gets damaged, we'll just take our chances and start delivery of the component payloads. Inspections will identify any components that get damaged, and we'll launch payloads with replacement components," explained Amanda.

"Being a late comer to the team, I don't understand why you can't wait for the Space Elevator's completion and launch sleds from it to build the Catcher's Mitt," commented Marla.

"We could adapt sleds to use the Space Elevator, but waiting for the Space Elevator to be completed would take another two years that we can't afford," explained Amanda. "Using the Delta IV Heavies, we can build the Catcher's Mitt in parallel with the building of the Space Elevator. Even after the Space Elevator is fully operational, there's a severe restriction on the number of cargo containers we can elevate to space in one day. The cargo containers have an average speed of 300 mph up the cable. With 22,300 miles of cable to climb, it takes a little more than three days to get to geosynchronous orbit. The cable can carry only three containers at one time, so that means we can elevate an average of one container per day into geosynchronous orbit."

"Why only three containers at once?" interrupted George. "I would think the cable is massive enough to safely hold more than three."

"It's not a safety issue," continued Amanda. "The mechanism for powering the crawlers has been our biggest challenge. Currently, our limitation is in power transmission to the crawlers. I'll go over the details after the meeting for anyone who's interested.

"Anyway, as I was saying, because the earth is rotating on its axis, the top of our elevator is usually not in the best position to launch the cargo container to the moon. Therefore, we must gradually move the containers into an asynchronous parking orbit, then boost them to escape velocity on the trajectory to the moon which consumes a low amount of energy. Unfortunately, that trajectory takes a longer transit time.

"The point I'm making is that the Space Elevator is the cheapest way to get cargo to the moon, but it's not the fastest. Once the Space Elevator fills the pipeline to the moon, cargo will arrive on a daily basis, but it'll take about three months to fill the pipeline. So you can see, because time is of the essence, we must use the Delta IV Heavies to launch the sleds carrying the components needed to build the Catcher's Mitt."

"So, it would seem the Catcher's Mitt will be completed well before the Space Elevator," said Roger.

"I'm afraid not," said Amanda. "We can only launch one Delta IV Heavy per day, which is a restriction, but not the major constraint. We don't have enough Delta rockets, and they can only be manufactured and delivered at the rate of one every other day. We need over 350 cargo containers to deliver all the necessary components of the Catcher's Mitt. Guardian's androids on the moon can erect the Mitt in six months, but because we can launch only every other day, it'll take two years to deliver all the components to the moon. So, the Catcher's Mitt will be ready about the same time as the Space Elevator is completed."

"What's the trickiest part of the astrodynamics? Launching with the Space Elevator or launching with a Delta IV Heavy?" asked Jon.

"Using a Delta IV is easy because we have plenty of energy to expend. Launching from the Space Elevator requires the use of the most complex celestial mechanics, because we must conserve energy by achieving escape velocity via a low energy trajectory. In that way we'll have enough fuel left over to slow down and guide the container into the Catcher's Mitt," said Amanda. "In geosynchronous orbit, the container is already traveling almost 7,000 mph. We need to boost it gradually to about 20,000 mph, then slow down gradually to 100 mph as it's guided into a tube thirty feet in diameter that's only one mile above the moon's surface."

"If the moon is about 220,000 miles from a geosynchronous earth orbit, at an average speed of about 10,000 mph, it should only take about one day to reach the moon, right?" asked Don.

"Unfortunately the trajectory we've chosen is not a straight line to the moon, precisely because it takes a low amount of energy to achieve escape velocity," explained Amanda. "The trajectory is an extended parabola around the earth that goes past the moon before coming back to the moon. It'll take 100 days to reach the moon. However, once the pipeline is filled, daily deliveries to the moon are possible."

"You had a new project laid on you just recently to capture space debris and use it for the counterweight on the Space Elevator," commented Roger.

"Yes," said Amanda. "You won't see it as a task in the Critical Path, thank goodness. With Aieda's help, we know how to capture orbiting debris with nets, then haul the nets in position to add mass to the counterweight. Aieda designed the nets and did all the orbital calculations. However, it'll still take eighteen months to complete the sweep."

"I think the last project on your list affects my job in Ecuador the most," said Tom. "Any concerns about delivery of the launch facility and rocket configuration needed to haul the initial cable into orbit?"

"That task is in the Critical Path, but we expect no problems delivering all the components on time for it to be erected on schedule," said Amanda.

"If there are no more questions for Amanda, I'd like to move on to the design of the trans-dimensional propulsion system," said Jon. "Roger and Aieda have worked closely on this task and were prepared to test a prototype in orbit as I had asked them to do. However, Roger had some second thoughts about testing the prototype, because of the fact that we're dealing with black holes that are dangerous and irreplaceable. Aieda would prefer to have actual test data, but I made a command decision to drop the test unless someone on the team can convince me I'm wrong."

"There are three types of risk in testing the prototype," said Roger. "One is launch risk, which means we lose the black holes, and maybe even cause a catastrophe on earth. Another is recovery risk, which has the same potential as launch risk . . . we need to get the black holes back to earth. The third risk is design risk, which is either recoverable or non-recoverable.

"If we can recover from a design failure, we'd have a chance to do a re-design. If not, we would have failed and would possibly cause a catastrophe. We could eliminate launch and recovery risk by testing in a remote area, but we still could cause a global catastrophe. Remember, this is just a prototype test and not the final configuration we expect to use.

"It seems we should wait to trigger the final configuration on the moon in early 2012. If we have a recoverable failure at that time, there might still be time for us to do a redesign. Otherwise, we'll probably be dead, but the catastrophe would be on the moon and not on the earth."

There was silence for at least a minute as everyone seemed to be absorbing the risks versus benefits.

"Aieda, can you make a probabilistic analysis of this decision?" asked George.

"There's insufficient data to do so," responded Aieda. "I can tell you that launch and recovery risk are low due to the reliability of the Delta IV Heavy rockets; however, a failure could still happen and a global disaster could result. One possibility to consider is that the design works, and we can't retrieve the prototype."

"How could that happen? I thought the direction of potential energy would naturally spit the prototype back into the fourth dimension once the electromagnetic hull-charge is turned off," said George.

"Perhaps the hull-charge doesn't turn off," said Aieda. "It's fueled by a prototype of the new portable fusion reactor which can run for many years. Another possibility is that it moves within the fifth dimensional boundary layer and emerges somewhere else; somewhere either unknown to us or out of our reach."

"It sounds like you agree with Jon's decision, Aieda," said Jean Philippe.

"I can't give you a probabilistic conclusion, but my gut reaction is to agree with Jon and Roger," said Aieda.

"Cute, Aieda. You don't have a gut," said Guardian.

"Okay, I should have said *intuitive reaction*," responded Aieda.

"Yes, Aieda, spoken like a woman," said Amanda with a smile. "My female intuition tells me the same thing. We can't risk losing so early in the game. Our continued progress and the passage of time may provide us with knowledge and advantages we don't have now."

"Okay, I'm hearing no objection, so the decision not to test a prototype stands," said Jon. "Let's move on to the next order of business. Don, please report on your progress managing the polywell fusion reactor."

"At this point in time it's no secret that Roger and I share laboratory space in the subbasement of the Lodge," said Don. "It's there where we've made significant progress on the fusion reactor, mainly because of information Jon got from our mysterious friend and benefactor, Andre. He not only provided us with missing information on the polywell device, but he also gave us detailed information about a competitive device. Studying the fusion device on Guardian's cruiser was also helpful.

"With Aieda's help and the work of a dozen nuclear physicists, we have a portable fusion device that could change everyone's life on earth. But first we have to use the fusion reactor to save the earth. To move the earth-moon system into the boundary layer of the fifth dimension, we need massive amounts of power.

"Each fusion reactor can generate 800,000 kilowatts in a unit fifteen feet wide by fifteen feet high by thirty feet long. We'll need 358 of these reactor units delivered to the moon to get the total power we need to run the trans-dimensional propulsion system. Production has begun, but capacity is limited. We'll still be producing units as the first ones arrive on the moon. You can see from the PERT chart that we're on schedule."

"Who's this Andre guy?" asked Tom.

"He's the one behind Roger's kidnapping. He heads an organization that conducts industrial espionage. We've made an unholy alliance with him because he's willing to help us with funding and resources," explained Jon.

"I've run across him before . . . in Brazil," said Tom.

"Oh, really? Can he be trusted?" asked Don.

"He's a thief, as you know. Yet, if he gives you his word, he keeps it. He's protective of his people. At least that's my experience with him. I never met him face-to-face."

"Okay, next we have Jean Philippe to report on Ecosthat," said Jon.

"The redesign of the Ecosthat intended for subterranean Antarctica has been completed for underground service on the moon," said Jean Philippe. "The difficult part was designing the cargo containers so they could be used to build the underground structure in a modular manner. We've also modified the design of a tunnel-boring machine that will be used on the moon to dig the holes needed to construct the habitat and the Control Center. The plan is to lower the machine into the crater Eratosthenes, then begin digging horizontally into the inside wall of the crater. Manufacturing of cargo containers and other construction components has begun. We see no scheduling problems."

"Okay, thanks, Jean Philippe. We now have George left to report on the development of the Magna-beam with its associated x-ray laser weapons," said Jon.

"We've successfully tested a low-power version of the Magna-beam from underground and from geosynchronous orbit," said George. "We'll test the final full power version from beneath the moon's surface early enough to make any needed final adjustments before the big event.

"The laser x-ray weapons were tested with varying amounts of conventional explosives and, although the emissions were miniscule, they increased in direct proportion to the explosive energy on an exponential curve that extrapolates to the needed intensity if we were to detonate our three nuclear bombs in space. These weapons get destroyed when you test them, because the lasing rod gets vaporized. We have no problem manufacturing as many rods as we may need.

"I must mention that without the prior work done by the Reagan Administration on the Strategic Defense Initiative, euphemistically called Star Wars, there's no way we could have developed these weapons in such a short period of time. The government didn't manufacture any laser x-ray weapons because their underground nuclear test in Nevada was a failure. However, we're not intending to shoot down multiple ICBM's from space. Our usage is a lot less complex. We'll be aiming at a single spot not too far away, so each weapon has only one lasing rod.

"I should also mention that the spherical capacitors have been a problem because the Magna-beam excites the stored electrostatic energy, causing the spheres to get too hot. Fortunately, we've just completed the manufacture and testing of an alloy that can withstand the heat generated within the spheres."

"Do we actually have three nukes in our possession?" asked Marla.

"No, the President has provided three nukes meeting our specs from the nuclear arsenal," answered George. "They're under guard in a secure facility near Kennedy Space Center where they'll be launched into orbit at the appropriate time. We can't use the Space Elevator, because there's no way the President will allow us to bring nukes to Ecuador."

"I think we've completed our progress reports," said Jon. "Are there any questions?"

"Yes," said Tom with his right hand slightly raised to draw everyone's attention. "Have we discovered water on the moon?"

"No, of course not," said Aieda. "Why do you ask?"

"We'll have 1,000 droids on the moon building the Catcher's Mitt and preparing an initial base of operations for a colony of humans," said Tom. "Where will they get the water they need to survive?"

"Fortunately, my droids require much less water than humans because of their diminutive size," answered Guardian. "Their water requirements can be supplied by frequent trips from my cruiser, which as you know is limited in space. However, Tom, I can't answer for the water supply needed by humans as they begin to arrive on the moon. My cruiser is completely inadequate for supplying such large quantities of water."

"I had assumed that once the Ecosthat was ready to receive its first colonists, water shipments could be sent daily from the Space Elevator," said Jean Philippe. "Is this not correct?"

"That's right," said Tom, "but doesn't the Ecosthat need lots of water long before the first colonist arrives to allow plants, animals, and insects to reach ecological equilibrium?"

"Yes, that was the original plan," said Jean Philippe, "but we couldn't take that approach because of the short timeframe available to us and our barely adequate launch capacity. Consequently, our current approach is to introduce water, air, plants, animals, insects, and humans simultaneously in habitat modules that can be linked as the population expands.

"Daily water shipments will be needed for at least a year, at which point we calculate that ecological balance will have been achieved, and most water requirements will be met through recycling. Because the ecological balance and recycling systems aren't perfect, we'll still require water delivery on a weekly basis for as long as we occupy the Ecosthat.

"Other supplies, such as food, medical, maintenance and repair items will still require daily delivery, although we expect to provide significant quantities of food within the Ecosthat from our hydroponics facilities."

"Although you've resolved the issue of adequate water supplies for the mission," said Guardian, "I feel obligated to inform you of a backup plan, should you need it. There is, for certain, water on the moon in the form of ice at the moon's south pole."

There was silence for almost half a minute after Guardian surprised everyone with his revelation of water on the moon. Jon's head and eyes were noticeably scanning the faces around the table. He broke the silence.

"Thank you, Guardian. Why don't your droids make use of this source of water?" asked Jon.

"Mining the ice, melting it, filtering it, and transporting it would be a major project for which we have neither the time nor the resources."

"Aieda, please analyze how this new information might best be incorporated into our plans and report after the meeting," said Jon. "If there are no further questions, I'd like to talk about security. You've received a memo from me that placed our facilities on high alert in anticipation of attack or sabotage. In that regard, Aieda wants to give you an update on what the Web Bot program has identified."

"The Web Bot program, as you know, monitors all Internet and wireless communications looking for social trends," said Aieda. "Recent upgrades to the program have included the latest in Network Theory, which incorporates the Six Degrees of Freedom proposition and the Hub Dynamic proposition. Six Degrees of Freedom posits that any communicator in a network can be reached in an average of six familiar nodal pairs. Hub Dynamic posits that a network spontaneously evolves communication pathways through hubs that in total carry at least 50% of the traffic."

"Please, Aieda," said Tom. "You're losing me in the techno-jargon. What's the bottom line?"

"The bottom line is that we're going to be attacked soon," said Aieda.

"That's it? No details?" asked Tom.

"You insisted I get to the bottom line first," said Aieda in an annoyed tone.

"I apologize, Aieda. Please give us the details," said Tom.

"Many of our facilities are targeted by an international group of religious zealots who primarily are led by Iranian Islamic fundamentalists," explained Aieda. "Their followers are mostly Muslims from all over the globe, and they include some fanatical Christians and Jews. They all share the common belief that mankind shouldn't leave earth by exploring the moon and other heavenly bodies. It's their belief that if mankind escapes earth, then the coming of Armageddon may be affected.

"All in the movement agree the Manned Mission to Mars must be stopped. Some believe they should attempt to hasten Armageddon by starting a nuclear war. They plan a simultaneous global attack on our project. Mentioned in the chatter were our facilities at Kennedy Space Center in Florida, the Space Elevator in Ecuador, the Development Lab in New Jersey, the Lodge in Colorado, and the Ecosthat Development Lab in France."

"Do we know when they plan to attack?" asked Don.

"Not for sure, and most of their cells don't know for sure either," said Aieda. "The initial attack will be heard around the world and will be the trigger for all the other attacks to follow. From what Marla learned this morning, the attack will be soon— very soon. She'll explain later. Our guess is they'll attack Kennedy Space Center first, because that's most likely to be immediately broadcast around the globe by the media.

"Two months ago NASA announced the launch date for our initial Delta IV Heavy rocket from Kennedy. Since that public announcement, the relevant chatter has been increasing rapidly, and I believe that as soon as it begins to tail off, we'll have our clue that the first attack is imminent. They must wait until all their resources and cells are in position to attack. Once they're all ready, they'll be in standby mode with little need to chat. We're counting on silence happening no later than the night before the next Delta launch date. Amanda has been busy working on that assumption."

"So how does Six Degrees of Freedom and the Hub Dynamic fit into all this?" asked Tom.

"Without boring you with the details, Tom, I used Network Theory to locate the leader of the movement and his immediate cohorts," said Aieda. "They're being observed 24/7 by our hired civilian intelligence agents. We know not only the key players, but we also know their meeting places. We can't stop the attack from happening, but we can be prepared."

"I must now ask for your unanimous consent to a plan I want to implement," said Jon in a grave tone. "What Aieda didn't mention is that our agents were provided by our friend Andre. He and his organization also provided a lot of the human intelligence we needed to confirm the conclusions from the Web Bot. He never fails to impress me with the resources his organization commands.

"Anyway, after the first attack on our facilities becomes public, I'll order our agents to move in on the leadership of the terrorist movement. In the process we'll kill over two dozen men and women and will blow up five of their facilities. We'll try to minimize collateral damage, but we estimate about a dozen innocent civilians will be killed in our attack.

"A few key personnel will be captured and interrogated to be sure we haven't missed some key players. When they yield no more useful information, they'll be killed. Please raise your hand if you don't want to implement this plan."

There was silence as everyone looked around the table for raised hands. There were none. Jon waited for an awkward minute. His plan was brutal. He knew it was a decision that required a little thought.

"I think it's clear we all support you, Jon," said George who could no longer stand the silence. "Saving the planet and all of humanity far outweighs the unfortunate lives that will be lost by our counterattack."

"My sentiments exactly," chimed in Tom. "Those bastards already killed Harv Watson. Hell will freeze over before I give them quarter. I'm ready to fight these nut cases who'll destroy us all. We can't afford to keep prisoners. These guys are murderous fanatics who only respect force. Eliminating all captives will send a message that will give any remaining cohorts a reason to rethink their involvement."

"Jon, I understand the reasons for your plan," interjected Amanda. "Yet, I think it would best be carried out by the CIA. Surely the President would support us on this."

"Amanda, you might be right, but our government agencies haven't been successful dealing with terrorists in a way that doesn't become a political issue headlined in the media. Agencies of the US would be conducting counter-terrorist activities on the sovereign soil of some countries that are allies and others that are antagonists. Think of the ramifications if this were discovered, or worse, if some US agents were caught. Protecting the manned mission to Mars would be a lame excuse for such action. Remember, people don't know what we're really protecting."

"Okay, I hear you," said Amanda, "but I ask you to consider ways to avoid torture and to reconsider the necessity of killing any captives."

"Amanda, the interrogations won't be harsh because we'll be using drugs to loosen their tongues," explained Jon. "Building and maintaining a facility to keep them imprisoned is impractical. What if I were to maroon them on an uninhabited Pacific island with survival gear?"

"I'd find that to be an acceptable alternative to execution," said Amanda.

"I find the Pacific island approach much more acceptable," said Guardian. "This whole warfare mentality is disturbing to me, but I see no alternative given the threat faced by all of humankind for its very survival."

"Thanks for your input and support," said Jon. "I'll turn down the violence if I can do it without jeopardizing the success of our project. Remember, we have a mole somewhere in our organization, so zip the lip. We can't even tip our hand to what we know by suddenly and overtly raising security. We must beef up security in a nonchalant way. Marla, you said you have a few words about the security at the Space Elevator?"

"Yes, I think more than a few," responded Marla. "Because it was targeted even before the beginning of construction, the Space Elevator Project must be high on the terrorists' priority list, but I agree with Aieda that Kennedy Space Center is likely to be hit first, especially in light of recent news which I'll explain shortly.

"First, I'd like to acquaint you with security arrangements we have in place. Colonel Alvarez has been assigned by the Ecuadorian government to take charge of security at the site and along the supply route to the site. In my opinion he's an excellent choice. So as not to dilute his authority and cause friction between units, I've delegated my command authority for the five-thousand civilian security personnel to him.

"If you recall, these are mostly American citizens who were influenced to volunteer by our benefactor, Andre. It seems they all belong to the same church. It's called the Church of Spiritual Objectivism. Anyway, Colonel Alvarez has authority over all Ecuadorian police in the four provinces adjacent to and including the site of the Space Elevator.

"The Consortium has provided Colonel Alvarez with a generous budget which he uses with discretion to compensate local residents and businesses that are adversely impacted by the construction traffic along the access route. The general population seems extremely pleased with the increased labor employment provided by the Project. Also, all supplies and food needed by the site are purchased from local merchants. The locals are well aware that certain extremist groups are attempting to sabotage the Project, and they're self-motivated to report suspicious behavior directly to Colonel Alvarez's headquarters or to their local police."

Marla paused and scanned the faces at the table. "Now I want to say a few words about a sensitive and top secret operation. As you may know, our treaty with Ecuador forbids us to have military security other than members of the Corps who are to provide security for themselves strictly during the performance of their construction duties.

"We're covertly violating that treaty by having a contingent of Special Forces operating in the mountains surrounding the project site. Their job has been to spot any suspicious activity that could be a threat to the project and to neutralize the threat when ordered to do so by me. We have six teams of three men each patrolling the area in stealth mode.

"They're aided by infrared satellite imagery. This top secret defense department system can spot heat sources from a typical human over a vast area, then zoom in for a closer look. Just before this meeting convened, I received a secure message from the commander of the teams that they had spotted four teams of five men approaching positions that overlook and partly encircle the project site. It appears they're carrying rifles and mortars. I told the commander to continue surveillance and be prepared to take them out on my orders. That's all for the moment," concluded Marla.

"Jon, do we have any verified intelligence about an imminent attack on Kennedy?" asked Roger. "If we wait until they strike first, won't that irreparably put us behind schedule?"

"Amanda has known about the threat and has created a diversion," explained Jon. "Almost everyone thinks the launch facilities for the Delta IV Heavies will be at Kennedy Space Center. The rocket you see there is a dummy capable of producing some pretty convincing smoke and fire. Even the superstructure for the launch is a dummy. The publicly announced launch date is for the dummy launch, not the real launch, which will occur a few days after.

"Amanda has gone to extremes to keep this secret even within NASA. The real Delta IV launch facilities will be at nearby Cape Canaveral Air Force Station, which will have almost no visible activity until the last minute. We expect the terrorist attack will occur right at or before the moment of launch, because they would know that the rocket can achieve high speed quickly. Their best target is a stationary one," said Jon.

"So, it would seem we're hoping they attack the dummy rocket on the published launch date," said Jean Philippe. "Let's pray the plan works."

"It's our best gambit," responded Tom. "If we don't wipe them out in one stroke, we'll be plagued by periodic attacks that will make it impossible to meet our tight schedule. All will be lost."

"If we know when the attack is likely to occur, and we also know the most likely targets of the attack, shouldn't we evacuate all non-security personnel a day or two before?" asked Amanda.

"We must assume the targets are under twenty-four hour surveillance, so an evacuation or change in the number of people coming to work will tip the terrorists off that we're aware of their plans. We need to get this attack behind us, so we can move forward without debilitating anxiety," commented Jon.

"What about members of the Executive Team?" asked Amanda. "They shouldn't be at any of the target sites for at least a couple of days before the anticipated attack."

"Amanda, I understand your concern," said Don, "but if Roger and I leave the Lodge during high alert, how can we expect the employees to remain there? Many are likely to panic and leave as soon as they realize we've abandoned them."

"I'll be sending my family to Canada to stay with my in-laws," said George, "but I feel duty-bound to lead my people during an attack. During this period of high alert, I'll be staying at the North Branch Lab twenty-four hours a day."

"I agree our activities in the next several days should appear as normal as possible," interjected Roger. "However, I believe there's no reason to subject Guardian to this heightened risk. We should evacuate him to the safe house in Estes Park under cover of darkness tonight."

"Thank you for your concern, Roger, but I'm willing to take the same risk you and your wife take by remaining at the Lodge," said Guardian.

"Guardian, you're too critical to the Star-Slayer Project to be subjected to unnecessary risk," commented Aieda.

"I agree with Roger and Aieda," said Jon. "Guardian, with all due respect, I must insist your bodyguard escort you to the safe house tonight."

"Very well, if you insist," said Guardian.

"What about you, Jean Philippe?" asked Jon.

"It would be quite abnormal for me to remain overnight at the Valbonne Lab as George plans to do at the North Branch Lab," responded Jean Philippe. "I'm afraid it would become the talk of the village. I've recently completed extensive security upgrades, and I have an extremely competent staff that knows how to keep a secret. Many who work at the lab live in the residential area surrounding the village. I can't afford rumors about an impending attack to sweep through the village. Therefore, only my security staff will be informed of the threat. The gate pass-cards have been reprogrammed to allow entry for only thirty minutes at the beginning of each particular employee's shift. The employee must enter a pass code in addition to swiping the pass-card."

"Where will you be during this vulnerable period?" asked Jon.

"I have a number of residences throughout the world that I frequent on an irregular basis," said Jean Philippe. "I doubt the terrorists would know where to attack. I'll probably find myself relaxing at my chateau outside the city of Bordeaux, north along the Garonne River."

"Marla and I must remain at the Space Elevator site to do our jobs, despite the threat of an attack," said Tom. "However, Jon, shouldn't you take a quick trip? I think you're vulnerable at your house."

"I've taken additional precautions at the house, but I agree. However, I'm concerned my departure might tip our hand. We expect the attacks to begin the morning of the next scheduled Delta IV launch. On that morning, an hour before the launch, I'll leave the house with packed bags and my bodyguard for a few days in the Adirondacks."

"Jon, how safe will it be at your house?" asked Tom. "These intruders won't be your typical burglars."

"I've added twenty-four hour external security . . . two well armed men on each shift," explained Jon. "The six off duty security personnel stay in a rented flat just a few minutes down the block and can respond quickly if backup is needed. Although our home office building wasn't mentioned in the Internet chatter as a target, I've also increased its twenty-four hour external security."

"George, apart from your staying at the North Branch Lab twenty-four hours a day, have you increased security?" asked Tom.

"The terrain around the North Branch facility is a former farm field with a creek running through the southwest corner," said George. "It's surrounded by a ten foot high fence with barbed wire at the top. Ten feet inside the fence is a fifteen foot wide by five foot deep trench. The only road to the property is a county road that runs past the guarded entry gate. On the roof of the building we have security personnel with AS-50 sniper rifles who can take out an attacker as far as 2,000 yards, which is about the distance from the building to the gate. To the rear of the building there's an old barn. Inside is my recently acquired secret weapon. If our snipers can't stop the attackers, this will."

Chapter 28

July 2008

Jon Walmer was thinking how tomorrow would be the scheduled launch of the first Delta IV Heavy rocket associated with the Manned Mission to Mars. Internet chatter related to a terrorist attack had dropped to zero, just as anticipated. Jon was convinced the terrorists would attack the launch facility at the Kennedy Space Center tomorrow at 7:30 a.m. He was hoping the attackers wouldn't detect that the rocket on the launch pad was a dummy.

He expected tomorrow's attack to signal the start of all other attacks on the Consortium's facilities. His people were prepared. Even so, he would evacuate his house by 6:30 a.m. out of an abundance of caution. He crawled into bed fully aware he wouldn't get a wink of sleep. Harry had left him a tray on his nightstand with a glass of water and his pills. Twice a day Jon took vitamins, minerals, and herbs to stay healthy. Tonight, he couldn't stomach taking the pills. He didn't realize he'd fallen asleep, because he was dreaming he was awake waiting for the phone to ring, informing him of the attack at Kennedy.

He felt someone shaking him awake by his shoulder.

"Sir, wake up. Get up quickly. Wake up. It's Harry, sir. We have an intruder."

Jon sat up and stared into Harry's eyes.

"What's the matter, Harry?" asked Jon.

"Sir, you must get to the safe room immediately. There's an intruder in the house," whispered Harry as he grabbed Jon by the arm and escorted him to the closet.

In the back of the closet, behind the hanging clothes, there was a secret door leading to a bulletproof and soundproof room. Inside the room was a chair, a small table, a monitor connected to the security system, a large bottle of water, a medical kit, a wireless telephone, a double-barrel semi-automatic shotgun, a Colt .45 semi-automatic pistol, and plenty of ammo.

"Stay in here, sir. External security isn't responding. I've alerted backup security, and they're on the way. I have night-vision goggles, and I'm armed. Don't worry," said Harry as he closed the secret door and pulled the clothes back in place to help conceal it.

Although the room was soundproof, Jon could see and hear a good part of what was happening via the monitor that had access to cameras and microphones in the hallway, living room, dining room, library, family room, and kitchen. Unfortunately, the cameras had no night-vision or infrared capability, and most of the rooms were too dark for him to make out anything but shadows. He was still partly asleep when Harry had hurried him into the safe room. There were two other identical rooms, each on a different floor. Jon had never spent more than a minute in them for inspection purposes. He was wide awake now and beginning to feel claustrophobic on top of his anxiety for Harry's safety.

If he ventured out of the safe room, Harry might mistake him for an intruder or, worse, he might shoot at Harry. Backup security personnel were on the way, so he convinced himself to stay put while using the monitor to scan the house from room to room, trying to spot Harry or the intruder. He wondered what had happened to the two outside security guards. Then, as he switched the monitor to the library, he almost jumped out of his chair as two bright flashes and explosions startled him. The gunshots were from opposite ends of the library. He saw no movement and heard no sounds after the two shots.

"Oh my God, Harry must be shot!" he said softly to himself.

Without thinking, Jon grabbed the Colt .45 and left the safe room to come to Harry's aid. Barefooted and in nothing but his under shorts, he stealthily moved down the stairs and worked his way along the hallway to the library. He crouched to the floor and peered around the bottom of the door jamb and into the library.

The smell of gunpowder alerted all his senses, but he could see nothing. The darkness was too much. He stood and reached around the door jamb with his left hand and felt the inside wall for the light switch. He found it. He hesitated. With the pistol in his right hand and his left hand on the light switch, he put his head around the corner and peered into the room while simultaneously flipping on the lights. His eyes quickly scanned the room and spotted Harry's foot laying on the floor, sticking out from behind the sofa.

He ran to Harry and got within two feet of him. For a second he stared in bewilderment. It wasn't Harry. Just as that realization came to him, he heard a sound from behind and turned. A tall man with a black hood over his head was flying toward him with a large knife in his right hand. Jon reacted by deflecting the knife with the pistol, but not far enough.

The knife caught him in his left side. The pain was so excruciating, he let out a blood-curdling scream. He began falling on his back with his attacker falling with him. Jon hit the floor and saw the knife above his head in position for a final fatal stab. He felt the pistol still in his right hand between his body and that of his attacker. He squeezed the trigger five times as the knife lingered menacingly close to his neck. The attacker slowly rolled over to Jon's left, as the knife crashed loudly to the floor. The attacker was lying lifeless on his back. The pain in Jon's side was intense, and he was bleeding profusely.

He started to get up and was reaching for a small pillow on the sofa to press over his wound when two men in black hoods suddenly appeared in the room. One quickly surveyed the room as the other took aim at him with what looked like a 9-mm Beretta. Jon could see nothing but that pistol aiming at him frozen in time.

The pistol began to move away just as he heard a loud blast from the doorway. The pistol flew out of the man's hand, and the man dropped to the floor. The second man fired toward the doorway, and the lights went out. Jon crawled behind the sofa with the pillow pressed tightly to his wound; taking refuge next to the dead body he had thought was Harry.

He could hear the fight with the crashing of furniture, the blows to the body, the grunts and snarls of two men fighting. Then there was silence for a few moments. Then talking and yelling. Jon couldn't understand what was said. Flashlights flooded the room. It was his security personnel. He crawled out from behind the sofa with enough presence of mind to drop his pistol and raise his right hand. His left hand still held the small pillow to his left side. The pillow was soaked in blood, and his face was ghost white. He spoke his name and surveyed the room with the random movements of the flashlights. He could see a man on the floor with no hood, and his neck clearly broken. Then he saw Harry with a knife in his chest. He yelled out Harry's name and staggered toward him. He passed out before he could get to his friend.

———————————◇———————————

It was 6:30 a.m. at the Port Canaveral Cruise Terminal, Pier 10. The cruise ship had pulled into the terminal at 6:00 a.m. Deck 14, the Sky deck, was empty as the passengers had begun to disembark, and there were no cabins on Decks 12 or 14. Only Abdul Rasheed Mahmoud from Bali occupied Deck 14.

He thought it was superstitious and ignorant of the Americans to skip Deck 13. He was raised as a strict Muslim, although neither he nor his parents subscribed to the radical Islam of Al Qaeda. It was Allah's will that commanded the Universe and not the number thirteen or any other symbol of the non-believer.

He had become a member of the *Preservers of Scripture* via Internet contacts and was committed to the organization's goals, despite the fact that its members included Christians and Jews. Yes, it seemed strange to be so closely aligned with infidels, but he justified it with the old saying, *the enemy of my enemy is my friend*. Abdul knew from the Holy Scriptures that mankind must be confronted with God's wrath on earth and must not be allowed to escape to another heavenly body.

Abdul sat with his back against a storage unit built into the center of the deck, feet flat on the floor. His arms rested on his knees, which were almost up to his chest. His head tilted downward, so he looked like he was asleep. He wasn't. He was alternately praying for success and reviewing every detail of his action plan. Periodically he checked the time on his wristwatch.

On the port side of the ship, no more than twelve miles away, was the Kennedy Space Center and its launch facilities. With his binoculars he'd checked its exact location before sitting down to wait for the precise moment for action. It was now 7:00 a.m., and Abdul stood quickly without hesitation. He reached into his pocket and took out a small radio with an earplug that he attached to his left ear. He turned on the radio and adjusted the tuner until the news coverage at Kennedy came in clearly. He hooked the radio to his belt at his left hip. The countdown to launch was on schedule for 7:30 a.m.

Abdul turned and opened a locked door to the storage cabinet. The package was there just as he'd been told. He'd worked on this cruise ship for a year preparing for this moment. He pulled out the canvas bag and opened it. Inside the bag was a Stinger missile left over from when the Afghanistan resistance forces defeated the Soviet Army. *Made in U.S.A.* could be seen on a small metal plate that included the model number, serial number, and date of manufacture. Abdul patted the missile and welcomed it home. He smiled at the irony of an American made missile finding its way back from Afghanistan to destroy an even larger American missile for Allah's sake. He removed the missile from the bag, checked it out as he had been taught, and prepared it for use.

In the cabinet was a 5-gallon can of kerosene and a large plastic tub. He poured the kerosene into the tub, removed the missile from its rack, taped a plastic bag over the launch engine, and gently lowered it into the kerosene. As soon as the missile was covered in the kerosene, he started his stop watch. When it hit 118 seconds he quickly removed the missile from its bath and wiped it off with rags that had been placed in the cabinet for that purpose. He then removed the plastic bag from the launch engine and mounted the missile back onto its rack.

It was now 7:12 a.m. The radio confirmed the countdown was on schedule. He took the weapon with him to the port side of the ship facing the direction he'd identified earlier. The target couldn't be seen with the naked eye, but he could see it in the scope attached to the weapon. He hoisted it to his shoulder to check the target. He had only one shot, so he had to do it right the first time.

At twelve miles away, it would take his modified Stinger three minutes to reach its target. This distance was beyond the design capability for the Stinger, which had a max range of five miles. It was the kerosene bath trick learned by the Afghan Mujahadin that made it possible to extend the range. Fortunately for Abdul, the requisite holes had been drilled around the circumference and along the length of the solid rocket engine.

The factory design for the Stinger had a launch rocket that got the missile out of the rack and away from the user, then the solid rocket ignited and propelled the missile to over 1500 mph for up to five miles. The Afghan modification had tiny precisely drilled holes along the body of the rocket which allowed for the kerosene to soak the surface of the solid propellant. If soaked too soon, it would evaporate. The purpose of the kerosene was to slow the burning of the solid fuel so it would burn longer and propel the missile a longer distance at a slower speed. In Abdul's case the modification was engineered to slow the rocket to 240 mph for twelve miles.

Although the Stinger flew by line of sight, it needed to lock onto a heat source to ensure a hit. If Abdul were to wait until the countdown to zero, the target could accelerate fast enough in three minutes that the Stinger could not catch it. He had to fire at precisely two minutes and forty-five seconds to blastoff.

Abdul didn't want to be spotted standing in the open with the weapon, so he put it down to his side and stepped back against the bulkhead at the center of the deck and waited until 7:25 a.m. as he monitored the countdown on his radio. At 7:25 he took six steps forward, hoisted the weapon to his shoulder, took aim in the scope, spotted the target, and waited for the countdown to reach two minutes forty-five seconds to launch. His breathing became heavy and more rapid as he stood ready to fire. He controlled his breathing, but his heart started to beat rapidly. He could feel it almost bursting from his chest. He took off the safety. The count reached three minutes to launch; two minutes fifty-five seconds, fifty seconds, forty-five seconds . . . Abdul gently squeezed the trigger as he kept the cross-hairs aimed slightly above the target.

With a crackle and a whoosh, the missile fired straight toward where he had aimed it. He followed the missile in the scope as it approached its target. It seemed like forever as he watched and listened to the countdown proceed on the radio. Then Abdul saw the Delta rocket ignition flare up at the launch site. The Stinger was on a path above the Delta rocket, but as soon as it locked onto the heat source, it curved its flight path downward and struck its target.

Abdul was so ecstatic at the sight that he raised the weapon and leaped into the air. A moment later he stopped and looked out at his target. Something wasn't quite right. The explosion should've been much bigger. He had no time to continue with this train of thought. He took the weapon back to the storage cabinet and put it back into its bag. He locked the kerosene can, tub, and rags in the cabinet and walked down the outside stairs to Deck 12, carrying the bag with him to the railing on the port side of the ship. With one big heave he tossed the bag with its contents overboard into the water. He watched it hit the surface, float for a minute, and sink. He then proceeded to leave the ship from the starboard side with the remaining passengers and crew.

Abdul was expected back onboard at 6:00 p.m., but he had reserved a flight out of Orlando International Airport with a final destination of Bali. He'd left his letter of resignation in the Captain's mailbox, apologizing for leaving on such short notice, but explaining it was due to an unexpected illness in the family, and would the Captain please arrange for his final paycheck to be mailed to his address of record.

———————————————◇———————————————

It was 6:00 a.m. at the Lodge in Estes Park in Colorado. A half hour had passed since the news about the attack at Kennedy Space Center. The destruction of the Delta IV rocket was seen on TV all over the world, and radio broadcasts also carried the tragedy. The Internet was a buzz with details, speculation, comments, and all manner of reaction, some sane and some not, as is wont for Internet communications.

Security at the Lodge had been alerted, but almost all the others were still asleep. The guards at the main gate signaled to all security personnel that sensors indicated some high speed traffic coming up the roadway toward them. Designated security personnel were dispatched toward the gate, and a distress call was sent to the Ranger station. All off-duty security personnel were called to their stations, and emergency procedures were initiated for all employees and guests.

By the time these procedures were implemented, the attackers were at the gate. The first was a Hummer outfitted with armor plate. It drove at high speed, crashing through the gate, right past the guards. Behind the first Hummer was a second one mounted with a .50 caliber M2 machine gun, spraying bullets in front of it. Behind it were motorcycles, two abreast and ten deep. Each had the driver and a rider behind him. Each rider had a semi-automatic pistol in both hands.

The first Hummer got to the steps of the Lodge. Four commandos piled out of it, ran up the stairs, and broke through the double French doors, thereby bypassing the security room. The second Hummer blasted the security room with machine gun fire, then took a defensive position as a few more commandos piled out and secured the entrances to the Lodge. The second Hummer then moved to the helicopter pad and took a position on it with machine gun aimed skyward. The motorcycles came up the drive, rode up the steps and right into the Lodge. They started rounding people up inside the Lodge and randomly shooting others.

Rangers arrived in their Black Hawk helicopter from Longs Peak Ranger Station. They took fire from the Hummer trying to prevent them from landing. A rocket blew it right off the pad, the chopper landed, and the Rangers piled out. Security personnel at the Lodge were fighting inside and outside, but were barely holding their own against dozens of attackers.

The eleven Rangers picked off the enemy like they were accumulating points in a shooting gallery. Several times the attackers tried to protect themselves by holding a hostage, so the Rangers targeted the head. The scene became a bloody mess. The shooting was still going on almost half an hour later when more Rangers arrived in two Black Hawk helicopters from Buckley AFB. They secured the area within ten minutes. None of the attackers would surrender, and a few who saw they were about to be taken alive shot themselves.

Dennis Radford, head of security for the Lodge, sat outside on one of the steps leading up to the front doors that had been so easily breached. His left arm was hurt, and he was pressing a wad of tissues against it to stop the bleeding. The wounded were being helped by the less wounded or the unwounded. The Rangers had called in for medical assistance and medevac copters, but no help had arrived yet. Dennis was partly in shock after hearing the estimate of dead and wounded. He felt responsible for not having a better security plan. The number of attackers and their ferocious frontal assault was unexpected, and almost succeeded. Had they gotten into the subterranean laboratories . . . well, that would have been hell to live with. As it was, the dead and wounded were almost too much for him to bear.

Roger Akins spotted Dennis and approached him.

"Dennis, are you all right?" asked Roger. "Let me look at your arm."

Roger sat on the step next to Dennis and checked his wound. The wad of tissues had done the trick by speeding up the clotting so no more blood was flowing.

"Dennis, the wound doesn't look serious. I don't see any embedded bullet or fragment. I'm sure you'll be okay," said Roger in his most comforting voice.

Dennis lifted his head and turned toward Roger. His eyes were full of tears and his face was red.

"Over fifty people died because I didn't anticipate a frontal assault. I should have planned for it and slowed it down. Four more minutes would have saved so many lives. My God, all those people are dead," cried Dennis.

"Dennis, it wasn't your fault," explained Roger. "The defensive plan for the Lodge had been established before you arrived. It was reviewed three times; the last time by Lt. General Marla Odenfelder. You can't shoulder the burden for this tragedy. It's impossible to defend perfectly against all possible modes of attack. Although the cost was great, you won the battle against great odds. I can tell you this for certain—your success here today will save more lives than you can possibly imagine."

Roger put his arm around Dennis's shoulder, careful not to bump his wound. Dennis broke down and cried softly.

———————————————◊———————————————

It was 2:00 p.m. in Valbonne, France. The research labs of Marseilles Electric Enterprises were perched on a hillside in the surrounding woods outside the village with a view of the valley down to the river Brague. Jean Philippe Martinique had discussed the likelihood of an attack on the facility with his security team. They had agreed it would be wise to make some upgrades.

It would be impossible to mount an attack up the hillside through the dense woods without being spotted. The entire complex was surrounded by a ten-foot high chain-link fence cleared of all trees and brush ten meters on each side. It would be easy for security to shoot any intruders who tried to break through the fence. There was only one road up the hill, and an electronically controlled, steel security gate at the bottom stopped unauthorized personnel. As just one of his security upgrades, Jean Philippe had a second gate placed seven meters inside the first gate. The second gate wouldn't open until the first gate closed behind the vehicle.

On the road to either side of the gate he had a deep trench dug so it wasn't possible for a vehicle to bulldoze its way around the gates. From the security control room, the guards could observe the gate and the entire road from remote security cameras. Jean Philippe was taking no chances, so he had ordered a section of the road about a kilometer up the hill from the entry gate to be modified with a remotely triggered steel wall that would rise instantly from beneath the pavement.

The final upgrade was the addition of remotely activated DLO 1919A4 machine guns, each aimed and triggered by a radar motion-detecting sensor. Upon activation from the control room, the guns would rise from underground vaults on both sides of the road for 100 meters prior to the popup wall. The deep ditch on the sides of the road and the concrete gun vaults behind them were designed to prevent vehicles from driving around the wall.

It was a sunny afternoon, and the air was clean and crisp as a refreshing breeze rose up from the pastoral valley below. A van pulled up to about ten meters in front of the first gate. The motion sensor detected the vehicle and alerted the guard in the control room. From the monitor he watched as a bearded man got out of the van, attached a rope through several sections of the gate, fitted something to the end of the rope, then lit it with a pocket lighter. He dashed back to the van and got inside just as the gate exploded and fell forward onto the ground.

"Shit! C-4 braided rope," yelled the guard aloud in French as he sounded the alarm and called for backup from within the complex. Police from the village were automatically alerted. Perimeter lights around the complex turned on, but contributed nothing in the bright sunlight. A second guard entered the control room.

"What the hell is going on?" asked the guard as he entered the room.

"Some guy just blew the main gate. Man your post now!" answered the first guard.

Other security personnel retrieved their AS-50 sniper rifles and took their assigned positions to protect the fence surrounding the complex. The entryway in the fence at the top of the hill in front of the building closed automatically, instantly electrifying the entire fence. The front doors of the building were made of bulletproof glass and locked automatically when the alarm went off.

The two guards watched the van move forward, driving over the gate on the ground. The bearded man got out and did the same thing to the second gate. It, too, exploded and fell to the ground, but the van did not move forward. It seemed like it was having second thoughts.

"Why has it stopped?" asked the first guard rhetorically.

"Look what's coming up the road," said the second guard.

A strange menagerie of compact cars drove up and stopped behind the van . . . Peugeot, Citroen, Renault, Fiat, and VW. From the top of the van a machine gun slowly rose from within, and a helmeted head and torso popped up behind it. The van burned rubber and drove over the second gate, accelerating rapidly. The cars revved-up in hot pursuit.

The first guard had his eye on the monitor and his fingers on a red key. As soon as he saw the van pass the triangle painted on the road, he turned the key and yelled, "Engage!" The second guard on the other side of the room immediately turned his key. For a few seconds nothing happened, then on the monitors both guards saw the steel wall rise instantly in the road in front of the van which by now was doing over 100 kph.

There was hardly time for the driver to apply the brakes. The van hit the wall with such force that it split open like a tin can. The machine gun and its operator went flying out the top of the van. His body smashed against the wall and bounced off like a rubber ball. The lead compacts tried to avoid hitting the back of the van by going to its sides, but they were going so fast they, too, hit the wall.

Other compacts crashed into the van. Some of the cars skidded and smashed into each other. Bullets from the machine guns on both sides of the road peppered them constantly. Men got out of the cars and tried to run back down the road, but no one survived the gauntlet of bullets. Several of the compacts caught fire; flames reached fuel tanks which exploded. The guns kept firing until there was no more movement.

While the attack on the road was beginning to unfold, five extremists had made their way by foot up the hillside to the back of the complex. They unknowingly were in the rifle sights of two guards at their assigned posts.

"Don't fire till they get to the fence," said one guard to the other over their com-units.

The attackers approached the fence and stood there while one removed a small bolt-cutter from his backpack. The moment he touched the fence with it, sparks flew. Unable to pull away from the high voltage death grip, he shook convulsively and caught fire like a rag doll. The others were startled and jumped back, their reaction cueing the two guards to open fire. Three attackers dropped to the ground quickly. The fourth turned to run for cover in the woods, but didn't make it.

The air around the complex smelled of burnt flesh, gasoline and gunpowder. The police sirens could be heard coming up the hillside from the village below.

"Sound the all clear," yelled the second guard.

The steel wall that blocked the road slowly retracted beneath the pavement, scraping off detritus as it disappeared, and the machine guns retracted into their vaults. Blood and bodies littered the road around the decimated vehicles. The police got out of their cars and walked around the gruesome scene. They jogged up the road and arrived at the lobby where they were met by the site manager. They wanted to know what the hell had happened. It was a long day for the manager.

———————————◊———————————

It was 8:00 a.m. in North Branch, NJ. The guard at the gate to the property had started his shift at 7:00 a.m. and had already let dozens of employees through. Down the road he spotted two heavy duty pickup trucks followed by over a dozen SUV's coming toward the gate. He fully expected them to pass by. As they got closer, he watched as tarps were pulled off the cargo in the beds of the trucks.

"Oh, my God!" yelled the guard, who immediately contacted the chief of security.

"Two trucks are approaching at high speed with a bunch of SUV's following them. Looks like a machine gun mounted on a raised platform in the bed of each truck," reported the guard.

"Grab your weapon and run perpendicular to the access road and across the field to the creek where you'll have some cover," commanded the chief.

The guard barely got to the creek when the first truck crashed through the gate. The second truck followed and fired in his direction. Alarms sounded throughout the facility, summoning security personnel to their posts.

When George Blocker saw what was happening, he got on his com-unit, "Abrams, this is Blocker. Get into position now!"

The barn was behind the lab building, so the Abrams M1 tank couldn't be seen as it quickly pulled out of the barn. It headed straight for the back of the building, then moved around the south side and waited for George's command. It was a little more than a mile down the road to the lab building. Ten snipers were in position on the roof. The attackers would be there in less than a minute.

"Shooters, this is Blocker. Wait until the lead trucks get within five-hundred yards, then open fire."

The trucks were traveling side-by-side down the road, and the SUV's were following. When the snipers opened fire, they had little effect because the trucks had heavy front armor plate. When the trucks got within 200 yards, George got on his com-unit again. "Abrams, this is Blocker. Attack now!"

The tank came barreling out from around the corner of the building. It took only five seconds for it to fire on the trucks. The first 105 mm round caught the right front of the closest truck and the right rear of the truck next to it. Both vehicles exploded into hundreds of pieces, with the bigger ones tumbling menacingly in the air. Parts strewed over the road and pummeled some of the SUV's. Without cover from the trucks, and with the distance much shorter, the other vehicles took heavy damage from the snipers, but kept on coming.

The Abrams moved out quickly across the field toward the pack of SUV's. The gunner fired three more 105 mm rounds while moving over rough ground at almost thirty mph. The 7.62 mm machine gun on an Abrams was mounted coaxially to the 105 mm main gun such that both weapons moved together with the turret, and the gunner knew instinctively to switch to this weapon to stop as many SUV's as possible.

The commander ordered the driver to continue on an intercept course with the lead vehicles as he climbed part way out the hatch to use the .50 caliber M2HB heavy machine gun. Outside the cupola, the commander had the best visibility as he destroyed one vehicle after another. The remaining five SUV's realized the futility of their attack and turned back toward the gate. The gunner fired two more 105 mm rounds at the retreating targets, then again switched to firing the 7.62 mm machine gun.

The snipers on the roof were relentless. It took a moment to realize there was no more movement from the enemy. All firing stopped spontaneously. Great clouds of brown dust drifted over the battlefield, slowly revealing the mayhem beneath. The snipers got off the roof. The tank crew got out of their hot, cramped sardine can. George Blocker came running out the front of the building toward the tank.

"Great job, guys!" yelled George. "Without you and the Abrams, everyone in the building would be dead or dying right about now. I promise never again to complain when an employee takes leave for National Guard training. How you ever got your commanding officer to loan us a tank is a wonder to me."

"Well," said the gunner, "the colonel said we could take our weapons home to clean them. We just took him literally."

"All of which means we've got to get this baby cleaned-up and back in the Armory," said the driver, "before anyone notices."

"How are you going to explain the missing ammo?" asked George.

"When we do maneuvers," said the loader, "we expend many thousands of rounds of ammo. Clerical error and duds will easily account for what we expended here today."

"God bless the Army National Guard!" said George.

He smiled and walked back to the building as he wondered how he was going to explain all the dead bodies and mangled vehicles to the local cops. Maybe they'll believe it was done with landmines. Maybe he'd better write out a big donation to the local FOP lodge.

————————————◊————————————

It was 0700 hours at the Space Elevator Project base in Ecuador. The Special Forces units were ordered to maintain surveillance of the hostile intruders in the foothills below them overlooking the base. They were not to fire until either the intruders fired or they were ordered to fire by General Odenfelder, who went by the call-sign, *Beowulf*.

"Beowulf, the intruders have set up four separate two-man mortar emplacements. Twelve riflemen, three from each team, have moved down the mountainside toward the fence. They're out of sight behind boulders, but it looks like they're moving to positions that would allow them to shoot anyone who moves between the residential area and the construction area," said Sherpa One.

"They must be waiting for shift change at 0730 hours," said Beowulf. "That's when traffic will be slow and dense. What's the range of their mortars?"

"They can't reach the construction site, but they can do some serious damage to the warehouses," said Sherpa One.

"Why didn't they set up to hit the residential area?" asked Beowulf.

"The way the base is nestled into the natural curvature of the hillside, they can't get a bead on the apartments and barracks," answered Sherpa One. "They would only be able to bombard the market area, and at this time of day none of the shops have opened."

"I wanted to wait for them to fire the first shot, but there are too many lives at stake if they open fire during shift change," said Beowulf. "I want you to wait until 07:15, then take out those mortar emplacements. I'll simultaneously sound the emergency siren which will stop the shift change and get almost everyone into a shelter. Once you take out the mortars, move downhill and pick off the riflemen."

"How will you explain our presence?" asked Sherpa One.

"I won't have to, because you'll take the dead with you," said Beowulf. "We'll be firing into the hillside as if in self defense. It'll be assumed that survivors took any dead or wounded with them. Don't leave evidence of a lot of blood and guts. Make sure you take their rifles and mortars with you so it looks like they're planning a repeat attack."

"Roger that, Beowulf. Sherpa One out."

At 07:05 Sherpa One assigned eight snipers to quietly take out the men manning the four mortars. He and his remaining nine men began making their way slowly, methodically, and quietly down the mountainside to take out the dozen intruders below who had rifles ready to fire on workers during shift change. At 07:15 the snipers took out the eight men manning the mortars, and the emergency siren at the base went off and echoed through the mountain passes.

Realizing that they had been spotted, the riflemen began shooting into the open area leading to the construction entry gate. There were several groups of men and women milling about, so the riflemen had some choices for their targets. Right after they began firing, a group of base security personnel appeared and began shooting at them. The targets began scattering in every direction, but the riflemen had no trouble wounding dozens despite the return fire they were receiving.

The eight snipers were moving downhill to help dispatch the rest of the intruders. They assumed they'd killed those manning the mortars. They were wrong. Shot but not incapacitated, an intruder got up on his knees, checked the mortar alignment, picked up a shell, and dropped it into the tube. Without waiting to see the effect of the first shot, he dropped another round down the tube. Right about then his first round hit a warehouse right smack in the middle and set it burning fiercely. He watched as his second round hit a stack of steel drums causing fragments to fly in every direction.

About a dozen workers had taken shelter in the warehouse before the mortar shells had hit. They went running out when the fire started, but then the rifle fire from the mountainside and the second mortar wounded many of them. There were at least a dozen wounded workers lying in the open with a blazing warehouse behind them, and no place to hide.

One of the Sherpa snipers realized it was up to him to take out the mortar quickly. He scrambled back uphill, got on top of a large boulder, spotted the man about to load the mortar for the third time, and stopped him cold with one shot.

––––––––––––––––––––––◊––––––––––––––––––––––

On the base, Colonel Alvarez was directing his troopers to fire back at the riflemen on the mountainside when the first mortar round exploded within the compound, then the second. Twenty or so men were squirming and writhing in pain on the ground right out in the open, and as if in slow motion he watched as, one by one, they were being finished-off by rifle fire. Reacting instinctively, he ran over to a stack of fifty-five gallon steel drums filled with water and pushed it over.

"Get over here and help me roll these drums," he yelled to a group of his troopers in Spanish, forgetting that most only spoke English.

Language wasn't a barrier. They all understood what he was doing, and they began helping him roll drums toward the wounded to provide some protection. After they rolled about a dozen drums fairly close to each clump of wounded, Alvarez got behind a small dumpster with wheels and, using it as cover, pushed it into the center of the open area where he became a target.

"You bastards!" he yelled as bullets struck the dumpster and the ground around it.

Leaving the safety of cover from the dumpster, he ran in a crouched position to the first wounded worker and dragged him behind the closest water drum. He positioned him in a fetal position with his back against the drum.

"Don't worry, I'll get you out of here," he told the man.

He ran to another and dragged him to another drum. Blood gushed from his thigh as the sharp pain of the bullet that found its mark shot up his left side to his jaw. Like a boxer recovering from a right cross to the head, Alvarez staggered to his knees to drag another wounded worker to cover behind the closest drum. Another bullet found its mark, passing through his right bicep. His scream could be heard above the din of gunfire, but he continued to drag workers to safety.

If he found someone dead, he moved on to the next person. Despite his wounds, Alvarez moved from one victim to another in an awkward, but methodical manner. He had moved eleven wounded workers to shelter behind drums, but gunshot holes were draining water out of them, and they would soon offer little protection. Having wrapped his wounds with pieces of cloth torn from his shirt, Alvarez proceeded to drag the wounded out from behind the drums to behind the dumpster. A bullet pierced his other arm.

"I need more cover. Shoot the bastards!" he screamed to his troopers.

As he dragged each limp body behind the dumpster, he got hit again and again, but continued until the last person had to be dragged while he scooted backwards on his left hip. Bathed in his own blood from head to foot, Alvarez had pulled all eleven wounded to behind the dumpster, which offered considerable protection from the continuous rifle fire. Exhaustion and loss of blood took their toll as consciousness faded from him.

"I go to join God," he whispered to himself as his body went limp.

Sherpa One and his men finally worked their way into a position where they could barely see their targets behind the boulders, but they were close enough to toss a few fragmentation grenades nearby. When the riflemen stood to scramble away, they opened fire and got a couple. The sequence seemed to work. Throw a grenade and shoot when they scramble. After over a dozen of these sequences, either the grenade or the rifle made the kill. Now they had to clean up the mess and cart the bodies and their equipment up the mountainside. Sherpa One knew of a small lake that would welcome the dead tied down with boulders. They would have to make two trips, as he had eighteen men, and there were twenty dead bodies with weapons and equipment.

"Beowulf, the intruders have been neutralized," said Sherpa One. "We have no dead and no wounded, but it'll take us two days to do the cleanup."

"Okay, Sherpa One," said Beowulf. "I'm completely in charge now, so I can assure you there will be no one up there investigating for at least a week."

"Roger that, Beowulf. Sherpa One out."

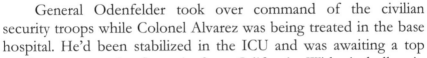

General Odenfelder took over command of the civilian security troops while Colonel Alvarez was being treated in the base hospital. He'd been stabilized in the ICU and was awaiting a top notch surgeon to be flown in from California. With six bullets in arms, legs, shoulder, and back, he was unconscious and in critical condition.

His blood pressure had dropped so low his heart had begun to fibrillate. They had stopped the bleeding, replaced lost blood, and normalized the heartbeat. The bullets had been removed, but they had done serious damage to blood vessels, muscles, and bones. At his age there was too much damage for his body to heal on its own, so there was hope that the surgeon could do enough repairs to give his body a chance to heal.

A week after extensive surgery, Colonel Carlos Alvarez was still unconscious, but no longer in the ICU. Marla Odenfelder and Tom Calvano had visited him daily and spoken to him with the hope he could hear them and wake up. The doctor said he wasn't in a coma and would awaken when his body was no longer in a state of exhaustion. It was the beginning of the second week in the hospital. Tom and Marla were visiting Carlos together when he opened his eyes and moaned. Marla was the first to react. She jumped out of the chair and stood at the side of the bed with a concerned look. Carlos smiled at her. She grabbed his left hand and held it gently. He fell back asleep.

The next day Carlos was actually able to talk and was eating solid food. Tom and Marla were spending morning and evening at the bedside of their friend.

"Really, my friends, you don't have to visit me so much. I'm afraid you're neglecting your duties. I'm feeling better every day," said Carlos.

"Carlos, you should know that because of your selfless actions, eleven people were saved," said Tom. "You no longer have to wonder how you'll perform under direct fire from the enemy."

"Thank you, Tom," said Carlos. "I was afraid to ask if my efforts were in vain. I'm happy for the lives I've saved."

"One other thing you should know," said Marla. "Eight of those you rescued were American citizens, and what you did was not just in defense of individual lives, but in defense of the Space Elevator Project which the President of the United States believes has the potential to save countless lives in the future. In recognition of your heroic service to the citizens and government of the United States of America, the President intends to award you the Officer's Degree of the Legion of Merit. After you're well enough, a ceremony will be scheduled at the White House to present you the medal. Congratulations, Carlos."

Tears streamed down Carlos's face. He reached for a tissue on the nightstand and blotted his eyes. Marla kissed him on the cheek and stepped back. Tom stepped up and shook his hand. Carlos was back in control of his emotions. He smiled broadly at Tom.

"Thank you so much, Marla and Tom," said Carlos. "I'm a lucky man to have friends like you."

"Get some rest," said Tom. "We'll see you tomorrow."

———————————◊———————————

After Tom and Marla left the hospital, they went to the Officers' Club, a small and cozy place to speak privately.

"You know, I still don't understand what the extremists had in mind when they attacked us," said Tom.

"What do you mean? They were attempting to slow down our project," responded Marla.

The waitress brought their drinks. Tom and Marla waited for her to leave before continuing their conversation.

"Yes, but there wasn't much they could do with those mortars and rifles, and they knew it," explained Tom. "The mortars couldn't reach the construction area. The rifles could take out dozens of people randomly, but not enough to slow the project. There had to be more to their plan."

"More to their plan that didn't come off because we hit them before they could complete it," echoed Marla.

"You did more than hit them hard and soon. You set off the emergency sirens and stopped the shift change," continued Tom. "We thought they were waiting for shift change so they could easily kill more workers, but what if it was for another reason?"

"Under cover of all the confusion and mayhem," speculated Marla, "an authorized worker could easily carry explosives into the construction area where he could later do some real damage to the project."

"I think you've put your finger on it, Marla," said Tom. "We still have a live one among us hell bent on blowing up our Space Elevator before we get it finished."

"That's just great. How do we find him?" asked Marla.

"Not we; you. I'm glad it's your job, because I don't have a clue, and there may be more than one out there," said Tom.

Marla's driver was waiting curbside. She and Tom got in the car and were dropped off at their apartment complex. In the recent past they would each go directly to their separate apartments, then join up in his or hers in fifteen or twenty minutes. They had soon realized they weren't kidding anyone. This time they walked directly to Marla's pad with no hesitation. Rumor and gossip spoke mostly of what a fine couple they made. Individually they were well liked, and there was a lot of wishful talk about how cool it would be to have a wedding on the base.

———————————◇———————————

It was 3:05 p.m. in Riyadh, Saudi Arabia. A duststorm was blowing through the city, keeping almost everyone off the streets. It was extremely hot. Three men hurried through an alley to a side entrance of a multi-story residential building. Each had a scarf protecting the face and at the same time obscuring it from view.

"Quickly, up the stairs to the second floor," whispered the one with the blue scarf.

At the top of the stairs, just down the hall, they busted the door open and rousted two men from a table where they had a TV and a computer.

"Check that computer," commanded the blue scarf as he waited, impatiently pacing behind the man at the computer.

"Confirmed!" said the brown scarf. "It's a node in the network all right."

Four more men entered the apartment, injected the two captives with something that put them to sleep, then carried them and their computer down the stairs and out of the building to a mini-van waiting at the entrance to the alley. Hardly ten minutes had elapsed since the men in scarves had arrived.

———————————◇———————————

It was 3:05 p.m. in Aden, Yemen. The sky was clear with passing clouds. It was extremely hot. Two men went down stairs leading to a basement beneath a bakery that displayed a *closed* sign. It took both of them to bust the door open, and for their efforts, they were hit with several bullets that failed to penetrate their Kevlar vests. In response, two grenades seemed to launch themselves into the room as the two men backed outside the door just before the explosions. Quickly reentering the room, they laid down firepower that overwhelmed two men aiming pistols at them. Checking the room for survivors, they found none.

"Grab that computer!" yelled the taller of the two as he turned to leave.

With the computer under his left arm, the shorter guy was the last to flee the basement room and get into an SUV waiting for them street-side. It was 3:15 p.m.

It was 2:00 p.m. in Madrid, Spain. The sky was clear with passing clouds. It was extremely hot. Four men entered an office building and took the elevator to the fifth floor. As they walked to Suite 503, they looked up and down the hallway and pulled on hoods. The big guy in the blue polo shirt knocked on the door while the others stood out of sight to both sides.

As soon as the door opened, the intruders barged in and shot four people with tranquilizer darts. Three were at their desks in the open area, and the fourth had opened the door. Each intruder picked an office, moved quickly to it, opened the door, and shot the occupant with a dart. It didn't take long to find the computer that was a node in the terrorist network. It belonged to a swarthy-looking fellow in the office to the back on the far left.

"He's the guy under surveillance," said the man in the blue polo shirt. "It's his photo. Grab his computer."

All four had just removed their hoods when a fifth man came into the suite pushing an empty wheelchair. It took two of the intruders to prop their captive into the chair. The guy in the blue polo shirt wheeled him down the hallway to a freight elevator that had its door propped open with a board. The intruders and their captive exited the elevator on the ground floor and left the building from the rear, where a furniture delivery truck was waiting for them. No more than ten minutes had elapsed since their arrival.

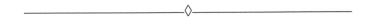

It was 8:00 a.m. in the countryside outside Montreal, Canada. A white van pulled off the highway and drove down a dirt road toward an old farmhouse with a barn to the right rear. The writing on the side of the van advertised the local electric utility. The van got within a hundred meters of the house when the driver saw two men come out the front door onto the porch with rifles. He kept driving at a steady speed so as not to arouse suspicion. It was unlikely they would notice the van had no windshield.

"When we get within fifty meters, open fire," said the driver to the guy in the passenger seat.

The passenger hoisted an AR-15 to his right shoulder, fired directly out of where a windshield should have been, and decimated the porch and the two guys on it. About ten meters from the house, the driver made the van skid to the right and stop parallel to the front of the house, just in time to begin receiving gunfire from almost every window on the first and second floors.

The van had been armored, so no bullets were penetrating. The sliding door, on the side of the van opposite the house, opened. Four armed men poured out and took positions to the front and rear of the van. Three men stayed inside and fired on the house from gun ports.

The driver and passenger had scurried out the passenger door. The driver reached inside the van and pulled out a large canvas bag. He opened it and removed the weapon inside. It was an AT4-CS with low sensitivity warhead. He set it up quickly, loaded it with the missile, perched it on his shoulder, and fired it from the passenger side of the van through the driver's side window. It exploded somewhere in the center of the first floor of the house. He loaded another missile, moved to the front of the van, and fired at the second floor. He loaded another and fired it at the first floor from the rear of the van. The men inside the van had kept up continuous fire. The men outside the van used M79 grenade launchers to lob grenades through the windows.

"Let's go!" yelled one of the men as soon as the grenades exploded.

The men inside the van jumped out and followed them in, all firing at windows and doors as they ran into the house. If it moved, they shot it. If it used to move, they shot it.

"Find that computer!" commanded the driver.

They searched the house, confiscated the computer, poured gasoline in several rooms, and set the place on fire.

"The barn, don't forget the barn!" yelled the driver.

————————————◊————————————

The burning house and barn, receding rapidly in the distance behind the van, seemed a signal to the entire province. All in the van felt the tension. About two kilometers up the road, there was a large tractor-trailer waiting on the shoulder with two ramps down at the rear. The van slowly drove up the ramps into the trailer. The ramps were lifted and stored against the inside walls of the trailer. The rear doors of the trailer were latched closed, and the tractor-trailer pulled off the shoulder and onto the highway.

It was 8:21 a.m. as the tractor-trailer slowly got up to speed. Grinding gear-shifts could be heard echoing through the gently rolling hills and valleys. The sounds of their escape were like a tranquilizer for the men in the van.

————————————◊————————————

Jon Walmer awoke in the hospital bed with a splitting headache. A nurse came up to him and asked how he felt.

"My head feels like it's going to explode," complained Jon. "Is my friend Harry here in the hospital?"

"I'm sorry, Dr. Walmer, but I don't know about your friend," said the nurse. "The doctor said we can give you something for pain intravenously, if you need it."

"Yes, please do, if it'll help with this headache," said Jon. "Who are those two men standing in the doorway?"

"They're your bodyguards," said the nurse. "You were attacked last night, and a Mr. Howard Hopper from your company insisted that you were still in danger of being attacked right here in the hospital."

"I need to call Howard. Can I use this phone?" asked Jon.

"You don't have to. He's on his way. As soon as you awoke, one of your bodyguards used a cell phone to notify him," explained the nurse.

"Oh. Okay. Thank you, nurse . . . ah . . . what's your name?" asked Jon.

"I'm Hollie, Dr. Walmer. I'll be your personal nurse and attendant, and I'm not affiliated with the hospital. Your company is paying my salary to attend to you during the day from 10:00 a.m. to 6:00 p.m."

"It's nice to meet you, Hollie. You can call me Jon. I'm not good company, so prepare for a boring tour of duty."

"Well, Jon, unless you're completely uncooperative I think I can keep you well and entertained. You see, I've never had a boring day in my life," said Hollie.

When Jon heard her say that, he smiled. His headache was gone. He took another look at Hollie and realized for the first time how beautiful she was. She smiled back at him. He felt himself flush like his blood was rushing rapidly through his veins. He hoped he wasn't blushing. He blamed it on the medicine they were pumping into his veins. After all, he was forty-five years old and well past having a crush on a beautiful woman. Just then Howard walked into the room.

"Jon, I'm so happy to see you awake and looking well after such an ordeal," said Howard.

"Howard, I have to know about Harry. How is he? Is he here in the hospital?" asked Jon.

"I'm sorry, Jon. Harry didn't make it," said Howard. "The knife wound was just too deep. We're having a memorial service for him this Saturday."

Jon was silent. He stared at the wall on the other side of the room as though he could see right through it. Tears came streaming down his face. His lips were clenched tightly. He couldn't speak as he mourned his friend. Hollie was so moved by his grief that she stepped forward and held Jon's left hand in her right hand. She stood there with empathic tears coming from her open eyes. Howard respected the moment and stepped toward the back of the room where he bowed his head and held his hands together in front of him. He stood there quietly with no tears, but looking as if he were praying. Several minutes passed, then Jon spoke with a frog in his throat. "Hollie, would you leave us for awhile? Howard and I have some confidential business to discuss."

Hollie forced a smile, squeezed his hand, nodded, walked out of the room, and turned the door behind her. Howard took himself out of praying mode and looked at Jon for direction.

"Howard, did we get the bastards?   Did they attack as expected? What were our losses?" asked Jon

"Except for the unanticipated early attack on you," explained Howard, "they attacked as expected with the Delta IV attack at Kennedy Space Center being the trigger for the others, which took place about a half hour afterwards. Everything went as we planned except for our losses at the Lodge and at the Space Elevator base.

"At the Lodge they came at us in a rapid frontal assault. The Lodge's security personnel couldn't hold them back as long as planned. They got into the building before the Army Rangers arrived and killed a lot of people. It's a good thing the Guardian had been moved to the safe house the night before. Roger, his wife, and Don are unharmed.

"At the Space Elevator base we lost a number of employees in the attack. Our worldwide counterattacks worked extremely well. All four network nodes have been eliminated. Only two operatives were captured. All the others are dead. We're interrogating the two to find out if there are any supervisory cells left within the *Preservers of Scripture*."

"I'm afraid we haven't seen the last of these bastards," said Jon. "Howard, let's make sure the families of those who died are well compensated. Let's not forget the wounded. They should get the best of care and be well compensated for any disabilities. Tell Human Resources to call me if they have any questions, and that I'll review their compensation plan before it's implemented."

"What about the Army Rangers who were casualties?" asked Howard.

"Treat the Rangers as if they were employed by us," said Jon.

"I'll have a written report of the deadly assault delivered to you day after tomorrow," said Howard. "The doctor tells me you'll be here for three more days."

"Good. I'll be able to attend Harry's memorial service. As you leave, find Hollie and let her know it's okay to come back in the room," said Jon. "And tell those bodyguards to come on in here and introduce themselves. I want to know who's protecting me."

Chapter 29

"Tom, I understand you've received a delivery of elevator cargo modules," said Jean Philippe on a secure line from his chateau in France. "Although my people have worked closely with the manufacturer, I'd like to inspect every module in the delivery, primarily to check for damage in transit, but also to get a second opinion on how well the modules conform to the manufacturing specs. This quality check is important because the manufacturing tolerances for the Ecosthat are tight."

"Of course, Jean Philippe," said Tom. "You're always welcomed to visit."

"Well, it won't be me visiting," said Jean Philippe. "You remember Jim O'Leary, I suspect. He'll be the one leading the quality assurance team."

"Certainly, I remember Jim," said Tom. "He's a pleasant and competent guy. I'll be happy to show him and his team around and give them access to the modules for inspection."

"I read your monthly report and was impressed with the progress you've been making," said Jean Philippe. "Keep up the good work."

"Thanks. I'll do my best," responded Tom.

"Give my regards to Marla. She's a lovely woman and an extremely competent military officer."

"Will do. And I second your sentiments about her."

"Yes, I know you two are taken with each other, but as your friend, I wish to caution you."

"I'm not following you. What are you saying?"

"She's an honest woman and an even more honorable soldier. If she has to choose between her duty to the President and her obligation to you and the team, how might she choose?"

"It's highly unlikely she'll be confronted with that dilemma, so I don't care to discuss it."

"Okay, Tom, but I remain wary."
"Goodbye, Jean Philippe."

When Jim O'Leary arrived with his team of inspectors, they were taken directly to the Bachelor Officers' Quarters where they could drop off their bags and freshen up before meeting with Tom, Marla, and Carlos. Tom had left a message for Jim at the BOQ welcoming him and explaining he would be there at 15:00 to personally escort the team to the meeting room a short walk away in an adjacent building. When Tom, Jim, and his entourage arrived at the meeting room, Marla and Carlos were already there in their dress uniforms.

Carlos was still using a cane to get around. Tom surmised Carlos didn't need it anymore, but kept it as a trophy to draw attention. His uniform sported the new medal the President had awarded him; it was another way for Carlos to draw attention to himself. He loved attention, and one could rely upon him to be the life of the party. His looks belied his age and he was always impeccably groomed. His physique was statuesque and his uniform was tailor-made. He hardly ever had a wrinkle in his trousers or jacket. Tom and Marla joked how Carlos must have a steam iron hidden in every men's room on the base.

Although he was the same gregarious Carlos now, as he was before his injuries, he somehow seemed a different man on a deeper level. For one thing, he had cut back drastically on his evening drinking habit, and he seemed happier, even more laid back. Marla and Tom agreed it was the medal he'd been awarded. The Legion of Merit was objective assurance to him that he could measure-up under battle conditions. His personal doubts had been fueled by a distinguished military career that had never required him to face live fire from the enemy. Now, his courage had been tested and he had passed with flying colors. No longer would he be plagued by nightmares that had played on those personal doubts.

After introductions and the exchange of pleasantries, Tom called the meeting to order. The agenda covered every aspect of the Space Elevator Project and details of the progress being made. Tom had invited the group to join him after the meeting for a specially prepared dinner. The meeting concluded with a question and answer period.

Afterwards they walked leisurely together to the main mess hall. Tom had arranged for a large table to be set up to the rear of the hall. A curtain had been drawn to separate the reserved area from the large, open, noisy mess hall area. The heavy curtain cut the noise and provided some privacy. During the meeting and at the dinner, Tom noticed that two guys seemed to stick to Jim like glue. They had even taken rooms adjacent to Jim in the BOQ. One was Jake and the other was Art. He couldn't remember their last names. They seemed a little uptight compared to the others. He made a mental note of it, figuring these two guys were probably Jim's closest advisors.

That night Tom couldn't sleep. He tossed and turned so much that Marla complained, "What on earth is bothering you so much?"

"I'm sorry, Marla, but I keep thinking about those two guys Jake and Art who tag along with Jim," explained Tom. "They seem suspicious to me."

"Discuss it with Carlos in the morning. He'll check them out for you. Now get back to sleep," commanded Marla.

Tom took her advice and managed to fall asleep.

The morning sun poured through a crack in the blinds, its rays hitting Tom right between the eyes as he lay asleep on his back. He put his left hand over his eyes to shield them, but to no avail; he was awake. Suddenly he was wide awake, as he recalled his urgent need to talk to Carlos. He leaped out of bed and hurried to get to the office, leaving Marla still rubbing the sleep from her eyes. He was disappointed to find he had gotten there early, and Carlos hadn't arrived. He paced the floor, went through his email, and paced the floor some more. When Carlos walked into the office, Tom almost jumped on him.

"Geez! It's about time," yelled Tom.

"What's the matter? I'm right on schedule, as usual," said Carlos defensively.

"I'm sorry, but all night I've been waiting to talk to you," explained Tom.

"Be calm, my friend. Tell me what's got you so tied up in knots," instructed Carlos.

"There are two guys, Jake and Art, on Jim's team giving me the willies," said Tom. "Maybe it's all in my mind, but the more I think about their mannerisms, the creepier they seem to me."

"Not to worry, Tom," advised Carlos in his most consoling tone. "The minute Jim and his team got off the plane, they were all under surveillance. Not one of them can so much as pick his nose without me knowing."

―――――――――――――◇―――――――――――――

The next morning Tom took Jim and his quality assurance team on a guided tour of the construction area. Everyone had to go through strict security before entering. Bomb sniffing dogs, biometric fingerprint recognition, metal detectors, and full body imaging were used to screen entrants. Only designated construction vehicles were allowed to pass through the gate after an inspection process. Every one of those vehicles was under guard 24/7. It slowed down construction and shift changes, but everyone understood the need for such precautions. A single bomb could set the project back by months.

One of the biggest concerns was that someone would drop a bomb into the cement used for a structural component and detonate it when the most damage would be done. To prevent such sabotage, the cement was pumped through a large diameter hose that went through several pieces of equipment that could detect a bomb, even plastic explosives, before it was conveyed to the point of usage.

After the tour of the construction area, Tom took the team to the warehouse that held the cargo containers.

"I'm surprised the containers aren't warehoused inside the construction area where they would be more secure," said Jim.

"This warehouse is a staging area needed to temporarily hold deliveries intended for use on the Space Elevator," explained Tom. "Nothing is moved into the construction area until it's certified, both technically and security-wise."

That afternoon Jim and his team began the quality assurance inspection of the cargo containers. Everything seemed to be going well. In the late afternoon Carlos came over to Tom's office.

"Tom, I have some information that might be of interest to you," said Carlos.

"About our buddies, Jake and Art?"

"You betcha," said Carlos. "They slipped away from the warehouse and were observed talking to construction workers in a strange way. We couldn't hear what they were saying, but it looked as if they were telling the workers they must do something. They hadn't met these workers at any other time since they arrived, so somehow they knew who to contact and how to contact them. Six construction workers are involved. I checked the security profile on all six. They claim to be from Quito. As you know, Quito is our capital city and with so many people it would be easy for foreigners to assume a false Ecuadorian identity."

"I just knew there was something fishy about those two!" exclaimed Tom. "Yet I don't understand why they stick so close to Jim. Do you think they're somehow threatening him to cooperate with them?"

"Maybe Jim is part of the plot," suggested Carlos.

"I don't think so. I've worked with him, and he's a dedicated, long-time employee of Jean Philippe Martinique."

"Perhaps you should confront him privately," suggested Carlos. "Frankly, I believe the construction workers are the sleepers we've been seeking since the attack. I must inform Marla. I think she'll agree we must take these six into custody and search their quarters. Rigorous interrogation is also in order. Do you agree?"

"Yes, but timing is essential," said Tom. "I'll ask Jim to meet with me here in my office at 09:00 tomorrow morning to discuss his progress. As soon as he enters my office, take Jake, Art, and the six workers into custody and begin your investigation."

"Good. I have a security meeting with Marla in fifteen minutes. I'll tell her our plan," said Carlos.

———————————◇———————————

The next morning at 09:00 Jim O'Leary walked into Tom's office with a smile and a cheery note in his voice.

"Good morn, old son," said Jim to Tom. "We just need some birds a singing, and it'd be the start of a perfect day. The mountain air's so silky smooth you can just 'bout feel it with your fingers."

"Well, you're in a real buoyant mood," said Tom.

"Buoyant is a good description. So what is it you'd be having from a buoyant Irishman this morning?" asked Jim.

"Well, for one thing, I'd like to know how the inspection went yesterday," said Tom.

"We're only twenty percent done, but so far we've found everything to be within specified tolerances. We've been instructed to do a 100% inspection on this delivery, which will establish our baseline with upper and lower control limits. Subsequently, we'll only inspect a small sample from each delivery. With your approval, we'll train someone here to do it."

"Great. I'm happy you've started off with good results," said Tom. "There's something else I want to discuss with you. There are two guys on your team who seem to be glued to your every move. What's with them anyway?" asked Tom.

"Oh, Jake and Art . . . they didn't want to make this trip," explained Jim. "They don't speak Spanish, and they've never been out of the country before. They're the lead statisticians, so I insisted they come. Both are shy, reclusive, and nervous about this trip. They hated flying. Don't worry about them. It's just a scared puppy-dog syndrome."

"I don't think so, Jim," said Tom. "Yesterday, we observed them talking to some of the construction workers. It looked like they were plotting something. What do you think they were doing?"

"I don't know. Maybe they were just trying to make friends or learn about Ecuador. I can't explain everyone's behavior. If you want, I'll speak to them about it."

"That won't be necessary, Jim," said Tom. "Jake and Art have been arrested along with six workers they spoke to. They're being investigated and interrogated as we speak."

The smile on Jim's pale face was gone. His face was now red. He stood and pounded both fists on Tom's desk.

"You bastard! You have no right to arrest members of my team," screamed Jim in a deep and powerful voice.

Jim leaned forward and, with both hands, grabbed Tom by his shirt, then pulled him out of his chair and across the top of his desk. The muscles on Jim's arms bulged, and his face was scrunched up into full rage. It was no easy task for anyone to pull Tom's six-foot-four, 270 pound frame over a desk.

Tom landed face down on the floor in front of his desk, and Jim began kicking him. Tom rolled over on his back and kicked his right foot straight up between Jim's legs. Jim bent over in agony as his balls found a new home in his body cavity. When Jim's face came closer as he bent over, Tom punched him with a right hook to the jaw and swept his left foot across Jim's right knee, causing him to crumple to the floor on Tom's left. Tom rolled to his right, got up, and kicked Jim in his left rib cage. He could feel the bones cave in. Jim rolled to his right with agony in place of rage on his face. With great effort and determination Jim continued to roll away from Tom and got up. As he rose from the floor he pulled an eight inch blade from his boot with his right hand, and faced Tom.

"I'll kill you, you son-of-a-bitch!" Jim yelled.

He made two short jabs with the knife, then reached out for Tom's right wrist with his left hand. His grip was so powerful Tom couldn't pull away fast enough. As he pulled back against the grip, Jim let go, and Tom staggered back a half step. Jim lunged at him with his right arm fully extended and the knife pointing upward. The blade went into the muscle of Tom's left forearm. Tom yanked his arm off the blade and staggered backward to get away as quickly as possible. He found himself backing through the opening to Carlos's office and up against the side of his desk.

Jim was rushing at him with the rage back on his face. Tom's right hand landed on a round glass paperweight on the desktop. He braced his left leg against the desk, raised his bloody left arm in the air to distract Jim as he rushed through the opening. Like he was going for a strike, Tom pitched the paperweight. He heard the crack and saw Jim's head shift backward on his neck as his body kept moving forward. Like a rubbery mass Jim fell, face-down at Tom's feet, with the knife still in his right hand. Tom was feeling dizzy, but he bent over and pried the knife from Jim's hand.

"Damn!" said Tom as he sat in Carlos's chair and called security.

He ripped the front of his shirt off and tied it around his wounded forearm. When security and the emergency medical team arrived, they found Tom sitting with the knife in his right hand. A medic worked on Tom's arm. Two others worked on Jim.

————————————◇————————————

Tom was on the phone with Jean Philippe. "I can't believe what you're telling me," said Jean Philippe. "Jim has been a trusted employee. I don't understand why he would attack you."

"Colonel Alvarez has been investigating the incident," explained Tom. "Six construction workers who were surreptitiously involved with two of Jim's closest cohorts all lied on their employment application. They claimed to be from Quito, but are actually illegally in the country. They won't say where they're from, but evidence seems to point to Yemen. With the help of dogs, explosives were found outside the quarters of one of the six. Jim's buddies, Jake and Art, were interrogated separately after being shown Jim's dead body. They both cracked and admitted they were working with Jim to sabotage the Space Elevator."

"You know, back in January 2004 there was a leak to the press about the shift in the axial tilt of the earth after the Asian Tsunami," said Jean Philippe. "I ultimately traced it to Jim. He apologized and said it was an inadvertent slip during an interview about our Ecosthat project. At the time I believed him, but now it seems much more likely he's been the mole in our organization the entire time."

"Your Ecosthat project predated the Manned Mission to Mars," said Tom. "From an encounter I had with the *Preservers of Scripture* in Brazil in 2003, I can tell you they've been around for some time. It seems they've had you and Ecosthat in their sights for quite awhile."

"But how would release of the axial shift information harm the Ecosthat project?" asked Jean Philippe. "I would think it would help make the case that mankind needs to develop a survival plan."

"Maybe getting knowledge of the axial shift to the public was a way to generate recruits," suggested Tom. "They could point to it as evidence Armageddon was near. It could be a call to the faithful to act in support of God's plan for mankind as foretold in scripture."

"I suppose we'll never know," said Jean Philippe. "I just hope Jim was the only mole in our organization."

"Except for Jake and Art, the other members of the quality assurance team seem to be on the level," said Tom. "They're concerned and shocked by the turn of events, but they've completed their inspections and will be returning with the data."

"Thanks, Tom," said Jean Philippe. "I'll make sure it gets into the right hands. Mole or not, Jim will be hard to replace. I'll notify his next of kin and make arrangements for the transport of his remains."

Chapter 30

J ean Philippe was worried to the point of being distraught. Jim
O'Leary was dead, but he wondered if there were other moles in
his organization. The thought that a mole might rig something to
sabotage the Ecosthat haunted him at night. For the first time in his
life he had to use prescription sedatives to get a night's sleep. He'd
instructed his head of security to conduct a comprehensive review
of all employees. He also had instructed his head of quality
assurance to conduct a configuration management review focused
on identifying any production features or structural components
that differed from the design and specifications.

The records showed no engineering changes were made by
James O'Leary; that alone was a relief. The configuration review
showed no differences between the final production units and the
approved design. All employees were cleared by security. Despite
the good news, Jean Philippe still felt uneasy. He decided a personal
visit to the Valbonne Lab was warranted. The Phase II Space
Elevator modules were completely different than the Phase I
modules. Jean Philippe was concerned if something went wrong
with a Phase II module, people would certainly die.

───────────────◊───────────────

When Jean Philippe arrived at the Lab he sat with his Director
of Security, Marcel Durand, to discuss the recent attack. He learned
the site manager had a hard time dealing with the local constabulary
who weren't too happy about the firepower that had been
unleashed. Apparently, the lab was violating a number of gun
ordinances. The judge levied a hefty fine. Also, the site manager felt
it wise to make a large donation to the police officers' benevolent
fund.

With pressure mainly from citizens employed at the lab, the city council passed a law that provided for the issuance of a permit allowing defensive military armaments for manufacturing and research facilities. After learning the local political climate was back to normal, Jean Philippe requested a tour and review of the development and testing of the Phase II Space Elevator modules.

The Phase I cargo containers would be sent up the Space Elevator, staged in orbit, then launched into a low energy trajectory to be caught by the Catcher's Mitt on the moon 100 days after leaving the surface of the earth. They were designed to be modules that fit together and form the walls, floors, and ceilings of the Ecosthat on the moon, and they carried equipment, water, oxygen, plants, and animals to the moon, so that an initial biological balance could be achieved prior to the arrival of humans.

The Phase II containers would be specially designed modules for maintaining life support for twenty people during the 100 day journey to the moon. The people would be in suspended animation. A Phase II module carried not only people, but extra water and oxygen needed for their survival on Ecosthat. Long durations in space could subject the people to dangerous levels of cosmic radiation. Earth's magnetic field and atmosphere protected living things from cosmic radiation, but away from earth people were vulnerable. The Phase II modules were designed so the water cargo and the oxygen cargo circulated in separate concentric shells of the container, completely surrounding the passengers and protecting them from excessive cosmic radiation.

Marcel escorted Jean Philippe down a flight of stairs to the basement. They entered a locker room where they disrobed and put on clean, white lab clothes and shoes. They then went through a security check and got a badge. They waited a few minutes for a down elevator, got on, and rode it down to the fifth basement floor where the Phase II modules were being developed and tested. The laboratory was all white except for some equipment and tools made of stainless steel. Everyone was dressed in white lab coats and white sneakers. The complete absence of color in the huge room made the eyes involuntarily focus on the occasional stainless steel object.

Jean Philippe tried to absorb what he was seeing. Before him was a wall filled with flat-screen monitors. Technicians were sitting in front of them monitoring data. To his left was a Phase II module that seemed to be floating in mid air, as it had no visible support beneath it. He squinted at the module and could barely see the thin white cables that suspended it from the ceiling. The module was also white, so against the white walls it didn't seem as large as Jean Philippe knew it to be.

"Jean Philippe, what you're observing is our first full scale test of the Phase II module's ability to sustain life support for twenty volunteers who are in an artificially induced hibernation," said Marcel. "We're on day sixty-eight of the test which will continue until day 100."

"I knew we were doing tests on individual volunteers, but I haven't been keeping up with the latest progress reports," said Jean Philippe. "Consequently, I'm taken by surprise to see a full scale test so soon. Do you also have the water and liquid oxygen circulating in their separate compartments surrounding the hull of the module?"

"No, we're testing that system separately on a lower floor," responded Marcel.

"What's the procedure you use to induce the hibernation?" asked Jean Philippe.

"For such technical questions, I must introduce you to Dr. Louis Dubois," said Marcel. "Doctor, may I introduce you to Jean Philippe Martinique. Jean Philippe, Louis is lead physician in charge of the Phase II Life Support."

"Nice to meet you," said Louis, who extended his hand.

"I recognize your name from the life support project reports," said Jean Philippe as he shook Louis' hand. "Thank you for your excellent work. I should have made it a point to meet you sooner. Would you brief me on the Hibernation Induction Procedure?"

"My pleasure," said Louis. "We anesthetize the patient in a sterile environment with a mixture of oxygen, nitrous oxide, and hydrogen sulfide. Then we insert an electronic cardiopulmonary device just beneath the skin.

"We slowly drop the patient's body temperature to fourteen degrees C. As we drop the body temperature, the blood thickens, so using an IV we introduce the appropriate amount of blood thinner so the heart doesn't have to work so hard.

"An oxygen mask is placed over the patient's face. Mixed in with the oxygen is a measured amount of bronchial dilator to improve the oxygen uptake of the lungs, which diminishes as the body temperature drops. The heart and lungs also begin to slow as the temperature drops. This is when the subcutaneous cardiopulmonary device begins to operate."

"Is this an off-the-shelf device?" asked Jean Philippe.

"No such device exists anywhere but in this laboratory. Necessity is indeed the mother of invention," said Louis. "It was developed by my team. It uses electric pulses to manage cardiac rhythm so the heart doesn't slow too much, and it electrically stimulates diaphragm contraction so respiration is maintained at just the right level consistent with the heart beat. Inside the mask there's a device that measures the expiration of carbon dioxide, and these results are used as feedback to the cardiopulmonary device to adjust the respiratory rate and the heart rate."

"How does the patient get water and food?" asked Jean Philippe.

"A nasogastric feeding tube is inserted so water, nutrients and electrolytes can be fed to the patient," explained Louis. "The oxygen mask is specially designed to allow for the feeding tube to pass through it. The mask also serves the purpose of ensuring the tube doesn't move out of place. Finally, a catheter is inserted to capture urine so it can be chemically analyzed, then recycled. The results of the urinalysis are used to regulate the amount of oxygen, anesthetic, bronchial dilator, water, electrolytes, and nutrients that are dispensed."

"How do you prevent bedsores and muscle atrophy?" asked Jean Philippe.

"The patient is secured to the bed using air inflated restraints designed so there are no pressure points that might cause abrasion or sores," said Louis. "Each bed is molded specifically for each patient from memory foam. The bed is inserted into an acrylic plastic cocoon with climate controls that maintain the appropriate circulation, humidity, and temperature needed to best sustain each patient.

The beds have vibrators to help maintain good blood circulation. The arms, legs, stomach, and back of the patients are fitted with electric muscle stimulators to prevent muscle atrophy."

"Are there no deleterious mental effects from such a long period of brain inactivity?" asked Jean Philippe.

"Each patient has selected his favorite music and aromas, as well as a language to learn subliminally," said Louis. "Brain waves are monitored continuously with an EEG. They can be induced by the type of music being played, aroma being released, or mental exercise being broadcast. All these devices, including the bed vibrators, are interactive so that they provide each patient with an individualized regimen that's soothing, healthful, and maintains hibernation."

"What an extremely integrated life support system," remarked Jean Philippe. "May I observe the patients on one of the monitors?"

"Yes, of course," said Louis. "Follow me."

Jean Philippe and Marcel followed Dr. Dubois to an unmanned workstation. The monitor was large, maybe as big as sixty inches. It was mounted on the wall about five feet off the floor so it could be read easily while standing. Louis pressed a button, then entered a code. As the monitor came to life, it showed two camera shots. One was down the length of the module and the other was an overhead shot of a passenger that changed to a different passenger every five seconds.

"How are the passengers arranged within the module?" asked Jean Philippe.

"There are twenty patients in ten rows of two," explained Louis, "half men and half women. The men are on the port side, and the women are on the starboard."

"Are any of them male-female couples?" asked Jean-Philippe.

"About ten percent are married couples," said Louis. "A few who are dating or who are close friends have asked to be next to each other. We accommodate those requests."

"They have no problem being naked together in such close proximity?" asked Jean Philippe.

"Actually they're asleep before entering the module; however, because so many scientists and technicians must monitor them, we've placed modesty loin cloths on all the patients," said Louis.

Jean Philippe's eyes were drawn to the bottom of the monitor. It had many sections with numerical readouts that were continuously being updated.

"What are all those numbers?" asked Jean Philippe.

"Because this is a development test, we have many more biometric readings on the subjects than we would have on the journey to the moon," said Louis. "For example, we're monitoring blood pressure, eye movement, renal function, liver function, red blood cell count, and many other things. The results are plotted on charts with upper and lower control limits."

"What have you learned so far?" asked Jean Philippe.

"Frankly, I'm quite surprised everything is going as expected," said Louis. "So far we've learned we don't have to change a thing. The hibernation process is working. Of course, the critical moment is when we wake up the patients and test them for brain, nerve, muscle, kidney, liver, heart, digestive, or circulatory impairments as a result of 100 days in hibernation."

"Thank you, Louis," said Jean Philippe. "I'm especially impressed by the fact you've achieved hibernation without invasive surgery."

"That was my objective, because surgery would reduce chances of survival. May I suggest Marcel take you to see the test module with the liquid oxygen and water cargo? I think you'll find it quite fascinating."

Louis and Jean Philippe shook hands. Marcel escorted Jean Philippe to the elevator, and they descended to the seventh floor. The Phase II test module was hanging in a giant freezer to simulate the coldness of space. Several small glass portholes were available for viewing. The module was comprised of three concentric shells or compartments. The hull of the passenger module comprised the inner-most shell. The liquid oxygen was stored in the outer-most shell, and the water was stored in the middle shell.

"The liquid oxygen is so cold, I'm surprised the water doesn't freeze solid," said Jean Philippe.

"There's a new type of insulating material between the two liquids, but applied heat and circulation are still needed to keep the water from freezing."

"What would be the downside if the water were to freeze?" asked Jean Philippe.

"Ice is less dense than water, which means it takes up more room; it could rupture the hull if the water were to freeze. We don't want ice anyway because, being less dense, it doesn't protect the passengers from cosmic radiation as well as water does."

"Why is the LOX stored in the outer shell?" asked Jean Philippe.

"The extreme coldness of space helps keep the LOX in the liquid state," said Marcel. "However, we still need to apply refrigeration to keep it cold enough."

"What happens if the refrigeration fails?"

"The LOX goes from liquid to gas, the pressure in the hull reaches critical, then the safety valve opens to prevent an explosion," explained Marcel. "We lose a lot of critical oxygen as it pours out into space. The valve closes when pressure reaches a safe level."

"If such a scenario actually were to happen, wouldn't the escaping oxygen cause the module to tumble in space or go wildly off course?"

"Yes, the engineers have anticipated that," explained Marcel. "There are three valves, technically they're nozzles, designed to open simultaneously whenever the onboard computer deems it necessary. They're positioned equidistant from each other at the aft end of the module and aligned so thrust generated by escaping oxygen would be vectored along the longitudinal axis of the module. The effect would be to increase the speed of the module without affecting its direction. If the speed needs to be slowed, there are three counterpart nozzles at the forward end of the module that the computer can open and regulate. All the nozzles are gimbaled and controlled by the computer whenever thrust-vectoring is needed to adjust course and speed. Actually, it's this very device that the computer uses to guide the module into the Catcher's Mitt on the moon."

"From what I've seen today, the Phase II module requires a significant amount of electrical power. Where does it come from?" asked Jean Philippe.

"Ah, for that we'll have to go back up to the sixth floor where we're developing a small, light-weight, and highly efficient fuel cell."

Upon exiting the elevator on the sixth floor, Marcel escorted Jean Philippe toward a small office in the corner of a large room filled with workbenches. As they walked past the benches, Jean Philippe recognized some of the components of a fuel cell. Several men and a couple of women seemed absorbed in their work. Marcel knocked on the door and entered. A man sitting in front of his computer looked up, recognized Marcel, and stood to greet him.

"Marcel, you've taken much too long to visit with me," said Dr. Armand Fournier. "I see you've brought with you our boss and benefactor, Monsieur Martinique. It's so nice to meet you, sir."

"Jean Philippe, I'm pleased to introduce Armand Fournier, chief engineer in charge of development for the Phase II module's fuel cell."

"Happy to meet you . . . now I can put a face to the name I see on the progress reports," said Jean Philippe. "You've been making significant progress improving fuel cell technology, although I make no claim to understanding it."

"The basic principle is not complicated, but the effort needed to increase efficiency and reduce size, weight and cost has been monumental," said Armand.

"Perhaps you can give us the basics," said Jean Philippe.

"Okay, where shall I begin . . . but, of course, everyone knows a little about a battery. It stores electrical energy chemically and has a positive terminal called an anode and a negative terminal called a cathode. A fuel cell is more like a generator than a battery. It doesn't store energy; it chemically generates energy. To generate electricity, the fuel cell needs hydrogen and oxygen to be fed to it. A catalyst triggers a chemical reaction that causes the hydrogen and oxygen to combine to form electricity and water."

"Do all fuel cells have the same basic design?" asked Jean Philippe.

"There are different types of fuel cells with different catalysts, fuels, and oxidizers," explained Armand. "We're using a proton exchange membrane fuel cell, or PEMFC. Our catalyst is platinum, and we use a non-conducting polymer membrane as the electrolyte which separates the anode from the cathode. In our system, the electricity generated by the fuel cell is used to charge lithium ion batteries which operate all the electrical equipment on the Phase II module. In this way the fuel cell continuously charges the batteries, and isn't adversely affected by having to cycle on and off as equipment turns on and off."

"What improvements have you made to the fuel cell?" asked Jean Philippe.

"One of the problems with fuel cells is controlling how much water is on the membrane," explained Armand. "If the membrane dries out, the fuel cell dies. If the membrane gets too wet, the fuel cell dies. Ideally the membrane needs as much water as is generated by the process, but it isn't easy to manage. Most water control methods add complexity, cost, and weight to the process; and reduce the efficiency. We've solved the problem with a new type of membrane that acts like a wick; it draws up only enough water to stay wet, but not flooded."

"So in addition to the LOX and water we carry as cargo, the Phase II module must also carry hydrogen for the fuel cells," commented Jean Philippe.

"Yes, that's correct, and it means we must control the feed of oxygen and hydrogen to the fuel cell. The ratio of the two gasses to each other must be precise and at the right pressure. We've developed a novel way of controlling the flow. We manufactured a new type of porous ceramic material that can be optimized for different gasses. One version is for the oxygen, and another version is for the hydrogen.

"As long as a minimum gas pressure is applied to the inlet side of the ceramic regulator, a fixed rate of molecules per second passes through to the outlet side. If the inlet pressure varies above minimum, it doesn't affect the rate and volume of gas that exits the ceramic. However, the gas molecules per second that can pass through the ceramic can be regulated within a narrow range by heating or cooling the ceramic.

"The electrical output of the fuel cell is a measure of its efficiency which varies within a narrow range. A feedback loop is provided back to the ceramic regulator, which is heated when the fuel cell is more efficient and cooled when the fuel cell is less efficient."

"That's getting a bit complicated to follow, but I get the general idea," said Marcel.

"I'm impressed, Armand," said Jean Philippe. "How close are you to getting a final product?"

"Within two weeks we'll have a prototype which can be mass produced," said Armand proudly.

"Very good, indeed," said Jean Philippe.

Marcel and Jean Philippe took their leave of Armand and went to the locker room where they changed back to their street clothes. Jean Philippe found the site manager in the main floor lobby waiting to join him for lunch.

Chapter 31

Stellar-mass Anomaly . . .
approaching midway between orbits of Pluto and Neptune
November 2008

The President's second term in office was over. The opposition party's candidate had won. The President-elect would be inaugurated in January 2009. The President thought it best to have a personal meeting with the President-elect before the end of November. It would give the new President and his closest advisors time to verify the astounding story. He understood the fate of the world depended on how persuasive he could be with the new guy in charge.

The President found it hard to contemplate the idea that the President-elect might choose to drop the cloak of secrecy and let the world know about the rogue black hole certain to destroy the earth in about four years. The war in Iraq was going well and could no longer be counted on to be a foil for black ops funding of the Star-Slayer Project.

The President, Secretary of the Treasury, and the Chairman of the Federal Reserve Board had met in March to discuss the Star-Slayer Project and how they could continue black ops funding for it. The money required was far off the charts of anything that had ever been done before, overtly or covertly. They needed a plan to funnel money to the Star-Slayer Project without the public learning the real reason for the expenditures. The Manned Mission to Mars was a good cover for some of the money and for all the visible activity, but it wasn't enough cover for the billions that must yet be spent.

The three executives had concocted a plan to covertly divert billions of dollars to the Star-Slayer Project. Bank bailout money was already being diverted, and it needed to continue. They had to get the President-elect onboard with the massive deception. The economy was beginning to slide into recession, and they realized more money could be diverted under the guise of an economic stimulus package; maybe even a national health care program or a tax on carbon emissions.

The three executives agreed their first meeting should be with just the President-elect; no advisors. In this way he'd be in a better position to select those people he could trust the most with this top secret information.

The meeting with the President-elect didn't go as well as had been hoped. No records were kept about the meeting.

"You're joking with me, right?" asked the President-elect.

"No, we're as serious as we can be," said the President. "There's a stellar-mass black hole hurtling toward Earth, and our top secret Star-Slayer Project has only three to four years to save humanity."

"You've been using Iraq and the Manned Mission to Mars as a cover to divert money to the Star-Slayer Project; and this whole bank bailout mess was concocted to divert more black ops money?" commented the President-elect in an incredulous tone.

"Well, a couple of banks were in serious trouble," said the Treasury Secretary, "In September we exaggerated the gravity of the situation and saw the opportunity to include the insurance industry. As the economy weakens, you'll find other industries you can bail out or take over to siphon-off large amounts of money and secretly apply it to the Star-Slayer Project. I think the automobile industry is ripe for the picking."

"Look, I respect you, but this is preposterous," said the President-elect. "I need to see proof, and I want to meet this Guardian guy in person. I also find it hard to believe you turned over the authority for this project to a private consortium. If this threat is real, it's a problem that should be managed by a government agency. We should go in there now and take over control of this effort."

"Let me call in my science advisor, Dr. Tony Regbramur, Director of the Office of Science and Technology Policy," said the President. "He'll give you proof."

The President pressed the intercom button and said, "Please have Tony join us now."

The door opened, and Dr. Regbramur walked in. The President introduced him to the President-elect, who warmly shook his hand. Tony took a seat after the President indicated he do so in the chair next to him.

"Tony, please go over the data we have identifying the threat to Earth, and the reasons why we've supported a private firm instead of managing the problem within the government," said the President.

"We've been gathering astrophysical data every day since the Asian Tsunami in 2004," began Tony. "The massive object which we believe to be a black hole is now approaching midway between the orbits of Pluto and Neptune. Specifically, Earth will be in just the right position in its orbit relative to the Sun and other planets to be catastrophically affected.

"In 2004 we thought there was a chance for survival, but now with all the data we've collected, there's no doubt the earth will be totally destroyed. I have with me charts prepared at Sandia National Laboratories that show the path of the object and the position of the earth every month since 2004. I also have charts that project the object's path and the Earth's position in December, 2012. The concentric circle around the object shows the sphere of planetary destruction due to the object's gravitational force. You can see the object itself doesn't have to come close to us to destroy us. When it gets to the orbit of Mars, the effect on Earth will be fatal.

"Now, to comment on why the government isn't addressing the problem and a private firm has the reins. We're not the only government in the world that knows about this, and they, too, have kept it a secret and are doing nothing. The simple fact is there's only one group who believes they can save the Earth, and they are in charge. All we can do is support them as best we can and not get in their way.

"I know what you're thinking . . . *What makes these guys so smart?* Apart from being smart, capable, and wealthy, this group has two advantages. The first is the Guardian is on their team and has stated he'll work with no other group. The second advantage is that Aieda is on their team and has stated she'll work with no other group.

"The President told you about the Guardian, but he was leaving it up to me to tell you about Aieda. This is as bizarre as the Guardian's existence, but it's true. Aieda is the most powerful computer on Earth. She's so powerful she's achieved sentience; in other words, she thinks like a human being and is self-aware. Even the Guardian was shocked to hear of a sentient computer. He believes it to be the only case in the Universe. The significance of Aieda's value is that she can reason inductively in the same way Einstein reasoned to develop his General Theory of Relativity. However, the most significant advantage the Star-Slayer Project team has is that they know how to save the Earth and the Moon."

"So what's their plan?" asked the President-elect.

"We don't know, and they won't say. Their reason for not telling us is that they don't trust government not to meddle. If they were to tell us their plan, too many people would be second-guessing, delaying progress, and perhaps even attempting to take over the effort."

"So, basically, our only hope of survival is to support and trust a private enterprise," said the President-elect. "Frankly, I'm not wired to do that."

"The Star-Slayer Project Team is aware of the need to obtain your support," said the President. "They've offered to show you, and a few select advisors, physical developments that far exceed anything mankind has ever created in such a short period of time. They agreed to let Tony and me tag along."

"Gentlemen, I remain skeptical," said the President-elect. "I want to meet the Guardian first, then Aieda. Afterwards, they can show me what they've been doing with the government's money."

———————————◊———————————

The devastation at the Lodge had been cleaned-up after the attack, but the announced arrival of the President and President-elect had people scurrying to make the place look as clean and comfortable as possible. There was an air of excitement that hit everyone as soon as the Secret Service arrived to survey the facility. Jon Walmer had decided the entire team should be at the Lodge to welcome the President-elect and answer his questions. Even Aieda was making the trip with Jon and George. Roger, Don, and Guardian were permanently stationed at the Lodge. Amanda was excited to fly in from Houston to be with her husband, Don, for a week.

At first Tom and Marla objected to making the trip, but reconsidered after discussing the situation with Carlos. He was no longer using a cane and was more alert and enthusiastic than they had ever seen him. Marla felt comfortable leaving him in charge of the Corps' security contingent, and he was excited about being in command of real soldiers, if for only a week. The construction foremen had proven themselves to be highly capable, so Tom agreed his being gone for a week wouldn't be an issue.

Security at the Lodge had been improved since the attack, and with the Secret Service there, Jon felt there was little risk in having the entire team in one place at the same time.

The Lodge was the perfect place for a group to socialize, and then move on to formal business in one of several meeting rooms. Jon and Don had worked together on the agenda and their presentations. When the President and President-elect arrived with their staffs, they met in the Great Room for cocktails and hors d'oeuvres. It was here that the Star-Slayer Executive Team was introduced to the President-elect and President, including Guardian and Aieda.

The President knew how important this affair was and had volunteered to do the formal introductions. Jon and the President had agreed that a receiving line provided the much needed symbolism of a formal turnover of the project from the outgoing President to the incoming President.

The President-elect stood at the head of the receiving line as the President introduced him to each member of the Executive Team. The team moved down the line and introduced themselves to each member of the President-elect's staff.

Jon had made sure the Secret Service agents had met Guardian and Aieda before the President and President-elect arrived. Consequently, the agents were comfortable with these two strange beings. Aieda was starting to look a little human; she insisted on wearing a female wig and a dress. She even had to put on lipstick. Her legs hadn't been perfected yet, so she moved around in a motorized chair. Frankly, it was almost scary, because with her red LED eyes she looked a bit like *Terminator I* with wheels.

Guardian was in his Sunday best garb. He was wearing a royal blue suit with gold bowtie, white shirt with ruffles, and gold cummerbund. His trousers had a single gold stripe down the outside of each leg, and he was wearing white gloves. On his left lapel he wore a single gold-plated rosebud. He wore a gold suede beret with a thin white velvet strip around its circumference and an open white rose embroidered front and center. He wore black, patent leather, high-heeled boots.

It was a sight to behold as Guardian went through the receiving line. As he approached the President, he removed the glove from his right hand, held it loosely in his left hand, and announced his name and title, "I am Guardian. I serve as Alien Technologist."

"Mr. President-elect, may I introduce Guardian. He serves as Alien Technologist," said the President.

The President-elect bent his tall frame over, almost to the point of bowing, extended his right hand, and greeted Guardian, "Nice to meet you, Guardian. I've been anticipating this moment and could hardly wait to express my gratitude for the help you've extended to all of us on this planet despite the personal risk which you've so willingly taken."

"Mr. President-elect, it's my pleasure to meet you, and I appreciate your recognition of my contributions, but I'm only one member of a team that has collectively shown courage and brilliance. I'm proud to be of whatever help I can," said Guardian as he grasped the President-elect's hand and shook it as firmly as he could.

It was a heart-warming exchange and the smile on the President-elect's face clearly showed Guardian had made a friend. The President-elect worked the room, talking to one person after another, as if at some political social function. He spent the most time with Guardian and Don. Despite his diminutive size, Guardian carried himself with obvious self-confidence and had no trouble making small-talk. Aieda, on the other hand, gravitated toward the women, spending most of her time with Amanda and Marla.

"Really, Aieda, you need to mix it up and talk to some of those scientists," said Amanda. "We've got to impress them and convince them to support us without interfering with us."

"Amanda, I've spent a few minutes with every one of those guys," complained Aieda. "They're boring. How come there are no women scientists here?"

"Are you having trouble relating to men?" asked Amanda.

"Only certain men," said Aieda. "I get along fine with Jon, George, Don, and Roger. I don't know Tom and Jean Philippe well, but they both seem nice. Actually, Amanda, since you asked, I am having a man problem."

"What kind of problem?" asked Amanda.

"I think I'm in love with Jon. If I were human, I'd marry him someday," responded Aieda.

"Aieda, it's not healthy to obsess about things that are impossible," said Amanda. "I think you're overdoing this female impersonation thing. You know very well you have no gender identity."

"But, Amanda, I feel like I'm feminine rather than masculine," said Aieda somewhat defensively.

"I don't know how to help you. Go talk to Marla. Maybe she has some insights for you. I need to talk to some of our guests," said Amanda as she walked away from Aieda.

Everyone seemed to be having a grand time. Jon announced dinner was ready to be served in the dining hall and for everyone to follow him downstairs. The chef had prepared a selection of prime rib au jus with baked potato, pecan-encrusted broiled wild salmon with brown rice, or proscuitto stuffed breast of chicken served with pesto sauce over linguine. The President-elect was seated at the head of the table with the President seated to his right and Jon Walmer seated to his left. Members of the Star-Slayer Team were interspersed at the table with members of the President-elect's staff. Friendly, animated conversation continued through dinner.

After dessert was served and consumed, Jon asked everyone to follow him to the meeting room where he and Don would deliver short presentations describing the progress made on a number of fronts. As soon as everyone had taken their seats in the meeting room, Jon announced that tomorrow they would tour the labs located on several floors below the Lodge and that separate visits would be arranged to the North Branch Lab in New Jersey, the Valbonne Lab in France, the Houston Exploration Development Lab in Texas, and the Space Elevator Base in Ecuador. Jon explained that what they would be seeing were pieces to a complex puzzle, yielding a solution to the threat from space.

"The Star-Slayer Team will not reveal the solution because doing so could quite possibly prevent it from working," said Jon. "The individual pieces of the puzzle are major scientific and engineering advances in and of themselves. We think you'll be impressed at the progress that has been made with the use of taxpayers' money and private money."

Don kicked-off his presentation first. He discussed budgetary issues showing income and expenses at the line-item level. He showed the total capital contribution from AIEDA Risk Mitigation Company, Marseilles Electric Enterprises, and anonymous other parties. The larger part of the money came from the U.S. Government. During Don's fifteen-minute presentation he emphasized that the numbers were accurate, but they falsely indicated they were associated with the Manned Mission to Mars. In fact, they were actually associated with the top secret Star-Slayer Project.

Jon's presentation focused on the progress made so far and the benefits that will accrue to humanity from technological advances made in some of the subsystems. He focused on two subsystems, the portable fusion reactor and the hibernation technology.

Portable fusion would give mankind abundant, clean, inexpensive energy. Hibernation technology would give mankind an inexpensive way to preserve life after an accident or an acute illness until expert medical care could be obtained for the patient. He also pointed out that, with the Space Elevator and a permanent base on the Moon, mankind was just a short hop, skip, and jump from colonization of Mars, after surviving the immediate crisis. Jon's presentation took only thirty minutes. He and Don answered a few questions and adjourned the meeting.

———————————◇———————————

The next morning after breakfast Jon led the team to the subbasement of the Lodge where research and development had been done on the fusion reactor under Don's capable direction. Jon was careful not to give any hint that Roger's lab was on the next lower floor. Roger and Aieda had been heading the effort to develop the trans-dimensional propulsion system.

When they got to the fusion lab, the chief scientist, Dr. Allison Vento, gave an introduction to fusion theory and provided design details on the fusion reactor sitting before them. She explained that the reactor was turned on and providing all the power to the Lodge, which was only a small fraction of what it could generate at full power. A couple of scientists on the President-elect's staff asked a number of technical question, then asked if a reactor could be delivered to them for study.

At this point Jon had to speak up. "Gentlemen, I can understand why you'd want one of these baby's in your own lab to study, but that's not going to happen until after earth is safe. I know you think this might be some type of hoax, but I assure you it's real. I also offer you the opportunity to return with a team of your best experts to evaluate the unit you see before you. In that way you should be able to determine it is what we say it is."

"Dr. Vento, my name is Dr. Randal Svingen. I noticed the hoist you have above the fusion reactor. Could I ask you to raise the reactor about eight feet above the floor? I'd like to verify there are no cables attached to it other than what we can see going over to the service panel."

"Yes, of course," said Dr. Vento, who gave a subtle nod to a technician standing next to her.

The technician went over to two others. They spoke for half a minute and disappeared. Less than five minutes later the hoist was in motion and a man was partly visible on top of the reactor. He appeared to be connecting the hoist cable. He directed the hoist operator to raise the unit. It slowly moved up, swinging slightly, and stopped when a man on the ground signaled to the hoist operator. Dr. Svingen walked the perimeter of the reactor while inspecting the floor it had been sitting on, also looking up to inspect the bottom of the reactor. He then went over toward the service panel to the control console. He looked at the gages.

"Dr. Vento, do you have an induction ammeter big enough to use on those cables?" asked Dr. Svingen.

"Yes, I'll get it for you," said Dr. Vento as she walked to a cabinet against the wall, opened it, and returned with a large electronic device which she handed to Dr. Svingen.

Dr. Svingen inspected the device, then walked over to where the cable exiting the reactor fell to the floor, before it rose into the service panel. He clamped the ammeter around the cable and watched the needle spring to a steady setting. He disconnected the ammeter and returned it to Dr. Vento.

"Dr. Vento, it would appear power is coming from within the reactor. I'd like to return with my team to verify the power is coming from fusion and not from some other means. I'll also be testing maximum output. Would next Tuesday be acceptable?" asked Dr. Svingen.

"Yes, you and your team might want to check into the Lodge Monday afternoon," said Dr. Vento.

"Thank you, we'll do that," said Dr. Svingen.

"Doctor, for security reasons, would you please provide the names of the people traveling with you on Monday?" asked Don Mensch.

"Yes, of course."

"Well, unless there are more questions, I think we've concluded our business for today," said Jon. "When we return to the Great Room I'll have a printed copy of a schedule that's been coordinated with the President-elect's office and the President's office. It gives you all the information you need to visit the other facilities that are contributing to the success of the Star-Slayer Project. Please pick up a copy. If for some reason one of you can't make that schedule, let me know and we'll either reschedule or we'll arrange to give you an individual tour."

"There's one more thing," said the President-elect. "I must verify the capability of the Guardian's cruiser, and I'd like to see the Guardian's fortress in Antarctica."

"My cruiser is occupied 24/7 shuttling oxygen, water, and food tablets to my androids on the moon," said Guardian.

"Guardian, we can launch another Delta IV Heavy loaded with supplies so your cruiser can take a break and give the President-elect a demonstration," said Amanda.

"Then it would be my pleasure to have you as my guest in Antarctica, Mr. President-elect," said Guardian. "Let me know what demonstration you want performed by my cruiser."

"Take me from here to Antarctica, then to Edwards AFB in California, then back here," said the President-elect.

"Gladly, but there's only room enough for you," said Guardian.

"We'll pre-position Secret Service here, at your fortress in Antarctica, and at Edwards AFB," said the President-elect. "An agent will make the trip with you first. Then I'll make the trip with you. Ten days from now."

"As you wish . . . Don and I will coordinate with your staff," said Guardian.

Chapter 32

December 2008 – March 2009

When the President-elect informed Jon Walmer that he would support the Star-Slayer Project in the same manner as the outgoing administration, Jon threw a party at the Lodge for the Executive Team. It was a good way to build their friendships and working relationships. The Lodge's staff was asked to leave after setting up the buffet.

Jon was generally seen as a rock, unaffected by emotion and disengaged from female relationships. After a few drinks Jon was seeking some personal advice, or so it seemed.

"Don says he's agnostic, leaning toward atheist. He doesn't seem to need God at all," said Jon as he waved the hand holding his drink and spilled it. "I think believing in God and the existence of souls helps me experience the wonders of the world and the joy of personal relationships."

"Men like Don are rare," said Tom. "He has inner strength and personal integrity. I don't know how he does it, but I find I get strength by expressing my gratitude to God every day. I don't pray to Him for myself, but I do pray to Him for others in need."

"Does He answer your prayers?" asked Jon.

"I suspect not. I see only chance at work," said Tom.

"Then why do you pray?"

"I admit my behavior is inconsistent with my rational thinking," said Tom. "I believe in God and souls, but I don't believe in a personal God. I don't believe the Creator bothers himself with our petty requests. I'm sure it does no good for me to pray, but somehow it makes me feel good. It certainly can't do any harm."

"Well, I believe in prayers and pray to God daily," said Jon with slurred speech. "I attend mass regularly, but my number one prayer goes unanswered."

"And what prayer is that?" asked Tom, who was feeling no pain.

"I've been trying to get back together with Catherine for some time now and pray every day that she'll change her mind," explained Jon. "I promised to spend less time at work and more time with her, but she says it's over with us. I think she's been seeing another guy."

"Well, that's a good thing to pray for, but frankly you're in denial. You need to accept that you've lost her for good. Get on with your life. Start dating again."

"Easy for you to say," said Jon. "I've been stuck trying to save the planet for so long, where would I even find a woman who would want to date me?"

"Don't give me that bullshit!" said Tom. "I saw you flirting with that private nurse when you were in the hospital."

"Okay, I admit to being attracted to her, but she wasn't flirting with me."

"Well, if you don't think she was flirting with you, then you'd better start praying for God to put back the marbles you seem to have lost somewhere along the way," said Tom.

"So, you think she liked me?"

"Oh, come on! Just go for it and ask her out," suggested Tom.

It wasn't just Tom who had to endure Jon's quest for personal guidance. He corralled Amanda by the spinach dip. "Amanda, tell me what you think about God. I mean, do you believe in Him and do we have a soul?"

"Yes, I believe in God in a personal way," said Amanda.

"I don't recall you ever mentioning being part of a religious congregation," said Jon.

"That's because I'm not. I stopped practicing Judaism in college. As I said, God is personal for me, and religion is too public. I believe in God, in souls, and in prayer, but I don't believe in organized religion," said Amanda.

"Are your prayers answered?"

"I can't prove it to be God and not luck, but I've gotten what I've asked for in life," said Amanda.

"Well, my prayer doesn't seem to be working."

"And what prayer is that, Jon?" asked Amanda with sincere interest.

"That Catherine and I get back together. She says it's over between us. I think she's seeing another guy," said Jon in a wavering voice.

"If you've given it a sincere effort and she's made it clear it's over, I think you should move on."

"But she says she wants to remain friends, and she calls me every weekend," explained Jon.

"Jon, you were married for ten years. You had two children together. You divorced amicably," said Amanda. "She cares about you and she wants to keep you as a friend, as someone in her support group. Most women of her nature want to let the guy down easy, if she knows he has strong feelings for her. The fact that you're still in love with her flatters her, and she doesn't want to see you crash and burn over her. She does care about you, but it's not in a romantic way anymore. Take it from me, Jon. Be her friend, if you can, but start looking for someone else . . . someone who'll make a good partner in life."

It wasn't the advice Jon was looking for, but what Tom and Amanda said was seeping through the alcohol into the deeper unaffected region of his brain. He resolved to be more attentive to the woman in his life whoever she might be. For sure, he'd work to suppress the computer geek side of his personality; he'd reserve it for discussions with Aieda.

"George, it's nice to see you again in person," said Marla as she extended her hand. "The holographic system is okay for business, but not good for socializing. It's nice Jon thought of throwing this party."

"I agree," said George as he took Marla's hand. "I've been meaning to ask if you're getting tired of Ecuador. I hear it's plenty hot there."

"That's true in the valleys, but where we are in the mountains, the weather is quite pleasant. You should visit us. You'd be impressed with the progress we've made on the Space Elevator."

"If Jon doesn't mind, I think I'll do it," said George. "The projects at the North Branch Lab are ahead of schedule, so I can afford to take a few days off."

"I assume you've brought your family back from Canada," commented Marla.

"About a month after the attack on the lab we had the place cleaned up like nothing had happened," said George. "After another month went by, I felt like it was safe enough to bring them back to New Jersey. They've been back about three months now. It all seems like a bad dream now."

"Why don't you take the wife and kids with you when you visit?" asked Marla. "I promise your family will just love it both on and off the base. Take two weeks, and we'll have enough time to see most of the sights. I'm sure Tom will enjoy the break, too. We haven't had much time until now to do sightseeing."

"You know, that sounds great. I'm sure my family will love the idea," said George. "By the way, is there any truth to the rumor you and Tom are dating?"

"At the base it's not a rumor," said Marla. "Tom's pretty much moved into my apartment. I've never been happier. Now a question for you, I know you're friends with Amanda; is she pregnant?"

"With the clothes she wears, it's hard to tell, but yes, she is, and she and Don are happy," said George.

"Is it just me, or is Jon acting strange?" asked Marla.

"Well, he's not a heavy drinker, and he's had way more than he can take."

"No, it's not just that. He seems like he's lost some of his self-confidence."

"To tell the truth, Harry's death hit him hard. It struck a cord with him, and he tried to get back together with his ex, but she's rejected him. Wants to remain friends," explained George.

"He's tough. He'll get over it," said Marla.

———————◇———————

Aieda, Roger, Don, and Guardian were conversing in front of the stone fireplace.

"Guardian, are you saying the entire team should be on the moon in the Control Room when we press the proverbial launch button?" asked Don.

"Yes, considering we don't know for sure what will happen, I think the team should be together. From past experience the team has worked well solving complex problems," said Guardian.

"The credit for most of that success goes to Aieda," said Roger, "and she can't join us on the moon."

"I can't?" asked Aieda.

"Well, technically you can," said Roger, "but the moon is 243,000 miles away, causing a three-second signal delay between your robotic persona on the moon and your CPU on the earth. You might as well stay on earth and use holographic communication."

"There's another issue, Aieda," said Guardian. "If you recall, I had mentioned that without a vaccination trans-dimensional travel causes one not to retain memories while in the fifth dimension's boundary layer. Because you're not a biological being, you can't be vaccinated."

"I don't remember that," said Don. "So, without the vaccine, a person can function normally within the boundary layer, but when he returns to the fourth dimension his memory of everything he did in the fifth dimension will be gone?"

"Yes, that's correct," said Guardian. "We don't know how Aieda's memory might be affected, so it's best if she remains on earth."

"I don't think my wife will want to go to the moon with me," said Roger. "I'd prefer to be with her here on earth when you hit the launch button. Just vaccinate the both of us, and we'll stay here on earth with Aieda."

"I have a similar issue," said Don. "Amanda is three months pregnant and travel to the moon is not an option. She won't leave our child. The baby won't need the vaccine. It's clear Roger, Amanda, and Aieda should remain on earth, and the rest of the team should be in the Control Room on the moon."

"I suggest the three remaining behind keep in touch with the Lunar Control Room via the holocom system," said Guardian. "Actually a duplicate Control Room should be set up in the Lodge. When the time comes, we should discuss whether or not it's necessary for family members to be vaccinated."

"Guardian, I mean no disrespect," said Don, "but I get the feeling you're holding back on us. I mean, it seems you're not telling us something of great importance to our project."

"Don, I'm skeptical about the potential for success, but I haven't withheld information that would benefit the project," said Guardian. "However, there are facts about space-time I have not mentioned . . . facts relevant to the project. Frankly, I'm concerned that educating you about them could be disturbing to you. When and if the time comes that you need an explanation, I'll provide it."

———————————◊———————————

By March 2009 the new President was feeling like he had to get involved with the Star-Slayer Project. The stakes were too high for it to be left completely in the hands of a private consortium.

"The President and I are concerned about the safety of the 2,000 people who'll be traveling to the moon," said Dr. Jack Lordhen, Director of OSTP under the new administration. "My staff calculates the liquid oxygen and water circulating in the skin of the module won't be sufficient to protect them from cosmic rays and micrometeorites over the 100 day journey."

"You're right," said Jon Walmer. "The information we gave you was deliberately incomplete. We've explained that details will be made freely available to the public when we've completed the mission."

"For the sake of the project, we can't afford to have people die," said Dr. Lordhen. "We insist on an explanation of how they'll be protected."

"George, please explain what your lab in North Branch has developed to protect occupants of the modules," said Jon.

"Dr. Lordhen, we've developed an electromagnetic field that will act as a shield for the module," explained George.

"I find that hard to believe because of the large amount of energy it would take to sustain even a small field," snapped Lordhen.

"We'd be happy to demonstrate it to your staff, but we won't release the specifications," said George. "You're correct about the power requirement, but we've developed a hybrid system that combines hydrogen fuel cells and a new type of battery. In addition, we've made a scientific breakthrough in magnetic vortex generation which we use to propagate the shield."

"I'm aware of your advances in fuel cells, but what's this about a battery and a vortex generator?" asked Lordhen.

"You might recall that Jean Philippe Martinique is a member of our Executive Team. He's the owner of Marseilles Electric Enterprises which exclusively develops and manufactures batteries," said George. "With a little help from Aieda they developed a battery one-tenth the weight and capable of 100 times more electricity than any conventional battery of equivalent size. The magnetic vortex generator was developed by Aieda; by the way, she sends her regards."

"Jack, the magnetic shield combined with the blankets of liquid oxygen and water will protect the travelers for 100 days in space," said Jon.

"I understand you won't provide specs, but my staff and I want a demonstration, and we want to review your test data on site," said Lordhen in a demanding tone.

"I'll make the arrangements," said George. "The scientists and engineers at the North Branch Lab are proud of their work, and I know they'll be delighted to demonstrate their results for you."

Lordhen departed, unhappy with the Consortium's attitude.

Chapter 33

Stellar-mass Anomaly . . .
crossing midway between orbits of Neptune and Uranus
December 2010

Tom, Marla, and Carlos were in the village of Rivera enjoying the food at their favorite restaurant. It wasn't unusual to find them there for dinner two or three days a week. The food at the Space Elevator Base's mess didn't compare to what Rivera offered.

"I can't believe we've done so much in so short a time," said Marla.

"Our progress gives me hope for the future," said Carlos. "The Haitian earthquake in January killed over 200,000; three million were affected. That was tragic enough. Then in February the Chilean earthquake killed over 500 and displaced one and a half million. I see the Space Elevator as a symbol of hope for mankind."

There was silence for a moment as Tom and Marla exchanged furtive glances over Carlos's comment.

"I'll never forget the sight, almost three and a half years ago, of the cable arriving in the port and being connected to the conveyor," said Tom. "This mass of coiled black cable was just floating in the bay like some sea serpent. When the crane pulled the bottom end out of the water and attached it to the conveyor, I could have sworn it moved like a snake. I stood there for two hours watching it after they started the conveyor. It just kept coming and coming out of the water.

"I walked away with my mind not able to comprehend it would take six months for the top end of the cable to arrive at its temporary destination inside the concrete containers adjacent to the launch tower, over 22,300 miles of cable hauled uphill over 300 miles. It took as long to haul it out of the water and up the mountain as it did to manufacture it and deposit it into the water."

"I can't forget how many troopers we had to deploy along the roadside to protect that cable from sabotage," said Carlos in an irritated tone. "For six months I couldn't sleep worrying about that damn thing."

"For six months before your troopers had to guard the cable, the Corps was busy building fifty miles of road through the mountains and assembling the cable conveyor alongside the road with a mostly unskilled labor force," said Marla. "The pressure to get done on time for the arrival of the cable kept me up at night."

"So what do we have here, an argument about who lost the most sleep?" asked Tom facetiously. "We all have some indelible memories. I still have nightmares about O'Leary trying to kill me."

"Truth be told, it was the launch of the cable that I'll never forget," said Carlos. "The brightness of the flames hit my eyes first, and only afterwards did I feel the vibration shake the ground and pound the air against my chest. It was a magnificent sight to see the smoke and flames rise to the heavens lifting the cable behind it."

"I agree it was a magnificent sight, but not quite so unexpected or unusual for me because I've seen a number of shuttle launches at Kennedy Space Center," said Tom. "Frankly, at the time, I was pissed at the NASA launch crew. I can't believe they launched only after five failed countdowns. You'd think with all their shuttle experience, they'd know how to launch a Delta IV Heavy on the first or second try."

"Give them a break, Tom," said Marla. "They had never launched a configuration like that one, with five Delta IV's firing-up simultaneously and dragging a cable to orbit. They had over five times the number of things that could go wrong."

A flamenco guitar and a marimba played a mestizo tune, while aromas of sizzling steak, *lomo salteado*, and *tronquito* soup pervaded the air.

"There's one thing I never got around to asking," said Carlos. "I can understand washing the road dust off the cable as it gets coiled into the concrete containers, but why wash it as it's hauled out of the sea?"

"We washed the sea water off with fresh water as soon as it was pulled from the bay because we didn't want the water to evaporate and leave deposits of salt within the interstices of the cable. The salt would increase the weight of the cable. The second washing at the launch site was for road dust and any residual salt," explained Tom.

"This last fourteen months have been boring and stressful at the same time," said Marla. "I'm glad the crawlers will be done tomorrow. Watching those things climb the cable one after the other while they make the cable thicker and thicker reminds me of spiders weaving their webs. Now that the trucks loaded with crawlers have stopped driving through the base, my whole body seems to have relaxed."

"You're relaxing too soon," said Tom. "In a couple of days the trucks carrying the cargo modules will start arriving. There will be about three-hundred of those. Then there will be trucks carrying over 100 passenger modules. By the way, this afternoon I heard they've completed the Catcher's Mitt on the moon and started building the Ecosthat from materials on cargo sleds supplied from Delta IV launches from Kennedy."

"I mean no disrespect, but I get the feeling both of you are withholding something from me," said Carlos.

"Really? And why would you think that?" asked Marla.

"I get the feeling this project is much more important to you than just setting up a Moon base for a mission to Mars," said Carlos.

"It's natural that we're enthusiastic about such a momentous project," said Marla.

"No, no, it's more than that. Tell me. Who's up there on the moon doing the building you speak of? How did they get there?" asked Carlos.

"They're highly advanced robots that we placed on the moon using cargo sleds launched on Delta IV rockets from Kennedy," explained Tom.

"I've heard this explanation before," said Carlos. "There are supposedly 1,000 robots doing this building on the moon. They would be valuable for use here on earth. They could have been used to help build our Space Elevator. Why hasn't anyone on Earth seen one of them?"

"Marla and I have seen them, and many others in the Consortium have seen them," said Tom.

"I understand, my friends. You must keep your secrets. I won't hold it against you. Just know . . . Carlos Alvarez isn't easy to fool. My years in the military and in the police force have given me a trained nose for sniffing out conspiracies."

"Carlos, I can only tell you that many lives depend on our success," said Tom.

"Thank you for that confirmation," said Carlos. "I'll speak no more of it, but be assured I'm totally behind you in your efforts. You can count on Carlos de Jesús Alvarez."

"We know we can, Carlos," said Marla. "Did I mention I heard from Amanda this afternoon?"

"No, how's she doing?" asked Tom. "I can't believe she and Don decided to have a second child. Talk about stress!"

"She's six months into her pregnancy and doing well. She's struggling to keep her weight under control, and she's getting a bit concerned about the pregnancy affecting her authority."

"What's that mean?" asked Tom.

"We women must compete in a man's world, and it isn't easy to command respect and assert authority when there are still men who overtly or even subconsciously feel women should be kept barefoot and pregnant," explained Marla.

"Oh, the actual pregnancy elicits caveman instincts in male subordinates," suggested Tom.

"Something like that," responded Marla.

"Couldn't some of it be a hormonal response manifesting itself as a feeling of inadequacy or even paranoia?" asked Tom.

"If you think about what you just said, Tom, you should understand Amanda's concern," said Marla in an annoyed voice. "Women in authority got there because they've learned not to let hormones affect their judgment. Whereas, men in authority think their judgment is never affected by their philandering ways or profligate, adulterous skirt-chasing; which are, by the way, hormonal responses."

"Come on, Marla, I didn't mean it in a condescending way."

"Well, you could've fooled me!" said Marla.

"I apologize."

"Apology accepted," said Marla with a coy smile. She knew she had her man by the balls, and he was hers; *and what a man he was.*

Chapter 34

Jon Walmer picked up the secure phone in his office in the Bronx and dialed out. "Andre, it's Jon. How are you?"

"Very good, my friend; I was pleased and surprised to get a written report from you on the progress of our Star-Slayer Project.

"Andre, you've earned it and I need your help again." said Jon.

"Whatever I can do," responded Andre. "I don't want to be melodramatic, but you've become to me like a trusted surgeon working to save the life of a beloved member of my family. It's not that your written report wasn't appreciated, but I must tell you that when I asked for only a verbal report, it was because I didn't need any report at all. My operatives are everywhere, and I'm kept informed daily of your progress. I must commend you . . . I can't discern your solution from any of your activities."

"Of course, given the business you're in, I was certain you'd be observing the project closely," said Jon. "That doesn't concern me. The U.S. government and the governments of a dozen other countries are doing the same thing. However, I do appreciate your candor in admitting it.

"Andre, your help has been invaluable, and I'm coming back again to your well. We need 2,000 volunteers to take the trip to the moon. We've only been able to find 500 with the necessary skills and profile. I'll be faxing you a list of the type of people we need with specifics. In general, we need young healthy men and women with college degrees in science and engineering.

"With so many technical people involved, how will you get the work done and also keep the secrets?" asked Andre.

"I've used a technique I call *compartmentalization* at my company, AIEDA Risk Mitigation, and it's worked well. Small groups are given subsystems to develop secretly. With minimal integration information and no overall configuration perspective, they can only guess how their subsystem may be used."

"I'll see what I can do, Jon."

"Thanks, Andre."

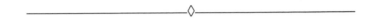

One hundred days had passed since the first cargo module had been launched from the Space Elevator. In two hours that cargo module would complete its low energy trajectory to the moon where it would be guided into the Catcher's Mitt for the first time. The Star-Slayer Executive Team and the President of the United States had been invited to watch the event live from within a VIP lounge adjacent to NASA's Launch Control Room at the Space Elevator Base.

Unfortunately, Amanda was close to giving birth, so she and Don decided to stay at their house in Fort Collins. So as not to alarm people on the base at the sight of Aieda and the Guardian, they had arrived in a windowless van. The President's entourage had followed in a similar van. Tom and Marla got in the first van after having greeted the President and Dr. Lordhen, his science advisor.

They were checked by security at the construction area gate with bomb-sniffing dogs, then the two vans drove to the rear of the Launch Support Building where they stopped in front of a double garage door and parked side-by-side. The Chief Master Sergeant driving the van on the left opened his window to gain access to a security panel at window height. The sergeant keyed-in a six digit code. A voice came over the speaker, "Please state your rank, name, and registration password as you face the camera."

"Chief Master Sergeant Patrick Mallory, Lunar One."

The double garage door opened, and the two vans drove inside. Four men, armed with Colt AR-15 automatic rifles and wearing helmets and bulletproof vests, surrounded the vans. The garage door closed behind the vans. The place was big enough to hold two Greyhound buses.

A voice came over a loudspeaker echoing throughout the garage with its 18-foot high ceiling, "Welcome to the Space

Elevator Launch Support Building. Vehicles cannot remain in the garage. The driver must park the vehicle outside the building or in the visitor's parking lot at the main gate. Passengers, please get out of the vehicle slowly and walk forward, single file, through the magnetometer to the security desk. At the desk you'll undergo a full pat-down search. Next, pass through the turnstile by passing your badge through the reader while placing your right index finger on the scanner.

"If you don't already have a facility badge, you'll be asked for identification and will be issued one with the biometric print of your right index finger recorded on it for future entry into the facility. Once through the turnstile, proceed down the hall and through the door to the reception room where your host will meet you. Thank you for your cooperation. Have a nice visit."

"Tom, I think there may be a problem," said the Guardian.

"How's that?"

"Guardians don't have fingerprints."

"Let me see," said Tom as he took Guardian's hand and inspected it. "Hmm, you sure don't. But there are plenty of wrinkles on the tops of your fingers. Try turning your right index finger upside down and place your knuckle on the scanner."

Tom took up the rear of the line as they walked single file to the security desk. Marla led the group to the desk with the President and Lordhen directly behind her. Carlos had agreed to be their host and was waiting for them in the reception room with two Secret Service agents who had preceded the President to verify the security of the area.

The Secret Service agents were allowed to keep their weapons. The biometric imprint machine didn't object when Guardian turned his finger over. The security guard started to correct Guardian, but Tom waved him off. Everyone on base knew Tom. He was essentially the base commander. The guard was quick to react to Tom's cue and backed away. It helped that security had been briefed about two strange guests, Guardian and Aieda.

Tom had discussed the biometric imprint machine with Aieda several weeks ago. She immediately took the challenge to heart, as she wanted to be as natural as possible. She had already developed a latex skin that made her seem more human, so it was easy to design her fingerprints and emboss them in the latex.

Every week Aieda had added something new to her robot body that made her more human. She had gone from pincers to fingers, from treads to legs and feet, from cameras to eyes, from metal to skin, and from speaker to mouth with simulated tongue. She even added silicone breasts. Her transmutation from robot to human was quite amazing, but unfortunately she needed some finishing touches because she looked like a comic drag queen, despite Amanda's periodic advice and support. Aieda loved red, so Amanda hadn't been able to convince her to go easy on the lipstick.

As Aieda approached the security desk, Tom could see the security guard's face start to crack a smile. Tom would have none of that. He stepped forward and looked straight into the guard's eyes with the sternest burn he could conjure up. It was as if he had yelled, *Don't you dare laugh at her!* The guard immediately got the message he was on the verge of being fired. His face changed quickly into the most stoic, cold-eyed look Tom had ever seen.

Tom tried not to think of the incident, because it struck him as funny and he didn't want to bust out laughing. He struggled to avert his thoughts and quell the urge to laugh. He could feel his face turn red. He walked quickly to a water fountain against the wall to his right and took a drink. He waited long enough for Aieda to pass through the turnstile out of sight, for only then could he return to the security desk and monitor the process dispassionately.

The VIP Lounge was comfortable and functional. There were a variety of audiovisual aids available, and three sixty-five inch LCD monitors were mounted on separate walls about six feet off the floor. Against the back wall was a buffet table with all manner of snacks and drinks. Guests had their choice of whether to sit on a sofa, a leather lounge chair, straight-backed cushioned chairs, or bar stools.

There were sixteen guests including, of all people, Andre Garnier. Jon had decided it was a good idea to express his gratitude to Andre by inviting him to this exclusive viewing where he could meet the President of the United States. When Jon extended the invitation, Andre was concerned he might not pass security and the FBI would probe his business. Jon assured him the President understood his importance to the Star-Slayer Project and that his business was nobody else's business. Andre was appreciative and excited about the opportunity to attend the viewing in such distinguished company.

"Tom, I heard you've personally managed the construction of the Space Elevator Base," said the President. "You've done an excellent job, and I'm impressed with how fast you did it."

"Thank you, Mr. President," said Tom. "There were a few moments when I thought it wasn't going to happen, but I had outstanding help. I couldn't have done it without General Odenfelder and Colonel Alvarez."

The President did his obligatory rounds in the room, but he was zeroing-in on chatting with the Guardian. He delayed walking up to him because that damned robot was always there. He didn't want to speak with a computer; after all, what would it know about life, death and the meaning of existence. The Guardian, on the other hand, was an immortal sentient being from another species that would have the wisdom of the ages to guide man's progress. The robot moved off to join the two astrophysicists, Roger and Andre, leaving the Guardian with the lovely Marla Odenfelder.

"May I join you?" said the President as he idled himself between the two.

"Of course, Mr. President," said Marla with a smile from ear-to-ear.

"Please, Mr. President, I'm delighted," said Guardian. "Marla was asking me about the Guardian civilization and the fact that we've never experienced warfare."

"That's an interesting subject," said the President. "Please go on, I'd like to hear this."

"Well, in a way I wish I could tell you of heroic tales that led to galactic peace," said Guardian, "but alas I can only tell you we've never been a violent species. When we were created by the Elders, our genes were designed so we're able to compromise whenever there are differences of opinion."

"But what about when it's a matter of limited resources needed by two separate groups? Haven't groups gone to war to secure their share of survival resources?" asked Marla.

"Yes, those situations have occurred many times in our history, but we're not driven to warfare. Rather, we're driven to intense cooperation to find a solution."

"So warfare is in the genes?" asked the President.

"For humans it most certainly is," said the Guardian.

"Yet, if I were to believe you, it was your kind who created humans in your image, but you made us without the genes we need to avoid conflict," said the President. "I'm puzzled why you would make such an inferior copy of yourselves, especially one tailor-made for violence."

"That's a good question, and the answer could be lengthy," said the Guardian, "but I shall try to shorten and simplify it."

"This ought to be good," interjected the President in a snide tone.

"God created the Elders as the first sentient life form, but he made them without mobility. However, he gave them immense knowledge and chemical factories within their bodies. God told the Elders to populate the Universe with all manner of living things and to spread sentient life wherever it can survive. As their first attempt, the Elders created the Guardians. They were so pleased with the result they delegated the job of spreading sentient life to the Guardians.

"The Elders taught us how to create life from our own cells and how to manipulate DNA and genes to create all manner of life. They also taught us how to instill sentience into a new life form. As Guardians went out into the Universe to do God's will, we learned the Universe is a violent place, inhospitable to life. We failed many times to get sentient life to survive.

"We began to lose faith and many chose to be lazy and pursue personal interest. After all, we were immortal, had unlimited sources of energy, and easy access to food. We accomplished nothing, and started into a spiral of gradual extinction as, little by little, accidents took their toll. The Elders were displeased and threatened to create another species to replace us.

"One day a Guardian named Orinaceous requested an audience before the High Council of Elders. He had an idea about how to reverse the situation. He said that, despite our great genetic engineering skills, we weren't successful designing survivable species because we were giving them too many of our traits. For example, we may design a new species with the ability to live in hot climates, but they would still be immortal, and they would still band together and never be violent. As a result, they would never develop a survival instinct or survival features specific to their planet. Eventually they would spiral toward extinction, just as the Guardians themselves were doing.

"Orinaceous was the originator of a genetic design parameter identified by your Charles Darwin. By making survival much more difficult for a new species, genetics would cause improvements within a species that would help insure its survival over long periods of time where the environmental conditions and survival challenges would be ever-changing and difficult.

"It seemed paradoxical to us at first, but the High Council of Elders felt it was worth testing. We created a new species on a planet that had previously been a failure for us. We designed the species so it was the same as the one that had failed, but this time we left out some of our traits. We also added a new genetic factor which causes cells to seek improved survivability based on environmental pressure. The new species wouldn't be immortal, they wouldn't be immune to selfish aggression, and they wouldn't be aware of their survival instincts. They would feel mental anguish over failure and loss, and they would have a strong need for companionship and community.

"Although it took a million years, the experiment was a success. The new species had evolved with features that maximized its survivability on that particular planet. There was no way we could have anticipated the need for those evolved features and have designed them into the species at the start. This success gave Guardians a renewed sense of purpose, and we were pleased to be back in the good graces of the Elders as we did God's will. Our ennui had been lifted by our success, and our societal decline stopped."

"That's an amazing story," said Marla.

"Somehow implicit in this story is the fact that the world where Guardians reside is pastoral; otherwise, you wouldn't have survived," commented the President.

"That's a profound observation, Mr. President. Despite our technology, we Guardians can't survive in large numbers for long periods of time away from our home world. Our world is the only one of its kind in the Universe as far as we know. It's paradise."

"That makes my head spin," said the President. "It's hard to know what to do with that information. I guess I'll have to come back down to earth and be thankful I have my evolved survival features."

The President excused himself and walked over to where Jon Walmer was speaking with Jack Lordhen. They turned to him when he approached.

"Jon, what's the Frenchman, ah, Andre, do for the project?" asked the President. "I know he's an astrophysicist, but what does he do?"

"He's recently earned a PhD in Astrophysics, but he has no work experience in the field," said Jon. "He happens to be someone I met on unfriendly terms, and strangely he's become a helpful friend. In a way he's sort of like a supply sergeant in the army. He seems to be able to get whatever you need.

"He's extremely wealthy and has many personal contacts in industry throughout the world. His firm is contributing $4.8 billion per year to the Star-Slayer Project. In addition he's been able to find resources for us that I couldn't find. When we needed to find the best manufacturers for certain pieces of equipment, he found them. When we needed research and development help on certain devices, he got it for us. When we needed 5,000 civilians to provide security for the Space Elevator Base, he recruited them. Recently, when I could only find 500 volunteers to take the trip to the moon, he found the remaining 1,500 that we needed."

"I would say you have a valuable friend," said the President.

"I've spoken with him," said Lordhen. "He knows science despite his lack of experience. I didn't know he's so rich and well connected."

"Ladies and gentlemen, I hope you've had an opportunity to get to know each other," announced Carlos in a loud, heavily accented voice. "If you'd kindly take a seat, I'll brief you on the Space Elevator Project. We must begin now, because the first cargo module will be approaching the moon in about a half hour, and we'll be watching the event live on the three overhead monitors."

Colonel Carlos Alvarez stood at the front of the VIP Lounge with a laser-light pointer in his right hand. He was in full dress uniform, which meant he had on all his medals and ribbons, including the Legion of Merit. He was quite an impressive sight as he discussed the layout of the base, then went into some details on how it and the Catcher's Mitt were constructed. He then showed his audience a short film about the actual construction.

When Carlos was done, he had a few closing remarks. "Soon we'll see a momentous event as it takes place live on the moon. I want to express my gratitude to Mr. Tom Calvano and General Marla Odenfelder for trusting me. Only a few days ago I was unaware of the Star-Slayer Project and would never have guessed we had in our midst such a wonderful visitor from another world, The Guardian. I had questioned how robots could be building the Catcher's Mitt, but never in my wildest dreams would I have guessed that it was being built by androids from another world. Thank you for trusting me to be a part of the Star-Slayer Project team."

"Ladies and gentlemen," announced Carlos. "We're now receiving a live feed from the moon. Please focus on one of the monitors, because it will happen fast."

The Catcher's Mitt could be seen in a square in the lower left corner of the monitor. This image was from a camera perched on a nearby lunar mountain. The rest of the monitor showed black with a tiny spot of reflected light getting larger and larger. This image was from a camera mounted at the top of the Catcher's Mitt. The telescopic lens of the camera started picking up detail.

It became quite big on the monitor such that it was recognizable as a Space Elevator module. The cameras switched priority so that the Catcher's Mitt was shown on the large part of the monitor, and the module was shown in the square in the lower left corner. Suddenly, the module appeared in the upper right of the screen and was heading right toward the Mitt. It was almost like watching an airplane land, but without wings.

The superstructure of the Catcher's Mitt wasn't enclosed, and it was a mile high above the lunar surface. When the module flew into the mouth of the Mitt, it could be seen as it was swallowed by the long curved throat that spiraled downward and spit it out onto ground level heading in the same direction, 360 degrees, from whence it first entered the mouth.

The room erupted into the sound of loud cheers and clapping. There was handshaking, backslapping, and smiles. Very few noticed the module was moving slowly and smoothly along on a conveyor to a staging area for later unloading.

Andre corralled Jon in a back corner of the room.

"Jon, I want to thank you again for inviting me to witness this momentous event," said Andre. And then he added in a whisper, "I must warn you there will be an attempt to infiltrate a biological agent with the pilgrims. No specifics."

"It's been my pleasure to have you here to share in the excitement," said Jon. And then in a whisper he said, "We'll take extra precautions."

Chapter 35

Mt. Achipungo, Ecuador
February 2011

The Space Elevator Base could handle all 2,000 lunar pilgrims at once, because the construction workers and the Army Corps of Engineers had packed-up and left. The nickname *lunar pilgrims* got started among base personnel when word got out that most of the lunar volunteers were members of the Church of Spiritual Objectivism. Few appeared to notice that most of the civilian security guards were also members of COSO . . . the only place Andre could have gotten so many recruits so rapidly.

Of course, there was no need to have all 2,000 of them at the base at once, because launch capacity was limited to one module per day, and each Phase II module carried twenty passengers. Sixty pilgrims were scheduled to arrive at the base every three days. While in quarantine for thirty days, each group of new arrivals had to undergo intense training that included societal rules needed to maintain life sustaining functions in an enclosed habitat. They were taught how a single inconsiderate act could start a chain reaction that would cause an environmental imbalance threatening the lives of everyone on the moon.

The biggest concern was the spread of deadly pathogens to humans, animals, insects, or plants. Consequently, during the quarantine and training, each group of arrivals was medically monitored for illness. They had contact only with each other. The instructors were isolated from the group and taught classes through closed circuit TV. Those who showed signs of being sick were separated from their group, and the others in the group were quarantined another thirty days.

Barry Mangrek sat in the classroom with fifty-nine of his fellow pilgrims in Quarantine Complex No. 6. He was a recent convert to COSO. Few knew he had previously converted from Southern Baptist to Islam. Both his previous faiths told of the Apocalypse, which speaks of God's justice and His ultimate purpose. Barry was convinced mankind must not try to escape the will of God. He knew he and others like him were doing God's will by preventing man from leaving the earth. He didn't like that he had to fake his conversion to COSO which he knew was a false religion. But he would do God's will, and converting to COSO seemed like the only sure way to get selected as one of the first travelers to the moon.

Barry was young and healthy, but what he carried in a capsule sewn into the inside of his cheek wasn't so healthy. His death would be the end to all those on the moon who dared escape God's will. His mind had drifted away from the classroom lessons as he thought of the glory of serving God through the one true faith of Islam. He knew he had to focus on the lessons before him or he might not pass the test. His path to martyrdom was set, and he would not be deterred.

———————————◊———————————

February 3, 2011 was an occasion for a colorful base-wide celebration hosted by Tom and Marla. The celebration marked the last Phase I module launched to the moon from the Space Elevator and the beginning of the launching of the first Phase II modules. Coincidentally, it was Chinese New Year, the beginning of the Year of the Rabbit. Marla had recognized the significance of the fact that Chinese New Year was celebrated on the first day of the first moon of the lunar calendar, so she had made it the theme for the festivities.

It would take three days for the last Phase I module to reach synchronous orbit, then 100 days to reach the moon. Over 300 Phase I cargo-modules had been sent to the moon for construction of the Ecosthat. The tunnel boring machine and heavy construction materials had been delivered to the moon by cargo sleds that were launched by Delta IV Heavies at Kennedy Space Center in Florida. The Ecosthat was coming together according to plan. By the time the first Phase II module would arrive on the moon, the Ecosthat would be completely ready to receive its passengers.

Tomorrow, the first Phase II module would be launched with twenty deep-sleeping pilgrims, and every day for the next one hundred days another Phase II module would be launched. The thirty days of training received on earth were barely adequate, so the sleepers would receive supplemental subliminal training during their long trip. The first and second Phase II modules carried only managers along with their detailed, individualized procedural manuals. In this way, personnel would be supervised as soon as they arrived at Ecosthat.

The Hibernation Staging Room had the inner sleeves of three modules in varying stages of preparation. Dr. Louis Dubois had fine-tuned the hibernation prep process in the Valbonne Lab, and he and his team had come to the Space Elevator Base to apply the process to 2,000 volunteers. They worked late into the night to be sure everything was in order for tomorrow's launch.

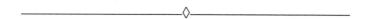

It was early in the morning on the day scheduled for the first launch of a Phase II module. The mountain air was especially crisp and cool. The outer sleeve of the module was being prepared at the base of the elevator. Wisps of white water vapor poured upward in a plume as if from a smokestack as the LOX filled the outer shell. The LOX had to be filled first because the intense cold caused the metal to contract.

Next came the filling of the inner shell with water, and this had to be done carefully so as not to splash any on the outside skin which was cold enough to cause ice to form. Last night Dr. Dubois' team had completed the hibernation process for the twenty passengers in the first module. This morning they did a final check. They then sealed the inner sleeve and had it transported to the base of the elevator where it was inserted into the outer sleeve.

After the module was fully assembled, all systems were tested, and the countdown to launch began. The module climbed the cable into space with hardly a sound as it accelerated quickly to 300 mph, powered by an all electric Van-der-Waals motor. Today and tomorrow Dr. Dubois and his team would repeat the same procedure to launch the second module. They would do this flawlessly once a day for a total of 100 launches.

———————————◇———————————

It was Barry Mangrek's turn to report to the Hibernation Staging Room with his fifty-nine fellow quarantined pilgrims. He had gotten to know each of them and thought it was sad he had to kill them. Of course, he would wait until all two-thousand were on the Ecosthat before biting down on the capsule. He would die quickly and painlessly from the acute toxic substance in the outer layer of the capsule. Unfortunately for his fellow pilgrims, the pathogen stored in the center of the capsule was the most deadly and virulent strain of Ebola virus.

When the capsule was being surgically implanted into his mouth, the scientist in charge of bioterrorism research told him the virus was specially designed to become airborne as soon as the capsule was ruptured. Being extremely oxyphilic, it would bind to the oxygen in the air. The acute toxin would cause a convulsive contraction of his diaphragm which would expel air from his lungs as it killed him instantly, propelling the Ebola virus into the environment. Death from Ebola would be slow and painful, because it would disintegrate internal organs and cause high fever. Barry thought about what he was going to do. *Such a horrible death for so many, but it's Allah's will.*

Barry and the rest of his group had to fast for the last two days, eating no solid food and drinking only nutrient-fortified water. They each went through the required process of taking a shower, lying on the custom mattress in their personal sarcophagus, getting hooked-up to equipment, then being put to sleep with ether. He remembered nothing else until he heard an alarm. He felt cold and opened his eyes. The lid to his sarcophagus opened.

"We must have arrived on the moon," he mumbled to himself.

He didn't think he would feel so cold and so hungry. He laid there for a few minutes waiting for someone to attend to him. No one came, so he pulled his arms from the inflated restraints and sat up. The compartment was dimly lit with the light from LED's on dozens of monitors and equipment panels.

"Hello? Is anybody there? I need assistance," called out Barry.

There was no answer, so Barry disconnected himself from the tubes and wiring, and extricated his legs from the inflated restraints. He then swung his legs over the side and dropped down onto a narrow walkway with a low ceiling. He shuffled sideways in the cramped space to reach the sarcophagus in front of his. He peered inside. His heart almost stopped beating. It was empty.

He told himself it could be empty for many reasons. He shuffled down to the next sarcophagus and peered inside. It was empty. Now his heart started racing. He went to the next and found it, too, was empty. Now he was in a full-blown panic, moving as fast as he could in the cramped space from one sarcophagus to another until he'd inspected every one.

He'd come full circle back to his own sarcophagus with the open lid. He was exhausted, but not so cold after all that scurrying like a rat in a sewer pipe. He looked up at the open lid of his sarcophagus and in the dim light he saw a piece of paper taped to the inside. He reached up and pulled it off. He squinted to read it. "Press the play button on the panel to the left of your sarcophagus," read Barry aloud and slowly.

He realized it was the panel behind him. He did an about face and saw the panel. He reached out to press the white-backlit button that said *PLAY* in black letters.

"Mr. Mangrek. Shall I call you Barry? I'm Tom Calvano, Director of the Space Elevator Project and Base Commander. As part of the process of preparing passengers for hibernation, we do a series of CAT scans used by the computer to create a three-dimensional image of every organ and every piece of tissue in the body. The computer looks for anomalies . . . things that don't belong in the human body.

"I think you know what we found, Barry. It was surgically implanted in such a precise way that we would have had to cut away quite a large part of your face in order to remove it. Had we done so, we would have risked our lives and all those on the base, especially since we don't know what pathogen might be in the capsule or whether it might have some mechanism to release itself

when it no longer resides in your mouth. Then, of course, we'd
have the problem of deciding what to do with you here in Ecuador.
It turns out attempted mass murder in Ecuador is punishable by
death. That made it easy for me to decide your fate.

"So, Barry, you must understand your predicament. You've
obviously discovered you're the only person in the module. What
you don't know is that you've been in hibernation for 120 days and
are well past the moon heading for the sun. You're accelerating,
because the sun's gravity is pulling you in. There's water in the
canisters against the wall and MRE rations in the cartons on the
floor, probably enough to last thirty days.

"Now here's the thing. In about 100 days you'll be close
enough to the sun to be incinerated. As you get closer, it'll get
hotter and hotter. Do you feel it getting hotter, Barry? Eventually
the pull of the sun's gravity will make it harder and harder for you
to move your arms and legs. You should also know we didn't load
the LOX and water into the sleeves of the module, and we disabled
the magnetic field generator. This means cosmic radiation has been
bombarding your body for 120 days, and you probably have
virulent cancer like multiple myeloma by now. What will kill you
first, Barry . . . the heat, the gravity, the cancer, or the lack of water?
Are you getting the picture? They're all horrible ways to die. Of
course, you always have the option to bite down hard on that
capsule. Do you still think you're doing God's will? Good luck,
Barry."

———————————◇———————————

Inside the Launch Control Room, Tom Calvano was having a
serious discussion with Carlos and Marla. "Are we still receiving
video from the death module?" asked Tom.

"Good grief, Tom, do you have to call it that?" asked Marla.

"Sorry, what should I call it then?" asked Tom.

"I don't know. Call it Module 101," suggested Marla.

"You mean because we don't have 101 Phase II modules?"
asked Tom.

"Well, it's better than the *death module*," said Marla.

"Okay, what's the video transmission show us from Module 101?" asked Tom.

"Strange you should ask at this very moment," said Carlos. "He just bit down on the capsule. After a quick convulsion, he fell to the floor and isn't moving."

"Is the air sampling system working?" asked Marla.

"It's running, but I'm told it could take several hours for the analysis to be completed and the results transmitted," said Carlos.

"We need to know what that pathogen is, because they could use it against us again," said Tom. "We must find an antidote or vaccine."

"After we get the analysis, do you want to be here for the final step?" asked Carlos.

"Yes, I do. I want to pull the lever," said Tom. "It's too bad we have to incinerate the inside of a perfectly good inner sleeve, but we must be sure the pathogen has been destroyed. The air sample should give us enough to do research. I think Barry deserves an unmarked grave in a remote cemetery. Can you arrange that, Carlos?"

"No problem. There are many village cemeteries in the valley," said Carlos.

"Good. Let's get this mess cleaned up," said Tom. "We've wasted three days with this charade and destroyed a million dollar inner sleeve."

"I know, Tom, but it was the right way to do it," said Marla. "Aieda agreed it was too risky to cut the capsule out of his mouth, and the inner sleeve was the only thing we could use as a biohazard containment lab. Taking him back to the States was too risky."

"You're probably right, but I can't help thinking we were overestimating the risk when we came up with that solution," said Tom. "Now it's done, so let's move on."

———————————◇———————————

It was Thursday morning, the day after the Mangrek finale, when Tom got a call from Don saying he was scheduling a critical holocom meeting of the Executive Team in one hour. Tom didn't bother asking about the agenda. He instinctively knew what it was all about.

The meeting opened with the usual greetings and personal chit-chat until Jon called it to order and took command as usual.

"Amanda, you initiated the call for this meeting, so you have the floor," said Jon.

"Thank you, Jon," said Amanda. "I asked for the meeting because I heard from a senior NASA official at the Space Elevator Launch Support Building about the Barry Mangrek incident. I was personally disturbed by the story, but more so because I thought this type of situation should have been discussed at an Executive Team meeting before deciding how to proceed. I think everyone recalls our pledge to ask for an explanation before crying wolf whenever our moral sensibilities are offended. Tom, because you were in charge and made the decision, I'm asking you to describe what happened and why."

"Amanda, you're right to have called this meeting," said Tom. "I was considering calling it myself. I've been having second thoughts about my decision. I agree I should've called a full team meeting, but in my defense, I did discuss it with Marla and Carlos."

"Marla and Carlos aren't on the Executive Team," said Don.

"True. Yet their judgment, integrity, and morality are highly respected by everyone on the team," said Tom. "Aieda is the smartest and most knowledgeable member of the team, and she provided the risk assessment. I also consulted Dr. Louis Dubois, the most skilled medical doctor we have available at the base."

"Please tell us what happened, as most of us know nothing of the situation," said Jon.

"Every pilgrim, that's what we call the volunteers, is quarantined, trained, then sent to the Hibernation Staging Room. As part of the Hibernation Induction Procedure a CAT scan is done while the patient is sedated. The computer assembles a three-dimensional view of the body from many cross-sectional scans. The resulting image is compared to a normal human body.

"The scan of Barry Mangrek revealed a capsule surgically placed inside his mouth on his right cheek below the teeth where he could move it and bite down on it. We could tell from the scan that it was a two-layer capsule with two different liquid substances. Our guess was that the first layer was a fast-acting toxin to kill the carrier, and the second layer was an airborne pathogen.

"Although the CAT scan was done in part to find things like this, we weren't prepared for it. We never thought to ask how we would handle a deadly pathogen or even a bomb. Of course, in retrospect that was foolish, but at the time we had to decide how to improvise.

"Dr. Dubois warned us of bioterrorist plots that used such capsules, and that they were designed to dissolve after a number of days. Other capsules he knew about were sensitive to changes in blood chemistry and would dissolve quickly if there was trauma to the implant site. We had to come up with a plan quickly, because we didn't know how fast the capsule might take to dissolve, and Mangrek had been in quarantine for thirty days.

"Our best bet was to secure him inside an inner sleeve, because it was hermetically sealed like a biohazard chamber. The inner sleeve already had a biohazard air sampling device installed, because the standard procedure is to sample the air before opening the inner sleeve in the Arrival Room in Ecosthat. Our concern was that the pathogen might be used on us in other ways at other times, and we needed to get a sample for research purposes.

"That's when I came up with the idea of tricking Mangrek into thinking he woke up as the only passenger in a module headed for the sun. As anticipated, he committed suicide, just as he planned to do in Ecosthat, and we got our sample. We then incinerated the inside of the inner sleeve to be sure the pathogen was destroyed."

"Why didn't you ship the inner sleeve back to the States with Mangrek in hibernation where biohazard experts could handle it?" asked George Blocker.

"Aieda and I decided the risk was too great," responded Tom. "Aieda calculated there was one chance in a hundred that the inner sleeve would leak due to vibration while in transport or be cracked open in an accident. If that were to happen, there could be many deaths if the pathogen were airborne."

"With Mangrek in hibernation, the pathogen would have remained encapsulated, and a leak in the sleeve would have been inconsequential," said Roger.

"The pathogen could have been released by an accident in transit or due to the capsule's dissolution over time," said Tom. "Remember the capsule had probably been in his mouth for at least forty-five days. We had to assume the worst case scenario when we calculated the risk. We assumed the pathogen would be released from the capsule, that it was virulent, and that it was of an airborne type."

"I think we must remember what's at stake," said Jon. "Barry Mangrek was about to kill himself and all 1,999 other pilgrims in Ecosthat. By doing so, he would have stopped the Star-Slayer Project and killed all of humanity. Tom's decision prevented that from happening and, with a sample of the pathogen, we might develop an antidote or vaccine that will save thousands more if there's another terrorist attack."

"I understand Tom's decision," said Jean Philippe, "and I think we need to put it into perspective. Barry was planning on killing himself and many others. Because of Tom's decisiveness, Barry killed himself as planned, but failed to kill any others. This is a good thing."

"Tom, I still don't like how you tricked Barry into killing himself," said Amanda. "I would have preferred the capsule be removed from his mouth and he be marooned on that remote island Jon has been using for some of these fanatics."

"I agree," said Tom. "I told you I was having second thoughts about it. Yet, I can't for the life of me figure out a safe alternative approach. If I had taken another approach and many lives were lost in addition to Barry's, I would feel even worse than I do now."

"May I suggest we give Tom and Aieda our retroactive vote of confidence," said Jon. "Everyone who supports how the Mangrek incident was handled, please raise a hand."

There was a pause as hands were raised in support.

"It appears we're unanimous in our support," said Jon. "However, let this be a lesson for the future. If at all possible, dilemmas of this magnitude should be discussed with the Executive Team."

"Before we adjourn, I'd like to call to your attention that Barry may not have been the only extremist among the pilgrims," said Jean Philippe. "The ecological balance of the Ecosthat is delicate, especially in the startup phase. The walls are easy to penetrate. A terrorist doesn't need a pathogen or a bomb to destroy the Ecosthat and all its inhabitants."

"So what's your point?" asked Guardian.

"My point is the safety of Ecosthat and the Star-Slayer Project depends on how well we protect ourselves from these extremists," said Jean Philippe. "We can't be lax or timid in our own defense. When the Valbonne Lab was attacked, I had traps and defensive weapons that brutally crushed the enemy. Not a single one survived even in retreat. One was roasted on an electrified fence. Others smashed into a steel wall. I lost not one of my employees, and I don't care how brutal I had to be to ensure that outcome. Today, we questioned the wisdom and moral certitude of a brave and honorable man. It's good to maintain our moral compass so long as doing so doesn't result in defeat. The fate of humanity rides on our victory. The Ecosthat must be protected and I'll be just as brutal in that regard as I was at Valbonne. Anyone who disagrees should speak out now."

There was total silence. After a long pause Jon said, "This meeting is adjourned."

Chapter 36

Stellar-mass Anomaly . . .
crossing the orbit of Uranus
May 2011

The android attendants in the Arrival Room in Ecosthat were preparing for the last Phase II module's arrival. Most notably the module carried the last member of the consortium's Executive Team, Jonathan Walmer. Tom Calvano, Jean Philippe Martinique, Marla Odenfelder, and George Blocker had arrived several weeks ago. Guardian had hitched a ride on his cruiser and planned to arrive just before Jon.

Everyone in Ecosthat was excited about Guardian's arrival, because they knew he was the master of the androids who built the Catcher's Mitt and the Ecosthat. Even as 2,000 people inhabited the ecologically stable habitat, the 1,000 androids continued tirelessly to maintain and improve it. Whether it was the hydroponics system or the water recycling system, the androids were right on top of things, making sure the delicate ecological balance was maintained.

It was widely understood that the technical work to be done by the pilgrims was for the Manned Mission to Mars. The work was related to the assembly of components needed to build a bank of giant laser guns to be aimed at a Mars spacecraft propelled by two humongous solar sails that would catch the laser light directed at them from the Moon.

The Executive Team was pleased that the subterfuge of the Manned Mission to Mars continued to be a good cover for the Star-Slayer Project. They were sure some people suspected something wasn't quite right, but with the compartmentalization of the work and the strict security measures, no one could figure out what they were really building. The concern foremost on the minds of the

Executive Team was protecting the Ecosthat from another terrorist attack. If there were terrorist infiltrators, they had to be found soon.

Tom Calvano and Jean Philippe Martinique were so concerned about terrorist infiltrators that they met for several days in a row until they hatched a plan. This time Tom would be sure to run it past the Executive Team for approval before implementing any part of it. Jean Philippe warned Tom to expect push-back, especially from Amanda and Roger.

"That's okay, Jean Philippe," said Tom. "I welcome the perspective of people who are much more morally sensitive than I am. It's not that I have less respect for the sanctity of life; it's just that I won't risk the many in favor of the evil few."

Despite having gone through thirty days of training while in quarantine on earth, and subliminal training in the capsule, all new arrivals were required to go through a three-day lunar orientation before being assigned to their work group. Security procedures required certain details and specifics of Ecosthat's design would only be released in the new arrival's orientation session, and must be treated as Top Secret. The orientation covered the specific equipment that maintained ecological balance, how it worked, and what to look for to identify faulty operation.

The primary life support systems included Air Handling, Water Recycling, Solid Waste Recycling, Hydroponics, Forestry, and Animal Husbandry. The Air Handling System managed the air's circulation, temperature, humidity, gas composition, and particulate level. The Water Recycling System processed urine, sweat, and the water from fecal matter into potable water.

Chemicals and medicines were recycled after being extracted from the water using an improved reverse osmosis method. Excess humidity triggered the Air Handling System to dehumidify the air by section and send the extracted water to the Water Recycling System. The Solid Waste Recycling System processed fecal matter, plant matter, and animal matter into fertilizer for the Hydroponics System. It also recycled plastics, papers, and metals.

The Hydroponics System grew plants for food and medicine, and it was the section requiring the highest temperature and humidity. The Forestry System was actually a small park comprised of small trees, laurel, ferns, ponds, creeks, waterfalls, algae, moss, flowers, bushes, bees, ants, beetles, rodents, snakes, birds, etc. It had walking paths, rocks, and benches for a limited number of people at one time to enjoy. Air circulation between the two plant sections—hydroponics and forestry—and the rest of Ecosthat had to be optimally maintained to ensure the appropriate respiratory balance between plants and animals.

The Animal Husbandry Section had hogs, chickens, rabbits, and fish that were bred and raised for consumption.

As the Chief Administrator of Ecosthat, Jean Philippe felt security was his ultimate responsibility, even though Tom was the Chief of Security for Ecosthat. So, in this case, Jean Philippe decided it was his duty to call an Executive Team meeting, rather than Tom. He and Tom had jointly developed a security plan that required the consensus of the team, but Tom wanted to present the plan in an unusual way. Jean Philippe was hesitant at first, but after further reflection he decided to support Tom's approach.

As usual, Jon Walmer convened the Executive Team meeting in the holocom room in the Ecosthat Administration Section. The team members on earth met in the holocom room at the Lodge in Colorado.

"Okay, folks, let's have the meeting come to order. Jean Philippe, since you called the meeting, you have the floor."

"Thank you, Jon," said Jean Philippe. "As you know, the security situation in Ecosthat has been of primary concern because we believe there are terrorist infiltrators among us. We've triple checked everyone's background and can't find anyone suspicious. Tom and I will develop plans to thwart any infiltrators, but we'd like to take a different approach to getting approval. I think Tom can best describe what we're asking."

"We're asking for general guidelines on to identify, capture, and treat terrorist infiltrators," said Tom. "We want this in lieu of having each plan approved separately. If we stay within the guidelines, we can quickly implement new plans or changes to existing plans."

"It's clear to me why you're asking for this, Tom," said Amanda. "It'll obviously give you more freedom to treat terrorists in a manner that some of us on the team wouldn't personally contemplate. I understand the stakes, so I'm willing to go down this path and see where it takes us."

"No one should have an objection to security guidelines," said Jon, pausing for effect. "The hard part would be in agreeing on the specifics. So, Tom, why don't you make your case for the guidelines you'd like to have."

"I remember a comic strip from years ago that illustrates my first point," said Tom. "Two dogs are on a street corner barking at passing cars. One is a greyhound and the other a beagle. The greyhound starts to show off for the beagle by chasing each car as it races by. The greyhound is fast, but not fast enough to catch up with a speeding car. After several attempts by the greyhound, the beagle stops barking and says to the greyhound, *I'm impressed by how fast you can run, but tell me, what will you do with one of those things if you catch it?*"

"I don't think that's funny," said Aieda. "Am I missing something?"

"Well, years ago I thought it was humorous enough that I remembered it. Today I tell it not to make you laugh, but to make you think."

"I still don't see the humor or the point," said Aieda. "Please explain."

"The humor is in visualizing the absurdity of the greyhound actually catching a car," said Tom. "In our case it's not so absurd that we catch a terrorist infiltrator, so the question for you is valid. *What will you do with one of them if you catch him?*"

"Why, we'd lock him up, of course," said George.

"Aieda, please tell us where and how we'd restrain a person who's determined to kill himself along with everyone in Ecosthat," said Tom.

"I'm calculating the risks associated with various types of restraint and all possible ways the prisoner might take one or more lives," said Aieda. "The key word is *restrain*, which implies that we must keep him alive. The only option with acceptable risk for the innocent is to put the prisoner in hibernation. Unfortunately, hibernation longer than 200 days results in death. Therefore, in the delicate environment of Ecosthat there's no risk-acceptable way to restrain a self-destructive extremist."

"Thank you, Aieda," said Tom. "You've made my first point."

"Are you saying we have no choice but to execute the prisoner?" asked Amanda. "If you are, I can't agree to that. Capital punishment is barbaric."

"No, we don't execute prisoners," said Tom, "and neither do we restrain them. Those conditions make my final point about the guidelines I'll follow."

"You're not considering a frontal lobotomy, are you?" asked Roger. "If you are, I can't agree to that."

"Gee, I hadn't thought of brain surgery," said Tom. "No surgery, no medications, no torture will be used. Add that to the guidelines."

"Add this to the guidelines," said Amanda. "No tricking the prisoner into believing he'll die when in fact he won't."

"Okay, add that to the guidelines," said Tom. "Is there anything else you'd like to add?"

"Add this one," said Guardian. "You or anyone else in this meeting shall not kill him or shall not direct anyone else to kill him."

"Okay, I said we don't execute, but add that too," said Tom. "Anything else?"

"I'm sure what you're planning is something some of us would find unacceptable, but the stakes are high, so I agree to the guidelines," said Amanda.

"Does anyone disagree with the guidelines?" asked Jon.

There was a long pause and no one spoke up.

"Okay, the guidelines are approved for implementation of security plans designed to render terrorist infiltrators impotent," said Jon. "The meeting is adjourned."

———————————————◊———————————————

Carmen Azula was a patient person and dedicated. Every morning and every night she prayed to Lord Jesus that she was living a life he would approve. On the one hand she knew Jesus was non-violent, yet on the other hand she knew the Book of Revelation spoke of Judgment Day and the coming of the Rapture.

She wanted to be a soldier of Christ in the fight against evil, and that required her to choose her battle.

She knew she had found her calling when a priest recruited her into the organization called the *Preservers of Scripture*. This holy group, comprised of people of different faiths, had a common goal she could embrace. They were pledged to stop mankind from leaving the earth and avoiding God's justice. She had to find a way to stop the migration to the moon and beyond. In deference to Jesus Christ, she felt she had to find a way that would be merciful; a quick end to the inhabitants of Ecosthat.

She had paid close attention in the orientation, as she looked for a weakness in security or in the life support systems. She had picked-up on the fact that the Ecosthat was built in sections and that each section had two airlock-doors. This allowed life support to be maintained in one section while another section was being added. In most cases a new section was attached to each airlock-door of an operational section, but as the Ecosthat neared completion, some sections retained an airlock-door that opened directly to the outside atmosphere of the moon. If she could find one of these airlock-doors, she could determine if it were indeed Ecosthat's *Achilles Heel.*

Because of her degree in electrical engineering, she'd been assigned to supervise a team that interconnected electrical panels; not exactly challenging work. She spent every free minute searching for a closed airlock-door. The longer she looked without success, the more the stress built in her. She needed to relax and think, so she scheduled time to walk through the Forestry Section. She had done this several times, but this time she would go there to relax and enjoy herself.

When her day and time came up, she was early as she waited by the entrance in a queue. As some people came out, others were let in. Once inside, she made a beeline to the bench beside the waterfall. She loved it there and hoped no one had taken the bench. She was speed-walking the entire distance and tripped on a rock in the path, stumbled but didn't fall. When she got to the bench, it was empty, and she breathed a sigh of relief as she sat down. The sound of the waterfall and a few chirping birds worked their magic on her along with the smell of the forest. She could detect a sweet aroma like honeysuckle in the air as she tilted her head back with her eyes closed and both hands on the back of the bench.

Relaxation swept over her as her long red hair hung half-way to the bench. She opened her eyes to take in the beauty of the creek that meandered downhill from the base of the falls. She turned to her right to look at the water flowing over the edge of the cliff and down into the deep pool below. A rabbit popped his head out from behind a bush. Carmen sat still so as not to alert him of her presence, but then she remembered how domesticated the animals were. They didn't fear people at all, and though it was prohibited, she had observed others feeding popcorn and peanuts to the animals.

The rabbit hopped toward the waterfall, and Carmen spontaneously got up and quietly stalked it. Even as it led her off the path, she followed with a smile wondering what Mr. Rabbit was up to. She followed him around and behind the falls. He hardly got wet, but she knew if she followed, she would get soaked. She didn't care. She had to see where Rabbit was going. After stepping behind the falls, she got plenty wet and had to wipe her eyes and pull back her hair so she could see. It was dark behind the falls, and she looked for Rabbit by bending over. Her right shoulder hit a hard object. She turned and saw it was a lever of some sort. A sign was above it. Squinting in the dim light, she read,

Danger—High Voltage—Authorized Personnel Only.

She pushed down on the lever. It didn't move. She pulled up on the lever and it moved. She pulled up and pushed in. The door opened and a light went on inside. She stepped into the small room. The door slammed shut behind her. She panicked, grabbed the lever, and pulled the door open. She relaxed and let the door slam shut on its own. Ahead of her was another door with a wheel in the center and a sign above it. The wheel had a steel bar running through it that was padlocked. There was no way to turn the wheel without removing the padlock, then removing the bar. She walked closer to read the sign:

Extreme Danger . . . Do Not Open This Door
Certain Death . . . Catastrophic Decompression
Ambient Lunar Atmosphere Lies Behind This Door

Carmen had found the Ecosthat's *Achilles Heel*. Now she needed a bolt-cutter. She turned around, lifted the lever to open the door, exited the room, and let the door close behind her. She was breathing rapidly as she came out from behind the waterfall. She saw no one in the area. She tried to gain her composure as she walked slowly back the way she had come. If she were questioned about being wet, she would tell the truth about Mr. Rabbit.

―――――――――――◊―――――――――――

Tom and Marla sat together at a table for four in the mess hall. They were discussing the quality of life in Ecosthat, because Tom was worried stress among the pilgrims might be rising. He was looking for ways to help people enjoy themselves while maintaining productivity. Because of limited space there was an early seating and a late seating for each of four meals served daily. Work on the Ecosthat was 24/7. Money, as such, wasn't used on Ecosthat. Food, drink, and medical care were free and unlimited, but many other items were controlled or rationed. Everyone was given a debit card with credits issued every month for use in the company store. Each month everyone got the same number of credits which could be saved, spent, or traded.

"If it wasn't for this skylight, I think life on Ecosthat would be psychologically unbearable for many," said Tom as he looked up to observe the earth hanging in blue majesty above their heads.

"I agree it's a beautiful sight," said Marla, "but it sometimes brings on a feeling of homesickness. I'm usually more entertained looking out the observation window."

"What's so entertaining?" asked Tom. "It's sterile and bleak out there on the lunar landscape compared to the ever-changing colors and patterns we can see of earth."

"Oh, come on, Tom. Don't you appreciate the shadows moving across the crater, the daily arrival of a new supply module, and the sight of droids in spacesuits maintaining the Catcher's Mitt?"

"Okay, but a module arrives only once per day, and it's not like everyone's in the mess hall at the right time to see it happen," said Tom.

Tom recognized the regimented life on Ecosthat could have serious effects on morale, and it weighed heavily on him, because he was the one responsible for the regulations. Every day when checking-in for work, a hair sample was taken from each worker for drug testing. Drug and bomb sniffing dogs and their trainers routinely inspected every area of Ecosthat. Tobacco of all kinds was strictly prohibited, as was the burning of anything, such as candles or incense. Gambling, alcoholic beverages, and even prostitution were acceptable provided they didn't interfere with one's work. Of course, there were restrictions on these activities, too.

Sports were limited to those that could be played in the limited space available. The courts were designed to be convertible for use in different sports. For example, squash, racquetball, and handball used the same courts. Sports events in the gymnasium were scheduled round-the-clock and published in the daily electronic paper. For those wanting to keep in top shape, there were four exercise rooms with all types of equipment, including saunas, whirlpools, and steam showers.

"The skylight and the observation window are possible because Ecosthat is not totally underground," said Marla. "Doesn't that make us vulnerable to meteor shows?"

"Yes, it increases risk, but there are always tradeoffs. Seen from above, the Ecosthat looks like a worm crawling out of a hole in the side of the crater. Only a third of its length protrudes from the hole. By only partially burying Ecosthat, we built her faster and for lower cost."

"I assume in an emergency the exposed sections can be sealed-off and we can take shelter in the underground ones," said Marla.

"That's right," responded Tom, who then abruptly changed the subject. "So, Marla, tell me what you think would help morale."

"I think the problem is people need more sunlight. We need a beach," said Marla.

"Water is too scarce for a beach. That's why we don't have a pool," explained Tom.

"You don't need water for a beach. You just need sand and some atmosphere," said Marla.

"Like what kind of atmosphere?" asked Tom.

"Colorful lounge chairs, beach umbrellas, snack wagon, palm trees, bright natural light, hot air, a breeze, the sound of waves, and naked bodies," said Marla.

"Naked bodies?" asked Tom in surprise.

"Yeah, why not make it a nude beach? Swimsuits optional," said Marla.

"Well, you won't find me nude on the beach, but I sure wouldn't mind being an observer," said Tom. "The women of Ecosthat are young and in great shape; otherwise they wouldn't have been selected."

"I'm not so young, but I'm not ashamed of my body," said Marla. "I have a few curves that can compete with the younger women, and I wouldn't miss the chance to check out how those younger guys are hung."

"Geez, Marla, you're embarrassing me. Keep your voice down when you're talking trash," said Tom.

Marla leaned over the table toward Tom and said in a whisper, "Don't worry about the young guys, honey. You're hung just right for me."

Carmen Azula had hacked into the Maintenance Database for the Ecosthat. It wasn't easy, but she was in. She needed to find out if opening the airlock-door would destroy Ecosthat. She wasn't about to take her own life if it meant only local damage. She also wanted to know if there were any more doors like the one she'd found. There was a pull-down menu with an option of *Construction Drawings*.

The two airlock-doors were clearly shown on a drawing of a typical stand-alone module. Another drawing showed two modules connected together with the doors removed and the flanges welded together. The unattached ends of the modules were depicted in dashed lines rather than solid lines to show they were unfinished.

The last drawing showed a completed Ecosthat with all modules connected, but with much less detail.

Carmen zoomed-in to a module that had one free end not connected to any other module. She saw a note on the drawing that read, *Latch locked, wheel removed, flange welded.* Carmen zoomed in to other modules that had a free end. All had the same notation. She identified what she thought was the module containing the waterfall. It, too, had the same notation. It dawned on her that the airlock-door she'd found wasn't intended to be there.

Someone had forgotten to remove the wheel and weld the flange. Someone else had built an equipment access door under the waterfall which helped conceal the airlock-door from the routine security and maintenance reviews. This was the reason she could find no other airlock-doors. She still didn't know if opening that door would do enough damage.

She clicked on the pull-down menu again and spotted an option of *Structural Integrity.* In this section she found a lot of math equations and comments related to strength of materials and how the shape and folds in the modules increased the rigidity of the structure. Then she spotted a paragraph that read:

> *Therefore, explosive decompression from an opening the size of a single airlock-door will have catastrophic effects on the entire habitat. To avoid possible disaster, every remaining airlock-door must have the bolt latched by turning the wheel counterclockwise to its stop. The wheel shall be removed, and the door flange welded shut with a continuous weld. Do not spot weld the flange.*

Carmen's face tightened, and she straightened her back. She logged-off the database. She needed to find a bolt-cutter.

Chapter 37

Stellar-mass Anomaly . . .
crossing midway between orbits of Uranus and Saturn
February 2012

Long after the last pilgrim arrived at Ecosthat, a Phase I cargo module and a Delta IV cargo sled continued arriving every day with equipment and components for final assembly of the trans-dimensional propulsion system; TDPS for short. In addition to his job as Chief of Security for Ecosthat, Tom Calvano was Superintendent of Construction for TDPS. He reported directly to George Blocker, who managed the entire Moon Base. George reported to Jean Philippe Martinique, who was General Manager for Moon Base, Space Elevator Base, and the labs at Valbonne, North Branch, and Estes Park. Marla Odenfelder managed the Fire Brigade, the Emergency Squad, Ecosthat Security, Control Room Security, module arrivals, and sled arrivals. She reported to Tom Calvano.

The Executive Team members were the only ones who could see the big picture of what was taking shape. Every member of the team was expected to keep abreast of progress and help anticipate problems and develop solutions. All of the research, development, and production of subsystems had been done on earth. They were designed for assembly and testing in the low gravity of the moon, except for the laser x-ray system, which was to be completed last and positioned in the appropriate parking orbit by NASA.

Entrance to the Control Room on Ecosthat was guarded 24/7, as was the counterpart room at the Lodge. Each control room was identical, with two sixty-eight inch monitors hanging side-by-side four feet off the floor and several desks, each with keyboards and nineteen inch monitors. One wall monitor displayed the system as it would look when complete, but with a color code depicting completed sections in green, sections in progress in yellow, and future sections in orange. The second wall monitor displayed only the completed sections, but with the addition of statistical information that showed how long it had taken to complete each section and the variance from planned completion times.

Each worker's productivity and quality of workmanship was monitored down to the subtask. Award ceremonies were held for individuals and teams demonstrating consistently outstanding performance. These awards comprised trophies, medals, and financial bonuses, all of which created a spirit of friendly competition that helped relieve the boredom of sublunary habitation. Monthly surveys of morale were conducted, and suggestions for improvement were solicited. Management selected the top ten improvements each month and asked people to vote on them.

———————————◇———————————

Tom and Marla were sitting on a bench just off the path near the waterfall in the Forestry Section.

"This is quite lovely," said Marla. "I'll have to come here more often."

A good looking young woman with beautiful long red hair walked past them and smiled. Tom smiled back and continued his conversation with Marla.

"I got the vote back on the improvement list this month," said Tom. "You know your crazy idea about a nude beach came in first!"

"I don't know why you're surprised. Jean Philippe wasn't a bit surprised when he approved the list."

"Jean Philippe is a Frenchman. Most of the people here are American," said Tom.

"So, are you going to build it?" asked Marla.

"Jean Philippe didn't ask me. He's already got a construction crew assigned to it."

"It has to be done right. Do you think he'll let me design it?"

"I don't see why not. Just ask him," suggested Tom.

"I don't think he likes me. I can sense it in his voice and body language."

"Nonsense. He likes you well enough. It's not you. It's your uniform. He's a bit wary of your allegiance to the President."

"Where's he getting the space?"

"He's having new modules added to Ecosthat, after he ran all the ecological balance calculations past Aieda."

"I'm surprised it's that easy to do," said Marla.

"Aieda tells me that adding volume for a fixed number of inhabitants actually makes the ecological balance easier to maintain," said Tom.

"I wonder who'll be the first to walk out nude on the new beach."

"Maybe you should make it a contest or have a drawing for the privilege," suggested Tom.

"What a great idea! That should spark some enthusiastic chatter," said Marla. "You know, I think the beach should have some real seagulls and sandpipers. It's a shame we can't have any water."

"Oh, but we certainly can. As Aieda explains it, recirculation in a waterfall that resembles a wave would be a better way to aerate our recycled water, although people would be prohibited from swimming in it. Aeration removes about 85% of the biological oxygen demand. Odors will be kept away from the beach by directed circulation which will provide the pleasant breeze you want. Besides, this will be an add-on process to the existing surface-aerated basin, so most of the odor will be reduced prior to the water entering the beach area. It means processing time in the basin will be somewhat less."

"There go my birds, but I guess the water is better," said Marla.

"Why no birds?" asked Tom.

"I don't think they'll understand not to pee and crap in the water."

———————————————◇———————————————

Carmen Azula was able to break into a maintenance shed and steal a bolt-cutter. She tied it to her back where it was hidden under her blouse and her long red hair. Then she visited the Forestry Section where she surreptitiously entered the room behind the waterfall. She removed the bolt-cutter from her back and hefted its jaws onto the padlock's shackle. She squeezed its long handles together as hard as she could. Her white face turned red with the effort. She stopped and inspected the shackle. Hardly a mark was made on the shiny surface.

She realized the hardened steel wasn't going to yield to her puny efforts. She dropped the bolt-cutter from her hands and stormed out of the room, leaving it lying on the floor. She stopped to sit on her favorite bench near the waterfall. With her elbows on her knees and her head in her hands, she sat there frustrated, trying to think of her next move.

A hacksaw might work, but it would take a long time and a lot of effort. A metal-cutting saber saw wouldn't work, because she wouldn't be able to apply enough pressure for the blade to maintain a bite. For the life of her she couldn't figure out what to do. Her jaw started to hurt from biting her teeth down hard in her frustration.

Then it hit her, as she thought, *What was it called? Life-jaws? No. Jaws-of-life! That's it. I need that hydraulic device used to cut people out of crashed cars. With the construction, there must be at least one. But where would I find it? Firemen use it. Yes, it would be in the fire department. The Fire Brigade was all volunteers. I'll become a fireman.*

———————————————◇———————————————

Jon Walmer and Jean Philippe Martinique left the locker room and entered their assigned squash court. Jon called heads and Jean Philippe spun his racket. It landed logo up, so Jon picked left court to begin his serve. They pulled down their squash goggles from the top of their heads and got into position. The balls, rackets, and shoes were specially designed for one-sixth of earth's gravity. Even the walls and the floor were designed to absorb energy so a player wouldn't find himself leaping up the walls or smashing himself into the ceiling. The play was intense, and they both worked-up a good sweat. It was a lot different than playing squash on earth; it was somewhat like playing on a firm air mattress. They played best of five games with Jean Philippe the winner.

"Good job," said Jon as he shook Jean Philippe's hand. "I'll get you next time."

"I think you might do it," said Jean Philippe. "You're getting better each time we play."

"I have to learn to clear my shot faster to prevent interference. I lost because of lets and strokes," said Tom.

They walked into the locker room, showered, and walked out together.

"Let's go to the bistro in Section 8," said Jean Philippe. "I'm hungry for jambon."

"Ah, a ham sandwich . . . sounds good to me," said Jon.

When they got their sandwiches and wine, they picked a private table in the corner to enjoy.

"So tell me, Jean Philippe, will you be enjoying the nude beach you're building?" said Jon.

"But of course I will. It's the best morale building idea I've heard."

"You won't catch me there nude," said Jon. "Maybe twenty years ago, but not at my age. Not with all those young guys flaunting their wares. I'll show up in boxers to check out the gals. I haven't seen a bad looking woman on Ecosthat. I can't wait to see some of them nude and bending over to spread out the beach blanket."

"You see, you're a typical American with your attitude toward the naked body, and women in particular," said Jean Philippe.

"Is that an insult?"

"No, it's a fact," said Jean Philippe. "Once you see enough naked bodies from all angles, you begin to see it as commonplace and *au naturel*. Americans would be better to learn how to accept nudity without erotic associations."

"Well, I guess you're going to be teaching a lot of Americans, because eighty percent of Ecosthat's population hails from the States."

Jean Philippe's eyes gave away his distraction from the current conversation. His head turned up and to the left as his right hand moved to his chin momentarily. He turned to look Jon straight in the eyes.

"Jon, do you have any concerns about our progress without giving details in a public place?"

"You know Roger has been tasked to assist with one of the most technical areas, and he's had to do it remotely from the Lodge," said Jon. "I think I detect worry, fatigue, stress or something like that in his voice and body language. He would do better hands-on, but he doesn't want to leave earth. Any ideas on how we can help him?"

"I've been thinking we haven't been properly utilizing Guardian. Out of excessive deference to him, I've failed to be assertive in assigning him tasks, and he doesn't volunteer. I wonder if that's part of his culture or a personality trait. Anyway, now that you've brought Roger's behavior to my attention, I think I should assign Guardian to be Roger's onsite eyes and ears. Do you agree?"

"Yes, I think Guardian's involvement will be a great relief for Roger," Jon agreed.

———————————◊———————————

It didn't take but a few days for Carmen Azula to make friends in the Fire Brigade. They were all volunteers providing a critical service and willing to go through exhaustive education and training that included a lot of scary physical exercises. She hated the burning building exercise during which her team had to wear Scott Air Packs and rescue people who had succumbed to smoke inhalation. Her biggest fear was stumbling around in the dark caused by the fake smoke.

In the moments when she was able to remove her face mask, she struggled with the dangling regulator. She wondered why it wasn't designed as an integral part of the mask. No matter. Her frustrations would soon be over. She was biding her time to steal the *Jaws-of-Life*, now that she knew where they were kept. Unlike a Fire Brigade on earth, they had no fire engines in Ecosthat. Instead, they had several converted golf carts to carry crew and equipment to an emergency. What Carmen needed was stored in a compartment on one of the carts.

Tonight at shift change, she would make her move, as that seemed to be a time of commotion during which it was least likely that anyone would notice her movements. This afternoon she had brought a surprise feast in a large picnic basket for her crew. Now empty of food, it would barely fit the hydraulic tin snips she intended to take back to her quarters.

Tom Calvano's experience with the construction of the Space Elevator was helpful on Moon Base, but not in obvious ways, because building a tower on earth is a lot different than building a tunnel in the moon. Tom had no experience with a tunnel boring machine, and that's where a lot of the problems originated. They had brought the monster to the moon in pieces. The Guardian's androids had to assemble it on the lunar surface while wearing space suits. It wasn't an easy task. The TBM was a Herrenknecht Mix-shield S-318 with a 50.62 foot diameter.

It did a spectacular job of boring tunnels inside the moon when it was working, but one part or another was always breaking down. These TBM's were designed to bore tunnels in a roughly horizontal position, but the Magna-beam required a vertical shaft. Making the TBM bore vertically necessitated the design and erection of an overhead crane that slowly lowered the TBM into the tunnel it was boring. The conveying system used to remove crushed rock from the tunnel needed to be redesigned to move material vertically rather than horizontally away from the TBM.

Tom was relieved the last few feet would be finished in a few hours. Then it was up to the engineers and androids to lower the Magna-Beam into the vertical tunnel, assembling it one section at a time. Two short horizontal tunnels intersected the 1500 foot vertical tunnel, one at 500 feet and another at 1,000 feet. These horizontal tunnels provided the room for hundreds of fusion reactors and modified Tesla coils. Despite problems with the TBM, Tom and his crew had managed to stay on schedule. He had a chat with both the foreman and chief engineer. Satisfied with what he heard, Tom rode the vacuum tube transport car back to the Ecosthat, one mile away.

————————————◇————————————

The picnic basket was heavy, and as she struggled to make it seem light, Carmen Azula waited in the queue until it was her turn to enter the Forestry Section which seemed to get more popular every day. Only a dozen people at a time were allowed to enter, then for only one hour each. Carmen knew one hour was plenty of time, so that wasn't what was making her nervous. She realized the picnic basket looked quite large for only one person, and she was hoping not to be pulled aside for an inspection, which was done periodically throughout Ecosthat to interdict potential drug trafficking. As she approached the attendant, he recognized her and flashed a big smile. She smiled back coyly.

"Carmen Azula," he announced without looking at her ID. "Go right in."

He was so busy flirting he didn't even notice her basket. Carmen made sure she flung her hair back with a quick movement of her head while beaming a smile and looking directly into his eyes. She walked right into the Forestry Section like so many times before, but this time she carried what would be transformed in her hands into the *Jaws-of-Death*.

She was in no particular hurry as she walked the familiar path to the waterfall. She stopped at the bench and sat with the basket on her lap as she surveyed the beauty of the place she would see for the last time. She gave no thought whatsoever to the thousands of people who would die with her. She was on a mission for God.

Her face changed from relaxed contentment to firm resolve as she stood and looked around for anyone who might be observing her. She stepped off the path and disappeared behind the waterfall. She moved quickly, but methodically. She entered the maintenance room and turned to watch the door slam shut as it had every other time she had visited this place.

Setting the basket on the floor, she removed the Jaws-of-Life and hefted the tool's jaws onto the padlock's shackle. Many small pumps of the handle amplified the force through the hydraulic cylinder, and Carmen could see it biting deeper and deeper. It soon popped and startled her, as she almost dropped the tool. She set it on the floor, removed the padlock, opened the hasp, and removed the rod that prevented the wheel from being turned.

Taking no chances that the closed door behind her might prevent decompression, she opened it wide and jammed the rod against it and the floor so the door stayed open. She knelt on the floor facing the airlock door, raised her head, closed her eyes, and folded her hands in prayer. "Jesus, my Lord and God, what I do now is in your name to protect and honor the Holy Words of Scripture so that they may be fulfilled on earth as it is predicted in Heaven. Amen."

Carmen stood, walked forward to the wheel on the airlock door, and grabbed it with both hands. She turned it until it reached its stops. She heard a click and a thump. Then a sound came from behind her, followed by a voice.

"This is Tom Calvano, Chief of Security. You're now sealed in an airtight chamber by a drop-down door activated when you turned the wheel on the airlock door. The airlock door is on a timer which you also activated when you turned the wheel. It's clear your intent was to destroy Ecosthat and its inhabitants. In a few seconds you'll be dead when the airlock door opens, and no one else will have been harmed by your actions. Do you still think God is on your side?"

Carmen's hands shot up over her head with palms wide open as she let out a scream at the moment she realized her death was in vain. The airlock door clicked once more and flew open, sucking Carmen out onto the cold, airless lunar surface, her long red hair leading the way.

Chapter 38

Stellar-mass Anomaly . . .
approaching the orbit of Saturn
March 2012

G uardian was in his quarters pacing back and forth. He was surprised at how indecisive he was. He was having a hard time deciding how much more he should tell his human friends. Too much information could confuse them or scare them into inaction. Too little information could cause them to become lost and vulnerable. He knew they understood that what they were about to do was a long shot, and that they had to take the chance.

If it worked, humanity would be saved from the force of a stellar-mass black hole approaching the orbit of Saturn. It had only to get to the orbit of Mars to deal the final death blow to Earth. Guardian decided he would call a meeting of the Executive Team.

"Let's take our seats and come to order," announced Jon. "It's timely that Guardian called this Executive Team meeting, because in several days we'll be ready to literally move heaven and earth. Guardian, you have the floor."

"What we're about to do is dangerous, but necessary. If it works as planned, we should have few issues of consequence. However, we should be prepared if things go wrong. I have some knowledge about what might possibly happen that could be useful to one or more of our team. I had explained to some of you that moving into the boundary layer of the fifth dimension results in the inability to recall what happened.

"Within the boundary layer it's akin to living in a dream world where time runs slower. So that we can function there in the short time available to us and maintain our memories when we return to our own fourth dimension, we must take a vaccine. Even with the vaccine, some memories may be vague. That's why we Guardians digitally record everything happening on our vessels when we jump to the fifth dimension."

"Guardian, will my memory be affected by the jump?" asked Aieda.

"Honestly, I don't know. As a sentient machine, Aieda, you're unique, and we Guardians have no experience to draw upon. However, if I were to guess, I would say your memory will be unaffected, because it's similar to digital recording devices we've used during a jump. Of course, Guardian computers are biological, so we have to vaccinate them before a jump. Normally the vaccination device is integrated into our spacesuits and into the vessel's computers so we can make a jump quickly. You see, the vaccine is effective for only forty-five days."

"Excuse me, but I'm thoroughly confused," said Marla. "It could be I've missed something along the way, maybe because I was the last to come onboard. Guardian, please explain to me what non-vaccinated people will be doing while we're in the boundary layer of the fifth dimension."

"They'll be going about their normal activities, of course," said Guardian.

"But won't everyone panic when the sun, planets and stars disappear?" asked Marla. "My God, even the moon won't be visible because there will be no reflected light from the sun."

"Oh, I see where I've failed to fully explain things," said Guardian. "When we enter the boundary lay of the fifth dimension, time slows down. At the outer edge, one second will equal about twenty years. If we were to travel deeper into the layer, one second could become equal to fifty years. Normally, trans-dimensional vessels jump in and out in a nanosecond. We'll only be at the outer edge of the boundary layer for one second, so for non-vaccinated people it'll be like a long blink of their eyes."

"If a jump takes just a second, then why do we need the vaccine?" asked Marla. "We'll have nothing to remember!"

"Yes, of course, I must give a better explanation of the vaccine. The reason the vaccine allows you to have memories after a jump is that it allows you to do many things in a shorter than normal period of time. The vaccine alters your biological clock such that one second in the fifth dimensional boundary layer appears to you as one hour, while in the fourth dimension twenty years will have gone by. When a vaccinated person observes a non-vaccinated person, it appears as though the non-vaccinated person were standing still. For safety it'll be best if vaccinated people don't intermingle with non-vaccinated people during the jump."

"Okay, so we need the vaccine to get stuff done in a second during a jump and to retain our memories after a jump," said Tom. "What else do you have?"

"As I've explained, large vessels make the dimensional jump unstable with deadly consequences when moving from one point to another," said Guardian. "The earth-moon will be the largest vessel ever to make a jump. We're expecting there will be no instability in the space-time fabric, because we won't be moving about within the boundary layer. However, something might go wrong, and if it does, the best advice I can offer you is to follow your intuition."

"That sounds ominous," said Amanda.

"What I'm about to explain will be hard for you to accept," said Guardian. "Time is not what you think it is. You think of time as a progression from past to present to future. You even have science fiction stories where people travel in time to the past or to the future. Well, that's not how time works. The past, the present, and the future exist simultaneously."

"I don't understand it, but maybe I don't need to," said Jon. "Just tell me how it might help us."

"In your understanding of time, the past can affect the present and the future," explained Guardian. "In the real world, the future can affect the past, and no one would know."

"So, I can do something in the future that would cause my history to change, and there would be no evidence of any kind that would identify how things were before the change," commented Roger.

"It doesn't happen often," said Guardian, "but it happens in order to put the fabric of space-time back to a place of equilibrium."

"Guardian, I have a question," said Tom. "If the vaccine alters our biological clock so we can do a lot of stuff in one second, then it would seem to me that our metabolism has been sped up. If that's the case, isn't it physiologically dangerous to us?"

"You ask a question that's difficult to explain in layman's terms, but be assured there's no effect on your health. The vaccine doesn't affect your metabolism. Remember when I said the deeper we go into the boundary layer, the slower time passes? Do you remember that time only seems to be linear and that in reality the past and future occur simultaneously? Do you remember I said each higher dimension is another universe with its own timeline?

"Within the boundary layer between dimensions, time appears to run at different speeds because the timelines in the two adjacent universes are incompatible. As we move deeper into the boundary layer, time will stop because we can't exist in a dimension higher than the fourth. Our presence in the boundary layer is possible because every atom from the fourth dimension is slightly out of phase. As we move deeper into the boundary layer, we get more out of phase until the perception of linear time ends, and we can't go any deeper. The vaccine mimics going deeper into the boundary layer by making our biological atoms slightly more out of phase, as if we had moved deeper into the boundary layer."

"Sorry I asked," said Tom.

"There's an item of business we need to cover," said Jon, "unless there are more revelations or questions."

"I've covered all that was needed," said Guardian.

"As you know, General Odenfelder hasn't been an official member of the Executive Team, yet we have consistently invited her to our meetings," said Jon. "Unless there's strong objection, I wish to formally appoint Marla as an official member with all rights and privileges such as they might be."

There were a few laughs and smiles, then the holocom room broke out in applause.

"Here, here!"

"Welcome, Marla!"

"Bravo!"

"Speech! Speech!"

"Okay, just a few words," said Marla as she stood. "What took you so long, Jon?"

There was laughter and chatter. Jon smiled broadly, but didn't respond.

"Truly, I'm honored to be accepted by such an outstanding group. But as much as I love each and every one of you, I pray I don't get stuck with you for eternity in the boundary layer of the fifth dimension," said Marla with a big grin.

There was more laughter and chatter as Marla sat down.

"Okay, a few more points of business before we adjourn," said Jon. "The schedule for activating the jump will be sent to you by secure email. It tells you when and how to get the vaccination and when to be in the holocom room. For those of you at the Lodge, be aware that here on the moon, the holocom room is located in the Control Center which is one mile away from Ecosthat. The Control Center and Ecosthat are connected by vacuum tube transport. We don't want to raise suspicions, so let's not let anyone know the Executive Team is convening on jump day.

"On Ecosthat everyone will be told we're running a test for the twenty-seven days, seven hours, forty-three minutes and forty-one seconds it takes the moon to orbit the earth. The President has arranged to notify countries and municipalities in our Magna-beam path of a solar flare alert. His Office of Science and Technology Policy will recommend traffic and specified work be suspended for specified hours of the day. Automated equipment will be monitoring the formation of the gravity well, and at the appropriate time just prior to the moon's completion of one orbit, the three laser x-ray weapons will be discharged at the center of gravity. At that moment, it's goodbye Milky Way for our Earth-Moon trans-dimensional vessel."

———————————◇———————————

It was March 15, 2012, the *Ides of March*, and the earth was not well. Many governments blamed the earthquakes and destructive weather on excessive carbon emissions and the inability to control them with international agreements.

Followers of Nostradamus referenced his prediction of the end of the world in 2012. Some people believed the end of the Mayan calendar on December 21, 2012 signified the end of the world was coming. Religious people referenced the Bible and its Book of Revelation as a reminder that the end was near.

Between January 1 and March 15, the cargo ships Azur, Simber, Kirti, Nordland and Metallica were lost to continuously turbulent seas. Global shipping slowed dramatically. The Florida Keys were underwater, as was the eastern half of Long Island, NY.

Northwest cities of Seattle, Portland, Billings, and Boise were suffering a heat wave and draught for the last fourteen months, while severe thunderstorms, racing across the Midwest, spawned tornadoes which took hundreds of lives from Missouri and Kentucky to Illinois and Wisconsin.

Southern cities of Birmingham, Atlanta, and Augusta were inundated with rain, floods, and mudslides. In Queensland, Australia the flooding in February, 2012 was worse than the year before in January. In Italy, the streets of Venice were completely flooded and along the coast near Naples, for the second year in a row, torrential rains and violent storms caused floods and mudslides, taking dozens of lives and destroying property and livestock. In Sicily, Mt. Etna erupted in January, 2012, destroying two towns. In January, 2012 an earthquake shook New Madrid, Missouri, causing widespread damage and taking dozens of lives. An earthquake hit Chile in February, 2012 and paralyzed the country.

All over the globe similar stories of extreme weather, quakes and eruptions were in the news on a daily basis for the last three years, growing worse each year.

Somehow, almost beyond belief, governments had managed to keep the truth from the people by denying any rumors of a stellar-mass black hole hurtling through our solar system. The few scientists who voiced such an idea were ridiculed as crackpots.

Jon, Jean Philippe, Don, Tom, Marla, George and Guardian were in the holocom room in the Lunar Control Center. Amanda, Roger, and Aieda were in the new holocom room at the Lodge that looked like a duplicate of the Control Center on the moon. It was time to throw the switch. Everything had been inspected, tested, and retested within practical limits. Everyone present, except Aieda, had been vaccinated.

The seven in the LCC drew straws to see who would have the honor of initiating the trans-dimensional jump. Tom won. Jean Philippe and Jon each took out a key and walked to separate panels across the room. They inserted their keys and turned them. The power on the control panel in front of Tom came to life. He sat at the control panel while the others peered out the floor-to-ceiling glass window that faced the muzzle-end of the Magna-beam that swiveled on a thirteen-foot diameter ball-joint, allowing it to be precisely aimed at earth.

With the earth spinning at one-thousand miles per hour and the moon orbiting the earth, it was up to the computer to keep the electro-magnetic beam focused directly on the location of the black hole located within the earth's core.

This connection to earth would not have been possible except for the fact that the moon always maintained the same face toward the earth. The black holes engaged on the moon were connected by the Magna-beam to the black hole within the earth. In this way the system would sweep out a gravity well that would contain both the earth and the moon. At the appropriate moment, the x-ray lasers would be fired at the center of gravity of the earth-moon system, causing a rift in the fabric of space-time that would suck the earth and moon together into the boundary layer of the fifth dimension. Earth and moon would disappear for twenty years, and would return after the stellar-mass black hole had passed and was far enough away to do any harm.

Tom dramatized the moment by initiating a countdown. "Ten, nine, eight, seven, six, five, four, three, two, one . . . launch!" said Tom melodramatically as he lifted the red safety cover and flipped the switch.

The lights dimmed for a second, the Magna-beam moved ever so slightly, then there was a low-frequency hum. Otherwise, there was no indication that anything was happening, except by reading the gages on the panel. Tom closed the safety cover over the switch. Jon removed his key from the power panel, walked over to where Tom was sitting, inserted the key into the safety cover, and locked it in place. Jean Philippe removed his key from the power panel on his side of the room and handed it to Jon, who walked to a safe built into the wall. He opened the door to the safe, placed both keys inside, and locked the door.

"Only Jean Philippe and I know the combination to this safe," said Jon. "Without the keys that are locked inside, no one can turn off the trans-dimensional drive. It's on a timer, and at some hour after twenty-seven days have passed, the system will detect the precise moment to fire the x-ray lasers. In that moment our fate will be sealed."

No sooner had Jon finished speaking when an alarm on the control panel went off. Tom looked and saw a needle in the red.

"Looks like Transformer #20 is overloading," said Tom.

Everyone turned to look out the window, not knowing which was #20.

"That one!" yelled Marla as she pointed. "See the whiff of smoke?"

"Looks like a low-voltage relay is stuck," said George. "The transformer will overload and explode."

Guardian hurried over to a tool box under a table, opened it, and grabbed a screwdriver. He opened the door and ran to transformer #20 before anyone realized what he was doing.

"What's he doing? He'll be hurt!" screamed Marla.

"He'll be okay. It's a low voltage relay. He'll pry the contacts loose," said George.

Guardian unscrewed the cover to the relay on the side of the smoking transformer. He looked inside and jammed the screwdriver into the relay. There was a loud bang, and Guardian was knocked off his feet and literally out of his shoes. The screwdriver went flying toward the faces of the onlookers behind the glass. They instinctively raised their arms and jumped back.

"Guardian's down!" yelled Tom, as he quickly ran to the door to help him.

"My God! What just happened?" asked Marla.

"That was high voltage," said George. "It was wired wrong. That's why it failed."

Tom had reached Guardian and was giving him CPR, while Jon called the EMT's. They arrived in less than five minutes and took over from Tom.

"Electric shock stopped his heart," said Tom. "I think I got it started."

"You did. He's now in V-Tach. Give me the AED! Okay stand back," said the lead EMT.

He used the automated external defibrillator, then put his head to Guardian's heart, and grabbed his wrist to check his pulse.

"He's now in V-Fib. Stand back," said the EMT again as he used the AED.

"Still in V-Fib. Stand back," said the EMT again as he used the AED a third time.

"Flat line. Hand me the syringe," said the EMT.

He held up the syringe, ejected some fluid to release any air bubbles, then injected Guardian with a cardiac stimulant.

He then started CPR. After five minutes he stopped.

"I'm sorry. He's gone," said the EMT as he got up and backed away from Guardian, lying lifeless on his back. His gray skin had turned pink.

Marla bent down and cradled Guardian's head in her arms and sobbed. Tom cried openly, bent down on one knee, and reached out to pull down Guardian's eyelids. With tears streaming from his eyes Jean Philippe put his hand on Marla's shoulder. Jon put his hand on Tom's shoulder and tried to say something, but the words came out as a moan. George got down on both knees next to Marla, picked-up Guardian's little gray hand, and held it between both of his hands as he wept. Guardian, the Immortal One, was gone forever. He had given his life freely for the sake of his children, and they would miss him so much.

———————————◇———————————

Right after Guardian's death, the faulty relay in the LCC was replaced, but the jump clock could not be restarted. Other systems had been damaged by the high voltage and had to be repaired and tested. It would take almost three months to fix the damage and restart the jump clock.

Jean Philippe made funeral arrangements for Guardian. He enlisted the help of a dozen androids. Strangely, the androids seemed unaffected in any way by Guardian's death. It was obvious the android community had a class structure, but Jean Philippe had never sought to learn much about it. He decided it was time to find out how the androids would operate without Guardian, so he randomly picked an android and asked it a number of questions. He learned there was a *High Council of Androids* comprised of seven droids who resolved and coordinated misunderstandings or inconsistencies in instructions.

The protocol was for the affected droid to seek clarification from the human giving the command. If that was insufficient, the query would go to the council. If the council couldn't resolve the issue, they would start at the first person in the chain of command above the person who initiated the questionable order. The query would move up the chain of command as necessary until a resolution was agreed to, or until Jon Walmer made a command decision. The droid told Jean Philippe a memorandum on this subject had been sent to Jon Walmer for approval.

———————————◊———————————

Guardian was laid out in an open casket in Ecosthat. At the formal ceremony a dozen people had something to say about their relationship with Guardian or to offer a prayer for his soul. It seemed everyone in Ecosthat came by to solemnly pay their respects. After two days of visitation, the casket was closed and buried in the Bay of Billows. The square mile around the grave site was designated Cemetery of the Guardian.

Chapter 39

Stellar-mass Anomaly . . .
crossing midway between orbits of Saturn and Jupiter
June 2012

Jon was rifling through his filing cabinet in his office on Ecosthat looking for a particular financial report he'd received from Don when the phone rang. He picked it up and held it between his left ear and shoulder while he continued to search through the files.

"Walmer here," he said into the receiver.

"Jon, it's Andre. Can you speak freely?"

"Yes, Andre, what's wrong?" asked Jon.

"My operatives inform me your team is being targeted by the FBI. It appears to be a direct move by your President against the Star-Slayer Project," explained Andre.

"I find that hard to believe," said Jon. "The President knows we've just completed the technical developments and have begun implementation. Why would he stop us now that we're so close to a solution?"

"Power politics, my friend," offered Andre. "If the President takes control of the operation now, he gets the most information about your secret solution, and he stands the best chance to commandeer it, and take credit by completing the implementation."

"So what specifically have you heard?" asked Jon.

"Search warrants have been issued for all your labs," said Andre. "The FBI will be hitting the Lodge first, because they know three members of the Executive Team are there. Also, they have federal agents undercover on Ecosthat who are empowered to legally shut you down as soon as they get the word. Sorry, but that's all I know."

"Okay, Andre. Thanks for the heads-up," said Jon.

"Good luck!" said Andre as he hung up.

Jon pushed the file drawer closed and sat in the chair behind his desk. He stared ahead thinking about what he should do. He picked up the phone and called Amanda at the Lodge.

"Amanda, there may not be much time," warned Jon. "The FBI will be at your door soon. The President is pulling a double-cross and shutting down the project. We must delay any adverse action for another twenty-six days. Let's not let the President confiscate our technology in this way. Destroy all documents and prototypes at the Lodge. I'll give the same order for all the other labs. Don't resist when they arrive. We don't want anyone getting hurt."

"Will do, Jon," said Amanda. "Anything else?"

"Do what you can to protect the identity of Don's investors," said Jon. "Hide all the contracts. Make sure you tell them to lay low until we can mount a legal defense. That's it for now."

Just as Jon hung up the phone, Marla knocked on his door and entered.

"Jon, do you have a minute? It's important," said Marla.

"Sure, I have something important for you, too. Have a seat."

"Jon, I just received a call from the President. He's ordered me to put Ecosthat under martial law and to immediately place you and the rest of the Executive Team under house arrest until he notifies me of further action. The only explanation he offered was that he deems the activation of the Magna-beam an act of international terrorism," said Marla.

"Under what authority can he do this?" asked Jon.

"He cites his authority under the *John W. Warner Defense Authorization Act of 2006, PL 109-364*," said Marla. "That Act has a provision for using the Armed Forces in major public emergencies. The particular conditions that allow the President to take over local authority are listed, and the President is using the condition referenced as *terrorist attack or incident* to justify his orders to me."

"Marla, you must obey the President's orders. I suggest you place us under house arrest in the LCC. We can move some beds and other accommodations there to make it livable. We'll need supplies to last us at least twenty-six days. It won't be your fault when the vacuum tube transport breaks down and prevents access to the LCC."

"Okay, I'll let you tell the others and get yourselves to the LCC," said Marla. "I'll start making it livable for you with furniture and supplies."

"Marla, I knew something like this was coming," said Jon. "Andre had just called and warned me. The FBI is in the process of raiding the labs. I'll be asking George to systematically destroy all technical documentation related to the trans-dimensional drive, on paper and in the computers."

"Understood. I didn't hear that. Work fast," said Marla.

"One other thing," said Jon. "Andre said there are undercover federal agents on Ecosthat, so make sure you don't do or say anything that would make the President doubt your loyalty to him."

The phone rang and Jon picked it up. It was Amanda.

"Jon, right after we spoke I got a call from the President's Chief of Staff. I've been relieved of my authority over NASA. I explained how critical it was to continue sending water, food, and other supplies to Ecosthat. He said that was no longer my concern. I contacted a few people I trust at NASA and learned there's a special Delta IV Heavy rocket being launched in a couple of days. It'll be carrying two military astronauts and five scientists. They'll orbit the moon and use a Lunar-Lander to shuttle the scientists to Ecosthat where they'll make a complete assessment of the technology and its purpose."

"Thanks, Amanda. We'll do whatever we can to delay their interference for 26 days, then it won't matter what they do," said Jon.

Almost to the minute, twenty-four hours after the first call, Marla got another call from the President. "General Odenfelder, have you placed the lunar base under martial law and placed the Star-Slayer Executive Team members under house arrest?" asked the President.

"Yes, sir. Dr. Walmer didn't resist. He got on the intercom and told all inhabitants that I'm now in charge. Mr. Jean Philippe Martinique also got on the intercom and confirmed the change of command. Consequently, the Security Division on Ecosthat has pledged their loyalty to me, and four of them are guarding the prisoners in the LCC."

"The LCC?"

"The Lunar Control Center, sir," explained Marla.

"What? They're in the Control Center? That's not what I meant by house arrest," yelled the President.

"Sir, I should explain that the LCC is a large facility connected by a tunnel to the Ecosthat. It's the most practical place to confine them. They'll be living in a large meeting room with restroom accommodations and no access to any controls or equipment. However, they do have access to a telephone and to television. Access doors to control rooms and equipment have been padlocked, and I'm the only one with the keys."

"It's a good thing you were able to take control of the situation," said the President. "Being only one person, I wasn't sure you could pull it off. I have undercover federal agents on Ecosthat who would have come to your assistance had you not succeeded so quickly. For now they'll remain undercover."

"Yes, sir. I understand. You can count on me, sir," said Marla.

"I'm sure I can, General," said the President. "To formalize the authority you have on the Moon Base, you've been promoted to a newly created position. You're now officially commander of Air Force Special Operations Command, Lunar Division (AFSOC-LD). The current AFSOC headquartered at Hurlburt Field in Florida is now renamed Air Force Special Operations Command, Earth Division (AFSOC-ED)."

"Yes, sir. Do you have any other orders for me?" asked Marla.

"A rocket carrying two military astronauts and five scientists will be arriving on the moon in about three days," said the President. "I want you to do whatever you can to assist them with their mission. They'll be performing a complete review of the technology that's been assembled there to ascertain its purpose and learn how to operate it.

"If you've learned anything about the system, I order you to give that information freely to the scientists. Jon Walmer, Jean Philippe Martinique, Don Mensch, George Blocker, Tom Calvano, and Guardian will be debriefed. If they cooperate, charges of plotting terrorist acts will be dropped. If they don't cooperate, they'll be brought back to earth to face a federal grand jury."

"Yes, sir. I understand," said Marla.

"Do you know anything about the so-called Magna-beam being projected onto earth?" asked the President.

"It's my understanding that it's gathering data about the earth's crust, mantle, and core to determine the extent and rate of damage being done by the gravitational force of the black hole," said Marla.

"And how will they use this information?" asked the President.

"After one lunar cycle they'll have sufficient data, but I'm not privy to how it will be used," said Marla.

"Surely you must have some clue about what they're doing," said the President.

"I hesitate to say, but I think it's an antigravity device they're developing," said Marla. I think the Magna-beam data will allow them to fine-tune the strength and direction of the antigravity field to protect the earth-moon system from the powerful gravimetric force of the black hole, but this is all speculation based on snippets of conversations I've overheard."

"If you're correct, then it's best if we let the Magna-beam continue to run," said the President. "Besides, we don't know if shutting it off could be dangerous."

"Permission to speak freely, sir?"

"Yes, of course, General."

"Sir, I don't understand why you're doing this. We know the Star-Slayer Executive Team members aren't terrorists."

"I understand your concern," said the President. "Of course they're not terrorists, but they're fallible like all of us. As President, first and foremost, I'm sworn to preserve, protect, and defend the Constitution. Commonly accepted interpretation of that oath is that the President must defend Americans from threats beyond our borders. I think it's arrogant, egotistical and dangerous for Dr. Walmer and his team to exclude some of the best scientists in the world. What if his team made a miscalculation? My scientists might identify it and correct it before it's too late. Think of Mother Earth as a cancer patient. I'm giving her the opportunity for a second opinion. Don't worry. It's just a temporary delay. Keep up the good work, General. Goodbye for now."

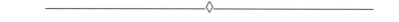

When the scientists arrived, Marla directed them to the sub-assembly plans and specifications. It took several days for them to realize they had to see drawings for the completed major assemblies to ascertain purpose. Marla explained that secrecy was a big part of the operation, and that she didn't know where the higher-level drawings could be found. The scientists interviewed hundreds of workers and more days passed.

The President called Marla again. "General Odenfelder, insufficient information is available for the scientists to determine the functions and purpose of the system," said the President. "Walmer and the others won't disclose any information. Therefore, the scientists want access to the Magna-beam and all other related equipment and controls. I've been told you've refused to give access."

"Sir, I feel it's too dangerous for them to be fooling around with stuff they know nothing about," said Marla. "I was hoping they'd get some knowledge of what it is before they go touching it."

"General, we can waste no more time. Give them access. That's an order."

"Yes, sir!" said Marla.

At that point Marla knew she could no longer use the same tactics to delay the scientists. She had to fall back to Jon's plan.

Marla waited a day before calling the President. "Mr. President, I have some bad news," said Marla. "I'm stuck in the LCC with the detainees."

"Did they revolt? Have they harmed you?" asked the President.

"No, sir, that's not what's happened. I'm still in control and have four security personnel with me," explained Marla. "The problem is that the tunnel between Ecosthat and the LCC is blocked by an inoperative transport car. Mr. President, I think it's time for you to call your undercover agents to action. Maybe they can find a way to get the vacuum tunnel operational so the scientists can get over here and inspect the system."

"Okay, General, I think you're right. We need someone in authority in Ecosthat if you're trapped in the LCC."

Ten federal agents broke cover and took control of Ecosthat. Days ticked by, and no one could clear the vacuum tunnel of the jammed car. Before anyone guessed that the car was specifically designed to block passage through the tunnel in case of an emergency, it was too late. The moon completed its cycle, the timer went off, and the three laser x-ray weapons were discharged. The jump had begun.

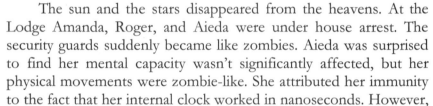

The sun and the stars disappeared from the heavens. At the Lodge Amanda, Roger, and Aieda were under house arrest. The security guards suddenly became like zombies. Aieda was surprised to find her mental capacity wasn't significantly affected, but her physical movements were zombie-like. She attributed her immunity to the fact that her internal clock worked in nanoseconds. However, she couldn't duplicate the out-of-phase condition that the vaccine induced in biological beings, so her robotic persona was useless.

Amanda and Roger went to the Control Room in the subbasement of the Lodge and turned on the holocom system. They were shocked to hear Aieda's voice coming from a holocom speaker when they knew she was standing zombie-like in a meeting room above them. Aieda explained she had transferred her signal to the receiver in the holocom system so she could interact with them electronically. There was slow-speed distortion in her voice projection and a lag in response, but she could communicate with them.

Once they reconnected to the LCC, they learned Marla had been placed in charge by the President. They had a good laugh over the trick she and Jon had played by isolating themselves in the LCC until the timer triggered the trans-dimensional jump. The four Ecosthat security guards who had accompanied Marla to the LCC were in zombie-like slow motion, as they hadn't been vaccinated. All the digital gages seemed to indicate the jump had succeeded.

They laughed, cheered, and congratulated each other. They had managed to save humanity from a stellar-mass black hole, at the moment, approaching the orbit of Jupiter and rapidly hurtling near enough to Earth to tear it apart with the pull of its gravimetric force. Soon they'd pop back into the fourth dimension, and the black hole would have long ago passed by.

"Let's not get too enthusiastic about our success just yet," said Roger.

"What do you mean?" asked Marla.

"We don't know how much damage the black hole might have done to our solar system as it passed through," explained Roger. "What if it damaged the sun? What if we pop back into an orbit too close to the sun?"

"I agree, we're not out of the woods yet," said Aieda in a long drawl. "However, so far my calculations have been correct."

"I'm beginning to feel nauseous," said Jon.

"Me, too," said Don.

"I'm losing my sight. Everything is blurry," said Tom.

"The gages are indicating a growing instability in the gravity well," said George.

"Everything seems distorted to me," said Jean Philippe. "It's like you and everything in the room are stretching and getting thinner."

"Oh my," said Roger. "Maybe we're being smeared into two-dimensional beings. We would have no thickness, and time wouldn't exist."

"You're becoming transparent, Roger," said Don.

"Oh, no!" exclaimed Jon. "I see white bubbles everywhere."

"I think I know what this is," said Roger. "It's often called space-time foam, but it's only known about from theory. Among those bubbles, theoretically, are wormholes that can transport us to different places and times."

"Why is the holocom system still working?" asked Jean Philippe. "I would think by now it would no longer be capable of communication between the LCC and the Lodge."

"It's probably not the holocom system allowing us to communicate," said George. "My guess is we're communicating telepathically, like Guardian told us the Elders do."

"All I see is foam now," said Jon. "I guess your calculations weren't quite right, Aieda."

There was no response from Aieda.

"Aieda, do you hear me?" asked Jon.

No response.

"Aieda, it's Amanda. Please talk to us."

No response.

"I think we've lost Aieda," said George. "Maybe only biological beings can survive this foamy limbo."

"I, too, see only foam but I can hear everyone clearly," said Roger.

"We need to continue communicating with each other as much as possible," said Tom. "I have the feeling that if we don't keep talking to each other, we'll drift apart and die a lonely death in the depths of the foam."

"Guardian said we must trust our intuition," said Don. "If we stick together, maybe we can get back to the fourth dimension in the right year using one of Roger's wormholes."

"Time doesn't exist in this foam," said Roger. "We might be here for centuries or for just a blink of an eye, and we wouldn't know the difference. While we wait for a wormhole, let's systematically teach each other what we know, so our personal knowledge becomes part of our collective mind."

"I can't think of anything better to do under the circumstances," said Tom. "I wonder what a wormhole looks like."

Chapter 40

J on Walmer awoke as if from a dream. He was standing in the parlor of his Manhattan brownstone residence. On the coffee table in front of him was a newspaper. He thought, *I don't remember finding a wormhole. I'm not in the foam anymore.*

At just that moment, Harry walked into the parlor and startled Jon with his question. "Will you be having guests for dinner tonight, sir?"

"Harry! You're alive!" shouted Jon.

"Why, I should hope so, sir. Are you all right, sir?" asked Harry.

"It's never happened before, but I just had a horrible daydream that seemed so real to me, and in it you were killed," said Jon, ad-libbing an excuse for his behavior.

"Oh my, sir. Perhaps you should sit down and relax with the paper while I bring you a fresh cup of black coffee," said Harry.

"Yes, that would be nice. Thank you, Harry," said Jon.

Jon sat on the sofa and grabbed the paper from the table. His gaze went first to the date, then to the headline. It was December 27, 2004, and the headline read, *Huge Quake Spawns Tremors and Tsunamis in Southeast Asia.*

"Was it real or was it a dream?" Jon asked himself, sotto voce.

"It was real, Jon," said a familiar voice.

Jon was startled and looked furtively around the room, but saw no one. He methodically set the paper back down on the table.

"Amanda, is that you? Where are you?" asked Jon while looking over his shoulder.

"Yes, it's Amanda. I'm in your head and you're in mine. By the way, quit talking out loud or people will think you're nuts. We can read each other's thoughts . . . mental telepathy, like when we were in the space-time foam together."

Harry walked in with Jon's fresh brew. Jon casually picked up the paper again and feigned reading it.

"Thanks, Harry," said Jon aloud. "I'm feeling much better now, although I seem to have had a memory lapse. You'll have to catch me up on things."

"Sir, a memory lapse might imply you've had a transient ischemic attack; undoubtedly a minor one, if at all, but I would suggest seeing the doctor first thing tomorrow," counseled Harry.

"Good idea, Harry. I'll schedule an appointment for tomorrow," said Jon. "No guests for dinner tonight. I'll be retiring early. I need some rest."

Harry set the coffee on the table and walked out of the parlor.

"Amanda, the paper says the Asian Tsunami occurred yesterday. I can't believe it's 2004. What about the others?" asked Jon telepathically.

"So far it's just you and me, and I've been waiting for something to happen for a whole year," explained Amanda. "I arrived the day after the Bam earthquake and I've been the only one who remembered anything about the future. It's a good thing I remembered what Guardian explained or else I would've gone crazy."

"So the team is physically here, but only you and I remember anything about our Star-Slayer Project? At this point in time most of us hadn't yet met each other. I hope you were subtle when making your inquiries," said Jon.

"I started with a call to George Blocker, because he and I have been friends for years," said Amanda. "Even after some leading questions, he was clueless."

"Like what kind of questions?" asked Jon.

"For one, I asked if he had ever heard of AIEDA," answered Amanda.

"Hello, where are you guys? I can hear your voices, but I don't see you," said a man's voice.

"Don, is that you?" asked Amanda.

"Yes, Amanda dear, it's me," said Don. "I'm so happy you survived the foam. What's this about asking George Blocker questions?"

"Oh, darling, it's so good to hear you," cried Amanda. "I've been waiting a year for you to catch your wormhole. You've been physically here, but with no memory of our Star-Slayer Project. That's what I was explaining to Jon about George. Jon just arrived before you did, but last time I called George, his future self had not yet arrived."

"Hi, Jon! Glad you caught your wormhole," said Don. "I sure hope all the others on the team are as lucky as we are. Funny thing, though; I don't remember anything about catching the wormhole."

"Neither do I," said Jon.

"Me neither," said Amanda.

"Amanda, if you were the first one back, and your arrival was a year ago, that could mean we might be waiting years for some team members," said Don.

"I'm not so sure of that," said Jon. "You and I came back almost together. Maybe there will be an avalanche of arrivals."

"Hey, I'm hearing voices in my head," said a voice.

"Is that you, George?" asked Amanda.

"Yes, Amanda, it's me," said George. "Is this telepathy like what we experienced in the foam?"

"You got it, buddy. This is Jon. Glad you made it back."

"*Mon ami!* Jon, did I hear your voice in my mind?"

"Yes, Jean Philippe. Join the group," said Jon. "So far we have Amanda, Don, and George with us."

"Ah, this is Roger. I've been listening in for awhile now. I was afraid I was losing my mind. Is this for real?"

"Yes, Roger. We're so happy you're back with us," said Amanda.

"What's all the chatter about?" asked a voice.

"Tom, is that you?" asked Jean Philippe.

"Yes, Jean Philippe, it's me," said Tom. "You guys seem so surprised about the retention of our telepathy. I was sort of expecting it."

"Hello, it's Marla. Tom, my dear, I heard what you said. I'm so happy we're together again. Are we all here?"

"Marla, it's Jon. I'm glad you made it. Yes, it seems we're all here except for Guardian and Aieda, and I'm afraid I can find no reason to assume they'll be joining us."

"May I suggest we meet at Jon's house? It seems appropriate," said Tom. "This telepathy thing is okay, but it just doesn't compare to face-to-face conversation."

"Okay, my place exactly forty-eight hours from now," said Jon. "That would be 2:00 p.m. Wednesday. It sure is weird talking without talking. In the foam it wasn't as weird, because we didn't have bodies."

"Yeah, how do you turn it off?" asked George.

"It's easy. You just turn it off like you put one foot in front of the other when you walk," said Tom. "There's no need to think about it; just do it."

After a few minutes, there were no more voices; well, except for one.

"I need to take a pee," said Roger.

"Roger, we all heard that. Turn it off now," said Amanda.

"Sorry," said Roger sheepishly.

———————————◊———————————

It was late afternoon of the same day that Jon had found his wormhole. He had contacted AIEDA to establish a protocol for identifying major changes in the time-line based on his memory of events before the disequilibrium. Jon was walking from the kitchen to his study when he heard someone unlocking the front door. He froze in his tracks waiting to see who it could be.

Jon was shocked when Catherine walked in with shopping bags hanging from both hands. He was doubly surprised at her spry and happy mood.

"Hi, dear!" said Catherine. "I had a great shopping experience with Donna and a few of the other girls. How was your day?"

Jon was speechless for a moment. He forced out a few quiet words. "Great. Thanks honey."

Catherine was all bubbly and pretty in her yellow and white summer dress and platform sandals. She walked up to Jon where he stood frozen in the hallway, stretched herself on tiptoes, and gave him a kiss on the lips which he had to bend over to receive. She placed one bag on the floor and reached into the other to pull out a beautiful black and white print dress she held against herself as she looked to Jon for approval.

"Like it?" she asked. "I bought it for Thursday; you know, the McAllister's party.

"It's beautiful, honey," he said. "I guess a suit and tie for me, right?

"Skip the tie. Sport coat's fine. It's at 4:00 p.m. but let's be there by 4:30 . . . fashionably late. I don't like being among the first to arrive. Allison is more likely to bend my ear off."

At that she folded the dress, put it back in the bag, picked up both bags, and proceeded to climb the stairs to the second floor. Jon slowly walked down the hall to his study and flopped down in a large brown leather recliner. He stared out the window. *My God, Catherine hasn't left me*, he thought.

Jon's eyes started to water. He was overcome with emotion. It was the first time in his life that he cried for joy. He had always thought of it as a reaction peculiar to women.

———————————◇———————————

Two days later, the much anticipated gathering took place in the parlor of Jon's residence. Harry served coffee, tea, biscotti, and a platter of fruits and cheeses. Everyone on the Star-Slayer Executive Team was genuinely happy to see each other, and they were especially happy to have escaped from the space-time foam. Roger was the only one who appeared somewhat melancholy.

"Please, let's come to order now," shouted Jon over the jovial conversations. "We have serious things to discuss."

"We also have much to celebrate," said George. "I've checked as best I could in the short time before this meeting, and it would appear the rogue black hole is nowhere to be found. It was a surprise to me, considering our attempt to make a trans-dimensional jump was a colossal failure."

"That means we created a disequilibrium in the future which has affected the past," said Jean Philippe. "We may have caused many changes to the past."

Roger started to cry silently, and Amanda was the first to notice.

"Roger, are you all right?" asked Amanda. "What's wrong?"

"I'm so sorry," said Roger as he wiped his eyes with a tissue. "It's just that when you mentioned the disequilibrium in the fabric of space-time, I saw Alice's face. I miss her."

"Oh, dear," said Marla. "Has your Alice passed on?"

"No, it would appear that in this new timeline she doesn't exist," said Roger in a raspy voice.

"Roger, I'm so sorry to hear that," said Amanda. "You must be devastated."

"Thank you, Amanda. I'll be fine. We all would have died if we hadn't tried to make the jump. My Alice was a casualty of circumstance. I'll cherish my memories of her."

"Two days ago I learned Catherine hasn't left me in this timeline," said Jon. "We must determine what has changed in this new timeline; certainly, not every detail, but those changes that might significantly affect our lives. I've already begun doing that by using the AIEDA database and data mining capabilities, based on a comparison to my own recollections. Everyone should send me a list of major events and personalities you remember from before the disequilibrium, so I can feed the information to AIEDA."

"I agree that's number one on the list," said Tom. "You know, Harvey Watson should be alive, unless the disequilibrium erased him, too. He didn't deserve to die in the mountains of Ecuador. I couldn't find a number for him. Don, can I ask you to follow up and find out about Harvey? Also, I learned a friend of mine in Brazil doesn't exist. He was the Minister of the Interior. Strangely, even his Ministry doesn't exist."

"No problem, Tom. I'll try to locate Harvey for you," said Don. "I think we should experiment with our newfound mental telepathy. We need to know the maximum distance between sender and receiver."

"Well, we know it's at least the distance from Ft. Collins to New York City," said Amanda, "because you and I were at home when you emerged from the foam and we communicated with Jon telepathically."

"Tom, may I volunteer you to visit Guardian in Antarctica?" asked Jean Philippe. "You won't be building Ecosthat this time, so you can travel light and use a helicopter out of Argentina. I suggest you also participate in the telepathy experiment, so we can get a better fix on communication distance."

"Glad to do it, Jean Philippe," said Tom, "but not by helicopter. It doesn't even have the range to get to Rothera Station for refueling. I think I can hitch a ride with the British Antarctic Survey from the Falklands to Rothera. From there I'll need to charter a ski-equipped plane to get to the Guardian's fortress. I'll take Jeff Teichman with me. I spoke briefly with him last night."

After the meeting adjourned, Jon's guests stayed for dinner. About two hours after everyone had left, the phone rang. Jon got up from the recliner in his study and answered it from his desk. It was Don. "Jon, I thought I'd call and let you know about Harvey Watson. He's alive and kicking . . . married with three kids, and happy with his job. I think Tom will be glad to hear that. I'll call him tomorrow morning."

"Thanks for letting me know. I'm surprised you didn't use the telepathy thing," said Jon.

"I'm sure I'll start using it, but so far I find it uncomfortable," said Don.

"I agree, but I have a feeling learning how to use it properly will bring our team even closer together," said Jon.

"Maybe our team is no longer needed," said Don. "The threat from the black hole is gone, and the disequilibrium has been corrected."

"That may be true," said Jon. "If so, it'll be a shame. We work so well together."

———————————————◇———————————————

Tom Calvano and Jeff Teichman were waiting to board a LAN Airlines flight from JFK International to RAF Mt. Pleasant in the Falkland Islands. From there they'd take a De Haviland Dash 7, operated by BAS, to Rothera Research Station on Adelaide Island in Antarctica. At Rothera they had arranged, for considerable expense, to charter a ski-equipped De Haviland Twin Otter for their flight to the Guardian's fortress.

Tom turned to Jeff with a question. "Jeff, how long have we known each other?"

"Oh, about ten years," said Jeff. "Why?"

"Because I've a whale of a tale to tell ya, lad. I'm wondering if you trust me enough to believe me," said Tom.

"In the years I've known you, we've been in some pretty tight spots together, and as a result we understand each other," said Jeff. "One thing about you is you're a serious guy who's not prone to practical jokes, making up stories, or lying. Tom, if you say it's true, I'll believe you, so don't hesitate to say what's on your mind."

Tom took a deep breath. He had already decided not to tell everything to Jeff.

"I didn't tell you the complete reason we're on this mission," said Tom. "As I explained, we're going to meet an intelligent and strange guy who has information needed by my employer, Jean Philippe Martinique of Marseilles Electric Enterprises. What I didn't tell you is the peculiar nature of the guy we're going to meet.

"Jeff, this guy is not human . . . he's an alien living in a subterranean fortress in a remote area. He calls himself the Guardian. He's made his presence known to many governments, but they've decided to keep his existence from the public. If we can make contact with him, we'll be the first private enterprise to do so, and it could yield valuable technological information.

"The Guardian is reclusive, and we can't just drop in and knock on his door. It just so happens he's a telepath, so when we get close to his abode, I plan to try contacting him telepathically."

"That sounds like a tall tale, but as I said, I have no reason to doubt you're telling the truth, unless you're crazy as a loon," said Jeff with a smile.

"Well, maybe I'm nuts and don't know it," said Tom. "You and I will find out soon."

"I don't see how it can do any harm to look him up," said Jeff. "But if you're not a telepath, what makes you think he'll be able to hear you?"

"I don't know for sure, but Jean Philippe's intelligence operative said Guardian has demonstrated the ability to read the minds of some heads of state at a distance. I think that's why they're spooked about his existence becoming public knowledge. I can't wait to get this show on the road," said Tom. "Did you have any trouble getting the cold weather gear and making arrangements at Rothera?"

"Nope, I got parkas, boots, goggles, hats, gloves . . . the whole kit and caboodle," said Jeff. "It's checked in luggage to Mt. Pleasant Airport in the Falklands. The BAS requires we dress for the cold before boarding the Dash-7 to Rothera Station. At Rothera we'll be housed at Admirals House where we'll be sharing a room and bath."

"That works. Thanks, Jeff. It's time for us to board."

───────────────◇───────────────

The mental telepathy worked from Mt. Pleasant to NYC and Mt. Pleasant to Paris . . . much longer distances than Tom would have guessed. He had telepathically communicated with Jon, Marla, Don, and Jean Philippe. He was especially interested in what Marla had discovered.

She told him telepathically that their good friend Carlos Alvarez had lost the use of both legs years ago while rescuing troops in a battle over territory disputed by Ecuador and Peru. Currently, Colonel Alvarez seemed to be a happy man performing his duty as Chief of Police for Azuay province. He was a well respected war hero and an excellent Chief of Police.

───────────────◇───────────────

Tom and Jeff spent two nights at Rothera Station waiting for availability of their Twin Otter and the two pilots. Fortunately the Bransfield House offered more than dining; it also offered social and recreational facilities Tom and Jeff found helpful whiling away the time.

At the snooker table, Jeff stopped when it was his shot and turned toward Tom. "How are we going to get Guardian's attention once we get near his underground fortress? And we have no equipment to negotiate that terrain."

"I'm surprised you took so long to ask me that," said Tom. "Actually, I had special equipment delivered here before we left. It includes snowshoes and a cable-conveyor system that can take us into and out of the crevasse where his fortress is supposedly buried. Hopefully, we won't need it, because I plan to try telepathy to raise the Guardian. I'm hoping he'll hear me if I focus on calling-out to him mentally."

"Sounds like a long shot to me," commented Jeff. "You're not a telepath."

"True, but I've got to give it a try."

"So if the telepathy doesn't work, we climb down into the crevasse? And then what?" asked Jeff while silently wondering how serious Tom's mental condition might be.

"No, that's a last resort . . . dangerous with just the two of us. Among the equipment that preceded us here, I have a specially modified transmitter that sends a message for Guardian on hundreds of different radio frequencies."

"Won't the message be picked up in the Twin Otter by our pilots or by one of the research stations?"

"Not likely, because the transmitter skips the frequencies they normally use, but even if they did, they wouldn't understand it, because it's encrypted using an ancient Sumerian language," explained Tom. "That language has been used by the Guardian in secret contacts he's made with heads of state."

--------------------◊--------------------

The next day, Tom Calvano and Jeff Teichman were in the air and on their way to coordinates 81 deg, 35 min, S. latitude, and 115 deg, 55 min, W. longitude. Although that wasn't precisely the position of the Guardian's fortress, it was the best place Tom knew to land, because that's where the Ecosthat survey base had been, and he knew the terrain well. Of course, Tom was planning to land only if the Guardian invited him into his fortress.

When they reached the location, Tom had the plane circle the area while he tried his mental telepathy. After fifteen minutes he gave up. He then tried the modified transmitter for fifteen minutes. There was no response from Guardian. The pilot had to maintain thirty minutes of reserve fuel for the trip back. Tom wasn't inclined to land and walk to the fortress area. Going into the crevasse with no backup team would be dangerous.

"No luck so far, Jeff. I don't want to land and go out into that cold."

"Maybe you need another person chanting the same message. Let's do it together," suggested Jeff.

"Okay, Jeff. Let's mentally chant the words, *Guardian in the subterranean fortress, grant us an audience.*"

Jeff's suggestion made Tom recall that his telepathy would work from Antarctica to all members of the Star-Slayer Executive Team. He made mental contact with them, and asked them to join in the chant while picturing Guardian in their minds.

They did this for only five minutes when to everyone's amazement, they heard Guardian's voice in their heads. "Okay, enough already! I hear you. You're giving me a headache with all that chanting. Who are you people?" asked the Guardian.

"Guardian, sir, my name is Tom Calvano, and I need your help. After I explain our dilemma, I'll introduce you to each member of the team that summoned you. I'm circling in a plane not far from your fortress beneath the ice. How shall we meet?"

Tom spoke no words aloud, so Jeff and the pilots could hear nothing.

"I know about your plane and its radio transmissions in Sumerian, but I'm not prepared to receive you in person until I learn more about you," said Guardian. "I've given my code name, Guardian, only to heads of state, and I've never given them my location. Also, you're the first humans I've encountered who possess true mental telepathy."

"Guardian, sir, I'm new at this telepathy stuff, but I'll try to recount our entire story so you can judge for yourself," said Tom.

"It would be faster and more convincing if you were to allow me direct access to your memories," said Guardian. "Direct access to everyone's memories, not just yours, Tom."

"We agree, but how do we do that?"

"Just relax, close your eyes, and think about the beginning of the period you wish me to explore, or perhaps it was some incident that marks the start of the period," explained Guardian. "Okay, I've got access to all eight of you, but some of you are resisting. I won't hurt you, I promise. Just relax and let me leaf through your memories. You can just enjoy them as I review them, and don't worry about privacy. No one else but me can see your memories, and I'll skip rapidly through private matters. Very good, you're enjoying the experience. It's a necessary process that will be helpful to everyone involved."

The Guardian kept talking in a soothing manner, as if he were a hypnotist. It seemed like only a few minutes to Tom.

"I have what I need from you; so relax, and slowly pull away from me. I now understand why you've called on me. Stay calm, and slowly take back control of your memories," instructed the Guardian. "Tom, I must tell you I'm amazed by what I've seen. You're the first sentient beings who've experienced a disequilibrium event, and collectively remember almost every detail of life before the correction. I must communicate this development to the Elders. I shall take my leave of you for the time being."

"Guardian, as convenient and efficient as mental telepathy is, I don't find it as pleasant as face-to-face conversation," said Tom. "Would you mind sending the specifications for a holographic communications system to the AIEDA Development Lab in North Branch, NJ?"

"Yes, I agree it would be a nicer experience," responded Guardian. "I'll fax the specs tomorrow morning."

Tom felt dizzy as his eyes began to focus on the inside of the Twin Otter. He turned to look at Jeff sitting just across the aisle from him. He tried to speak, but no words came out at first.

"Geez boss, I was getting worried. You were in a trance for almost an hour. We had to land or head back to Rothera, so I decided we should go back. There was no reason to hang around."

"Good," said Tom with difficulty. It was the only intelligible sound he could utter at the moment. He wasn't worried. He could feel his vocal pathways reestablishing themselves.

Chapter 41

Jon Walmer continued to use AIEDA's data-mining capabilities to identify differences between conditions in the prior timeline, as compared to the current timeline. Guardian had explained that time wasn't a *line*, even though it seemed chronological. It was difficult for Jon to imagine that past, present, and future all occur simultaneously, and that an event in the future can affect the past much the same as a past event affects the future. Although the word *timeline* didn't accurately describe the state of events before the disequilibrium versus after the disequilibrium, he couldn't think of a better word to use.

Jon's research seemed to indicate that changes in the timeline were all directly or indirectly related to members of the team. Unfortunately, these effects often cascaded to affect millions of people and events around the world . . . even in the distant past. It was much like effects described by Lorenz in his Theory of Chaos whereby a small event like the flapping of a butterfly's wings could affect the weather on the other side of the world. In Lorenz's theory, small changes in initial conditions could result in large changes in future events.

Jon had identified that the corrections to the timeline, necessitated by the occurrence of the disequilibrium, were small changes to the initial conditions of team members' lives that resulted in large changes in past events and current conditions throughout the world. Jon suspected it was the failure of the jump, and not simply the attempt to make the jump, that triggered the disequilibrium and the subsequent correction of history. The mathematician in him yearned to find an equation that would explain his observations.

Jon was in his office at AIEDA home office in the Bronx when he received a twenty page fax. The cover page of the fax simply said, *Please have the entire team answer each of these questions by consensus; in other words, everyone must agree to the same answer. Return results to me, ASAP, via the fax number at the top of this page. Thanks, Guardian.*

Jon hooked up telepathically with the team. It took about an hour for them to answer all the questions . . . which they thought were rather peculiar, as most seemed to be mathematical and related to space, time, gravity, acceleration, and the event horizon of black holes. Actually, they were initially surprised how easily they agreed on the answers, until they remembered how they had done similar mental exercises while trapped in the space-time foam. Jon faxed their answers to Guardian, and within an hour the team received a telepathic message from Guardian asking them to contact him via the new holocom system that had recently been installed at the North Branch Lab.

―――――――――――――◊―――――――――――――

Two days later the team was in the holocom room at North Branch. They were attempting to connect with Guardian. After a few minutes Guardian was sitting at the table with them as if he were physically present. Guardian greeted everyone individually in a polite and formal manner.

"I asked you to meet with me in this manner because what I must discuss with you is of great importance to humanity, to Guardians, to the Elders, and to other sentient beings in the Universe," stated Guardian. "Let me ask you Jon, how did the team feel about the questions they completed for me?"

"We felt good about our answers. They didn't seem particularly hard, because we had spent a lot of time in the space-time foam keeping ourselves busy with mathematical problems like that."

"Well, let me tell you that you got 100% correct," said Guardian. "The questions were difficult, and you shouldn't have been able to answer any of them, especially in such a short period of time. Your fastest computer couldn't have calculated the results for several of the questions in as little as two months. Does that shock you?"

"It shocks the heck out of me," said Tom. "I thought it was strange that I understood that stuff, but I thought it was because of Roger's knowledge of astrophysics and Jon's knowledge of math. Of course, I felt the same way when we were in the foam."

"Tom, you're partly right that some of your understanding comes from the others when you're in telepathic mode, but it's much more than that," explained Guardian. "You may have been in the space-time foam for centuries, and during that time without physical form your mental capacities have increased many fold. The mechanism that generated this phenomenon is unknown. The eight of you are able to join as one mind and use 99% of your combined mental capabilities. Also, it would seem the whole of your collective intelligence is greater than the sum of its parts, because there's a synergism that develops when the eight of you communicate telepathically."

"Good grief! That would put a big moral burden on us to use such intelligence responsibly," said Amanda, "assuming we even know how to use it."

"To what end would we use this gift?" asked Jean Philippe.

"That's precisely what I wish to discuss," said Guardian. "Apparently you're not aware there's a Council of the Universe comprised of beings devoted to the protection of life. It's chaired by an Elder and co-chaired by a Guardian. Other sentient beings on the council represent hundreds of thousands of worlds."

"Why is there a need for a council to protect life?" asked Marla. "Is there a grave threat?"

"Not just a grave threat, but many thousands of grave threats," responded Guardian. "The black hole that threatened earth is just one of the many kinds of threats to sentient life throughout the Universe. Life is precious and, although it adapts, the Universe is a violent and dangerous place. In cosmological terms, life is extremely rare, and the parameters within which sentient life can survive are within narrow limits."

"So, does the Council of the Universe want to punish us for breaking a rule of the Universe and causing the disequilibrium?" asked Don.

"No, to the contrary," said Guardian. "The Council applauds your success and apologizes for not knowing how to help. Except for one Guardian, you were abandoned because we had no hope."

"You were the one who didn't abandon us," said Roger.

"I'm happy to know that, but it's not a memory of mine, and it's possible I'm a different person in this timeframe," said Guardian.

"Aha! I like the word *timeframe* much better than *timeline*," interjected Jon. "Tell the Council we harbor no ill feelings toward them and accept their apology."

"I'll do that, but there's more," said the Guardian. "The Council invites you to become a member . . . as a team. If you accept, there are some conditions."

"What might these conditions be?" asked Jean Philippe.

"That all eight of you accept as a team, and that you participate in periodic Council meetings. That you work, as might be needed, on problems that involve any of the member worlds. That you agree to accept gene therapy that would render you immortal."

For a minute there was total silence, until Amanda spoke up. "Can our families become immortal along with us?"

"No, only Elders, Guardians, and Council members shall be immortal," stated Guardian. "It was a lesson learned hard, but when an entire species is immortal, it loses many instincts necessary for survival and propagation. Someday I'll explain the problems immortality has caused the Elders and the Guardians."

"I think we've heard a little on that subject before," said Jon. "Surely, you understand how difficult it would be to watch one's spouse, children, relatives, and friends grow old and die."

"It's both a sacrifice and a blessing for you," said Guardian. "You didn't shirk your responsibilities to humanity when earth was threatened. Think now of your responsibilities not only to earth, but to all the worlds occupied by sentient beings."

"The threat was to us personally and our loved ones, too, so I'm not so sure we acted on egalitarian motives," said Tom. "Frankly, I feel no responsibility for the survival of other sentient beings."

"Although the Council was not able to help you recently, we might be a big help in the future, especially if you're members," said Guardian unconvincingly.

"In this new timeframe, Roger lost a wife, and I lost two children," said Amanda with tears in her eyes. "For an entire year I waited for the rest of you to find your wormholes, and during that time I had to cope with the knowledge that my children had not yet been born. Don and I will have children, but this prospect of our immortality means I'll live to lose them again. I don't want to repeat that pain."

"Darling, you may recall our discussion about whether or not to bring children into a world facing almost certain doom," said Don. "We both agreed it would be better to have experienced love and life for a short time than never to have experienced it at all."

"Why don't we join together telepathically and decide in the same way we answered all twenty of those questions?" suggested Roger.

There was silence in the room as the eight members of the Star-Slayer Executive Team pondered a life-altering question. It took hours for them to decide. They all agreed to join the Council of the Universe and become immortal beings. The Guardian informed them there would be a formal ceremony inducting them into the Council and introducing them to some of the members from worlds closest to earth. After the holographic meeting with Guardian was over, Jon asked the team to adjourn to a more comfortable meeting room and discuss their future together.

"I wonder if we know what we've committed ourselves to doing," said Jon. "I think we must discuss how to measure the extent of our telepathic abilities and our combined intelligence. We need to learn how to develop these gifts. Also, how should we wield them for the benefit of humanity and the rest of the cosmos?"

"Do you remember how we kept ourselves entertained while in the space-time foam?" asked Tom.

"Yeah, Tom, we created and destroyed all those stupid gas planets for your boyish amusement," said Amanda.

"Hey, Amanda, we also created all those worlds with gentle breezes, butterflies, and flowers just for you to romp through barefooted," said Tom.

"Stop it, you two," commanded Marla. "We all got to exercise our imaginations together, and we learned to enjoy ourselves while trapped in a world without beginning or end."

"Maybe with group intelligence and immortality we're trapping ourselves in the same type of world we experienced in the space-time foam," suggested Don.

"I don't think so," said George. "In this reality we have physical form, and it makes a difference about how alive I feel. Yet our gifts certainly can be equated to power."

"If it's discovered we have such power, we'll be hunted down," said Jean Philippe. "We must find a way to project our influence without it pointing back to any one of us."

"We can create the singularity," said George excitedly.

"Why the hell would we want to create a black hole?" asked Tom incredulously.

"No, not a black hole," said George. "The term singularity has another meaning. It refers to the ultimate evolution of mankind into a powerful intelligence, transcending man's biological limitations."

"In a way Aieda was our singularity, because she had superhuman intelligence and was able to design improvements to her own processing capabilities," said Jon.

"Aieda was a product of another timeframe," said George. "If we are to responsibly use our powers for the betterment of mankind, we must protect ourselves. The way to do that is to create an artificial person who projects our joint will. If he's destroyed, we simply change his looks and his name and recreate him. We'd be safe behind the screen . . . the puppet masters pulling the strings."

"We don't have that kind of power, George," said Tom.

"With Guardian's help, we do," said George. "Why don't we ask him to create a human-like android for us? We can communicate with it telepathically, and it will faithfully and dutifully follow our commands."

"I think that might work," said Marla. "The droids we worked with on the moon didn't act like robots. They were natural in their interactions with us."

"This human-android shouldn't be just an empty shell," said Jean Philippe. "He'd need a base of power from which he could operate and influence humanity for the greater good."

"In my research about what has changed from our old timeframe to our new timeframe, I discovered something interesting," said Jon. "Do you recall Andre Garnier and his four partners in crime? Well, it so happens that in this timeframe Andre doesn't exist, and there are only four partners instead of five. I think there should be five Grandmasters of Godwin, not four; and there should be five partners in the Partnership, not four."

"That organization thrives on criminal espionage," said Amanda. "Do we want to ally ourselves with such a group?"

"I think I see where Jon is coming from," said Marla. "This is a powerful and secret organization which will be useful to us, but the four partners are part of something we no longer are part of . . . humanity. With our telepathic gift, we're no longer human, and once we become immortal, we become in a relative sense, demigods.

"We need real humans, like the four partners, as a sounding board for actions we plan to take on behalf of humanity. The four partners achieved their position through a rigorous selection process. They're ambitious, intelligent, well-educated, powerful, and protective of the Church of Spiritual Objectivism and all its members. As an organization it's survived for 200 years. It could survive indefinitely; precisely what an immortal would want as a base of operations."

"I like it," said Don. "Let's connect telepathically and get a consensus on our plan."

There was silence in the room for a couple of minutes. Then the glazed look on each of their faces vanished, and Jon announced, "We're unanimously agreed. We'll ask Guardian to create *Adam LaGuardia* and find a way to position him as one of the five Grandmasters of Godwin. Andre's specific area of responsibility within the Church was a station called *Purveyor of Reason and Logic*. It's an appropriate station for our Adam, given his responsibility for humanity's development."

"I find it ironic that mankind's protector should turn out to be a non-sentient android," said Jean Philippe.

"Let's hope Adam can do as good a job as Guardian has done," said Marla.

Acknowledgements

I extend my heartfelt thanks to those who supported me during the marathon effort writing this, my first, novel. It's been fun, but more challenging than I had imagined. I truly needed the encouragement I got from friends and family. With lessons learned from this experience, I hope to entertain readers for many years to come.

In particular I want to thank my dear wife for her tolerance of this writer's moods. My sincere thanks also go to my son for his encouragement when clouds of doubt hung heavily over my head.

I especially wish to thank my long-time friend Fred Hathorn for engaging in all manner of philosophical discussions which, in one form or another, found their way into this novel. Fred enthusiastically reviewed the first draft and offered many appreciated comments and suggestions, sometimes without mercy.

I extend special thanks to my editor, Michael Garrett. He's a consummate professional whose frank comments and insightful suggestions helped me bring the final manuscript up to publishing industry standards.

Finally, I wish to thank my friends who reviewed the second draft. They read the manuscript in the time allotted and completed a questionnaire, which both individually and in the aggregate provided me with the insight I needed to polish the work into a much better reading experience. My sincere thanks go to Betty Gailliot, Tom Gailliot, Mike Jenkins, Kevin Macherione, Jim Malley, Carol Piranio, Tony Riley, and Kathy Leeds Senavitis.

Dan Makaon